GUARDIAN

BY JOHN SAUL

John Saul

GUARDIAN

FAWCETT COLUMBINE • NEW YORK

A Fawcett Columbine Book
Published by Ballantine Books
Copyright © 1993 by John Saul

All rights reserved under International and Pan-American Copyright Conventions.
Published in the United States by Ballantine Books, a division of Random
House, Inc., New York, and simultaneously in Canada by Random
House of Canada Limited, Toronto.

LIBRARY OF CONGRESS CATALOGING-IN-PUBLICATION DATA:
Saul, John
Guardian / John Saul.—1st ed.
p. cm.
ISBN 0-449-90862-3
I. TITLE.
PS3569.A787G8 1993
813'.54—dc20   93-19002 CIP

Designed by Fritz Metsch

Manufactured in the United States of America
First Edition: September 1993

10 9 8 7 6 5 4 3 2 1

For Don Cleary and Stephanie Laidman—
Thanks for everything!

GUARDIAN

CHAPTER 1

*I*t was just the kind of day that never failed to depress her, even when she woke up feeling good. Today, the sense of impending disaster—the vague feeling of panic that had seized her when she first woke up—only worsened as the temperature skyrocketed and the hot, wet air closed around her like a straitjacket.

August in Canaan, New Jersey. Temperature, 93 degrees, humidity, 97 percent, and both climbing.

Canaan, New Jersey, where there were only two decent weeks a year—one in the spring and the other in the fall—and the rest of the time it was either too hot and muggy or too soul-numbing cold.

Canaan, where MaryAnne Carpenter had been born, and where she'd grown up, and where she'd gotten married, and where she'd had her children, and where, she thought wryly, it was beginning to look as if she was going to die.

If she wasn't dead already—which, this morning, seemed a definite possibility. And maybe not such a bad possibility, she reflected as she sipped at the coffee that had grown cold in the chipped mug. Except that if she *was* dead, then that meant she was now in Heaven and was due to spend eternity in a shabby two-bedroom house surrounded by a scraggly strip of brownish lawn, with a backyard just large enough to hold a rusting barbecue, some stained plastic lawn furniture, and a creaking swing set that neither of her kids had used for at least two years.

Obviously, if she was dead, this wasn't Heaven and she must have sinned a lot more than she realized.

The back door slammed open, and her daughter's voice cut through her brooding thoughts. "Isn't Daddy here yet?"

MaryAnne stifled the tart response that rose in her throat, determined not to let her anger and mistrust toward the man she'd married contaminate Alison's relationship with her father. "He said noon, but you know your father," she said evenly. "If he's an hour late, we count him as on time, right?"

Alison unconsciously twisted a lock of her dark brown hair around her forefinger, a habit MaryAnne had first noticed almost the day after she and Alan had separated. Alison glanced at the clock, then flopped into the chair opposite her mother. "So he won't be here for another forty-five minutes." The girl sighed. "Just like I told Logan." She began picking at the curling edge of the Formica-topped kitchen table. "Mom? Can I ask you something?"

The fact that Alison's eyes didn't meet hers warned MaryAnne that whatever the question was, she wasn't going to like it. But since Alison's thirteenth birthday last month she'd grown used to fielding questions she didn't quite feel comfortable about answering, so now she steeled herself and nodded. "You know you can always ask me anything you want, sweetheart," she said.

Alison took a deep breath. "Well, Logan and I are sort of

wondering. Are you and Daddy going to get back together again?"

Now, how on earth am I going to answer that one? MaryAnne thought. How do I tell her that the last thing in the world I want to do is go back to living with Alan Carpenter?

Except that maybe putting it together with Alan again *wasn't* quite the last thing in the world she wanted to do. Maybe—just maybe—it was the only thing she *could* do, given the circumstances. She realized now that at some level it was what she'd been thinking about all morning, though she still had no answers—for Alison or herself. No answers, just a jumble of feelings that were totally confused.

Confused not only by emotions, but by economics as well.

And economics, she knew, were not a proper basis for a marriage.

Hadn't she read all the articles in all the women's magazines on the glories of love?

Hadn't she read all the stories about the poor couples who found happiness in each other and rose above their poverty?

The novels about women who married for money, only to find true love in the arms of the chauffeur, or the gardener, or the pool man?

Everyone knew that love and money should properly have nothing to do with each other.

Then she'd looked around the house and begun to wonder. The paint on the outside was beginning to peel, and the wallpaper in the living room had finally deteriorated to the point that Logan's messy fingerprints could no longer be cleaned off.

"Didn't I tell you you should have painted in the first place?" Alan had asked when she'd called him to plead for enough money to replace the paper. "If you'd been practical at the start, you could just repaint. I just don't have the money for new paper."

But you had the money to take Little Miss Blondie to Bermuda, didn't you? MaryAnne had thought bitterly as she slammed the phone down.

She'd spent the rest of the day in a black rage, but by the next morning she'd calmed down enough to realize that Alan *hadn't* had enough money to take Eileen Chandler—or anyone else, for that matter—to Bermuda. Eileen must have paid for the trip herself.

Which had only made her mood dark again, and she'd spent the rest of *that* day engulfed all over again in the pain of losing her husband to a woman who was younger and prettier than she was, and had plenty of money of her own as well.

The worst part of it was her anger at herself for not having seen the separation coming. How stupidly loyal and trusting she'd been! How naive to believe every word Alan told her about working late so many nights to prove himself ready for a big promotion.

A promotion that would allow them to move into a bigger house in a better neighborhood, to take their first real vacation in years, and even to put away some money so when the kids went to college, they wouldn't have to plunge themselves into debt.

Blind. She'd been utterly, hopelessly blind—until the night six months ago when Alan had come home late, and without a word of apology or regret, had packed his suitcase and announced he was moving in with another woman.

"It's not something I can explain," he'd told her as she sat on the edge of the bed, staring wordlessly at him while tears streamed down her face. "It's just something that happened. She came in to talk to one of the architects, and something happened between us. Something I couldn't control." Finally he'd sat down next to her, gently putting his arms around her and talking quietly, his soft voice and warm brown eyes consoling her at the same time that his words cut into her soul. By the time he left, she was almost convinced that the whole thing was somehow her own fault.

The next morning she'd had to explain to Alison and Logan that their father had gone to live "somewhere else" for a while.

She'd evaded all their questions, explaining only that things like this sometimes happened between grown-ups, and that they mustn't worry about it. Everything would work out for the best.

By the end of the week she'd figured out just how stupid she'd been. There was no way Alan was going to be promoted without going back to school. True, he was a very good draftsman—the best the company had—but for him to go any further in the firm, he was going to have to get a degree in architecture. Why had that never occurred to her in the months he'd been sleeping with Eileen Chandler?

Because she hadn't wanted it to occur to her, of course. Because she hadn't wanted to believe that this man, whom she had believed in so completely for the fifteen years of their marriage, could be capable of so cruel a betrayal. From the moment she'd met him, the warmth of his smile and clearness of his eyes had convinced her that he would never lie to her.

Now, he had.

Still, as the months had gone by, she'd somehow refused truly to believe it, kept somehow believing it was a bad dream from which she would awaken, and somehow kept putting off filing for a divorce. The bad dream became reality the evening she finally glimpsed the other woman, very blond, very petite, very elegantly dressed, and very securely wrapped in Alan's strong right arm.

They were coming out of a restaurant. A very expensive restaurant which was far beyond Alan Carpenter's modest means.

So, MaryAnne thought, could anyone begrudge her the glee she felt when Susan Weinstock had called last month to say, "Guess what? Little Miss Blondie threw Alan out!"

Susan gushed on: "Would you believe it's another man? Apparently, the lovely Miss Chandler decided Alan wasn't quite what she wanted. So she traded him in for a richer model. Some guy with two middle names, a roman numeral at the end, and a trust fund! Isn't that great?"

And it was—for one completely, blissfully satisfying moment

of sweet revenge. Which quickly soured into confusion when Alan called to tell her that "things haven't worked out with Eileen, and I've moved out."

"Really?" she had replied, carefully revealing nothing of what she already knew, hoping her neutral tone concealed the collision of emotions inside her—the need to forgive and forget and have him back again warring with the longing to punish him for all the hurt he'd caused. "What happened?" she'd asked.

Alan barely hesitated. "It—Well, it was you, honey," he said, with the perfect amount of appealingly boyish repentance in his voice. "I—Well, I just couldn't get you out of my mind, and in the end, I found out it's you I love, not Eileen."

Another lie. MaryAnne felt her optimism shrivel as she silently hung up the phone.

But Alan was relentless, calling daily, pleading with her to give him another chance, begging her to forgive him, swearing that the affair had been a terrible mistake and that nothing like it would ever happen again. It wasn't until he'd admitted that Eileen had thrown him out that MaryAnne finally agreed to see him again.

Since then, her confusion had only grown. She no longer trusted him. She was bitterly angry about what he'd done. But she was just as attracted to him as she'd ever been, and just as susceptible to the charm that had made her fall in love with him in the first place.

And, of course, there was the question of economics.

But as desperate as she was to have her family whole again, she wasn't ready to take him back.

Not yet.

Maybe not ever.

But finally she'd agreed to this first family barbecue, a week before Labor Day, and her daughter's question still hung in the hot, muggy air.

"Are you and Daddy going to get back together again?"

As MaryAnne searched for the right words to answer Alison's

question, the doorbell rang, and a moment later Logan charged
in through the back door.

"It's Daddy!" the ten-year-old shouted. "He's early!"

MaryAnne's eyes went to the clock, and a faint smile curled
the corners of her mouth. Only half an hour late, which, for
Alan, was a record of punctuality.

Maybe, after all, he really had changed, really was sorry for
what had happened.

Or maybe he just figured it would be a lot cheaper to move
back into the house.

MaryAnne stood up to greet her husband, still not sure whether
she was glad to see him or not.

More than two thousand miles from the stifling atmosphere of
Canaan, New Jersey, Ted Wilkenson stepped out onto the front
porch of his house near Sugarloaf, Idaho, and breathed deeply
of the crisp mountain air. The day was perfect, the heat of the
summer already beginning to fade, the deep blue sky forming an
unblemished bowl over the valley in the Sawtooth Mountains in
which Sugarloaf nestled like a forgotten village from a century
earlier. His personal Shangri-la.

As he did every day, Ted paused to savor his good fortune in
having discovered the valley nearly fourteen years ago. It was
still no more than an unknown speck in the mountains north of
Sun Valley then, and the refugees from Los Angeles had not yet
realized that just beyond what they thought of as paradise was
the valley of Eden. The problem now was to keep it that way.
For the last five years, since the first developers had begun arriv-
ing to cut ski trails in the mountains above Sugarloaf, and build
their brick and stucco time-shared condominiums, Ted and a few
of his friends had begun buying up as much land as they could,
and passing zoning ordinances to protect the original beauty of
the place.

Ted's own ranch had grown from its original three hundred acres to more than a thousand. Tomorrow he would close on a deal to add another two hundred acres of land to his holdings. Two hundred acres straddling Sugarloaf Creek, which joined the beginnings of the Salmon River, ten miles farther down, where Sugarloaf Valley opened into the immense open space of the Sawtooth Valley. That should set Chuck Deaver—"Devious" Deaver, the locals called him—back a pace or two, Ted thought as he started across the wide yard that separated the rambling two-story log house from the weathered barn that was the only original structure remaining on the property. Beyond stymieing the developer, whose plans to use the site as the heart of a much larger project had finally goaded Ted into making the purchase, the acquisition would please Audrey and Joey as well. Both his wife and son had been pleading for the purchase for nearly a year, Audrey to protect the land from the continuing march of condos up the valley, and Joey because he couldn't wait to have his own private fishing stream. As of tomorrow, a good portion of the stream would be safe from Deaver's bulldozers, and Ted, with Bill Sikes's help, could begin moving fences to include the new land into the protected wilderness that was the ranch.

For wilderness was what El Monte was, since neither Ted nor Audrey had any interest in developing more land than was necessary to raise fodder for the three horses that were the sole occupants of the barn. The whole point of the ranch was to protect the valley in its natural state, and both Ted and Audrey were aware of the irony that their current low-tech lifestyle was a direct result of Ted's former high-tech experience in the overdeveloped morass of Silicon Valley. Now they were using the profits from the immensely successful software company Ted had founded in California to protect their private wilderness in Idaho.

Ted and Audrey had discovered Sugarloaf together, only a month after they'd discovered each other. Audrey had spent the summer working as a waitress at the Sun Valley Lodge, and Ted had come up for a weekend respite from the pressures of running SoftWorks, which had already grown into a major software company, employing three hundred programmers, though Ted was still only twenty-five. He had met Audrey the first night he was there, and wound up staying the rest of the summer, running SoftWorks by phone, and discovering in the process that he wasn't nearly as indispensable to his company as he'd imagined.

On the last Sunday morning of the summer, she'd joined him for breakfast on the terrace between the lodge and the ice rink, and before lunch they'd driven over Galena Summit and stared in awe at the Sawtooth Valley, revealed before them like a hidden treasure. Surrounded by towering mountains that protected it from the world beyond, the valley's floor was a vast sea of grass and wildflowers, dotted with clumps of aspens and cottonwoods, the streams that would converge to become the Salmon River seeping out of the marshes at the head of the valley, to meander slowly down toward Stanley, the town that lay at its foot. For a long time they gazed silently at the flanks of the mountains, heavily forested on their lower slopes but barren above the timberline, soaring up to the jagged peaks that had given the Sawtooth range its name.

"This is it," Ted had finally murmured. "This is paradise. Now all we have to do is find the perfect spot."

They'd driven down into the valley, explored the weathered old buildings of Stanley, then started back, turning up each road that wound into the foothills until finally they stumbled into the Sugarloaf Valley, a miniature version of the vast reaches of the Sawtooth, blocked at its eastern end by the rugged face of Sugarloaf peak.

The village, near the mouth of the valley, appeared as perfect as a set for a Western movie, with raised wooden sidewalks connecting the false-fronted buildings that flanked the unpaved road. Between the town and the face of Sugarloaf, the valley rose with increasing steepness, the wilderness broken only by a few cultivated fields, occasional long, twisting driveways leading to nearly invisible farmhouses which were the only signs of human habitation.

At the end of the road, they'd come upon a sign offering three hundred acres, together with a house, a barn, and outbuildings.

"Here it is," Ted had said.

"Here is what?" Audrey had asked.

"Here is where we're going to live after we get married," Ted replied, as if it were the most natural thing in the world for him to be proposing to a woman he'd known only a month, and deciding that they would live on a crumbling farm hundreds of miles from anywhere.

"Looks all right to me," Audrey heard herself reply. "Do you think we ought to look at the house, or should we just buy it?"

"Let's just buy it," Ted had said. Half an hour later he had done just that.

The farm duly purchased, they headed back to Sun Valley, but by the time they got there, they'd decided there was no reason not to finish the job they'd already started, so they continued on through the resort town and drove down to Hailey, picked up a license at the courthouse, and got married before dinner.

"You're sure there isn't anyone you want at the wedding?" Ted asked at the last minute.

There was only MaryAnne, her childhood friend and still her best friend, but MaryAnne was two thousand miles away. "No," Audrey had said. Then, with the sudden thought: "You sure you don't want to at least call your parents?"

Ted's laugh had filled the car. "No chance. My mother ran out on me about a week after my father dumped her. I haven't seen either of them since. And I'm not about to spoil the best weekend of my life by trying to find them."

As they stood before the magistrate, their hands clasped while they repeated their vows, it occurred to Audrey that after only a month in a resort town, she really didn't know much about Ted Wilkenson at all. But somehow it didn't matter. Since the loss of

her own parents to a junkie who had mugged them on the steps
of their apartment house on New York's Upper West Side, she
had felt just as alone in the world as Ted must have during the
years after his mother abandoned him. But in the four short
weeks since they had met, they'd come to feel as if they knew
each other perfectly.

And that feeling had never changed, as far as Ted was concerned.

Joey was born less than a year after they were married, and
Ted had essentially retired from SoftWorks, going back only often enough to explain his ideas for new programs and to get the
programmers to begin producing them.

The old farmhouse was torn down, and the log lodge built in
its place.

The ranch slowly grew, and the Wilkensons slipped easily into
the fabric of the town.

Both of them knew that through some strange fate, they had
found in one another the perfect partner.

And so Ted, not quite forty yet, was now living in his idea of
paradise, with a wife who was his best friend, and raising his
son far from the problems of the city.

His son.

The only fly in the ointment, Ted thought ruefully. Instantly
regretting the thought, he reminded himself that Joey seemed to
be getting better. Discipline was all the boy had needed, really,
and he had administered it. Not that Joey had ever been a truly
bad kid—he'd just let himself fall into moods of silence and for-
getfulness. Sometimes he wouldn't speak for hours at a time, or
would disappear from the house for an entire day.

Ted had finally put his foot down, a couple of years ago. "He's
not a baby anymore," he told Audrey before taking his belt to
Joey's backside the first time. "We've tried getting him to grow
up your way, and it hasn't worked. Now we'll try it my way."

That first time Ted used the belt, Joey had sulked for two
hours, until Ted explained to him that if he continued sulking,

more punishment would follow. It had straightened the boy right up, and soon afterward Joey stopped giving in to his strange moods.

Yesterday, however, Joey had disappeared after breakfast, leaving his chores undone and telling no one where he was going. When the boy finally appeared as the sun was setting, Ted hauled him out to the barn, explaining to him that what was about to happen was for his own good. He had taken off his belt as Joey cowered. But the boy hadn't resisted his punishment, Ted now recalled with satisfaction, and he hadn't gone crying to his mother. Instead he'd told her that he and his father had been feeding the horses. Well, that was that.

The boy hadn't complained, and he hadn't sulked.

He was finally growing up.

A feeling of well-being surged through Ted as he stepped into the barn to begin mucking out the stalls.

He led Sheika, the black Arabian mare that was his favorite, to the cross ties, tethered her, then began the process of mucking out the horse's stall. He'd barely gotten the soiled straw shoveled into the wheelbarrow when Sheika whinnied nervously and pawed at the ground.

"It's okay, Sheika," Ted called out, but instead of settling down, the horse pawed at the floor of the wash stall once again, then tugged her head against the restraining tethers.

"Hey, settle down, old girl," Ted soothed, leaving the stall and moving toward the horse.

Sheika ignored him, her eyes fixed on the open door of the barn, her ears laid back against her head as she snorted nervously.

"What is it girl? What's wrong?" Ted glanced toward the door, but the glare of brilliant sunlight outside blinded him and he could see nothing. "Joey? Sikes? Is someone out there?" But he knew his son had gone fishing, and he'd seen Bill Sikes, his caretaker, drive off toward town. What the hell was going on?

Suddenly he felt vaguely uneasy. For a while now, strange

things had been happening on the ranch. The horses had been spooking, and at times even he had experienced the unsettling sensation of being watched by unseen eyes. Just a couple of nights ago, telling Audrey that he felt like getting some fresh air, Ted had gone outside to have a look around. The horses were restless in their stalls that night, but they'd calmed right down when he talked to them, and he'd found nothing amiss in the barn.

Yet even as he'd returned to the house, he'd still had the distinct feeling that somewhere, hidden in the darkness, eyes were watching him.

Despite the warmth of the evening, he'd shivered, and found himself hurrying back to the brightness of the house.

Now, in the full light of day, he had that same uneasy feeling. Again he called out: "Who is it? Is anyone out there?"

There was still no answer. Ted at last turned back to Sheika, reaching out to take one of the tethers in his right hand while he stroked the horse with his left. For a split second the big mare seemed to calm, but a sound from the door startled her and she jerked her head, yanking the tether from Ted's hand. Instinctively, Ted turned to see who had come into the barn, but all he saw was a quick flash of movement before the horse whinnied loudly once again, then reared up, her front hooves striking out against the presence in the barn.

Sheika's right hoof struck Ted Wilkenson in the back of the head, felling him instantly. He was still conscious, but before he could roll away, the horse plunged back down, neighing loudly as the form in the doorway drew closer.

Her great left hoof, shod only the day before with fresh iron, smashed into Ted's right temple, the bone shattering under the immense weight of the animal.

The horse reared again, finally jerking free of the tethers, then lunged out of the wash stall, her hooves thundering on the thick planks of the barn's floor as she galloped toward the doors.

A moment later she was gone, racing across a field toward the woods beyond.

Inside the barn, the two remaining horses panicked, whinny-ing loudly, rearing up, their hooves striking the sides of their stalls as they reacted to the sudden danger. But then the presence was gone as quickly as it had come, and the horses calmed once more, only pawing nervously as they caught a strange coppery scent in the air.

And Ted Wilkenson lay dead on the floor, his head resting in a pool of his own blood.

———

MaryAnne Carpenter gazed out the kitchen window, her hand suspended over the soapy water in the sink. The scene outside looked for all the world like any normal American family enjoy-ing the end of a late summer day. Alison was clearing the last of the supper dishes off the outdoor table, and the embers in the barbecue were dying away, only a faint wisp of smoke betraying that there was anything but ash left beneath the grill.

Logan and Alan stood at opposite ends of the small lawn, hurl-ing a softball back and forth as if they'd been doing it every evening all summer. And indeed, for the kids, it was almost as if their father had never been gone. They'd fallen into their old patterns, vying with each other for their father's attention. After a while even MaryAnne had begun to let down her guard, won-dering if, after all, Alan might really have had a change of heart.

Except that suspicion, once learned, is difficult to put aside. Despite Alan's constant reassurances that a return to his family was what he really wanted, how could she be sure that if Eileen Chandler raised her finger, Alan would not happily trot back to her condominium, with its well-equipped gym—which, judging by his trim figure, he had obviously been using—and its swim-ming pool, which she had steadfastly refused to let Alison and Logan enjoy?

Despite her misgivings, MaryAnne had to acknowledge that she'd enjoyed the day, the easy comfort of having Alan back to tend to the barbecue and produce the perfectly cooked steaks that always managed to elude her, no matter how carefully she timed them. She'd even found herself falling into his discussion of the improvements they'd make to the house as soon as he moved back in.

"And you'll get your promotion, so we can pay for it all?" she'd been unable to resist asking.

He hadn't risen to the bait, and he'd had the good grace to blush with embarrassment at the question, and admit that he deserved the jab.

And now he was playing catch with Logan, as if the destruction of his marriage had never happened. The blissful look on her son's face tore at MaryAnne's heart.

"Mom?" Alison said anxiously as she came through the back door, a stack of plates precariously balanced in one hand, four glasses clutched with the fingers of the other. "Are you going to let Daddy come home now?"

The question jarred MaryAnne out of her reverie. She reached into the greasy water and fished out the skillet in which she'd fried the potatoes they'd had with Alan's steaks. "I—I'm not sure," she said, unwilling to shatter her daughter's hopes. "There's a lot to be discussed before that can happen."

Alison carefully set the glasses down on the counter. "But wouldn't it be easier to talk about things if he were here?" she asked, her eyes once more avoiding her mother's, just as they had a few hours before, when she'd broached the same subject. "I mean, Logan and I really miss him, and—"

"And I don't really want to talk about it right now, all right?" MaryAnne broke in, with more sharpness than she'd intended. "What's happening between your father and me is very complicated. I—I just can't discuss it with you right now."

"Then who should you discuss it with?" Alison demanded, her words taking on a petulant tone. "If you can't talk about it with me, who can you talk about it with?"

Audrey, MaryAnne thought. I could discuss it with Audrey—

except she's thousands of miles away, and wouldn't understand anyhow! I marry a man I knew for two whole years, and he ends up cheating on me, and she marries a man she's known for less than a month, and everything turns out perfect. It's not fair! Then she caught herself, realizing that she herself wasn't being fair. If anyone would understand what she was going through, it would be Audrey, her best friend since they had been children right here in Canaan.

"Aunt Audrey," she said out loud, with a smile for her daughter. "In fact, I think I'll call her tomorrow, and see what she has to say."

Alison's eyes lit up. "Really? You promise?"

MaryAnne cocked her head at her daughter. "Now why does that please you so much, young lady?"

"Because Aunt Audrey's crazy about Daddy, so she'll be on our side."

"Side?" MaryAnne repeated, raising her brows in an exaggerated arch. "Since when are you and Logan taking sides?"

"I didn't mean it like that," Alison said, backpedaling quickly. "I just meant that Logan and I really want you and Daddy back together, that's all."

Before the discussion could go any further, Alan strode through the back door, trailed by their son, who was begging for just five more minutes of catch.

"Don't you think I better help your mother with the dishes?" Alan countered, picking up a towel and starting to dry the pans that were draining in the rack.

"But—" Logan began.

"No 'buts,' " Alan said, cutting him off, snapping the towel at the boy, who leapt out of range. "Now scoot, and let your mother and me have some time to ourselves, okay?"

Logan's mouth opened as if to reply, but his older sister grabbed him by the arm and almost dragged him toward the living room. "Just shut up, Logan," Alison said. "For once in your stupid life, try not to say something dumb!"

"Alison, don't talk that way to your brother," MaryAnne automatically called to her daughter, but the kitchen door had already swung closed behind her children. And then, before she quite knew what had happened, Alan had slipped his arms around her and begun nuzzling at her neck. Even as words of protest rose in her throat, MaryAnne felt the familiar warmth of his touch begin to flow through her.

"Now was today so bad?" Alan crooned into her ear. "Come on, honey, admit it—you loved having me here as much as I loved being here. And what happened with Eileen is over. It's over and forgotten. There's no one for me but you, and there never will be again. All I have to do is pack up my clothes, and we can be together again."

MaryAnne wanted to tell him to be quiet, to leave her alone, to give her a chance to think things out. But his words crept into her mind, and his arms held her close, and she thought if she could just forget the last year, just put it out of her mind, things might be the same as they had been before.

He turned her around and pressed his lips to hers, and as the kiss deepened, she realized just how much she had missed him.

"Let me stay," Alan whispered. "At least let me stay for tonight."

MaryAnne felt her resolve slipping away, but before she gave in completely, she promised herself that tomorrow, in the clear light of the morning, she would follow through on her promise to Alison.

She would call Audrey Wilkenson.

Audrey would help her figure out what to do.

CHAPTER 2

*T*he shadows cast by the Sawtooth Mountains were already creeping down the valley as Audrey Wilkenson approached the gates to El Monte. Though it was almost fourteen years since she'd first seen this spot, she could still remember the moment as clearly as if it were yesterday. Not that the entrance to the property looked as it had back then, when she and Ted had stumbled across it. Where there had once hung only three sagging strands of barbed wire tacked to crumbling posts, with an opening blocked by a rotting wooden cattle guard, there now stood a split-rail fence, four feet high, extending off into the woods in both directions, as far as one could see from the road. The cattle guard had been replaced by a gate, double hung from two columns built of native stone, surmounted by a deeply carved wooden arch announcing the name of the ranch.

Even the forest flanking the road had changed, for during the first two years they'd been there, she and Ted had cleared out the underbrush and thinned the trees so that the most majestic now spread their limbs unfettered by the clutter of saplings that had originally crowded the landscape.

The gates stood open, for the first thing the Wilkensons had done was to sell off the cattle. They had resolved that as much of the land as possible would be allowed to revert to natural meadows and forests. Slowly, almost imperceptibly from year to year, the land had recovered from the farming that had once taken place on it. Now all that remained in cultivation were the two small fields necessary to raise food for the horses. El Monte had become a private park, a quiet refuge not only for the Wilkensons, but for the wild animals that roamed there. The few remaining fences were no longer designed to keep anything either in or out, but solely to let hikers know where the property began and ended.

Slowing the Range Rover as she started up the winding drive toward the house, Audrey anticipated the familiar sense of well-being that always came over her whenever she came back to the ranch, no matter how short a time she had been gone. But as she made the last turn, and the comforting mass of the rambling log house came into view, that accustomed feeling of security in homecoming failed to settle over her.

Instead, she felt a vague sense of unease, as if something had gone wrong.

Pulling the Rover up in front of the wide porch that fronted the house, she opened its door, dropped to the graveled ground, and slammed the door shut, leaving the keys in the ignition, as did nearly everyone in Sugarloaf. Unaccountably, she paused, staring at the house, a frown creasing her forehead as she tried to identify exactly what was bothering her. Just a feeling. Nothing was visibly wrong at all.

The house looked no different from the way it ever did, its two low wings extending from its two-story center in a welcoming V pattern. Shaking her head as if to toss off the uneasy feeling, she strode up the three steps to the porch, crossed it, and pushed the front door open.

"Ted? Joey?" she called. "Anybody home?"

Silence.

Which was not unusual, she told herself as she dropped her purse on the old wooden pew that sat just inside the front door. Joey was probably still off fishing, and Ted was undoubtedly in the barn, tending to the horses.

Yet the feeling that something was wrong wouldn't leave her, and her frown deepened as she toured the downstairs rooms of both wings, then started up the stairs toward the second floor.

She stopped short on the third step, her intuition telling her that the second story was as empty as the first floor.

Her strange sense of apprehension growing stronger, Audrey left the house and started across the yard toward the barn, glancing at the field and the woods beyond.

The field was empty.

No sign of Ted or Joey, nor even Bill Sikes.

She paused outside the open barn door, listening to the horses moving restlessly in their stalls.

If Ted—or even Joey or Sikes—weren't inside, then why were the doors standing open?

And if Ted *was* inside, then why wasn't he talking to the horses, calming them as he always did when something made them nervous?

Her apprehension congealing to fear, her intuition shrieking that whatever was wrong was inside the barn, she steeled her nerves, then strode through the open doors.

She saw him sprawled out on his back, his head twisted unnaturally to the right, his hair matted in a dark slime of drying blood.

"Ted?"

The single word slipped almost tentatively from her lips, her mind unwilling to accept the full meaning of what her eyes told her. Numbly, she took a step forward. "Ted!"

Suddenly she was running toward him, screaming his name, and a moment later she dropped down on the floor of the wash stall. "Ted! Ted, say something!"

As Audrey grasped her husband's shoulders, his head rolled to one side and his eyes fixed on hers. For an instant, just the tiniest moment, she felt a stab of relief.

He was all right!

He'd just fallen and hurt his head, but he was all right!

She grasped at the straw of hope, but as her eyes stared into Ted's, relief faded as quickly as it had come.

His eyes, a clear, deep blue, had gone flat.

All she could see in them was the unblinking gaze of death.

She froze, her gaze locked on her husband as she tried to understand what could have happened.

When she glanced up, her eyes fogging with tears, she saw the broken strands of leather dangling from the posts at the corners of the stall.

"No . . ." she breathed, the single word drifting almost soundlessly from her constricted throat. It couldn't have happened.

Not to Ted.

Not possibly to Ted.

He had a way with animals, the same way he had of instilling trust in any living creature, which she herself had sensed the moment she'd met him.

All he had to do was speak to an animal, or lay a gentle hand on it, and—

A wracking sob clutching at her chest, Audrey Wilkenson struggled to her feet and staggered to the door. It seemed to take forever, and with every step, her anguish built inside her. Then she was out of the barn, and a howl of grief erupted from her, bursting from her throat to shatter the quiet of the gathering evening.

Across the field, just emerging from the woods with his fishing pole slung over his right shoulder and his tackle box in his left hand, Joey Wilkenson stopped short as his mother's agonized cry rolled over him. At his knees, the German shepherd that was his constant companion laid his ears back and pressed his body against Joey's legs as if to protect his master from whatever creature had uttered the unearthly sound. A second later Audrey cried out again, this time shouting for help. Finally, Joey Wilkenson came to life.

"Go on, Storm," he commanded the dog. "Go get her!"

Obeying his master instantly, the big dog shot forward, flying away from Joey to race across the field toward Audrey, who had sunk to her knees, her face covered with her hands as she gave in to the grief that overwhelmed her.

Only when the big dog had thrown himself onto his mother, eagerly licking her face as he tried to soothe her, did Joey break into a run, loping easily across the field with the grace of a wild animal. And as an animal would have, he stopped short when he was still a few yards away from her, a sudden wariness making him hesitate.

Joey said nothing at all as Audrey brokenly told him what had happened. He listened in silence as he absorbed her words, and understood only one thing.

His father would never beat him again.

———

Though it seemed like an eternity, only an hour and a half had passed since Audrey Wilkenson's discovery of her husband's body. Now she sat in the tack room, staring straight ahead, the words of the people around her penetrating her consciousness in broken fragments.

"Somethin' musta spooked her . . ."

"Don't make sense . . ."

"Sheika's not the kinda horse to . . ."

"Can't believe it—not Ted."

But it *was* Ted.

She would never forget the deathly gray of Joey's face as she'd told him what had happened, nor the dark curtain that had closed over his emotions as he listened expressionlessly to what had befallen his father. When her words finally failed her, he'd turned and started toward the barn, as if unwilling to accept the truth unless he had seen for himself what had happened.

"D-Don't," she'd whispered, her voice hoarse. "Don't go in, Joey. Find Bill Sikes." Joey had hesitated, and Audrey had managed to speak again. "Just go get Sikes, Joey. There's nothing you can do in there."

Her son's eyes had fixed on her, but then he'd turned away and continued walking toward the barn. Only when he was at the half-open door was Audrey finally able to drag herself once more to her feet and return to the barn to pull her oddly silent son into her arms.

"Come on," she'd whispered to him, turning him away from his father's still body. "We have to get help, Joey. We can't just stay in here."

Almost in a trance, she'd led Joey back to the house, and called Bill Sikes, who was in his cabin a quarter of a mile away. The Custer County sheriff's office was located in Challis, more than seventy miles away, but the deputy's office was closer, in Sugarloaf, and the deputy, Rick Martin, like everyone in town, was a friend. Rick would know what to do.

"There's been an accident," Audrey said when Martin's voice came on the line. "It's Ted."

She couldn't remember much after that, except that within a few minutes the police car arrived, and an ambulance, and then the yard between the house and the barn had begun to fill up as word spread through the valley of what had happened.

It was Rick Martin who had led her to the tack room, Joey's hand clutched in hers, and told her to stay there.

"I can't keep folks away from you in the house, Audrey," he said gently. "Better if you're down here. No one'll come through unless you say the word."

Audrey nodded mutely, sank down onto the sagging leather sofa that was the tack room's main piece of furniture, and waited, Joey sitting silently next to her.

She did her best to answer questions, but was unable to tell Rick Martin any more than he'd been able to see for himself.

Half an hour ago, after they'd taken pictures from every imaginable angle, Ted's body had been placed in the ambulance and taken away.

And now, at last, Rick Martin was crouched on the floor in front of her.

"Audrey?" he said, his voice barely penetrating the mist that seemed to be closing around her mind. "Can I talk to you, Aud?"

Talk to me? What could he possibly say? Ted's dead. He's dead, and nothing can bring him back to life.

She felt a wave of panic well up in her.

What am I going to do? What am I going to do without him?

She wanted to throw herself into someone's arms—

—wanted to scream out the anguish she was feeling—

—wanted to let herself die, to give up her life to the grief that held her in an iron grip, choking her.

Help me, Ted! Please help me!

Though no sound escaped her lips, the plea echoed in her mind.

And one word emerged out of the confusion that engulfed her.

Joey.

An image of her son rose out of Audrey Wilkenson's roiling emotions, and abruptly her mind cleared.

She took a deep breath, then sat up straight, focusing on the deputy's concerned face. "What happened, Rick?" she asked, her voice calm and clear. "Do you have any idea?"

Martin shook his head. "Not really," he said. "From what I can see, he was mucking out Sheika's stall, and he must have parked the horse in the wash stall till he was done. Something must have spooked the horse, and when Ted tried to calm her down, Sheika must have reared up, knocked him over, then come down on his head. An accident, pure and simple."

Audrey felt another wave of emotion rise up inside her, but firmly held it in check.

"What could have spooked Sheika?" she asked.

Rick Martin shrugged. "Don't know. Could have been any-thing, could have been nothing at all. For all I know, a rat could have run through, or an owl dropped down from the rafters. You know horses. Practically anything can do it, if it takes 'em by surprise."

Audrey's head moved in silent acceptance of the deputy's words; then: "What about Sheika? Has anyone found her yet?"

"Not yet. I got a couple of guys out looking, but she could be anywhere. When we find her . . ." His voice trailed off, and his gaze shifted momentarily to Joey, who was still perched stiffly next to his mother.

"You'll shoot her, won't you?" Joey demanded.

Rick Martin's tongue ran nervously over his lower lip. "I'm afraid we don't have much choice, Joey," he said. "She—"

"She didn't do it on purpose!" Joey flared. He jumped to his feet, his dark eyes fixing angrily on the deputy, his dark hair falling over his forehead, making him look much younger than his thirteen years. "Maybe it wasn't her fault! Maybe someone came into the barn and spooked her on purpose! You can't kill her! You can't!" Turning, he bolted out of the tack room, leaving his mother and the deputy staring helplessly after him.

"I'm sorry, Audrey," Rick Martin said into the silence that fol-lowed Joey's abrupt departure. "I didn't handle that very well."

Sighing, Audrey pulled herself to her feet. "It's all right, Rick. You know how Joey is. He's always had this thing with animals. Even when he was at his worst, he always got along with them."

"Like Ted," Rick said, then wished he could retract the words as he saw the stricken look on Audrey's face. "I—I'm sorry, that was—"

But Audrey shook her head. "It's all right. But it's not like Ted at all. It's different. Ted could always keep the horses calm, but with Joey it's always been something else. Sometimes it's almost as if he can communicate with them."

Rick Martin shifted his weight uncomfortably, knowing there was nothing more he could do at the ranch right now, but not certain that Audrey should be left alone. "I got rid of everybody but Bill Sikes. Figured you can call anyone you want, but right now you don't need the place cluttered up with everyone in town." When Audrey made no reply, he went on, "Or I can call Gillie, if you'd like. I mean, I'm on shift this evening, so she could come up here and just sort of keep you company."

"That's nice of you, Rick," Audrey replied. "But I think for tonight, Joey and I might do better by ourselves."

Holding Rick's arm, she let him lead her out of the tack room and back through the barn, where she carefully avoided looking at the spot where she'd found her husband's body less than two hours earlier. Bill Sikes was still there, doing his best to settle the two horses who were still in their stalls.

"I'll take care of everything, Mrs. Wilkenson," Bill Sikes said as she passed. "You just try to get some rest, okay? That was the hardest thing after Minnie died—tryin' to sleep."

Audrey paused, smiling at the caretaker. His weathered face made him look older than his sixty years, but his wiry body still held the strength of a man twenty years younger. "Thank you, Bill. It'll be all right. Somehow, we'll all get through this."

"We will," Sikes assured her. "You need anything tonight, you call me. You never know what's wandering around here at night. And I got a bad feelin' lately, like there's somethin' up there in the mountains, watchin' us."

Audrey shivered even as she tried to reject Sikes's words. "I'm sure I'll be just fine," she said, lending her words more conviction than she truly felt.

"Okay," Sikes sighed, knowing it was useless to argue with her. "But you call me if you want. Anytime at all."

"I promise," Audrey said, though even as she spoke the words, she knew that she wouldn't call him.

Tonight, after Joey had gone to sleep, she would sit alone in the den that had been Ted's favorite room, trying to come to grips with what had happened and to figure out how she was going to get through the rest of her life without him.

Live without him.

It was a concept she had never considered since the moment she'd met Ted. Not even when the . . . problems had begun.

Now, for the first time, she was going to have to think about it.

She had no choice.

———

The ten o'clock news was over. As she clicked the television in the den off, Audrey realized she hadn't heard a single word of it. Through the entire half hour, she had sat staring numbly at the screen, vaguely aware of the images of the pretty blond woman and the plastic man who were reading from the TelePrompTers, but not absorbing so much as a syllable of what they had been saying.

Exhaustion had overcome her. She swung her legs up onto the couch, closing her eyes for a moment in a vain hope that she might drift off to sleep.

But all that came were images of Ted.

Working in the forest, his shirt off, his muscular body glistening with sweat.

Galloping across the field astride Sheika, gracefully soaring over the jumps they had set up when they thought they might get serious about riding.

Sitting in the easy chair next to the sofa, a book open in his lap, as he had almost every evening since they'd built the house.

And then another image of Ted came into her mind.

An image of her husband striking her son.

It had only happened once. Just once, she told herself. But that once was too much. She could still remember the horror and shock of it. Two years ago, almost exactly.

The moment Joey had come downstairs for breakfast, they had known that one of his strange moods had come over him. He was silent, barely responding even when she spoke directly to him, and after breakfast he had simply disappeared, going off with

Storm to wander in the woods. He didn't return until thirty minutes after the sun had set, by which time Audrey had been seriously worried.

That evening, Ted had taken Joey out to the barn and beaten him with his belt. It stunned Audrey, and when she saw the look in Joey's eyes when he came back to the house, her heart had nearly broken.

"I won't tolerate it anymore," Ted had told her. "He doesn't have the right to go off without a word to either one of us, and he's been coddled about it long enough."

"But he's only a little boy!" she'd protested.

"He's not that little anymore," Ted had said, his voice taking on an unfamiliar harshness. "He's old enough to take some responsibility for his actions!"

"But to whip him . . ."

Ted's eyes had darkened. "A couple of smacks won't hurt him, Audrey."

But it hadn't been "a couple of smacks." It had been a series of angry red welts across her son's back and buttocks, which Joey had done his best to conceal from her.

Just once, she repeated to herself now, just once. But she could not still the thought that kept creeping back into her mind.

Had there been other times?

Times that she didn't know about? How many times might Ted have taken Joey out to the barn and—

Audrey forcibly banished the image from her mind, the wounds of Ted's death still too fresh. It seemed wrong even to think about the faults her almost perfect husband had exhibited during the last couple of years.

Go to bed, she told herself. If you sit here, you'll wind up crying all night, and you still have a son who needs you. You cannot simply curl up and die, no matter how much you want to!

Determinedly, she planted her feet on the floor, then stood up and moved swiftly around the large room, switching off the lamps and locking the outside door.

Against what?

That was something else that had only begun over the last couple of years: a sense, once in a while at night, that there was something outside the house. Something they could never quite see, could never quite be certain was even there. And yet both she and Ted had begun to lock the house up at night. Now, she followed the habit they'd both established, moving through the rooms, locking every door and latching every window.

She was at the foot of the stairs when she sensed a movement above her. She looked up to see Joey, still dressed, starting down, Storm at his heels. "Honey? Why aren't you in bed?"

"The barn," Joey said. "The door's closed."

Audrey cocked her head in puzzlement. "It's always closed at night."

"But what about Sheika? What if she comes back?"

He was at the bottom of the stairs now, looking up at her, his dark eyes worried.

"She'll just stay in the field, sweetheart," Audrey told him. "And she might not come back tonight at all. If she was frightened, she could have run for miles."

Joey shook his head. "She'll come back," he said. "I know she will." His face set in the stubborn expression that told Audrey he was prepared to argue for hours, and she realized there was no way she could cope with a fight with her son tonight.

"All right," she said. "We'll leave it open. But we're going to make sure the stalls are locked. The last thing we need is to have the other horses gone tomorrow."

Together they went out the front door, leaving it standing open behind them. The moon was high in a cloudless sky, and a gentle breeze drifted down from the mountains above. Audrey reached out and took Joey's hand as they started toward the barn, and for the first time in months he didn't pull away from her with the self-consciousness of adolescence. But when they were halfway across the yard, he suddenly stopped, dropped her hand and pointed.

"Look! There she is!"

Peering into the darkness, Audrey gazed across the field toward the woods. At first she saw nothing. A second later, though, something moved, and then she saw the great form of the mare move out of the shadows of the forest into the brilliance of the moonlight. She halted, and lowered her head to graze, but as Joey called out to her, she looked up, her ears pricking and her tail arching gracefully.

"Sheika?" Joey called. "Sheika! Come on, Sheika!"

With Storm trotting after him, Joey started running out toward the field.

"Joey, stop!" Audrey called after him. "If we just leave the barn open, she'll go in!"

But even as she watched, the horse shied away and disappeared into the trees.

"Get a tether, Mom," Joey yelled. "I'll keep her in sight!"

Audrey stood rooted to the spot as the surrealism of the moment whirled around her. What were they doing outside in the middle of the night, only hours after Ted had died, chasing a horse?

It was insane!

It was ridiculous!

It was—

And then she realized.

It was exactly what Ted would have wanted them to be doing. She could almost hear him: *You're still alive, Audrey. And so is Joey. Go get her!*

The fatigue vanishing from her body, her mind finally overcoming the shock of finding Ted's body on the floor of the wash stall, Audrey breathed deeply of the night air, then ran to the barn, pulled the door open and slipped inside. In the tack room she found a lunging tether and a flashlight, then she left the barn and strode across the field toward Joey.

She caught up with him at the edge of the forest. He was

calling out to the horse, then listening carefully for any sound of the animal moving in the darkness of the woods.

His dog was nowhere to be seen.

"Where's Storm?" she asked, dropping her voice, although the two of them were completely alone.

"I sent him to find Sheika," Joey replied. A moment later they heard a sharp bark from somewhere in the forest. Then the tone of Storm's bark changed as the dog began trailing the horse. "Come on," Joey cried, charging down a path that cut through dense undergrowth that had never been cleared from this part of the woods.

Audrey switched on the light, following in the direction her son had taken, though he was already out of sight as he ran toward the sound of the baying dog. Then, as Storm fell silent, Audrey broke into a trot, stopping short when she came to a fork in the trail a hundred yards farther on.

Which way had Joey gone?

She listened for the sound of Storm's barking.

Nothing.

"Joey?" she called. "Joey, where are you?"

She waited, but there was no response. For an instant she felt a twinge of panic, but quickly put it down as she remembered where she was. Though the trail branched here, it came together again a few hundred yards farther up, where it ended at a bluff that overlooked the entire Sugarloaf Valley. The fork to the right was the easier one, the one to the left a little shorter. Either way, there were no other paths leading off the trail, and the under-brush was too dense even for Joey—let alone the horse—to leave the trail. Whichever path she chose, she would eventually come upon both her son and Sheika.

Sighing, she started the climb, choosing the right fork. She moved as fast as she could, pausing every now and then to call out to Joey and the dog, but it was as if the night had swallowed them.

She was still a hundred yards from the bluff when she began to worry.

What had happened to them?

Surely they must be able to hear her calling!

Was Joey playing some kind of morbid joke on her, tonight of all nights?

But what if he wasn't?

Her worry edging into fear, she hurried her step.

Abruptly, she stopped, sensing something close by.

Joey?

Storm?

What if it was neither?

What if it was a bear?

She froze, listening.

Silence.

She called out once more, but once again heard only the silence of the night. Though the wind soughed softly in the trees, she suddenly realized that she heard no sounds of birds rustling in their sleep, or insects chirping in the darkness.

Danger.

She sensed it all around her now, and automatically turned, instinct warning her to run down the trail and across the field to the safety of the house.

But she couldn't! Not with Joey still out here!

She pushed on, refusing to let panic overcome her, calling out every few seconds now, but still hearing nothing in reply. Then, as fatigue tugged at her, she burst out from the forest onto the bluff. Instantly, with the woods no longer enclosing her, and the full light of the moon flooding the valley below with a silver glow, her fear subsided. Any second, either Joey and Storm, or Sheika, or all three of them, would emerge from the other trail-head a hundred feet away, and then all of them would start back down.

She stepped out onto the edge of the bluff, gazing out over the valley. At the far end, the lights of Sugarloaf village twinkled in the darkness, and here and there, dotting the valley floor, she could see the lights of the houses between El Monte and the town.

How many times had she and Ted come up here when the moon was full?

How many times had they stood here together—

She froze, sensing that she was no longer alone.

"Joey?" Her son's name seemed to hang in the air for a moment, then died away into the silence.

She heard something, a faint rustling behind her.

She turned then, praying that whatever was there would be something familiar.

Almost invisible in the deep shadows of the trailhead, a dark form was slinking toward her.

She gasped, uncertain what the strange shape might be, but sensing the peril that emanated from it.

She stepped back, instinctively putting more distance between herself and the creature.

And then it leaped, hurtling out of the darkness toward her, its menace palpable in the night.

A scream of terror rose in Audrey's throat. She lurched back, the sudden movement taking her off balance, and realized a split-second too late that there was no longer anything beneath her foot.

She teetered for a moment, struggling to regain her footing. The scream in her throat finally broke free as she tumbled over the edge, scraped roughly against the bare stone face of the bluff, then felt herself dropping downward.

Her scream went on, only to end in sudden silence as she struck the rocks two hundred feet below.

CHAPTER 3

*M*aryAnne Carpenter jerked upright, her eyes opening wide as the sound of a scream echoed in her head. For a moment she felt totally disoriented, for the voice that had awakened her had been clearly recognizable.

Audrey.

Audrey Wilkenson.

But it was crazy—Audrey was in Idaho!

It must have been something else. Some other sound. A police siren on the street outside. A cat's strangely human cry. She started to get out of bed, and only then, startled for a moment, became aware of Alan, sound asleep next to her, the single sheet that covered them shoved down to his waist, one arm curled around his pillow.

Why hadn't he awakened, too?

She silently slipped out of bed, pulled on her robe and left the room, leaving the door slightly ajar, afraid that even the click of the latch might awaken her husband.

She moved into the living room, leaving the lights off, and dropped down onto the sofa.

She shouldn't have let Alan stay.

She should have simply sent him home when the kids went to bed last night, and not further confused the already complicated situation by letting him seduce her.

And that was exactly what it was—a seduction.

He'd helped her with the dishes, then suggested the four of them play a game of Monopoly. She almost groaned with the corniness of it—how many years had it been since the four of them had sat down to play a game together? She couldn't remember. Yet when Alan had suggested that it "would be just like old times," she had fallen right into it. But what old times had he been talking about?

The old times when the four of them had sat in front of the television, just like everyone else, staring at the tube and pretending that their comments on the shows were conversation? It had taken the kids half an hour even to find the Monopoly set, for God's sake! Who were they kidding?

Yet she had gone along with it, enjoying the unfamiliar closeness of the family, allowing herself to forget that an evening without television—and without a quarrel between Alison and Logan, for that matter—was something that had rarely happened before, and undoubtedly wouldn't happen again if she let Alan move back in. Instead, it would be back to business as usual, with the television filling the time between dinner and bedtime, and eventually Alan would begin working late again.

Working late!

Maybe that was what the scream in her mind had really been about. Maybe it had been a scream of protest that she was letting herself be sucked back into a marriage that only yesterday she had been quite sure was over. Until Alan had begun nuzzling her at the sink, and then, after the kids had gone to bed, beginning his campaign to spend the night.

And it had worked.

Oh, God, had it worked!

Even now, as she sat in the darkness, she could feel the warmth of his body against hers, the touch of his fingers on her flesh, the—

Stop it! she commanded herself. *Just stop it!*

The cry in the night hadn't been about herself at all.

The voice hadn't been hers: it had been Audrey's!

She realized, of course, that it hadn't been her friend at all. It had been her own cry, she thought, regaining a measure of control, that her dreaming mind had assigned to Audrey simply because she didn't want to face the true depths of her own confusion. What she really needed to do was to *talk* to Audrey. And not in the morning, either, after her subconscious had had a whole night to work her over and make her think that maybe everything wasn't as bad as it seemed right now.

Well, why not? What was stopping her?

She got up from the sofa, her mind made up. Going to the kitchen, she snapped on the light and glanced at the clock above the sink. One-thirty. Only eleven-thirty in Idaho.

Even if Audrey had already gone to bed, she couldn't possibly be asleep yet.

MaryAnne picked up the phone, dialing the number from memory. The instrument at the other end began ringing. On the eighth ring the connection clicked and she heard Audrey's voice.

Her recorded voice, saying she couldn't come to the phone right now, and to leave a message. When the electronic beep came, MaryAnne's words tumbled from her lips in a nervous staccato: "It's me, Aud. MaryAnne. I know this is really stupid—I just got a weird feeling—lots of weirdness going on just now—and I wanted to talk to you, right away. So I called, and you're not even home. Dumb, huh? Anyway, I really do need to talk to you. It's about—Alan and me. He— Oh, shit, I hate these machines! Call me in the morning, huh?"

As she hung up the phone, she heard the kitchen door open, and turned to see Alan, naked, standing in the doorway, squinting in the glare of the kitchen lights. "MaryAnne? What are you doing? Do you know what time it is?"

She forced a smile, her mind racing. "I—It's just one of those women's things. I woke up with the feeling that Audrey needs me, so I called her."

Alan's lips twisted scornfully. "Audrey needs you?" he asked, his voice etched with bitterness. "What would someone who married a hundred and fifty million dollars need with you?"

MaryAnne's jaw tightened, and Alan instantly realized his mistake. "I'm sorry, honey," he went on, his tone softening. "I didn't really mean it the way it sounded. I just—"

"Maybe you'd better just go home," MaryAnne interrupted. "I've never understood how you can hate a man you don't even know!"

"I don't hate him," Alan protested. "But you have to admit that there aren't many problems Audrey could have that Ted's money wouldn't solve."

"I can," MaryAnne shot back, her eyes boring into Alan's. "How about another woman? How would his money solve a problem like that?"

Alan looked instantly contrite. "You're right," he said quietly. "I guess I deserved that. And I guess I deserve a lot more, too. But I want to make it right, MaryAnne. I really do. Eileen was a mistake, and I only hope you'll be able to forgive me someday."

Don't listen to him, MaryAnne told herself. Don't believe him! He said it all when he talked about Ted's money. Revealed so much more about himself than even he knows. "I don't want to talk about it right now, Alan," she said. "I just want you to—"

"Let me stay," Alan pleaded. "Please? Yesterday and tonight were terrific. We had a good time. Let's not spoil it, okay? Let's just go back to bed, and we'll talk in the morning. We'll send the kids off bowling or something, and then we'll talk. Just you and me, MaryAnne. If we really try, I know we can straighten this mess out."

He slipped his arms around her, and once more she felt the familiar strength of his body, the reassuring croon of his voice.

And, once again, she felt her resolve to send him home fade away. "All right," she sighed, more in resignation than agreement. "Let's go back to bed. But tomorrow we talk. About all of it."

Twenty minutes later, though, when Alan had fallen back into a deep sleep, MaryAnne left her bed again, went to the living room, turned on a light, and picked up a book.

Sleep, despite the lateness of the hour, was the last thing on her mind.

"I think maybe you better come with me, Gillie," Rick Martin told his wife as he pulled the uniform he'd taken off only a few hours earlier back onto his large frame. "I don't know what's going on up there, but Joey sounded scared, and Bill Sikes isn't home."

His wife, who was as small as he was large, and as blond as he was dark, was way ahead of him. She had dressed while listening to Rick's end of his disjointed conversation with Joey Wilkenson, then made them both a cup of coffee while Rick called the station and spoke to his assistant deputy, Tony Moleno, telling him to meet him at El Monte Ranch. She handed him a steaming mug, unable to read the expression on his face. "What's happened?"

"Don't know," Rick replied. He took a swallow of coffee and, balancing the mug on the edge of the night table, turned to pull on his boots. "Joey was so upset he could barely talk, but it sounded like they were out looking for Sheika, and Audrey disappeared."

Gillie's mouth dropped open. "But that's—" She fell silent, floundering, trying to make sense out of Rick's words.

"It's nuts," Rick said grimly, finishing her sentence for her. "Why the hell were they out looking for a horse at this hour? And how could Audrey have just disappeared?" Strapping on his holster and picking up the mug of coffee, he started out of the bedroom. "We sure as hell aren't going to find out till we get there, are we?"

Less than ten minutes later the black and white Jeep that served as Rick's squad car drove through the gate of El Monte. Rick had to slow down as the paved road gave way to the narrow graveled drive that wound through the woods, to open out in the large clearing that held the Wilkensons' big house, the barn and sheds, and the field. A squad car was already parked in front of the house, and as Rick pulled his Jeep up next to it, the front door opened and Tony Moleno stepped out onto the porch.

"Joey's in the kitchen. He doesn't know what happened, but he—well, he thinks his mother's dead."

"Dear God," Gillie whispered, brushing past Moleno and hurrying inside to do what she could for Joey Wilkenson.

"What's he told you?" Rick asked, putting out a hand to restrain the assistant deputy as Moleno, too, started into the house.

"I told you—not much. Pretty much what you told me. They were looking for the horse, and they got separated, and he heard his mother scream but couldn't find her. So he came back here and called you."

"Okay," Rick said, his mind already working. "I want you to get up to Bill Sikes's cabin and see if you can find him. He didn't answer the phone, but that might just mean he got drunk and passed out."

"Sikes hasn't had a drink in ten years—" Moleno began, but Rick cut him off.

"And today his boss died, so who knows what he's up to? Anyway, I want you to find him, and then start rounding up some men. If something's happened to Audrey, and she's out there with a broken leg or something, I want to find her as soon as possible. After you've checked Sikes's cabin, come back here. I'll see what I can find out from Joey."

Nodding his acceptance of the other man's orders, Moleno trotted down the steps toward the squad car as Rick Martin went into the house, closing the front door behind him.

"Joey?" he said a moment later, as he stepped into the large kitchen where the boy was huddled on a stool at the breakfast bar, watching Gillie start a pot of coffee. "What happened? Can you tell me about it?"

At Joey's feet, Storm growled a warning to the deputy, but calmed down when the boy reached down to pat him on the head. "I don't know," Joey wailed, wiping his tearstained cheeks with the sleeve of his shirt, then blowing his nose on a piece of Kleenex he fished from a box on the countertop. "I saw Sheika, out in the field, and Mom and I were trying to catch her. But Sheika went into the woods, so while Mom was getting a rope, I sent Storm to follow her." Slowly, his voice quavering, he pieced the story together. He and his mother had gotten separated, and then he'd heard something in the woods. His dog had been with him, and whatever was out there had frightened Storm, so when he heard his mother calling him, he hadn't answered. "I was too scared," he admitted. "I mean, it was like something was hunting for me, and if I answered Mom, it could find me."

"But didn't you think your mom would worry if you didn't answer her?" Rick interrupted.

Joey's eyes shifted nervously toward Gillie, as if seeking help.

"For heaven's sake, Rick," Gillie said, "if you thought something was hunting you in the woods in the middle of the night, would you start yelling? Of course not!"

Rick felt his face redden as he realized she was right. "Is that when you came back here?" he asked, turning his attention back to Joey.

Joey shook his head. "Me and Storm just stayed where we were, and after a while we didn't hear anything anymore. And then—" His voice broke and he had to choke back a sob. "And then there was this scream—it was awful, like—" He fell silent. A tear ran down his cheek.

"Like what, son?" Rick asked, almost afraid to hear what the boy would say next.

". . . like she was falling. . . ." Joey sobbed, choking on the words.

As Gillie started around the end of the counter to comfort the boy, Rick held her back with a gesture. "Where were you, Joey?" he asked. When the boy made no response, he pressed a little harder. "When you heard your mother scream, where were you?"

Joey looked up, trying to swallow the lump that had formed in his throat. "We were on the trail to the bluff," he whispered. "And—and after I heard it, Storm and me—we went to look for her." He gazed down at the big dog, who was stretched out on the floor now, his muzzle between his front paws. As though he felt his master's eyes on him, the shepherd looked up expectantly. "I told him to find Mom," Joey whispered. "And I thought he did, too. He started wagging his tail, and I had to run to keep up with him. But when we got to the top of the bluff . . ." His voice trailed off.

"What, Joey?" Rick pressed. "What did you find when you got to the top of the bluff?"

"The flashlight," Joey breathed. "The one she got from the barn."

Joey stared down at Storm. As if sensing the boy's misery, the dog sat up and licked at his hand. Rick's eyes met Gillie's.

"I think I better go have a look at the base of the bluff," he said.

He left the house and started across the field toward the thin strip of lodgepole pines that grew at the base of the vertical face of Sugarloaf Mountain. The moon was still high, and he could see clearly the wide ledge two hundred feet above the valley floor. It was easily accessible by the trail that began on the south side of the field. Once, he recalled now, when he was eighteen, he and two friends had reached the top by scaling the face of the granite wall, using pitons and lines, and praying they wouldn't get caught before they made it.

Snapping on his flashlight, he made his way quickly through the stand of pines, then began climbing over the boulders that studded the land at the bluff's foot.

Within minutes he found Audrey Wilkenson's body, twisted and broken, lying facedown at the base of one of the boulders. Though there was no question she was dead, he checked for a pulse anyway, then snapped on his radio. "I've found her, Tony," he said. "I'm at the base of Sugarloaf. Get up here as fast as you can." No more than twenty seconds later he saw the headlights of Moleno's squad car come on, then watched as the car wove down the twisting drive from Bill Sikes's house, then headed across the field directly toward him.

"Was Sikes there?" he called as Tony emerged from the woods and began scrambling across the boulders.

"Oh, yeah," Moleno replied. "And you were right. Drunk as a skunk. Looked like—" His eyes suddenly fell on Audrey Wilkenson's body, and the words died on his lips. "Oh, Jeez," he whispered. "That poor kid."

"Start calling for help," Rick ordered, masking his shock and sorrow with gruff efficiency. "I'm going to have to go back to the house."

He started across the field once more, his steps deliberate, wondering how he was going to tell Joey Wilkenson that not only his father had died that day, but that his mother had, too. Except, he realized as his hand pushed the kitchen door open a few moments later, he suspected that the boy already knew. It would have been impossible to hear the scream Audrey must have made as she fell, without knowing exactly what had happened.

As he stepped into the house, Gillie looked at him questioningly, and he shook his head. "I'm thinking maybe you'd better call someone in the family," he said. Understanding exactly what he was saying, Gillie gasped, and slipped her arms protectively around Joey Wilkenson. "I'm sorry, Joey," Rick went on. "I—I found your mother. I guess—well, I guess she must have tripped." He watched Joey carefully, searching for any falseness in the boy's reaction, but there was none.

Joey only looked up at him, and when he spoke, his voice was hollow. "She was calling me. If I'd answered her . . ."

Gillie drew him close. "Don't think about it," she told him. "It wasn't your fault. It was an accident."

Joey gazed up at her. "But what if it wasn't?" he asked. "What if—"

"We need to call someone, Joey," Gillie broke in, wishing she could save the boy from the thoughts that must be racing through his mind. "Do you have a favorite uncle? Or aunt?"

When Joey spoke again, his voice was barely audible. "There isn't anyone," he whispered. "We don't have any relatives, except Aunt MaryAnne."

"Aunt MaryAnne?" Gillie repeated gently. "Who is she?"

"My godmother," Joey replied. "She's my mom's best friend, ever since they were little."

"Do you know where her number is?"

"In the book," Joey replied, his voice numb, his eyes fixed on the floor. "Under Carpenter. Over there by the phone."

It wasn't until Audrey Wilkenson's address book was already in her hand that Gillie Martin saw the message light blinking on the elaborate instrument that sat on the kitchen counter. Without thinking, she pressed the playback button, and a few seconds later the strained tones of MaryAnne Carpenter's voice filled the kitchen. In silence, Gillie and Rick Martin listened to the message Audrey Wilkenson's best friend had left no more than ten or fifteen minutes after Audrey herself had died.

It makes you wonder, Gillie thought as she found MaryAnne's name in the address book and dialed the New Jersey number. It makes you wonder if you understand anything that goes on in this world.

––––––––––

"You know, this is really nuts!" Alan Carpenter exclaimed, doing nothing to mask his fury as he watched MaryAnne throwing clothes into a suitcase. "Do you have any idea what time it is?"

MaryAnne glared at him. "Of course I know what time it is," she snapped. "It's almost four o'clock in the morning, and I have to be at the airport by five-thirty! Now, are you going to help me or not? Because if you're not, then just go home, and I'll call a cab!"

"For God's sake, MaryAnne, don't you think we should at least talk about this?"

MaryAnne dropped the pair of jeans she was holding into the suitcase, then turned to gaze steadily at Alan. "What is there to talk about? My best friend is dead, Alan. And so is Ted! How can I not go?"

"But what can you do?" Alan demanded, once again picking up the argument that had been raging ever since MaryAnne had awakened him after the call from Sugarloaf. "You can't bring them back to life!"

MaryAnne took a deep breath. Why couldn't he understand? It wasn't as if she hadn't already explained it a dozen times. Still, she tried once more. "There isn't anyone else, Alan. I'm all Joey has left. Ted hasn't heard from either of his parents since he was a boy, and you know what happened to Audrey's. Who else is going to take care of Joey?"

"There's got to be plenty of people out there," Alan replied. "Christ, they must have someone who'd take the kid in—"

"Joey!" MaryAnne uttered the word with such force that Alan was struck silent. "His name is Joey, and I made a promise to Audrey years ago, before he was even born. We were both pregnant at the same time, remember? She with Joey, and me with Alison. And we made each other a promise. We swore that if anything ever happened, we'd look after each other's kids. Well, something's happened, Alan! She's dead! They're both dead! Can't you get that through your thick head?" Though both she and Alan had tried to keep their voices low enough not to wake their sleeping children, now both Alison and Logan appeared at the door to the hall.

"Mommy?" Logan asked. "What's wrong?" Then, seeing the suitcase, the worry in his eyes turned to fear. "Are you going away?"

Suddenly her pent-up emotions broke free, and MaryAnne sank down on the bed, sobbing. Instantly, both the children were by her side, throwing their arms around her. She pulled them close, then struggled to regain control of her tears. "Something's happened," she told them, forcing her voice to stay calm. "Uncle Ted and Aunt Audrey have been in an accident, and I have to go out to Idaho and take care of Joey."

It was Alison who understood what her mother was saying. "Y-You mean they're dead?" There was a tremor in her voice, and her own eyes were already brimming with tears.

MaryAnne bit her lip and nodded.

"But why do you have to take care of him?" Logan asked.

It was nearly a full minute before MaryAnne trusted herself to speak. "Because there's no one else, sweetheart," she explained. "I'm Joey's godmother, just like Aunt Audrey was yours. And that means I have a duty to take care of him now."

Logan looked as if he were about to cry. "B-But who's going to take care of us? Can't we go with you?"

MaryAnne reached out and brushed a lock of blond hair out of her son's eyes. "I'm afraid not, honey. But I won't be gone very long." She shot Alan a glance over Logan's head. "And while I'm gone, Daddy's going to take care of you. He's going to move back in this morning, after he takes me to the airport. In fact, if you and Alison get dressed, you two can go along with us, then stop and get some of Daddy's things on the way back. How does that sound?"

Logan brightened immediately. "Really?" he demanded. "Daddy's going to live here again?"

"Well, who else would take care of you while I'm gone?" MaryAnne countered, unwilling to answer his question directly. Logan darted back to the room he shared with his sister, but Alison stayed behind.

"*Is* Daddy coming back?" she asked, glancing from one parent to the other. "Are we all going to be together again?"

Feeling both her daughter's and her husband's eyes on her, MaryAnne frantically searched for some kind of an answer, but found none. "I don't know," she finally said as the silence in the room grew strained. "I can't tell you right now, darling. We'll just have to see what happens, all right?"

Alison hesitated, then nodded and left the room, and a moment later MaryAnne and Alan heard their daughter sending Logan to the bathroom while she got dressed.

"It's my room, too!" Logan protested. "You can't just kick me out!"

"I can as long as I'm bigger than you," Alison reminded him. There was a slam as Logan stamped out of the shared bedroom, then another slam as he went into the bathroom to sulk.

Silently, feeling Alan's eyes on her, MaryAnne went back to her packing.

"We're going to have to work this out, honey," Alan said, finally starting to help her fold the clothes she'd laid out on her bed. "When you come back, we're going to have to decide what to do. If we get back together, and I can get rid of my apartment, we'll be able to afford a room for Logan. He's ten years old now. He should have a room of his own."

MaryAnne put the last of the clothes in the suitcase, closed it, and snapped the locks. "When I get back," she said firmly. "I won't talk about any of this until I get back. And then—" She hesitated, then shrugged helplessly. "Then we'll see."

Alan opened his mouth to speak, but MaryAnne held up a

hand to stop him. "Don't," she said. "Don't ask me any questions, and don't ask for any more explanations of why I'm going. I don't owe you any explanations at all, but you still owe me plenty."

By the time she got out of the car at the airport, she and Alan were, once more, barely speaking to each other.

CHAPTER 4

"How come you and Mom keep fighting?"

Alan emerged from the closet in the bedroom of the furnished apartment he'd rented after the break-up with Eileen Chandler, his three suits and a few shirts—still on their hangers—draped over his left arm. Though Alison appeared to be concentrating on packing his clothes into the battered suitcase on the bed, he could sense the tension in her body as she waited for his answer.

"It just happens that way sometimes," he said. And your mother's being pigheaded about giving me another chance, he didn't add, though the words were on the tip of his tongue.

"Did Little Miss Blondie really kick you out?" Logan piped.

"Logan," Alison groaned. "You're not supposed to call her that! We're not even supposed to know that's what Mom and Susan—" She clapped her hands over her mouth and turned to look at her father.

"Little Miss Blondie?" Alan echoed, not certain whether to laugh or be angry at the appellation his wife had assigned to his former girlfriend. But then, seeing the fear of a blow-up in both his children's eyes, he chuckled. "Well, Eileen *is* small, and she *is* blond, and she *is* still single, so I guess it fits, doesn't it?" As the children relaxed, and he began laying the suits and shirts into the suitcase, he tried to dismiss his transgression with a shrug. "And I guess the whole thing was just a stupid mistake. Anyway, it's over, and all I want to do now is make things right with your mother, and move back home so everything can be like it used to be."

"Then why don't we just move all your stuff?" Logan suggested. "That way, when Mom comes home, you'll already be there. I mean, you're going to be there anyway, aren't you?"

Alan reached out and tousled his son's hair. "I wish it were that simple," he replied. But as he glanced around the dingy room he'd been sleeping in for almost a month, he began to wonder. Why not? September's rent was almost due. It made far better sense simply to move out now, than to stay in this depressing place. The furniture in the living room, great sagging masses upholstered in some coarse green fabric that threatened to peel the skin off his fingers every time he touched it, should have been relegated to a Dumpster years ago, and the sagging bed wasn't any better. There was no real kitchen—only a converted closet barely big enough for one person, in the living room, which he suspected had been the dining room of a much larger apartment, back when the building was new, decades ago.

So why not just move back in? Even if MaryAnne kicked him out again when she got home, he could certainly find someplace better than this to stay until she came to her senses.

Besides, hadn't MaryAnne herself suggested it? What was he supposed to do for the next few days, come over here every time he needed something?

"You know, you're right, Logan," he declared, his mind suddenly made up. "Let's go down to the basement and find some boxes and pack everything up."

With the prospect of their father moving home permanently, the mood of both the children immediately lifted from the silent tension of the ride to and from the airport to one of noisy joy. Twenty minutes later the job was done, the few things Alan had acquired in the months since he'd walked out on MaryAnne barely filling two large cardboard cartons. After they'd stowed the two boxes and his suitcase in the car, Alan left a note for the manager, announcing that he'd left, stuffed the note and his key into an envelope, and slid it under the manager's door.

Twenty minutes later he was back in his own house, the suitcase open on the bed. His suits slung over his arm, he went to the large closet that had always been roomy enough to hold both his and MaryAnne's clothes, and slid some of his wife's dresses down to make room.

And found himself staring at an unfamiliar sport shirt, at least two sizes too large for himself.

"Alison?" he called. "Alison!"

A second later his daughter appeared at the bedroom door. The look on her face as her eyes focused on the shirt clutched in his hand made the message clear.

"What the hell's been going on around here?" he demanded. "What did your mother do, move her boyfriend in the minute I was gone?" As Alison stood frozen in the doorway, her younger brother hovering behind her, Alan hurled the shirt to the floor, then kicked it against the wall. Reflexively, Alison scurried across to pick it up.

"I-It's Bob's," she stammered. "I guess he . . ." Her voice trailed off as she saw the fury in her father's eyes.

"Who the hell is Bob?" Alan demanded. "What's been going on around here, anyway?"

Logan fearfully clutched Alison's hand, and her eyes glistened with tears. "H-He isn't anybody, Daddy," she said. "He's just a guy Mom went out with a few times, that's all."

"A few times?" Alan repeated, his voice crackling. "If she just went out with him a few times, what the hell is his shirt doing in my closet?"

"How am I supposed to know?" Alison was suddenly shouting, the tears of a second before giving way to anger. "Maybe he just left it, Daddy! Maybe he was helping Mom out with the yard-work, so she washed his shirt for him!"

"Yeah, sure!" Alan spat the words out bitterly, his rage ballooning. "How dumb do you think I am?"

Alison recoiled almost as if she'd been slapped, but held her ground. "Well, so what?" she shot back. "So what if he even spent the night with Mom? What were you doing? Why is what she was doing when you weren't even here any of your business? Come on, Logan. Maybe Mom's right! Maybe she shouldn't let Dad move back in!" Still grasping her brother's hand, Alison half dragged the little boy out of the room. A second later Alan heard her slamming the door of the room the children shared.

His fury only inflamed by his daughter's outburst, he snatched up the offending shirt and ripped it up the back.

What the hell kind of tramp *was* MaryAnne, anyway? And how many men had there been since he'd been gone? She'd probably had one waiting all the time. No wonder he'd fallen for Eileen Chandler, with MaryAnne ignoring him while she flirted with every man in town! It would serve her right if he didn't move back in at all. And trying to make him feel guilty over one lousy mistake! He ripped the shirt again, yanking one of the sleeves loose, then wadded the remains up and hurled them against the wall. What else had this guy left around the house?

He began jerking the drawers of the bureau open, pawing through them, then abandoned the chest in favor of the bathroom. He threw open the medicine cabinet, searching for anything MaryAnne's boyfriend might have stored away.

But all he found were his own things.

His shaving brush, still on the shelf where he always kept it.

His toothbrush, hanging in the rack, just where it always was.

His Right Guard was still there and his shaving cream; even the antibiotics Dr. Weinberg had prescribed two years ago when he'd come down with a bronchial infection. All exactly where he'd left them.

His rage began to drain away. As he stood gazing at the array of his things, things that hadn't even been moved aside while he was gone, a feeling of shame began to creep over him.

What the hell had he been thinking of? Alison was right—what business was it of his if MaryAnne had seen someone else while he was sleeping with Eileen Chandler? Maybe he should just count himself lucky that she hadn't actually divorced him. Leaving the bathroom, he went to the kids' room, and tapped softly.

"Go away," Logan said, his voice muffled by the closed door.

Alan knocked again, then turned the knob and opened the door a crack. "Kids? Hey, look, what I said just now—well, I guess it was pretty stupid. Anyway, what do you say we start over, huh? Let's pretend I just got here, okay?"

Alison and Logan glanced uncertainly at each other, then Alison spoke for both of them. "You're not mad at Mom anymore?"

Alan took a deep breath, then let it out in a sigh that was half resignation, half defeat. "No," he agreed. "I'm not mad at your mom anymore. But I guess she's still pretty mad at me."

Logan scrambled off his bed, grinning. "It'll be okay," he declared. "She gets real mad at me sometimes, but she still loves me. And I bet she still loves you, too!"

A few minutes later, as Alan resumed putting away the few things he'd taken with him when he left, Logan's words echoed in his mind.

What if MaryAnne didn't still love him? Then what would he do?

Bleakly, he realized he didn't have the slightest idea.

———

"Mrs. Carpenter? MaryAnne Carpenter?"

MaryAnne, her large purse slung over one shoulder and her single suitcase clutched in her right hand, had just stepped through the door into the gate area of Boise Municipal Airport. She instinctively ran her free hand through her hair, certain that she must look even worse than she felt. But the rugged-looking man striding toward her, arm outstretched to take her suitcase, seemed not to see the exhaustion she was feeling.

"I'm Charley Hawkins," he said, his deep voice resonating in the nearly empty waiting area. He looked to be about sixty, with salt-and-pepper hair and a craggy face that MaryAnne found oddly reassuring. "I'm sorry we have to meet under these circumstances." His voice trailed off, but then he plunged on. "But anyway, it seemed like I should be the one to come down and pick you up. I'm—I was Ted and Audrey's attorney. Or, anyway, their attorney up here. Of course, Ted had a firm in San Francisco that handled most of his affairs, but for the ranch, he pretty much always used me. This all the luggage you brought?"

Taken aback by the sudden change of subject, MaryAnne managed a nod, then let herself be steered along by Charley Hawkins's firm grip on her elbow.

"My car's right outside. It won't take more than a couple of hours to drive up to Sugarloaf." He kept up a steady patter of innocuous talk until MaryAnne's suitcase was in the backseat of his Cadillac, she was settled in the front next to him, and they were well away from the airport, heading northeast on Highway 21 toward Stanley.

"What happened?" MaryAnne finally asked when she felt ready to hear the details of her friends' deaths. "I can hardly believe they're both . . ." She left the sentence unfinished, even now knowing that if she said the final word, she might well lose the little control she still had over her emotions.

Charley Hawkins shook his head sadly. "Accidents, so far as anyone can tell," he began. For the next few miles, as the big car hurtled through the bleak landscape around Boise, the lawyer explained what details he knew of the tragedies that had befallen Ted and Audrey Wilkenson the day before. But all the time he spoke, the words of his first sentence hung in MaryAnne's mind.

"You said they were accidents 'so far as anyone can tell,' " she repeated when he was finished. "Is there any question about it? Is there some possibility that—well, that someone might have killed them?"

Charley Hawkins glanced over at her, but for a long moment said nothing. When he did finally speak, though, the timbre of his voice had changed slightly, and MaryAnne knew she was now listening to a lawyer, not merely a friend of Audrey and Ted's. "Like I said, as far as we know, they were both accidents. But there's a question about what could have spooked that animal. Sheika's always been the steadiest, gentlest horse around. Almost more like a dog than a horse, if you know what I mean. And as for Audrey, well, there weren't any witnesses, and it wasn't like she didn't know exactly where she was. With the moon last night, it had to be almost as bright as day up there, and Audrey wasn't the kind to take many risks. So I guess you could say there's a question of what made her fall. Not that we're ever likely to find any answers, but . . ."

But.

The word hung in the air between them. MaryAnne waited for him to finish his sentence. When he didn't, she turned in her seat to look more directly at him. "Mr. Hawkins, is there something you're not telling me?"

The lawyer's eyes remained steady on the road ahead as they began climbing up into the Sawtooth Mountains. "Whenever there are two deaths this close together, and a lot of money is involved, there are going to be questions, Mrs. Carpenter."

"But who—" And then, unbidden, a thought came into her mind. "You can't be talking about Joey, can you?" she demanded. "My God, he's just a little boy!"

"He wouldn't be the first thirteen-year-old to have killed his parents," Charley Hawkins replied. Then, catching a glimpse of MaryAnne Carpenter's suddenly ashen face out of the corner of his eye, he hastened to try to soften his words. "I'm afraid the police don't have any choice but to look at the situation with Joey, Mrs. Carpenter. That's not to say anyone seriously thinks the boy had anything to do with it, but unfortunately, when two parents die the way Ted and Audrey did, you have to look at the son. Too often these days, that's the way it turns out."

"But Joey was crazy about his parents!" MaryAnne protested.

When Charley Hawkins's expression hardened slightly and he made no reply at all, she pressed harder. "There wasn't a problem, was there?"

"Depends on what you mean by a problem," the attorney hedged. "Joey's just starting into his teens, and that always means some kind of problem, doesn't it?" He glanced over at her, smiling with more confidence than he actually felt. "He's a teenage boy, Mrs. Carpenter. Things aren't always great with teenage boys, especially when you're their parents. Now, I don't want you to start worrying," he added quickly. "All I'm trying to tell you is that I suspect the police are going to want to talk to Joey again, if for no other reason than to make sure he's told them everything. There might be something he doesn't even know he knows—something he saw or heard that might be a clue. So just don't be surprised if someone comes to talk to Joey, that's all."

"I see," MaryAnne breathed, easing herself back against the heavily cushioned seat. "But it seems so—I don't know—so *far-fetched*, I guess."

Charley Hawkins offered her a faint smile. "And it probably is, when you get right down to it. Anyway, there are a lot of other things you and I need to talk about, and I'm not much of a man for putting things off. I assume you know you're Joey's guardian."

MaryAnne nodded. "Audrey and I made an agreement years

ago. She didn't have anyone else, and I couldn't think of anyone but her taking care of my kids, so we did it. But of course, I never really thought it would ever happen."

"No one ever does, Mrs. Carpenter," the lawyer agreed. "But at least you and Audrey talked about it, and Ted and Audrey put it in writing. And a lot more, too."

His last words were said in a tone that left an uneasy feeling in MaryAnne's stomach. All through the flight out from Newark, she had sat staring out the window of the airplane, doing her best not to think at all. And she certainly hadn't thought about what was going to happen once she got to Sugarloaf. Had she assumed she could just help get Joey through his parents' funeral, pack his clothes, and take him back to New Jersey?

She hadn't even bothered to think about the ranch, or Ted's company, or any of the other details of his and Audrey's complicated lives. But from the way Charley Hawkins had just spoken, apparently Audrey and Ted had thought about it all. When she finally replied to his last statement, she chose her words carefully. "I assume the estate is complicated, and from what you just said, I'm beginning to suspect I must be the executor, too."

"Not quite," Charley Hawkins corrected her. "I'm the executor, which means I'm the one who will be dealing with all the paperwork. You're the trustee."

MaryAnne turned to gaze at him blankly. "The trustee?" she repeated. "I thought I was Joey's guardian."

Hawkins turned to smile at her, and she thought she detected just the faintest tinge of sympathy in his slate-gray eyes. "Oh, you are. But when an estate is the size of Ted and Audrey Wilkenson's, and the main heir is a minor, things get complicated. It was not sufficient simply to make you the boy's guardian, they also made you the trustee of his estate."

"Dear God." MaryAnne suddenly thought of the company in California in which Ted still had a major interest. "What does that mean?"

"Well, for one thing, it means you and I are going to be doing a lot of business together. Ted and Audrey and I became good friends almost the minute they arrived in this area, and they knew that if anything ever happened to them, you were going to need help."

The uneasy feeling in MaryAnne's stomach jelled into fear. "Just exactly what kind of help are you talking about, Mr. Hawkins?"

"Managing a fortune. And in the business Ted was in, they don't come small. As of this morning, Joey is a very wealthy young man. And you are a rather wealthy woman."

"Me?" MaryAnne asked, still dazed by the implications of what Charley Hawkins had just revealed. "I'm afraid I don't understand. . . ."

"It's pretty simple, really," the lawyer explained. "They decided that given the size of the estate, and the problems concomitant to raising the heir of the estate—that's legal jargon for Joey—the position of guardian should not be without compensation. It was put on a sliding scale, decreasing according to the age Joey had reached in the event he was orphaned. The sum they decided upon was one percent of the estate—"

"One percent!" MaryAnne exclaimed. "But that could be hundreds of thousands of dollars! It's crazy!"

"It's not crazy, MaryAnne," Charley Hawkins replied quietly. "When you think about it, it makes a lot of sense. It makes the guardian—you, Mrs. Carpenter—independently wealthy. A precaution, you might say, against Joey being resented for his wealth. It also prevents Joey from attempting to control you by holding money over your head."

"Good Lord," MaryAnne breathed. "How much is it?"

"A lot more than you're thinking," Hawkins replied. "Because it's actually one percent of the total for every year remaining until Joey's twenty-first birthday. Which means that your share is eight percent of the total."

MaryAnne felt a strange numbness forming in her body. "It's not possible," she breathed. "It's just not possible!"

Charley Hawkins chuckled hollowly. "Just be glad you were in New Jersey last night. If you'd been here, I'm afraid you'd be very high on my list of suspects."

MaryAnne gasped and turned pale. "You don't think—"

"A joke, MaryAnne," the lawyer told her quickly. "It was only a joke!"

"My God, everything's changed!" MaryAnne exclaimed as they drove through Sugarloaf on the way up to El Monte Ranch. The village was at least twice the size she remembered it from her single visit eight years before, although if she'd had to identify which buildings were new and which were original, she wouldn't have been able to, so perfectly had the recent structures been blended with the old.

"New money coming in," Charley Hawkins commented. "So far, we're managing to keep the flavor of the place, but it seems like a new developer comes in every week. I'm spending most of my time these days fighting off challenges to our zoning restrictions. And now," he added grimly, "I've lost my strongest ally. If Ted hadn't died . . ." He was silent a moment, then shrugged. "I guess we'll figure out a way to get by without him, won't we? Since we don't seem to have a choice."

They made the rest of the drive up to the ranch in silence, but MaryAnne was relieved, once they left the town behind, to see that the valley seemed much the same as she recalled. At last they pulled through the gate to El Monte, and up the narrow, curved drive to the front of the big, lodgelike house.

Bigger, MaryAnne, realized, than she'd remembered it.

She had just stepped out of the car and started toward the front steps when the door opened and Joey burst out, charging across the broad porch, taking the three steps in one leap and throwing himself on MaryAnne.

"Aunt MaryAnne? What are we going to do? Mom and Dad

are—" His words died on his lips, and MaryAnne hugged him close.

"It's going to be all right, Joey," she said softly, stroking his hair. "I'm here now, and it's going to be all right."

The boy gazed up at her, his eyes fearful. "Are you going to take care of me?" he asked.

"Of course I'm going to take care of you," MaryAnne reassured him. "That's why I'm here." She gently led him back into the house, with Charley Hawkins following behind with her suitcase. Standing in the doorway was a small friendly featured woman in her mid-thirties, clad in jeans and a plaid shirt, looking as tired as MaryAnne felt.

"I'm Gillie Martin," the woman said, offering MaryAnne her hand. "My husband's the senior deputy out here, and I came up with him last night when"—her eyes shifted to Joey for an instant, and she shook her head sadly—"when I heard about Audrey," she finished uncomfortably. "If there's anything I can do for you, you call me anytime. There's plenty of food in the kitchen—people have been dropping by all day—and I went ahead and got one of the guest rooms ready for you." She flushed slightly. "I hope that's all right."

"It's fine," MaryAnne assured her quickly. "If you've been here all night, you must be exhausted. You must want to go home—"

"Not until you're settled in, and I know you and Joey are going to be all right," Gillie said in a tone that left no room for argument. "I'll just call Rick—that's my husband. He can pick me up." She smiled warmly. "And I can hold him off for a while. I know he'll want to talk to you, tell you what happened here. But not today, right?"

MaryAnne nodded gratefully.

———

The house seemed to fill up with people, and MaryAnne, struggling to fight off the exhaustion of the last twenty-four hours, let

herself be taken care of by the throng of neighbors who had
arrived to offer her help with whatever might be necessary for
the next few days. By early evening, though, they had begun to
disperse, and finally she was at the front porch saying good night
to Charley Hawkins.

"You're sure you feel all right staying here tonight?" he asked.
"If you and Joey want to come and stay with me, I've got plenty
of room. Since Mabel died last year, I've just been rattling around
like the last bean in the coffee can."

"Thanks, but we'll be fine," MaryAnne replied. "Or as fine as
we can be, given the circumstances. But I think tonight Joey and
I need to be alone together, if you know what I mean."

"I do," Hawkins replied. "If you need anything—anything at
all—you just give me a call." As he started down the steps, a
thought that had been flitting through MaryAnne's mind for the
last hour suddenly came to the fore.

"Charley?" The rawboned lawyer paused at the bottom step
and glanced back. "I've been thinking. Obviously I'm going to
have to be here for a while. I wonder if perhaps I shouldn't have
my children come out."

Charley Hawkins grasped what she was saying. "Just let me
know. I'll arrange for the tickets. And I'll have a checking account set up for you at the bank tomorrow morning. If you come
into the village, just stop in and sign the cards, or I could bring
them up for you."

"I'll come in," MaryAnne replied. "And thanks, Charley. I'm
very glad that Ted and Audrey chose you to be their attorney."

A crooked smile creased Charley Hawkins's cheeks. "And I'm
glad they chose you to take care of Joey. Of course, I wasn't too
worried. One thing about Ted and Audrey—they were never
wrong about people. Have a good night."

When he was gone, MaryAnne closed the door behind her,
then leaned against it for a moment, finally releasing the steel
grip with which she'd held her emotions in check. For a moment

she felt as if she might faint, but then her strength came back to her, and she went upstairs to check on Joey. He was stretched out on his bed, fully dressed, his big dog lying beside him.

"Joey?" MaryAnne said, stepping into the room. "Are you asleep?" There was no reply from the boy, so she went over to the bed, pulled the large Pendleton blanket at its foot up to cover him, then leaned over and kissed him on the cheek. "Take care of him, Storm," she whispered as she switched off the light. "He needs you right now."

Almost as if he understood her words, the big dog thumped his tail on the bed and pressed closer to his master.

Leaving the door ajar, MaryAnne went back downstairs and began wandering through the rooms on the lower floor. In the den, her eyes came to rest on a double silver frame that held pictures of Audrey and Ted, and she made no attempt to wipe the tears that began to run down her cheeks.

Finally she settled herself at Audrey's desk, picked up the phone, and dialed her own number in New Jersey. On the third ring, Alan picked up.

"It's MaryAnne," she said. "I wanted to let the kids know I got here all right."

"I'll tell them," Alan replied. There was an uncomfortable silence, their quarrel that morning still fresh in both their minds. Then Alan spoke again. "Are you okay?"

"Considering the circumstances, I suppose I'm all right," MaryAnne replied. She hesitated, then went on. "But I'm going to have to be here for a while, and I think maybe you should bring the kids out."

She heard a dark chuckle from her husband. "Right," he said. "I'll just call the travel agent and order up some tickets. First-class. Jesus, MaryAnne, we barely have enough money to live on, and you want me to fly us all out to Idaho for a couple of days?"

"Alan, I've got some money," MaryAnne began, but before she could go on, her husband interrupted her.

"You're kidding! You mean you've been whining at me about money every month for the last year, and you've been *saving* it? What the hell is going on with you? You've been acting like you were at the poorhouse door!"

His words froze MaryAnne. Should she tell him what had happened, what the terms of Ted and Audrey's wills were?

And then she remembered Eileen Chandler.

I'll never be able to trust him, she thought. If I tell him about the money now, I'll never be able to trust him again. I'll never know if he wants to come back to me, or just to the money.

"It's been tight, but I've still managed to save a little," she said, her voice cold. "There's enough for the plane tickets, and I don't want to argue with you. But I want my children with me right now, and you can either bring them or send them. It's up to you."

Her tone of voice told Alan not to argue with her any further. And it also told him that if he hoped to put his marriage back together, he'd better go, too.

"We'll be there," he said. "I'll get the kids packed, and we can be on the same flight you took, tomorrow morning. Okay?"

MaryAnne let out the breath she hadn't realized she'd been holding. "Thank you, Alan," she said quietly. "I'll have the tickets waiting for you at the airport. See you tomorrow."

She put the receiver back on the cradle, then leaned back in the chair.

In the space of twenty-four hours her entire life had changed.

CHAPTER 5

Logan Carpenter snuggled deep into the soft mattress and pulled the down comforter right up to his chin.

"Ready for me to turn the light out?" MaryAnne asked, smiling down at her son.

"But it's only nine o'clock, Mom," Logan protested, though he already knew it wasn't going to work.

"And it's eleven where you woke up this morning," MaryAnne replied. "You were falling asleep in the den half an hour ago."

"I was not," Logan objected. "I was—"

"You were sound asleep, just like you will be in another five minutes," MaryAnne broke in. She bent down and kissed him, then snapped off the light that stood on the pine table next to his bed. "Want me to leave the door open?" she asked as she started out of the room.

"I'm not a *baby*," Logan protested with the full maturity of his ten years. Pointedly silent, MaryAnne pulled the door closed. As soon as Logan heard the latch click, he slid out of bed and dashed over to the window.

Idaho!

He was in Idaho, on Aunt Audrey's ranch, and there was no one in the bedroom except him!

He stared out into the moonlit Sugarloaf Valley, which seemed to spread away from the house forever. In the distance he could just see the glow of lights from the town at the mouth of the valley, and then, beyond that, a great black void hung over the Sawtooth Valley—he'd already memorized its name—and even farther away was the black silhouette of Castle Peak. The window was open—which never happened back home, where you always had to make sure everything was locked before you went to sleep—and the cool night air drifting down from the mountains caressed his face, entrancing him with the pure scents of nature, which were nothing like the sour smells at home that always made him want to hold his nose.

There were sounds, too, that weren't anything like the rumble of the trucks on the turnpike just a block from their house in New Jersey.

Now the quiet of the night was broken by sounds he couldn't ever remember hearing before.

The cry of an animal drifted down from somewhere up in the mountains, and Logan shivered as he imagined a wolf, sitting on one of the huge granite cliffs that soared above the house, howling at the moon.

There was a cracking sound, coming from the forest off to the right, and Logan was instantly sure he knew what it was.

A bear—probably a grizzly—was stalking something.

Maybe a mountain lion!

Suddenly he wondered if maybe he shouldn't close the window, after all. He peered down, staring at the roof of the porch, just a few feet below the window.

What if a bear got up on the porch roof and crawled into his room in the middle of the night?

Another crackling came from the woods, and Logan jerked his head up, a stab of panic shooting through him. But then, as he watched, a doe emerged from the forest, followed by two fawns, and trotted across the yard to the field beyond the barn. As he watched, transfixed, the deer and her young began grazing contentedly in the moonlight.

Finally turning away from the window, Logan went back to his bed, crawled in, and lay staring up at the peeled logs that supported the cathedral ceiling above him.

A ceiling so high, he probably couldn't touch it even if he jumped up and down on the bed.

Should he try it?

Why not? For the first time he could remember, bossy old Alison wasn't in the room to tell him what to do, and what not to do. For as long as they stayed here, this was *his* room, and he could do exactly what he wanted! A new thrill of excitement racing through him, he threw the comforter back and stood up again.

He flexed his knees, testing the springiness of the mattress.

Tentatively, he tried a jump, reaching up to see how close his hand came to the large beam that spanned the room and supported the smaller posts that braced the actual roof beams.

Not even close.

He jumped higher, stretching his arm upward, crouching lower every time he came down, until he had the rhythm right and each jump was higher than the one before.

He strained upward, but his fingertips still missed the beam by several inches.

Higher. Higher . . .

"For heaven's sake, Logan! What are you doing?"

Too startled to keep his balance, Logan collapsed onto the bed just as the overhead light went on and he saw his mother glaring at him from the doorway.

"Nothing," the little boy said, jerking the comforter back up, even though it was far too late to pretend he was telling the truth. "I wasn't hurting anything!"

"Well, from downstairs it sounded like the whole house was coming down!" MaryAnne told him. "And what are you thinking of, jumping on the bed? You know you're not allowed to do that."

"I-I was just trying to see if I could touch that," Logan stammered, pointing to the beam above his head. "I wasn't—"

"Don't say you weren't hurting anything again," MaryAnne cut in. "You could have broken the bed, or even worse, you could have fallen off and broken your arm."

"Aw, Mom . . ."

"And don't 'Aw, Mom,' me, either. Now just settle down and go to sleep. Okay?"

"But—"

"Okay?"

"Okay," Logan sighed. "But tomorrow, can I ride a horse? Joey says—"

"We'll see," MaryAnne interrupted. Given the chance, Logan would go on for at least five minutes about what Joey—who had instantly become Logan's idol simply because he was three years older and lived on a real ranch—had told him about the horses in the stable. "For now, just go to sleep! And no more jumping on the bed!"

Switching off the overhead light once more, she pulled the door closed, leaving Logan alone in the moonlit room once again. Go to sleep? How could he go to sleep? He was going to stay up all night, listening to the animals hunting in the woods. In fact, as soon as he was sure his mother wasn't listening at the door, he'd get back up and go look out the window again. The deer were probably still in the field, and he might even see a bear, or a wolf, or . . .

He drifted off to sleep, imagined visions of forest creatures still prowling through his mind.

And, because he was asleep, Logan Carpenter missed the dark form that emerged from the woods beyond the pasture a few minutes later, lingering in the shadows that rendered it all but invisible as it stared across the field at the lights glowing in the windows of the house. Lights that would soon go out, encouraging the shadowy figure to move closer. . . .

––––––––––––

"Maybe we ought to go back," Andrea Stiffle whispered. It was a little after eleven, and she and her twin brother were moving quietly along the trail through the woods that led up to El Monte Ranch, almost a mile farther up the valley than their parents' house.

"You scared?" Michael asked. He, too, was whispering, but Andrea could hear the scorn in his voice.

"No, I'm not *scared*," Andrea lied, for even though she and Michael had celebrated their thirteenth birthday last month, she still turned her night-light on every night, and had never quite gotten over the fear she always felt on the nights when clouds obscured the stars and darkness closed in around the house like a blanket, so the world beyond her window seemed to disappear completely. But tonight the moon was shining brightly, and she hadn't been about to admit to Michael that she was still scared of the dark, so when he'd suggested they go on "an adventure," she'd instantly agreed. Now that they were a quarter of a mile from the house, in the thickest part of the stand of aspens that covered this part of the valley floor, she'd begun to have her doubts.

Every time she heard something rustle in the brush, her heart leaped and she had to choke back the startled yelp that rose in her throat. But she still wasn't about to admit how frightened she really was. "I just don't want to get in trouble, that's all," she said, hoping she sounded a lot less scared than she was. "I mean, what if someone catches us?"

"Who's going to catch us?" Michael sneered. "Mom and Dad are both asleep, and there aren't any lights on at El Monte, either."

"How do you know?" Andrea demanded, her voice rising.

"Will you shut up?" Michael hissed. He glanced around quickly, betraying the vague discomfort that had come over him a few minutes before, when they'd moved from the pasture behind their house into the dense stand of trees. "I can see the house from my window. They shut all the lights off half an hour ago."

"You can only see the front of the house," Andrea reminded him. "What if someone's still awake in the back?"

Michael groaned impatiently. "Then we won't do anything, that's all. We'll just go back home, okay?"

"Promise?" Andrea demanded.

Michael glared at her in the darkness. "If you're going to chicken out, do it now," he told his sister. "If you want to go home, just go!"

For a second Andrea was tempted to do just that, but as she began thinking about having to walk all the way back to the house by herself, she changed her mind. "I'm not chickening out," she decided. "I just don't want to get in trouble. If we get caught, Dad'll ground us for a week."

"We won't get caught," Michael insisted. "So just shut up, okay?" Turning away from his sister, he started along the narrow path once again, so familiar with its twists and turns that he could have walked it blindfolded.

Her nervousness growing by the second, Andrea followed, staying as close to her brother as she could.

A few minutes later they came to the Wilkensons' driveway, and as she stepped out into the road, Andrea felt a little better. Here, at least, the branches of the trees were no longer brushing against her face and the underbrush wasn't tickling her ankles. But as they came into the wide, empty expanse in front of the house, she realized that anyone looking out the windows would be able to see them clearly in the moonlight.

"We'll go over by the barn," Michael whispered. "That way we can get a lot closer before anyone could see us!"

Dropping low to the ground, he scuttled across the yard toward the barn, and Andrea quickly followed. Within a few seconds they were crouched in the deep shadows behind the barn. Michael led his sister around the far side, staying close to the wall as they neared the building's front. From inside the structure, they could hear the horses nickering softly; one of them whinnied as they passed. Finally they came to the corner and peeped around it to gaze at the house, thirty yards away.

All the windows were dark. Except for the soft hooting of an owl, the night was silent.

"Come on," Michael whispered. "Let's do it."

"But which room is Joey's?" Andrea asked. "What if we do it at the wrong window?"

"It's the one over the end of the porch," Michael replied. "I've seen him at the window thousands of times. Just staring out, but not looking like he was seeing anything, you know? Me and Jeff Tate saw him a couple of weeks ago, and Jeff waved to him, but Joey didn't even see him."

"How come he's so weird?" Andrea asked.

"He just *is*," Michael said, his eyes rolling at his sister's denseness. "He's nuts. Jeff thinks he killed his folks."

"Really?" Andrea gasped. As she stared up at the window above the porch roof, she shuddered, imagining a weird, wild-eyed Joey staring back, and wondered once again if maybe they shouldn't just forget about what they were going to do and go home. "What if he sees us?"

Michael grinned maliciously. "Then maybe he'll kill you, too." Without waiting for his sister to reply, he darted away from the shelter of the barn and dashed across the yard toward the house.

Andrea, left by herself, hesitated a moment longer. Finally, the fear of being left alone in the darkness overcame her fear of being spotted from the house. Taking a deep breath—as if she were about to plunge into cold water—she ran after her brother.

Together they crouched in the shadows, catching their breath. Michael reached down and picked up a handful of the cinder rocks that covered the area between the house and the barn. Stepping away from the house, he threw them up at Joey Wilkenson's window, ducking back into the shelter of the porch roof even before the small rocks hit the glass.

There was no response from above. Michael had reached down to pick up another handful of gravel when Andrea grabbed his arm.

"I saw something!" she whispered.

Michael froze. "Where?"

"O-Over there," Andrea replied, her voice quavering as her heart began to pound.

Michael followed her pointing finger with his eyes, staring off into the darkness beyond the house. At first he saw nothing, but then, across the yard near the woods, something moved.

A deer. It had to be a deer. If he and Andrea held perfectly still, it would come out of the shadows of the tree into the moonlight, and they would see it clearly. He reached out to Andrea, his fingers closing on her arm, the forefinger of his right hand going to his lips to keep her from speaking again. Together the twins froze in the darkness, waiting.

After what seemed an eternity, the shadowy figure moved again, then emerged from the woods.

It wasn't a deer.

The form they beheld was large, like a tall, muscular man. He moved a few steps on silent feet, with the grace of a wild animal. The two children stared at him, barely able to discern the shape from the surrounding shadows. As the figure came partly into the moonlight, he suddenly stopped, freezing like a rabbit catching the scent of danger, and both of them were suddenly certain he was watching them.

"Oh, God," Andrea whispered, her voice barely audible. "Who is it?"

Michael said nothing, for something about the dark figure

made his blood run cold. The idea of trying to frighten Joey Wilkenson evaporating from his mind, he tightened his grip on Andrea's arm and began backing slowly toward the corner of the house.

A breeze came up, blowing down from the mountains, and a moment later one of the horses whinnied loudly in the barn, and then they heard the sound of hooves striking out against the wooden walls of one of the stalls.

"Let's get out of here," Michael whispered. Pulling Andrea along beside him, he ran toward the mouth of the driveway, no longer worried about being seen from the house, but only wanting to keep the house itself between him and the ominous figure that had come out of the woods. He'd only gone a few steps when Andrea jerked her arm loose from his grip and sped past him, her feet pounding on the ground as she, too, raced toward the driveway.

It wasn't until they were almost back to their own house that they finally slowed down, both of them gasping for breath. At last, with home in sight, Michael dropped to the ground, struggling to control his breathing, now frightened that his own parents might hear them. Andrea crouched beside him, and for a few minutes neither of them said anything.

Finally, Andrea, unable to stand the silence any longer, spoke. "Who was it?" she whispered, her voice ragged from the exhaustion of running for almost a full mile. "Was it Bill Sikes?"

Michael shook his head. "He was a lot taller than Sikes," he said. "He was huge."

"D-Did he see us?" Andrea wailed.

Michael glanced nervously into the woods behind him, listening for any sounds that might betray the man's presence. "I-I don't think so," he stammered. "At least, if he did, he couldn't have recognized us."

Now Andrea's eyes flickered nervously around. "Wh-What if he followed us?"

Michael struggled to swallow the lump of fear that had risen in his throat. "He didn't," he told his sister, sounding a lot more confident than he felt. But as he thought about it, he realized that she was right.

If whoever had been out there in the night, prowling in the woods, had wanted to follow them, he could have.

And he could have caught them, too.

Michael's skin began tingling, as if some unseen being were watching him. As the chill spread through his body, the last of his nerve deserted him. "Come on," he whispered, his voice cracking with fear. "Let's get in the house."

They darted across the pasture, scrambling through the window they'd left open and dropping onto the floor of Andrea's room. Instantly, Michael pulled the window closed and locked it. For several long seconds the two of them sat still on the floor, listening for any unfamiliar sound from outside.

But now that they were safely back in the house, everything beyond the familiar walls of Andrea's room seemed normal once more. After a few minutes, Michael left his sister and slipped back to his own room.

Outside, the shadowy form that had soundlessly followed them through the woods turned away, merging back into the darkness of the night so quickly that anyone who watched might have been uncertain that it was there at all.

But it *was* there—prowling the Sugarloaf Valley tonight just as it had every night for years.

Prowling.

Watching.

And waiting.

———

Alan Carpenter gazed out the kitchen window the next morning, his eyes bleary from lack of sleep, the cramping of his muscles from yesterday's long flight barely eased by the night in bed.

He wasn't sure he'd gotten any sleep at all. Part of his restlessness, he knew, had resulted from the fight he'd had with MaryAnne just before they'd gone to bed. All evening, he'd done his best not to confront her about the shirt he'd found in her closet, or ask her any questions about Bob—whose last name he didn't even know. Instead, he'd tried to listen patiently while she explained the terms of the Wilkensons' will, refusing to give in to the cold fury that had built inside him as he came to the realization that whatever amount of money they had left to Joey's guardian—and he assumed it must be a lot, though MaryAnne hadn't told him how much—had all been left to his wife alone.

What the hell was that all about? They'd known damned well MaryAnne was married to him and was the father of her kids. Didn't they think he was good enough to raise Joey, too? Apparently not. Still, he'd kept his peace, determined not to let anything spoil his reconciliation with MaryAnne. He'd even gone as far as apologizing for their fight just before she'd left New Jersey, although he knew deep down that it had been MaryAnne's fault far more than his own.

But when they finally went upstairs, she'd shown him to a room down the hall from her own!

"What's this all about?" he'd demanded. "Aren't we sleeping together anymore?"

MaryAnne had actually had the nerve to look puzzled. "Alan, we haven't been sleeping together for a year, except for night before last."

"Then what the hell did you ask me out here for?" Alan exploded, his voice rising. "I thought—"

"Will you keep your voice down?" MaryAnne rasped, her jaw clenching. "For God's sake, Alan, we don't need to let the kids hear us fight every time we see each other, do we?"

"It's not *my* fault," Alan shot back. "I'm your husband, for Christ's sake! I have a right—"

"That's enough," MaryAnne snapped. "Being my husband might have given you some privileges, but it never gave you any rights. And the *privileges* ended the day you walked out on me, so don't think you can just jump into my bed any time you want. And don't bother to argue anymore, because I'm going to bed! If I'm going to get through Audrey's and Ted's funeral tomorrow, I have to get some sleep." Before her words had quite sunk in, she'd hurried down the hall, slipped into her room, and locked the door behind her.

And Alan, his fury growing every minute, had gone into the small guest room she'd relegated him to, and tried to get some sleep. The problem was that aside from his raging anger, the whole place gave him the creeps.

The night was filled with noises he couldn't identify, and he missed the familiar rumble of traffic right outside his window. He'd finally closed the window, certain that if he didn't, a bat, or a raccoon, or some other wild animal, would come in and attack him while he slept. So he'd lain awake all night, wondering why he'd come out here at all.

Now, in the bright sunlight of morning, he felt no better. The kids were already out of the house, following Joey to the barn to help him feed the horses.

Horses, for Christ's sake! What did a couple of kids from Canaan, New Jersey, need to know about horses?

And MaryAnne was washing the breakfast dishes, putting things away just as if she'd lived here for years. "Don't get too comfortable," he said, his voice betraying his foul mood. "We're only going to be here another day. We go to the funeral this afternoon, and tomorrow morning we go back to New Jersey."

MaryAnne stopped working at the sink and turned to face him. "Oh?" she asked. "When did you make up your mind about that?"

Alan fought to keep his anger under control. "I didn't mean it quite the way it sounded," he began.

"Somehow, I think you meant it exactly the way it sounded," MaryAnne replied, her voice cool.

With an effort, Alan ignored both her comment and its tone.

"I just meant that we can't stay out here past the funeral. I've already used up my vacation time this year. If I take extra time, I'll get docked."

MaryAnne shrugged. "I just don't see how that's going to be possible," she said. "I talked to Charley Hawkins this morning before you came down. There's going to be a mountain of paperwork involved in settling the estate. And even if we decide to close the ranch—"

"We?" Alan broke in. "We being who? You haven't said a word to me about the ranch!"

"I mean Charley and I." MaryAnne sighed, finally dropping into the chair opposite Alan. "Look, Alan, there's something I've been thinking about that we have to discuss."

Alan's brows rose in a cynical arch. "Oh, really? So now who's been making plans without talking to anyone else?"

"I'm talking to you now," MaryAnne replied evenly. "And I haven't made up my mind about anything. But since you're talking about going home, this seems like the right time." She waited for a response from her husband. When there was none, she went on. "It seems as if it might be a good idea for me to stay out here with the kids for a while. You could move back into our house, which would save us a lot of money, and—"

"Money?" Alan repeated. "From what you said last night, I gather money isn't going to be a problem at all anymore."

MaryAnne spread her hands in a helpless gesture. "I didn't mean it that way. And I certainly have no idea how long it's going to take for the estate to get settled."

Alan's eyes rolled in disbelief. "Right. But I'll bet good old Charley can advance you whatever you need, can't he?" Seeing MaryAnne's eyes narrow with anger, he veered off in another direction. "Anyway, what about the kids? School starts next week, doesn't it?"

"I wish it did. But in case you didn't know, it doesn't. There's a strike on in Canaan, and it doesn't look like it's going to be settled for at least a couple of weeks. So it just seems to me that it makes sense for the kids to stay here with me. They haven't had a real vacation in years—"

Alan stood up abruptly. "You don't want to discuss a damned thing, do you? You've already made up your mind. Well, that's just fine!" Reaching across the kitchen counter, he picked up the phone, jabbed a series of digits into the keypad, then drummed impatiently on the countertop as he waited for the information operator to respond. As MaryAnne listened in silence, he made two more phone calls, then left the kitchen without another word.

By the time his shaving gear was cleared out of the bathroom and his dirty underwear was haphazardly tossed back into his suitcase, Sugarloaf's lone taxi—a maroon van with nothing more than a magnetic sign stuck to a door to advertise its purpose— was just coming up the drive. MaryAnne came out of the kitchen as Alan hurried down the stairs, catching up to him at the front door.

"You're really going to walk out without even saying good-bye to the kids?" she demanded.

Alan's eyes fixed coldly on her. "I didn't say good-bye to them last time, either, so I guess they should be used to it by now." He strode across the front porch and down to the driveway, tossed his suitcase in the back of the van, then climbed into the passenger seat.

"Boise," he said. "The airport."

CHAPTER 6

*M*aryAnne was just about to start getting ready for the funeral when a police car pulled up in front of the house. A uniformed officer strode up to the front porch and rapped loudly on the door. "MaryAnne Carpenter?" he asked as she uncertainly opened the door a few inches. She nodded, and the officer smiled at her. "I'm Rick Martin. I think you met my wife a couple of days ago. Gillie Martin?"

The instinctive nervousness she'd felt at seeing him evaporated. MaryAnne pulled the door open wide. "Of course. Won't you come in? I think I still have some coffee in the pot."

"No thanks," Martin replied. "Actually, I'm here on business." As MaryAnne's expression faltered, he quickly reassured her. "Nothing to do with the ranch this time. At least I hope not."

She smiled uncertainly. "Then I'm not sure how I can help

you. I don't think I've been away from the place since I got here."

"I was just wondering if anyone here might have seen something last night. Or heard something. There was an attack up at the campground."

"The campground?" MaryAnne said. "I'm afraid I'm not sure what you're talking about."

"Maybe I'll take you up on that cup of coffee after all," Martin told her. As they started toward the kitchen, he began explaining what had happened. "It's Coyote Creek Campground. It's up the mountains to the south, maybe a mile from here. It's not on the ranch, but it adjoins the property, and there's no fence." He chuckled softly. "Ted said the hikers wandering down here were getting worse than the yellow jackets. Anyway, one of the campsites got torn up last night."

MaryAnne, the coffeepot in her hand, looked up at the deputy. "My God! Was anybody hurt?"

Martin shook his head. "No one was there. The folks who were camped in the site had gone down to Sun Valley for the day, and decided to spend the night. They didn't discover what had happened until this morning."

"But what *did* happen?" MaryAnne asked as she set a steaming mug in front of the deputy, who had settled himself onto one of the chairs at the kitchen table.

The back door opened then, and Joey Wilkenson, followed by Logan and Alison Carpenter, came inside, Storm wriggling past them to sniff curiously at the policeman.

"These are my children, Alison and Logan, and of course you know Joey. This is Deputy Martin."

Though both Alison and Logan said hello to Rick Martin, Joey Wilkenson said nothing, and suddenly Charley Hawkins's words came back into MaryAnne's mind. *Don't be surprised if someone comes to talk to Joey, that's all.* The nervousness she'd instinctively felt at the deputy's appearance a few minutes before flooded back, and as she listened to what Rick Martin was saying, she could not keep herself from glancing at Joey every few moments, searching his face for some sign of how he was reacting. Had something really happened at the campground, or was Rick Martin actually here only to talk to Joey?

"I'm not sure what happened," the deputy began. "I got called up there about an hour ago, and I still can't figure it all out."

The campground at Coyote Creek consisted of only ten sites spread over five acres. The creek babbled through the center of the grounds, and while every one of the sites faced the water, not one of them was visible from any of the others. Until this morning, neither Rick Martin, Tony Moleno, nor any of the rangers who patrolled the area had ever experienced any trouble up there.

No complaints of drunken parties involving college kids on a weekend bender. No motorcycles disturbing the quiet of the summer nights. Not even any problems with fires left untended, or campsites left filled with litter.

But this morning a camper had appeared in town with a report that his campsite had been destroyed. Though Rick had suspected the man might be exaggerating, he'd followed him back up to Coyote Creek to take a report.

What he found had shocked him.

The tent, one of the old-fashioned kind made of thick canvas, was in tatters, and when he examined the frayed edges where it had been torn, Rick saw no signs of knife marks. Searching through the ruins of the tent, he found one of the sleeping bags, which had been torn nearly in two. Oddly, most of the feathers were still inside; indeed, when he turned it over, the down cascaded to the ground. Surely, if an animal had done the damage, the feathers would already have been spread all over the campground. All his life, growing up in one part of the mountains or another as his father had moved from sawmill to sawmill, he'd watched wildlife hunt, watched animals stalk their quarry, watched predators worry their prey once they'd caught it. They never simply ripped something open and then let it lay. Invariably, the animals he'd watched picked up their kill and began shaking it, just as his dog shook the occasional rat he managed to kill, instinctively trying to break the rodent's neck even long after it was dead.

Finally, after he'd examined the rest of the ruined camping gear and searched the area for tracks, he'd shaken his head uncertainly. "I want a couple of other fellows to take a look at this—see what they think—but I have to tell you, I'm not sure what we can do about it. Unless someone saw something, or at least heard something, I'm not real sure we'll ever figure out what did this."

"What about a bear? Or wolves?" the camper, whose name was Roy Bittern, suggested, unwilling to accept that he might never find out what had savaged his gear.

"Could be a bear, I suppose," Martin had agreed. "Except with this kind of damage, and no reason for an attack, you have to assume a rogue bear. And rogues don't stop. They just keep on rampaging, till someone comes along and shoots 'em."

Bittern had gazed speculatively at his shredded tent. "Unless this is just the beginning," he mused out loud. "What about wolves?"

Rick Martin had already thought about that possibility and dismissed it. "Not a chance. Wolves have a bad reputation, but as far as I know, that's all it is—just a reputation. They stick to themselves, and grab a sheep now and then, but that's pretty much the worst of it. Never heard of wolves doing anything like this. Best guess I can come up with is that it's a grizzly gone bad, and if it is, you're right. This is just the beginning."

Finishing up his notes on the incident, and assuring Roy Bittern that two rangers would be up to look over the vandalism within the hour, Rick Martin had gotten into his Jeep and started back down the rutted dirt track that led to the valley floor.

If it was a bear that did the damage, he suspected there would be another incident within a night or two. Once a bear went bad, it never stopped.

But if it was a bear, where were the tracks?

As he came to the main road, he thought of Joey Wilkenson.

Joey, who had always been a little odd, and who had now lost both his parents to "accidents" that neither Rick nor his assistant deputy, Tony Moleno, were yet willing to accept at face value.

Joey, who often took off into the woods on his own, with only the company of his dog.

Was it possible that Joey might have come up here in the middle of the night and wreaked havoc on the campsite?

On the spur of the moment, he'd decided to go up to El Monte and have a talk with the boy, and watch his reactions carefully.

"Lucky those people weren't there," he finished now, covertly keeping his eyes on Joey as he spoke. "If they had been, they probably would have been killed."

MaryAnne shuddered at the words, but didn't miss the fact that Rick Martin was watching Joey as he made the statement. Her own eyes shifted to the boy, who had listened silently to Martin's account.

Joey, though, said nothing, betraying no reaction at all.

"What I was wondering," Martin went on, "was whether any of you heard anything last night, or saw anything."

Now Joey stirred in his chair. "I did," he said. As everyone in the room turned to face him, his brow knit into a deep frown. "Something woke me up," he said. "I don't even know what it was. Anyway, I went to my window and looked out, and I thought I saw someone outside."

Rick Martin felt his heartbeat quicken. "You thought you saw someone?" he pressed. "Or did you actually *see* someone?"

Joey's eyes flicked toward MaryAnne for a moment, almost as if he was seeking her help, but then he turned back. "I'm not sure," he said. "It was just a sort of shadow outside. At first I thought it was a deer, but then I knew it wasn't. It was out in the pasture, and I could barely see it. But it looked like a man."

"Do you know who it was?" Martin asked.

Joey shook his head. "I told you—I could hardly see it."

"Why didn't you tell me about it this morning, Joey?" MaryAnne asked.

Joey shrugged. "I hardly even remembered it when I woke up," he explained. "I mean, it was almost like it happened in a dream, you know?"

"What did you do after you saw it, Joey?" Rick asked.

"I just went back to bed."

"You didn't go outside?" the deputy pressed. "You didn't go out and take a look?"

"Why would I do that?" Joey asked, his eyes narrowing.

Though he could sense MaryAnne Carpenter glaring at him, Rick decided to go on with his questions. "But you do that sometimes, don't you Joey? Your dad used to tell me you like to go out in the woods by yourself."

"Y-Yeah, I do that sometimes," Joey reluctantly admitted. "But I didn't go out last night."

"Are you sure?" Martin pressed. "You went out a few nights ago, didn't you? The night your mom—"

"Do we have to do this?" MaryAnne interrupted. "He told you what he saw last night, and he told you what he did."

Rick Martin hesitated, then decided that for now he'd gone far enough. But he'd watched Joey carefully while questioning him, and taken careful note of one thing.

The boy hadn't flinched at the deliberate mention of both his mother and his father.

Indeed, though the funeral was only a couple of hours away, Joey had barely reacted to the mention of his parents at all.

Didn't he care that they were dead?

Or was he still in shock?

As he left the house a few minutes later, Rick Martin knew that at the funeral, he would watch Joey Wilkenson very carefully. He still wasn't sure whether he believed Joey's story of having seen someone in the pasture last night, just as he still wasn't sure Joey had told him the whole truth about what had happened the day his parents had died.

That, in fact, was Martin's whole problem with Joey.

He could never tell when the boy was telling the truth and when he was lying.

────────

MaryAnne Carpenter stood in the graveyard on the edge of Sugarloaf, Alison and Logan on one side of her, Joey Wilkenson on the other. Her eyes were fixed on the twin coffins that stood at the edges of the open grave, and she determined once more not to give in to the sob that was rising in her throat. Her role here was not only that of the grieving friend, but that of the survivor's guardian, as well. For Joey's sake, she must not give in to the terrible sense of loss that had all but overwhelmed her last night, after the children and Alan had gone to bed and, unable to sleep, she had found herself alone in the cavernous downstairs rooms of the house. Finally she had retreated to the den, built herself a fire, and had herself a good cry.

Today, though, there would be no tears. She would bid her closest friend farewell, and then begin the process of building the new family that would, from now on, include Joey Wilkenson.

Not that it would be a difficult thing to do, she reflected. Already, Logan seemed to think of Joey as the big brother he'd never had, and Alison appeared to have taken to him as well, though MaryAnne suspected Joey's primary attraction for her daughter was his knowledge of horses. Horses, for Alison, had been at the center of her dreams for the last five years.

Dreams that, until two days ago, had been all but unattainable.

But for the last two days, with Joey showing her what to do, Alison had learned to groom the horses, saddle them, feed them, exercise them, and, MaryAnne had noted with amusement, muck out their stalls.

Now if only Alison would muck out her room, as well, she thought.

Suddenly she was aware that the murmuring of the crowd
around the twin graves—nearly the entire population of Sugarloaf—had ended and the service had begun. MaryAnne automatically reached down to take Joey's hand in her own as the
minister began the first prayer. When it was over, amens dying
away, the boy made no move to pull his hand away, but stood
silently staring at the caskets in which his parents' bodies lay, his
expression almost puzzled, his eyes dry. MaryAnne squeezed his
hand reassuringly, but if Joey was aware of the pressure, he gave
no sign.

Shock, MaryAnne told herself. He's still in shock.

And yet, though she tried not to let it even take form in her
mind, another thought wormed its way in as well.

It's almost as if he doesn't care.

She banished the thought instantly, wishing that Charley
Hawkins had never planted the tiny seed of doubt about the two
deaths in her mind, and that Rick Martin, when he had come to
the ranch this morning, hadn't nourished that seed with his questioning of Joey.

Her eyes flickered over the crowd. She found the deputy at
once, standing almost directly opposite her.

His eyes were fastened on Joey, his frown reflecting his own
suspicions of her godchild.

But Joey was a little boy, for God's sake. A little boy who had
loved his parents! Slipping her arm around him protectively,
MaryAnne pulled Joey closer, as if to shield him from the disturbing doubts that suddenly seemed to be hanging in the very
air of the cemetery. Indeed, as she scanned the crowd now, she
imagined that everyone there was gazing at Joey with veiled eyes,
their suspicions barely concealed, ready to boil to the surface at
any moment.

Even a couple of children his own age—a boy and a girl who
looked enough alike that MaryAnne was certain they had to be
twins—were staring at Joey, then whispering to each other as if
passing on some dark secret.

No! MaryAnne told herself. You're acting like a paranoid, and thinking like one, too! Steeling herself against the unsettling thoughts that had begun seeping into her mind, she turned her attention back to the service, forcing herself to concentrate solely on the words of the minister until he'd finished his eulogy.

Then, one by one, the people of Sugarloaf stepped forward to say a few words about Ted and Audrey, and MaryAnne slowly came to realize just how important a part of the village her friends had been. There didn't seem to be an organization in town that one or the other of them hadn't been a member of, nor an individual anywhere who at one time or another had not received a helping hand from them.

"I don't think Ted Wilkenson ever met a man he didn't like," Tom Granger, who owned the town's single grocery store, began. "And I sure as hell never met a man who didn't like him. Or, anyway, an *honest* man who didn't like him," he quickly amended himself when a murmur about real estate developers ran through the crowd. The murmur turned into a ripple of laughter. "All right, he didn't like developers any more than they liked him!" The laughter grew, and Tom Granger flushed with embarrassment. "Oh, hell," Granger finished. "You know what I mean! Ted Wilkenson was the nicest son of a bitch I ever met, and that's all I have to say!" Flustered, he retreated into the crowd, and someone else stepped up. But before the man could even begin his speech, a voice called out from the crowd.

"Hey, Phil! Tell 'em about the time Ted took you and me hunting, and he wound up talking us out of shooting anything!"

One by one people began telling their stories, and slowly MaryAnne came to comprehend the closeness of the town, the value that each of these people had to one another, and the loss the town incurred whenever someone died. For these people, their neighbors were their family. It would be a long time before the wound caused by the deaths of Ted and Audrey Wilkenson would heal. They would be missed, and they would never be forgotten.

After an hour, the last of the memories had been shared, and the final prayer was begun.

And Joey Wilkenson's hand suddenly tightened in MaryAnne's, his fingers digging into her flesh. Startled, she looked down to see Joey staring off into the distance. Following his gaze, she saw nothing at first. Then, barely visible in the trees at the edge of the graveyard, she thought she could distinguish the figure of a man.

A large, hulking man, with wild-looking hair and a full beard, whose clothes seemed not to fit him at all.

She looked again, straining her eyes to see him more clearly, but the figure was gone. Shaken, she wasn't quite sure she'd seen it at all.

A few minutes later the service was over, and MaryAnne led Joey back to the car that would return them to the ranch. Only when they were away from the cemetery did she finally question the boy about what she thought she'd seen.

"I think there was a man," Joey replied uncertainly. "I-I think he was watching me."

"Watching you?" MaryAnne asked, feeling a chill as she remembered Joey's words of a few hours ago, when he'd told Rick Martin about seeing a man in the pasture during the night. "Could it have been the man you saw last night, Joey?"

Joey was silent for a moment, but finally shook his head. "I hardly saw him," he whispered. "I-I was thinking about Mom and Dad." His eyes brimming with tears, he looked at MaryAnne worriedly. "But why would he be watching me?"

She slipped her arm protectively around the boy. "Maybe he wasn't," she tried to reassure him. "Maybe he was just someone who knew your parents and wanted to come and pay his respects." But the strange, fleeting image of the man stayed in her mind, and as the reception at the ranch went on through the afternoon, she began questioning people as to who the stranger might have been.

No one else, however, had even glimpsed the shadowed figure.

It was as if he hadn't been there at all.

MaryAnne went to bed early that night, worn-out from the funeral and the reception that had followed. But sometime near midnight she woke up suddenly, feeling something was wrong.

Something that had nothing to do with the events that had drained her energy that day.

No, it was something else.

Something about the house.

She lay still in bed for a moment, listening. Nothing but the normal sounds of the night.

And yet the sense that all was not right wouldn't leave her. She got out of bed, slipped into her bathrobe, and left her room, leaving the door open so that the light by her bed would spill out into the hallway.

Moving to Alison's door, she listened for a moment, then opened it a crack and peeped inside.

Her daughter was asleep, sprawled on her back, her hair spread out on the pillow. Silently closing the door, she went on to Logan's room. Her son, curled up with a pillow in his arms, was also sound asleep.

Finally, she hesitated at Joey's door, then tapped softly. When there was no response—not even a whimper from Storm—she opened the door and looked inside.

Joey's bed covers were thrown back. The room was empty. "Oh, God," MaryAnne whispered softly, hurrying to the window to peer out into the night. She scanned the yard and the field, searching for any sign of the boy or the dog, but there was nothing. Then a movement caught her eye and she turned to look at the barn.

One of its great doors was open, swinging in the wind.

What was he doing out there? Hurrying downstairs, MaryAnne clutched the robe around her as she left the house through the kitchen door and trotted across to the barn. Inside, the horses were whinnying nervously, and Sheika, who had reappeared on the day after MaryAnne arrived, was stamping at the straw that littered her stall. "Joey?" she called as she stepped through the open door. "Joey, are you out here?"

She listened, and for a moment heard nothing, but then there was a low sound, unidentifiable, from the far end of the barn. One of the horses reared up, snorting loudly.

"Joey—"

The sound from the far reaches of the barn swelled into a snarl, then something came charging out of the blackness toward her. Acting only on her reflexes, MaryAnne jerked back from the gaping darkness, slamming the door shut and dropping the bar into place just as the thing, whatever it was, hurled itself against the other side. Her heart pounding, she turned and fled back across the yard, slamming the kitchen door shut as soon as she was inside the house.

What was it?

What had been in the barn?

It couldn't have been Joey—it *couldn't* have been! Surely he would have answered her when she called to him. And Storm wouldn't have attacked her.

Would he?

But it was impossible! If anything, the big shepherd was too friendly, constantly licking people and begging to be petted!

Her pulse slowly returning to normal, she quickly checked the living room and the den, praying that Joey might have come downstairs in the night and fallen asleep on one of the sofas.

There was no sign of him.

Finally, she picked up the telephone on the table behind the stairs, and was about to dial the deputy's office when she heard the kitchen door open. For a moment she froze. Was it possible that whatever had been in the barn was now in the house?

"J-Joey?" she stammered, her voice choking in her throat. A moment later Storm bounded out of the dining room, his tail wagging, and threw himself on her, his paws resting on her chest as he tried to lick her face. A second later Joey himself appeared, dressed in jeans, a T-shirt showing under his denim jacket. "Get down, Storm," MaryAnne protested, twisting away from the enthusiastic dog. "Joey, get him off me!"

"Sit, Storm," Joey commanded, and the dog instantly dropped to the floor, his tail curling around his feet, his eyes fastening on his master.

"Joey, where were you?" MaryAnne demanded, the fear of a few minutes before now giving way to annoyance. "Do you know what time it is?"

Joey's eyes darkened. "It's only about midnight. I couldn't sleep, so Storm and I went for a walk."

"A walk?" MaryAnne echoed, Rick Martin's questions that morning loomed once more in her mind. "Joey, did you see someone again? Was it like last night?"

Joey shook his head. "I didn't see anything. I just wanted to go for a walk. What's wrong with that?"

MaryAnne felt disoriented. He was only thirteen, and it was the middle of the night, and God only knew what might be in the woods. Surely Audrey hadn't approved of—

And then she was sure she understood.

Only that day, he had watched both his parents being buried.

What must it have been like for him?

She couldn't even begin to imagine.

This night, the finality of the funeral still fresh in his mind, must have been an endless agony for him. She should have sat up herself, with her door open and her light on, in case he needed her.

But he hadn't wanted to waken her, hadn't wanted to bother anyone with his grief, she thought, fighting back the sting of tears as sympathy for this slight, solemn-eyed child overwhelmed her. So he'd taken his dog and gone for a walk.

But what about the barn? What had he been doing in there? And why had Storm come at her like that, scaring her half to death?

"Didn't you hear me when I called you in the barn?" she asked, her voice now devoid of any anger.

Joey's brows knit into a frown. "I wasn't in the barn. We just went along by the creek for a while."

Now it was MaryAnne's turn to frown. "But I was just out there, Joey. The barn door was open, and some—" She hesitated, then decided which word to use. "*Something* was inside. It came at me!"

Joey stared at her. "Well, there isn't anything out there now," he said. "I stopped to check on the horses just before we came in. Everything's fine."

With Storm at his heels, Joey bounded up the stairs. MaryAnne heard his door close.

Nonplussed, she turned off the downstairs lights. The darkness and silence of the night once more closed around her.

But tonight, the peaceful countryside, the darkness and silence of the ranch, had abruptly taken on an ominous feeling, a feeling that made MaryAnne shiver although the night was warm, almost balmy.

It was a long time before she fell asleep. Twice she got up to peer out into the velvet darkness beyond the window.

Though she saw nothing, heard nothing, she still had the uneasy feeling that something—*someone*—was out there.

Out there watching, and waiting.

CHAPTER 7

MaryAnne was up early on Monday morning, having made up her mind the night before that although it was Labor Day, she would begin the serious business of finding out just what was involved in running the ranch. Until now, all her energies had been depleted by grief over the loss of her closest friend, and by the demands of dealing with the double funeral, as well. But it was over now, and after the weekend spent hiking the ranch with Alison and Logan—and trying to remember as much as she could of Joey's continuous explanation of what they were seeing—she'd decided that this morning it was time to begin putting together some kind of routine, holiday or not.

Besides, she'd discovered yesterday that in Sugarloaf, Labor Day was celebrated on Sunday, regardless of what the rest of the country might do. "Ranches don't know anything about days off," Charley Hawkins had explained to her on Friday, "and

around here, it's just one last chance to milk the summer tourists." So the "traditional" picnic had been yesterday (open to
tourists at twenty-five dollars a head) along with the rodeo (another twenty dollars) and a "genuine square dance" in the evening (fifteen dollars, drinks five bucks a shot). "Then the stores
stay open all day Monday, just in case anyone has any cash left,"
Charley had explained. But following his advice as well as her
own instincts, MaryAnne and the children had stayed home. "It's
one thing to go on with your lives," Charley had counseled. "But
if I were you, I'd give it some time before I started doing much
of a social nature." Thus, the four of them had stuck close to the
ranch all day Saturday and Sunday, but when she'd seen Bill
Sikes coming back from town the night before, she'd gone out to
ask him to come to the house at seven o'clock this morning.

Sikes had pursed his lips in apparent protest. "Mr. Wilkenson
never wanted me in before eight—maybe eight-thirty," he'd
complained, but even as he uttered the words, MaryAnne had
sensed the first test of her authority.

In retrospect, she thought she had handled the situation pretty
well.

"I'm sure I'll do a lot of things differently from Mr. Wilkenson," she'd replied evenly, "so if you'll just come to the kitchen
at seven, I'll have coffee ready for us, and we can begin going
over things."

Sikes had said nothing, but MaryAnne took the tiny movement
of his head as agreement, and when she went to bed that night,
she set her alarm for six o'clock. She intended to be showered,
dressed, and ready for the interview—complete with the coffee
she'd promised—at least ten minutes before the appointed hour.

By seven-fifteen, when there was still no sign of Bill Sikes, she
began to feel annoyed with the man. Should she keep waiting
for him, or call him? Or even go looking for him?

What if she found him in his cabin, sound asleep, with an
empty whiskey bottle by his bed? Would she have to fire him?

And then what would she do? She couldn't run the ranch by herself—

A knock at the back door interrupted her thoughts, and when she looked up to see Sikes himself peering through the window, she instantly abandoned all notions of firing him. He'd come, and it was still forty-five minutes earlier than he'd been required to report to Ted—assuming she believed his story, although she wasn't at all sure she did. If he wanted to be a little late just to prove his independence, so be it. She'd deal with it.

She waved him in, pouring him a mug of coffee, then nodded toward the table in the corner of the large room. "Did you have a good night?" she asked.

Bill Sikes shrugged disinterestedly, pulled off the knit cap he habitually wore on his grizzled head, but made no move to settle into one of the chairs at the table. "I been thinkin'," he said without preamble. "I'm prob'ly gonna be quittin'."

MaryAnne froze, the mug of coffee she'd just poured hovering in the air. Quitting? But he couldn't do that! How could she manage without— And then a thought came to her.

He was testing her again, no doubt seeing if he could get more money out of her by threatening to leave her on her own. "I see," she said, keeping her voice calm, masking the twinge of panic that had seized her. "Well, why don't we sit down and talk about it?" Putting his mug on the table, she pulled one of the chairs out for him, then seated herself on another.

Sikes hesitated a moment, then almost reluctantly sat down. As he sipped his coffee, MaryAnne eyed him surreptitiously, trying to read the expression on his face. She still had no idea how old he might be, and his dark skin and black eyes suggested that at least part of his heritage was Native American. His skin had the leathery look of a man who had spent most of his life outdoors, and though he was no more than five-foot-six or -seven, there was a wiry power to his body. Was he angry about something? She searched his face, but realized that she couldn't tell.

If anything, he looked more worried than angry. "Why don't you tell me what's wrong?" she asked. "Perhaps if we discuss why you want to quit, we can work something out."

"Just doesn't seem right anymore, that's all," Sikes said, his eyes avoiding hers.

"You mean because of what happened to Ted and Audrey." MaryAnne nodded sympathetically, fighting back a wave of grief at the reminder of what had happened to her friends. "I know it must be as much of a shock to you as it was to me, but—"

"It's not just that," Sikes interrupted. "It's somethin' else, too. If I was you, I'd just put this place on the market, and take Joey back to wherever you came from. A woman like you can't run a ranch—"

"A woman like me?" MaryAnne cut in sharply. "Exactly what kind of woman would that be, Mr. Sikes?"

Bill Sikes's eyes narrowed to slits. "Don't get on your high horse with me, young lady," he said. "You know what I'm talkin' about. What do you know about running a ranch?"

"Not any more than Ted and Audrey did when they first came out here," MaryAnne shot back. "And I suspect that the man on this place who knew the most about ranching was you. If you could teach Ted and Audrey, I don't see any reason why you can't teach me, too." Though she was absolutely certain she had just given Bill Sikes far more credit than he deserved for the running of the ranch—and Ted and Audrey Wilkenson far less— the flattery seemed to work. Sikes sat up a little straighter in his chair, and his head tilted in acknowledgment of the compliment.

"I've learned a thing or two in my time," he admitted, then shaking his head, added, "Still, somethin's not right around here. I just don't believe what happened to Mr. and Mrs. Wilkenson was an accident. Mr. W. was good with horses. Good, and real careful, too. He wouldn'ta spooked Sheika. And somethin' about that accident with Mrs. W. ain't right, either."

MaryAnne felt her pulse quicken. "Have you talked to Rick Martin about it?"

·"Oh, yeah. Fact is, he don't like it any better'n I do. He's been up to see me twice now, askin' all kinds of questions." He glanced at MaryAnne as if expecting her to press him for more information, but instead of saying anything, she simply met his gaze with her own. Finally Sikes broke the look, shifting his gaze back to the tabletop in front of him. "Fact is, I don't know what's goin' on around here. But for quite a while now, things ain't been quite right." His eyes met hers again. "You ever think about the animals?" he asked abruptly.

Startled by the sudden shift of the conversation, MaryAnne could only echo Bill Sikes's last words. "The animals?"

Sikes nodded. "The animals whose land this is. The bears and wolves and deer. The raccoons. The beaver. All kinds of animals. An' it seems like lately all we're doin' is pushin' 'em aside, makin' more an' more room for ourselves. You ever think about that? You ever think about the animals when you look at all them condos goin' up in town?"

"I—I suppose everyone has, one way or another," MaryAnne replied uncertainly. What was the man getting at? A second later, he told her.

"Well, it seems like somethin's goin' on around here lately. Somethin' went into that barn and spooked that horse so's it kicked Mr. W. And somethin' gave Mrs. W. enough of a scare that she lost her balance."

"But it was dark," MaryAnne protested, unwilling to let Sikes's words nurture the seed that Charlie Hawkins had planted in her mind the previous week. If he starts talking about Joey, I'll fire him right now, she told herself. Right this very minute.

"Not that dark," Sikes insisted. "And Mrs. W. was up there hundreds of times. Best view of the valley we got. She knew every inch of it, and she wouldn't have lost her footing even if she was blindfolded. So somethin' made her fall. And there's the horses, too," he added.

Suddenly MaryAnne remembered the night before last, when Joey and Storm had gone out, and she had seen the open barn door. But she was almost sure that despite Joey's denial, it had to have been him in the barn. "I'm not sure what you're talking about," she said, steeling herself for the words she was certain were coming next.

"Somethin's spooking them," Sikes went on. "Seems like it's practically every night now. I can hear 'em from my cabin. Every night—at least once, sometimes a coupla times—they start snortin' and stampin' like somethin's after 'em. I been down there more'n once, but I can't never find out what it is. But somethin's out there, an' it's startin' to make me pretty nervous."

"Joey was out night before last," MaryAnne said softly, keeping her eyes on Sikes, waiting for him to rise to her bait.

But Sikes shook his head. "It's not him. Saw him myself. You was out, too. Heard you callin' him. He was up by the creek—I was keepin' an eye on him. Besides, the horses know Joey. They wouldn't spook just 'cause he was around. Not unless he wanted them to, anyway."

MaryAnne said nothing for a moment, turning Sikes's last words over and over in her mind, examining them from every angle. *Not unless he wanted them to, anyway.* Was he implying that Joey himself might have spooked Sheika, causing his father's death? Yet the man's expression betrayed nothing save admiration for Joey's ability to communicate with the animals. She let her guard down slightly. "But there was *something* in the barn that night. It snarled at me, then came at me. I slammed the door just before it got to me."

"I ain't sayin' there wasn't," Sikes replied. "I heard the horses, too. But when I checked the barn after Joey came back in here, there warn't nothin' there. Just the horses. Nervous. As if a grizzly was skulkin' around."

"What about a man?" MaryAnne suggested. "Joey thinks he saw—" She cut her words short as Joey himself came into the room, stopping in surprise when he saw Bill Sikes.

Saying nothing to the handyman, Joey went to the refrigerator. "Is there any orange juice?" he asked MaryAnne.

"In the pitcher," MaryAnne replied. Then: "Aren't you going to say good morning to Mr. Sikes?"

Joey glanced at Bill Sikes for the briefest of moments. "Good morning." He poured himself a glass of orange juice, then sat down at one of the stools in front of the counter.

Sikes, draining his mug, stood up and started toward the back door. "Maybe you and me better talk later on," he said. Before MaryAnne could reply, he was gone.

"What was he doing in here?" Joey demanded as soon as the door had slammed shut behind Sikes.

MaryAnne picked up the two empty mugs and took them to the sink. "We were having a talk," she said, suddenly annoyed not only at Joey's rudeness toward Sikes, but the tone of his voice when he'd demanded to know why the caretaker was in the house. "Is there something wrong with that?"

Joey's expression darkened. "He shouldn't be in here. In fact, he shouldn't be here at all."

MaryAnne's brows rose in surprise. "I beg your pardon?"

"Dad was going to fire him," Joey said.

"Fire him?" MaryAnne echoed, her eyes narrowing with uncertainty. "But he's been working here for years, hasn't he? Why would your father have fired him?"

Joey gazed steadily at her, and when he spoke, his voice was cold. "Because he's crazy. He makes up stories about everything. I bet he's even making up stories that I did something to Mom and Dad." Draining his orange juice, Joey slid off the stool and went out the back door, heading toward the barn. Stunned by his last words, MaryAnne made no move to stop him, no move to demand an explanation of what he'd just said.

All she knew was that the Joey she'd just talked to seemed nothing like the boy who had thrown himself into her arms when she'd arrived five days earlier.

This Joey seemed completely different.

He's still in shock, she insisted to herself once more. That's all it was—he was still in shock from Ted and Audrey's deaths. But even as the words formed in her mind, she knew that this time she didn't believe them.

This time, Joey hadn't been upset by anything, hadn't been angry about anything. He had simply stated what he believed.

Or what he wanted her to believe.

Suddenly MaryAnne Carpenter had an uneasy feeling that there was a dark facet to Joey Wilkenson's personality that she knew nothing about. A darkness she was just beginning to see.

CHAPTER 8

"**C**an we go into town, Mom?"

MaryAnne was sitting at the desk in the den as she tried to familiarize herself with the ranch's accounting system—a process which had so far involved five calls to an increasingly impatient Charley Hawkins, who had finally sighed mightily and suggested that she simply make a list of her questions and bring them to his office the next morning. She glanced up at Alison, who was standing in the doorway to the living room. "I'm not sure I have the time right now," she began, then caught sight of the large grandfather clock in the corner. "My God—it's already eleven!"

"You don't have to take us," Alison told her. "We can walk."

MaryAnne stared at her daughter. "Two and a half miles?" she asked. "You and Logan are going to walk two and a half miles to town, and two and a half miles back?" Back home in New Jersey, she couldn't remember either of her kids ever walking more than a few blocks. Anything farther, and they either took a bus or begged for a ride!

"It's not like at home," Alison said, as if she'd read her mother's mind. "It'll just be like going on a hike. And anyway, if we're going to start school tomorrow, we have to get clothes, don't we?"

Just as she had last year at this time, MaryAnne flinched at the thought of the expense of school clothes. But then she remembered: this year, things were different. For the first time, she could afford to buy the kids what they needed, without having to resent every penny the clothes might cost. Still, she hesitated. "I think I ought to be with you if you're going shopping—"

"We're not going to buy anything." Having neatly sidestepped her mother's primary objection, Alison pressed her advantage. "It'll save you a lot of time if we've already picked things out and tried them on." Warming to the idea, Alison rushed on, building her case. "All we'll do is have them hold the stuff we pick out, and then we can all go back later this afternoon and you can decide which stuff we should buy."

Though the entire speech sounded suspiciously like something Alison had carefully rehearsed before trying it out on her, MaryAnne had to admit that it made sense. Until she remembered Joey and his strange behavior this morning. "Honey, have you noticed anything different about Joey this morning?"

Alison suddenly looked guarded. "D-Different?" she stammered, her eyes darting to the left. "What do you mean?"

Then Joey himself stepped into the doorway, his dark eyes exhibiting nothing of the chill MaryAnne had seen in them early that morning. "We've already taken care of the horses, Aunt MaryAnne. Can't I take Alison and Logan into town? Please?"

MaryAnne studied the boy carefully. There was no trace left of the arrogance he'd exhibited toward Bill Sikes, nothing of the coldness with which he'd told her that his father had been about to fire the handyman. Once again, he was the appealing thirteen-year-old she'd come to know over the last few days. Whatever had happened this morning, she decided, must have been blown out of proportion in her own mind. "Well, I don't see any reason why not," she decided. "What time will you be back?"

Joey shrugged. "Three or four?"

"Fine," MaryAnne replied. "But if you're going to be later, call me. Okay? And remember—don't *buy*! Just *look*!"

By the time the kids had left the house, MaryAnne's attention was once more focused on the account books in front of her, and though she heard Joey's voice through the open window, the words he spoke didn't penetrate her mind.

"This is gonna be great," he told Alison and Logan. "Wait'll you see all the neat stuff they have!"

———

"How much farther is it?" Logan complained, coming to a stop on the trail they seemed to have been hiking along forever. When they'd started out from the house, walking into the woods and then along the creek, it had all seemed like a great adventure, but now, nearly an hour later, he was getting scared, though he'd never admit it. The woods were starting to feel like they were closing in on him, and they had crossed so many other paths that he was sure he could never find his way home. Alison grinned at him. "Afraid the big, bad wolf might get you?" she teased. Logan felt his chin start to quiver, but before Alison could say anything else, Joey pointed through the trees.

"We're almost there, Logan, see?" He held the smaller boy up so he could peer through a gap in the heavy underbrush. "We just go a little farther, then there's a trail to the left."

Sure enough, there was the town, only a little way off. Even if he got lost, all he'd have to do was start walking downhill and he'd be out of the woods in just a few minutes. As Joey put him back on the ground, he stuck his tongue out at Alison. "I wasn't scared," he insisted with far more conviction than he could have mustered a second before. "Come on!" Striking out ahead of the two older children, he took off down the trail, and sure enough—around the next bend was another path, winding off down the slope, just like Joey had said. Another minute and he burst out into the meadow that covered the valley floor, and ran over to the bank of Coyote Creek. "How do we get across?" he called back to Joey.

"We don't," Joey told him. "We just walk along it till we get to the cemetery. There's a bridge there."

At mention of the cemetery, the three children fell silent and their pace slowed, until finally they came to the stone wall that separated the graveyard from the meadow.

Joey climbed up onto the top of the wall, offering his hand to Alison while Logan scrambled up on his own. Spread out before them were two acres of well-kept lawn dotted with white-bark pines, which made up the Sugarloaf cemetery. The three of them stood silently staring at the spot on the far side, close to the forest's edge, where Joey's parents had been buried the day before yesterday.

"Do you want to go visit the graves?" Alison finally asked.

Joey hesitated, then shook his head. "They wouldn't even know I was there."

"They might," Logan said.

But Joey shook his head harder. "I don't want to, okay?" His voice was harsh. As Logan recoiled from the older boy's disapproval, and Alison flushed with embarrassment, Joey quickly added, "I mean, you guys are my family now, and when I'm with you, I feel good. But if I went to visit their grave . . ." His voice trailed off and he wiped his sleeve across his eyes, then fumbled in the back pocket of his jeans, pulled out a handkerchief, and blew his nose. "Let's just go into town, okay?" he asked. Without waiting for an answer, he turned and started along the wall, only dropping off it when he came to the spot that was closest to the bridge across the creek. As the three children crossed the bridge and headed along the narrow path toward the graveyard's entrance, none of them looked back at the place where Ted and Audrey Wilkenson had been buried.

"Where shall we start?" Alison asked as they came into the center of the little town a few minutes later. The shopping district occupied only two blocks, crowded with shops offering a brightly colored array of clothes, ranging from T-shirts to elaborate ski outfits, but almost everything displayed in the windows seemed calculated to attract tourists, not townspeople. "Where are the regular clothes?"

"The Mercantile," Joey told her. "And there's Conway's, too. You guys like western clothes?"

"I do!" Logan instantly declared, garnering him a scornful look from his sister.

"You don't even know what they are," Alison told him.

"I do, too!" Logan shot back. "The shirts are real fancy, with lots of snaps on them! I want a blue one! And boots! Can I get some cowboy boots?" he asked Joey.

"We can't buy anything," Alison reminded him. "You heard what Mom said. All we're doing is looking!"

"But Joey said—" Logan began. Alison cut him off.

"Logan, we don't even have any money! How are we going to buy anything?"

Logan's bubble of excitement began to deflate in the face of reality.

"Don't worry, Logan," Joey told the smaller boy. "We'll still get you some boots, and lots of other stuff, too." Holding Logan's hand, he started down the wooden sidewalk, with Alison scurrying to catch up. In the next block, hanging from one of the larger stores, she could see the sign identifying it as the Sugarloaf Mercantile. As they approached it, the door burst open and several boys and girls about her own age came out. They turned as if they were coming toward her, but abruptly stopped, looked at each other, seemed to make up their minds without exchanging a word, and headed without a backward glance across the street.

Joey, who had stopped stone still as the group came out of the Mercantile, watched them go but said nothing. And yet, from the look on his face, Alison was sure he knew them. "Who are they?" she asked. "How come they went the other way?"

Joey's eyes narrowed and his jaw tightened. "Just some kids," he said. "They don't like me, that's all."

"How come?" Alison blurted.

Joey's face reddened. "They just don't," he said. "How do I know why? Come on, let's go see what kind of clothes they have." He pushed the glass door of the Mercantile open and went inside, with Logan right behind him, but Alison hesitated, gazing across the street to where the group of kids was standing, now whispering among themselves and sneaking glances in her direction.

What is it? she wondered.

What was going on?

Why wouldn't they like Joey Wilkenson? What could he possibly have done to them?

For a brief instant she was tempted to cross the street, to walk right up to them and ask. But even as the thought came into her mind, she knew she wouldn't act on it.

For she knew exactly what would happen if she did.

None of them would say anything. They would just look at her, and then turn around and walk away.

"Alison?" she heard Logan calling from inside the store. "Come on!"

Turning away from the group across the street, Alison hurried into the store, where she found Logan and Joey examining a stack of brightly colored western shirts.

"We can buy anything we want!" Logan told her, his eyes sparkling with anticipation. "All we do is charge them!" Seeing the uncertainty cross his sister's face, he turned to Joey. "Isn't that what you said?"

Joey grinned at Alison. "It's true. We have accounts at every store in town. All we have to do is pick out what we want, and they send the bill to the ranch!"

"But Mom said—" Alison began. Joey didn't let her finish.

"Aunt MaryAnne doesn't know about the accounts. And if she says we shouldn't have bought something, we can bring it back. What's the big deal? We need school clothes, don't we?"

Alison hesitated, but then her eyes took in the massive display of merchandise spread out before her, and her resistance melted. As her fingers fell wistfully on a plaid cashmere scarf, she heard Joey speaking to her: "Buy it—it'll look terrific on you."

For the first time in her life Alison Carpenter abandoned herself to the joy of shopping.

The scarf instantly became hers and she decided she would always think of it as a gift.

A gift from Joey.

In the middle of the afternoon, MaryAnne closed the last of the ledgers on the desk, leaned back and shut her eyes.

She had done it!

She had gone over all the accounts. In the beginning the ledgers looked like nothing more than row upon row of meaningless numbers, but she had kept at it, and slowly come to understand just how much it cost to run the ranch. She understood the cost of keeping the horses, and the amount of money the Wilkensons had saved by raising most of their hay, rather than buying it.

More important, she understood just how much the ranch had cost Ted and Audrey, and the fact that it had never been intended to make money. Indeed, it had cost far more than it needed to, for the Wilkensons had spent considerable sums in rejuvenation projects, restoring once-cleared fields to their natural state and removing a culvert that had detoured the stream from its original course. That project had been particularly expensive, since it involved replacing a small forest of fully grown trees that had died when the stream had been diverted decades earlier, cutting off their water supply.

Yet no matter how much money the ranch absorbed, the books showed clearly that Ted Wilkenson's income was large enough to support it all, with sums, which heretofore had been beyond MaryAnne's wildest dreams, left over to support various conservation and environmental causes in the Sawtooth Valley area.

Though she covered several pages of the yellow legal pad she had found in the desk with questions, she had already struck several of them out as her understanding of the Wilkensons' financial structure had become clearer.

I can do it, she decided. At least this part of it.

She got up from the desk, stretched, then moved through the house, automatically straightening things as she wandered through the rooms. Going out the back door, she paused to bask in the sun for a moment, enjoying the feel of the heat on her aching muscles.

Exercise.

That's what she needed.

Maybe she should just take an hour or so and go for a long walk. She tipped her head back, surveying the soaring mountains that almost surrounded her. To the west, the stone face of Sugarloaf was just barely falling into the shadows of the afternoon, and as her eyes lingered on the ledge from which Audrey had fallen, she felt a chill go through her and quickly looked away. But there were huge granite outcroppings everywhere, and any one of them would provide a panorama of the whole valley. Surely the network of trails that led up the mountains would take her to one or another of them.

She was about to start off across the field when a loud whinnying came from the barn. Frowning, she headed across the yard, but stopped short, remembering the night of the funeral.

Another of the horses joined in the whinnying, and then from the house she heard another sound.

A dog barking.

Surely Joey had taken Storm with him when they'd gone to town? Except if the kids were going to be shopping— She looked up to the second floor, and there was the big shepherd, his fore-paws propped up on the sill of Joey's open window. He started barking again as the commotion in the barn increased. Mary-Anne ran to the back door, calling out to the dog. From the second floor Storm's barking turned into a frantic howl, and MaryAnne suddenly understood what had happened. Hurrying upstairs, she opened the door to Joey's room. The dog immediately bounded out, racing down the stairs. MaryAnne followed him, catching up to him in the kitchen, where the closed door had stopped him. As soon as she opened it, he streaked across to the barn, disappearing inside.

By the time MaryAnne made it to the barn, the horses had begun calming down, but still she stopped at the door. "Storm? Here, boy! Come on!" A second later the dog trotted up to her, his tail wagging. "What was it, boy?" MaryAnne asked, reaching down to scratch the big dog while she peered into the gloom of the cavernous barn.

The horses were quiet now, and when neither they nor Storm showed any further signs of nervousness, MaryAnne finally stepped inside, peering into the shadowed light. "Bill?" she called out. "Are you here?"

Nothing.

With Storm at her heels, she moved farther into the barn. The three horses were in their stalls, each of them with its head over the door, watching her.

"What was it?" she asked them. "Was someone in here?"

Though neither Buck nor Fritz, the two geldings whose stalls were closest to the door, made any response, Sheika nickered softly, her ears flicking forward. MaryAnne moved farther into the barn, frowning uncertainly at the big mare and remembering how Sheika had finally come back to the barn the day after she had arrived.

That morning, when she'd first looked out the window and seen the big horse calmly grazing in the field, she hadn't known where it had come from, and surely would have stopped Joey had she known it was the mare that killed Ted. But Joey had charged outside immediately, calling out to the horse. MaryAnne had watched in stunned surprise as the big mare stayed where she was as Joey ran toward her. Only as he'd come close had she finally walked over to him, then nuzzled his neck, licked his cheek, and followed him docilely back to the barn without his even laying a hand on her bridle.

She had had to call the sheriff's office, of course. Within the hour Tony Moleno had arrived with Olivia Sherbourne, the bluff middle-aged woman who was the local veterinarian.

While the vet had examined the horse, Joey pleaded with the assistant deputy not to have her destroyed. "She didn't hurt Dad on purpose," he insisted. "She's not like that! Something made her do it!"

Tony Moleno had said nothing until Olivia Sherbourne finished her inspection. "Well, what do you think?"

Olivia had shoved her hands deep in the hip pockets of her jeans, and met Moleno's gaze with a determined look. "I think putting this horse down is the stupidest idea I've ever heard. You *know* me, Tony! I've put down plenty of horses in my time, some of them because they were sick, but most because they were dangerous. And I never had any question it was the right thing to do. But I've known Sheika for a lot of years, and I've never known her to hurt anything. You could poke that horse with a sharp stick, and all she'd do is look at you. I think Joey's right—something gave her a hell of a scare, and all she did was react. It was an accident, pure and simple. If you want me to, I'll go roll around under her, and you watch what happens. All she'll do is snuffle my pockets, looking for sugar!"

Tony Moleno had taken a deep breath, but Olivia Sherbourne wasn't through.

"There's no law saying a horse has to be put down just because of an accident, Tony, and if you don't believe me, call Rick Martin or Charley Hawkins. It's just a custom, and with Sheika, I won't do it." Anticipating him, she added: "And if you put her down yourself, I'll see to it that every kid in town knows that you did it, and that I was against it!"

The assistant deputy had spread his hands in submission. "All right, Olivia. You've made your point, and you're the expert. If I wasn't going to listen to you, I wouldn't have brought you up here, would I?"

Olivia Sherbourne had snorted in derision and walked back to her truck. But as she pulled out of the yard, she'd stopped and stuck her head out the window, calling out to MaryAnne. "You have any trouble with him, you call me! In fact, if you have any trouble with anybody, you call me! I live just down the road." Then she'd driven away, leaving Tony Moleno chuckling in the cloud of dust she'd raised.

"She means it," the deputy had told her. "Olivia's a terrific vet, and a terrific woman, but I wouldn't want to cross her. The last guy that did wound up with a black eye and a dislocated shoulder. Deserved it, too. You couldn't have a better friend than Olivia, and there's not a soul around here who wouldn't agree with me."

"Including the man she gave the black eye to?" MaryAnne had asked.

Moleno's chuckle had turned into a roar of laughter. "He's not around here anymore. Stayed another month, then just left. No one's heard from him since."

Though that had been the end of any talk of putting Sheika down, MaryAnne had still felt leery of the big horse. Now, in the barn, she approached the mare carefully. "What was it, Sheika? Was there someone here?"

The horse nickered again, and stretched her head forward, and MaryAnne reached out to give it a tentative scratch. The horse's big tongue slid out, licking her arm, then she dropped her head lower, straining her nose toward MaryAnne's jeans.

"You want some sugar?" MaryAnne reached into her pocket, pulling out one of the lumps she'd already started taking from the sugar bowl each morning to feed to Buck and Fritz. Now

Sheika gently took the sugar from her hand, her lips barely touching MaryAnne's skin. "I think Dr. Sherbourne was right," MaryAnne said, patting the horse once more. "I really don't think you'd hurt anyone."

"Damn right I was," a voice said from the barn door. "And my name's Olivia. Nobody calls me Dr. Sherbourne, and I hope you're not going to start."

MaryAnne spun around to see the vet silhouetted against the bright sunlight outside. "My God! You startled me!"

"Down, Storm!" Olivia commanded as the big shepherd reared up to try to lick her face. Obediently, the dog dropped back to the ground, and the vet fished a dog biscuit out of her pocket, holding it down for Storm to snatch. "Greedy, aren't you?" She strode into the barn, speaking a few words to each of the horses, then stopped in front of Sheika. "Thought I'd stop by and see how my girl's getting along." She held the big mare's head in her hand, then peeled back her lips to check her teeth. Satisfied, the vet turned to face MaryAnne. "I assume you're not having any problems, since you haven't called me."

"Actually, I'm barely getting used to the place," MaryAnne replied. Then, remembering her conversation with Bill Sikes that morning, and Joey's words after Sikes had left the house, she found herself telling Olivia Sherbourne about it. "I'm not sure what to do," she said when she was done. "Was Ted really about to fire Bill?"

"Not that I know of," Olivia replied. "But I can't say he wasn't, either. And if Sikes wants to go, let him! There's plenty of people who could take his place, and probably do a better job. I liked Ted and Audrey a lot, but if this were my place, I'd do things differently."

MaryAnne frowned. "What's wrong with it?"

Olivia hesitated. "Well, now that you've put me on the spot, I guess I'm not sure," she said. "Just more of a feeling, you know? I've just had a feeling lately that something's not quite right around here."

MaryAnne felt a shiver go through her as she heard the veterinarian reiterating almost exactly what Sikes had said only this morning.

"Well, I don't mean it like he did," Olivia replied after MaryAnne repeated the handyman's words. "I'm afraid I don't buy into the idea of animals taking revenge. But there are all kinds of strange people around here. There are even a few mountain men still living up near the timberline."

"Mountain men?" MaryAnne echoed.

"Nut cases," Olivia replied. "Most of them have died off, but there are still a few left, scratching out a living God only knows how. For the most part, they're pretty harmless, but some of them are absolutely psychopathic."

Unbidden, the memory of the strange-looking man she'd seen at Ted and Audrey's funeral came into MaryAnne's mind, along with an echo of Joey's insistence that he'd seen someone in the pasture the night before the funeral. "Do any of them live around here?" she asked.

"Who knows?" Olivia replied. "They seem to live pretty much anyplace they damned well please, and do whatever they want to do." Seeing the look of worry that had come over MaryAnne's face, the veterinarian regretted her words. "Hell, I'm just talking to hear the sound of my own voice. I'm sure everything's just fine." Her eyes scanned the countryside, looking for something to distract MaryAnne from what she'd just said. Then, as though she'd had a sudden inspiration: "You had a full tour of this place yet?"

MaryAnne shook her head. "I haven't had time—"

"Then the time's just come," Olivia declared. "As it happens, I've got nothing better to do this afternoon than meddle in your life, so what do you say we get started?"

For the next two hours, they toured the ranch, first going through the barn and tack rooms, then each of the other outbuildings, Olivia identifying everything they saw, even promising to teach MaryAnne how to use the tractor. Their inspection of the buildings completed, Olivia taught her how to saddle a horse, and they set off on Buck and Fritz to ride the land. After they covered the property, Olivia glanced up at the mountains toward the Coyote Creek campground. "What do you say—shall we ride up and take a look at the campsite that got torn up the other day?"

MaryAnne hesitated, then shook her head. "It's getting a little late. I'd like to be at the ranch when the kids come home."

It was nearly four when they got back, but except for Bill Sikes, who was stacking firewood against the side of the house, the place was still deserted.

"When you get right down to it," Olivia said after they finished taking care of the horses and were settled on the front porch with glasses of wine, "I'm not sure what you need a full-time handyman for at all. If you decide to get rid of Sikes, or he just clears out—and believe me, he'll never do that—don't bother to replace him. One field, a pasture, and a barn. That's all that's left up here, and it doesn't take much work to keep them up. Between you and the kids, there shouldn't be any problem at all. And I can always lend a hand if you need it."

"I couldn't possibly ask—" MaryAnne began, but Olivia silenced her with a gesture.

"Don't tell me what you could ask and what you couldn't. We're neighbors, and that means we help each other. Besides, if it weren't for Audrey, I wouldn't be here, and I guess I feel like I owe her."

"Audrey?" MaryAnne repeated. "You mean you knew her before you came here?"

Olivia nodded. "We were friends in Sun Valley. I'm not certain we would have had much in common, except both of us were nursing broken romances." Suddenly she laughed, a great booming sound that rose from her chest, loud enough to flush a covey of quail from the brush by the creek. "I guess if I'm going to be completely honest, I'll have to admit I was kind of jealous when Ted came along. And let me tell you, when Audrey married him a month after she met him, I had plenty to say! Told her she was just on the rebound, that she hardly knew Ted—you name it, I guess I said it."

MaryAnne chuckled ruefully. "I guess I told her all the same things. But she proved us wrong, didn't she?"

Olivia nodded, sighing. "She sure did. Anyway, after they moved up here, I started driving up to see them practically every weekend, and the longer I spent here, the more I started hating Sun Valley. So finally I just packed up and moved. Took a beating in my practice, but it's been worth it. Or it was up until Ted and Audrey died." She fell into pensive silence, her eyes taking in the ranch, and the mountains above. When she spoke again, her voice was low. "Remember earlier, I said that lately there's been something about this place that hasn't seemed quite right?" MaryAnne nodded. "Well, I'm still not sure what it is. But there's a reason why the animals are spooking, and it seems to me we'd better find out what it is. The next time it happens, you call me. Okay?"

MaryAnne's brows rose skeptically. "In the middle of the night?"

Olivia Sherbourne threw back her head once again, her laughter echoing across the valley. "I get called in the middle of the night over a sick cat!" she declared. She finished her wine and stood. "Well, it's been fun, but all good things come to an end. I'd better go check my machine and see whose cattle are bloating and whose horses are colicky. Call me if you need anything, okay?"

"Okay," MaryAnne agreed. She walked Olivia out to the truck, but just as the vet was about to climb in, MaryAnne held her back with a hand on her arm. "Olivia, could I ask you a question? About Ted and Joey?"

Olivia Sherbourne seemed to tense, but the impression was so fleeting that when the vet dropped back down to the ground to face her, MaryAnne decided she had only imagined it.

"Ted and Joey?" Olivia asked. "What about them?"

"I'm not sure." MaryAnne faltered, suddenly wondering if she should have brought up the subject at all. "It's just—well, I'm wondering if there was a problem between them. Charley Hawkins said something I thought was a little strange, then tried to pass it off as nothing. But then Rick Martin was out here asking questions the other day, and—well, I'm just wondering if you know anything about it."

Olivia hesitated just a fraction of a second too long before she spoke. "I know Ted was pretty hard on Joey the last couple of years, but if you're asking me if Ted abused Joey, I'd have to say no." A sardonic smile curved her lips. "Of course, everyone has his own definition of abuse, doesn't he? So I suppose different people would say different things about it. As far as I could tell, though, Ted was just trying to get Joey straightened out and teach him some responsibility."

The reply raised more questions in MaryAnne's mind than it answered. "What about Audrey?" she asked. "Did she think Ted was too hard on Joey?"

For a moment MaryAnne wasn't sure the veterinarian was going to reply at all, but finally Olivia shrugged. "There was a lot Audrey never talked to me about and a lot I never asked her." She swung up into the cab of her truck and started the engine. "Look," she added, "don't go looking for trouble. If you do, I guarantee it'll find you first! See you soon." She put the pickup in gear and drove off, and MaryAnne waited until she had disappeared around the first curve of the driveway before starting back to the house. But as she picked up the glasses from the table on the front porch and took them to the kitchen, with Storm trailing after her, she realized what Olivia had just told her had done nothing to ease her worries.

What had Audrey not talked about, and Olivia not asked?

Something about Joey?

Or Ted?

Or something else entirely?

Then she decided that Olivia was right—it was stupid for her to go looking for trouble. If there were anything seriously wrong with Joey, or between Joey and his father, Audrey would have talked about it with her.

Wouldn't she?

Or were there things Audrey had kept even from her childhood friend?

CHAPTER 9

*T*he sun dropped behind Sugarloaf Mountain, and the afternoon shadows began their march down the valley. MaryAnne glanced at the clock above the sink.

Not quite five, and she had already made up her mind that she wouldn't start worrying in earnest until at least a quarter after. She turned on the oven and opened the big Sub-Zero refrigerator, taking a quick inventory of the possibilities for dinner.

She instantly rejected tuna casserole—there were still three, each of a different size, and each marked with a carefully lettered piece of masking tape that identified the name of its donor. But they'd had tuna casserole last night, and though the children had all eaten it, it was obvious they hadn't enjoyed it much. Moving past the tuna casseroles, and making a note to transfer their contents into other dishes tomorrow, so at least she could return the bowls to their rightful owners, she spied a large container on the bottom shelf, marked "Spaghetti—Olivia Sherbourne."

Perfect, she decided, pulling the Tupperware container out of the refrigerator, then turning the oven off again. She selected a pan from the long row hanging from an enormous wooden rack that was suspended by heavy chains over the cooking island in the center of the kitchen, emptied the spaghetti sauce into it, and began heating it over one of the six burners on the range. She was rummaging in the pantry, searching for spaghetti, when Storm bounded to the door, whining eagerly and scratching to be let out. MaryAnne glanced out, saw nothing, but opened the door anyway. The shepherd took off around the corner of the house, barking joyfully. Moving out into the yard, MaryAnne watched him tear down the driveway, disappear around the first curve, then reappear a moment later, his tail high, chasing a stick someone she couldn't yet see must have thrown.

"Get it, Storm!" she heard Joey call, and a second later Logan's voice chimed in.

"Bring it here, Storm! Bring it back!"

The dog snatched up the stick on the fly, whirled around, and charged back down the drive, skidding to a halt as the three children suddenly appeared.

Carrying packages.

MaryAnne's smile of welcome faded as the children came up the last few yards of the driveway, Logan already running toward his mother, a large shopping bag barely held off the ground.

"Wait'll you see what we got, Mom! I got new jeans, and two western shirts, and"—he came to a halt, his eyes glistening with pleasure, then stared down at his feet—"look at these!" he finished. "Real cowboy boots! They're Acmes!"

MaryAnne gazed at the boots, their brown leather polished to a high sheen, but instead of admiring them, her eyes shifted to Alison, who had stopped a few feet away and at least had the good grace to look embarrassed.

"I thought I told you not to buy anything," she said, beginning to add up the expenses that had to be contained in the bags not only from the Mercantile, but from Conway's as well. Logan's boots alone must have been more than a hundred dollars.

Alison's mouth opened, but no words came out, and her eyes instinctively went to Joey.

"It was my fault, Aunt MaryAnne," he said, his grin fading as he saw the expression in his godmother's eyes. "I mean—my mom, well, she's been letting me do my own shopping since last year, and we have accounts at all the stores, and . . ." His voice trailed off.

"They were having sales, Mom," Alison rushed in. "You know, for back to school. And we can take it all back. Joey said—"

"I don't care what Joey said," MaryAnne cut in. "I care what *I* said, and *I* said you weren't to buy anything. How are we ever going to afford—"

And then she remembered the books she'd pored over just that morning, and the balances that had shown in all the various ranch accounts.

Pages flicked into her mind, pages on which Audrey had carefully recorded every purchase in every store in which she shopped. Audrey's ideas of shopping had obviously borne no resemblance to her own thrifty habits. And why should they have? For Audrey, the money had been unlimited; since the day she'd married Ted, she'd never had to worry about what she spent. Obviously Joey had picked up the same habits, and, again, why shouldn't he have?

"All right," she said, her anger already melting. What the children had done wasn't going to bankrupt her, and their happy excitement was worth a fortune. "Let's go in and see what you've done, and decide what you're going to be taking back," she said, suppressing a smile beneath a stern demeanor. "Believe me, it will be the three of you who walk back to town with the things you're going to return! And I want your promise that you won't do something like this again. If I can't trust you to do as I ask, how can I trust you to go to town by yourselves again?"

Alison was staring at the ground now, and Logan's chin was quivering at the possibility of losing his brand new cowboy boots.

"It's not their fault, Aunt MaryAnne," Joey pleaded as the children followed her into the house. "Alison didn't want us to buy anything at all, but I talked her into it."

"I understand, Joey," MaryAnne told him gently. "I know your mother let you shop for yourself, but Alison and Joey never have before." She held the kitchen door open, letting the three youngsters go in ahead of her. "Okay," she said, pointing to the kitchen table. "Let's see what you've bought."

While MaryAnne filled a pot with water for the spaghetti, the three kids began opening their bags, spreading out the purchases they'd made. For Alison, there were three pairs of jeans, which MaryAnne recognized as a brand that had always been far beyond their means back home, along with three shirts, three sweaters, and some socks and underwear.

"Do you know how much those jeans cost?" MaryAnne demanded, pouncing on what were obviously the most expensive items.

"They're sixty dollars each, except they were marked down to half price," Alison told her. "And I got three, in different sizes, because I'm growing so fast now and the woman said they probably wouldn't be on sale again until next year."

Frowning, MaryAnne abandoned the jeans and picked up one of the shirts. It was one hundred percent cotton, slightly larger than the size Alison currently wore, but not so big it would look strange. The other two shirts were the same size, only their colors differing.

All of them had been marked down fifty percent.

The sweaters were all a soft wool, almost as velvety as cashmere, and in feminine shades Alison normally scorned—cornflower-blue, pale lavender, a pearly-pink the color of a delicate seashell.

"Where's all the stuff you usually want to buy?" she asked. "All the punk-look things we always argue about?"

Alison flushed. "I guess I figured I'd better buy good stuff," she said. "I sort of splurged on the scarf, though. I'll take it back, if you want me to."

MaryAnne shook her head. "It's gorgeous. And you're going to need it when winter hits, so let's just keep it all."

She turned to Logan's acquisitions and discovered that, like Alison, though he'd bought too well, he'd bought wisely. Everything he had chosen were things she would have purchased for him herself. Even his jeans were in a length that would have to be turned up at the cuffs for the first few months, but would certainly last him through at least a year. The shirts he'd bought were smaller versions of the ones Joey had bought for himself, except for a bright blue western shirt, shot through with silver and piped with black, a tight row of mother-of-pearl snaps running down the front, two more on each of the pockets, and three more on each of the cuffs.

"Isn't it cool?" Logan asked as she stared at it, his face alight with excitement.

"Where on earth are you going to wear it?" MaryAnne asked.

"He has to have one," Joey explained. "Everybody around here has one."

"And what about the boots?" MaryAnne asked, finally turning her attention to her son's feet.

"He has to have those, too," Joey insisted. "If he's going to learn to ride, he has to have boots, and everyone wears them all the time. And they aren't Tony Lamas. Dad says it's dumb to spend that much until your feet are done growing. Then you get the best boots you can, and wear them forever."

Dad says. MaryAnne's resistance crumbled. "All right, I give up," she said. "You didn't do what I asked you to do, but I didn't really think it through, either. Obviously at least two of you are old enough to shop by yourselves. And since you didn't just throw money away on junk, I don't see any point in taking any of it back. But next time, either you do what you promised, or you call me and tell my why you've decided not to. All right?"

"I can keep my boots?" Logan cried, ignoring the question.

MaryAnne sighed. "You can keep the boots. But if your feet hurt, don't blame me."

As she went back into the pantry to finish the search for the spaghetti, Joey winked slyly at Alison.

"See?" he whispered. "I told you we could get away with it."

The wolf froze, its body going rigid, one forepaw raised from the ground, its tail held straight out.

The man stopped instantly, only his eyes moving as he searched out the terrain indicated by the animal's point and found the object of the wolf's interest.

A rabbit was crouched in the shelter of a boulder, its senses alert, its nose quivering as it sniffed the breeze. The sun was gone, the blanket of darkness fast gathering over the field of heather that spread up the mountainside just above the timberline. Soon it would be safe for the rabbit to creep out into the meadow to nibble at the vegetation that spread over the ground, for the predators that soared in the sky would settle down into their nests for the night, and the threat to the rabbit's life would be reduced. For now, though, it held perfectly still, searching for an odor or movement that would betray the presence of the enemy it had sensed a moment before.

It sniffed again, but only the aroma of heather filled its nostrils. Finally, the urge to eat overcame the little creature's instinct to stay hidden until night had fully fallen. It crept forward, nipping at the tender grass that grew between the clumps of heather. As the light continued to fade, the rabbit grew bolder, venturing farther out into the field.

The wolf edged forward, its eyes fixing on the rabbit, but the man laid a hand on its sinewy flank, calming it. "Not yet," he whispered so softly that his words were almost inaudible. Now the rabbit froze, its ears standing straight up. As the seconds stretched out, it held perfectly still, becoming all but invisible in the gathering dusk, but when it heard nothing else, it finally dropped back down, relaxing, and began to feed again.

The man tapped the wolf. Instantly, it shot forward, bursting out of the clump of heather in which man and animal had been hidden, hurling itself on the rabbit almost before the smaller animal knew it was under attack. Seizing the creature by the neck, the wolf jerked its head back and forth, then dropped the twitching rabbit to the ground, held it down with one forepaw, and tore into its flesh with its sharply pointed canines.

The rabbit squealed in pain, then lay still on the ground. The wolf prodded it with a forepaw, snuffled at it, then picked it up in its mouth. The man, already on his feet, started back toward the woods, the wolf falling in beside him.

In a bulky pack that lay where he'd dropped it a few minutes ago when he'd decided to go after the rabbit, were the carcasses of two raccoons and a small otter, all collected from his traps that afternoon. The man paused to pick the heavy bundle up and sling it onto his back, then moved on, barely aware of the weight that would have made most other men stagger.

Coming finally to the shack in which he lived, he dumped the three carcasses from the backpack onto a rough-hewn table, picked up a knife and began expertly skinning them.

The wolf, with the bloody body of the rabbit clutched in its mouth, dropped to the floor near the door and began ripping its catch to pieces, tearing open the hide with its teeth, ripping out the entrails, devouring them even as they spilled from the rabbit's torn belly.

"Want some more?" the man whispered in his hoarse voice. Running the knife up the belly of the otter, he slit open its abdominal cavity, plunged his hand into the still-warm mass of organs and tore them free, tossing them to the ground a few inches from the wolf's muzzle.

The wolf, her jaws dripping with saliva, pounced, the bloody mass disappearing into her throat.

The man finished butchering his catch, tossing the hides out the open window, knowing that by tomorrow afternoon they would be gone, taken away by the creatures that prowled in the night, or picked clean by scavenging birds.

Whatever was left he would take away later, but for now, at least, there would be nothing in the cabin to attract the swarms of ants that lived deep beneath the ground.

He cut the carcasses up, the heavy knife chopping easily through the gristly joints, then lifted the top off the pot of stew that always stood on the stove.

He threw most of the meat into the pot, then stirred up the fire and added enough wood to keep it going while he went out into the night. By the time he got back, the brew would have been simmering for hours, the flesh falling away from the bones, which he would fish out and throw to the wolf.

He picked up the last leg of the beaver and was about to add it to the pot when he changed his mind. Clutching it in his hand, he tore into the raw meat with teeth that were almost as strong as the wolf's, the gamy flavor of the animal's flesh sharply sweet on his tongue, the smell of its fresh blood filling his nostrils.

Tonight, the hunger was on him fully, and he knew where the hunting would be best.

———————

MaryAnne started clearing the dishes from the kitchen table, pausing before she picked up Joey's plate. "You're sure you don't want any more?" she asked worriedly. All through dinner he'd barely spoken a word, withdrawing further and further into himself, jumping nervously whenever someone spoke directly to him, and replying only in monosyllables.

Joey looked down at his plate, still nearly full, the large portion of spaghetti covered with the thick meat sauce Olivia Sherbourne had provided all but untouched. He shook his head.

"I thought all kids loved spaghetti," MaryAnne commented.

"I guess I'm just not very hungry," Joey replied. "May I be excused?"

MaryAnne smiled sympathetically at the boy, certain his loneliness for his parents was overcoming him once again. "Of course," she said. "Alison and Logan can help with the dishes tonight. Go turn on the TV if you want to."

Joey slid off his chair, still not looking at her. "I think I'll go up to my room," he said. "I've got a book I've been reading."

MaryAnne's eyes shifted pointedly to her daughter. "Hear that?" she asked. "A book. You remember them, don't you? A lot of pages with print on them, between two covers?"

Alison rolled her eyes. "Come on, Mom. Just because I like TV—"

"Like it?" MaryAnne repeated. "How about addicted to it? When was the last time you actually read a book all the way through?"

"Mo-om," Alison groaned. "I get good grades in school, don't I?"

Joey, barely hearing the argument that was beginning, snapped his fingers softly, and Storm, who had been stretched out under the table, his head resting on Joey's feet, stood and padded after his master as the boy silently left the room. He was already halfway up the stairs when he heard MaryAnne speak to him from the foyer.

"Joey?"

He paused, turning to gaze down at her.

"Are you all right?"

Joey nodded, but said nothing.

MaryAnne peered uncertainly up at him. "Is there anything I can do? Anything at all?"

Joey shook his head. "I-I'll be okay," he stammered. Turning away before MaryAnne could say anything else, he hurried up the stairs and disappeared into his room. MaryAnne, feeling helpless, wanting to take the boy into her arms and comfort him, went back to the kitchen to help Alison and Logan with the dishes.

———————

In his room, Joey flopped down on the bed.

The feeling was coming over him again.

The feeling he thought he was finally done with.

But now it was back, stronger than ever.

He got up from the bed and went to the window, raising it all the way, so the breeze from the mountains blew into his face.

He took a deep breath, filling his nostrils with the fresh scent of the pine trees, his lungs with the cool air of the evening.

It was fully dark now, and the feeling had been gathering around him ever since the sun had fallen behind the mountains and their shadows had begun to creep down the valley. At dinner, as the last of the light had faded away, the feeling had grown stronger, and he'd had to resist the urge to jump up from the table and run out into the night.

But why?

He no longer felt the need to escape from his father, for his father was dead.

Dead and buried, so that he could never take him out to the barn again, never take the belt from his pants and whirl it over his head before lashing down on his bare buttocks.

When he had realized that his father was dead, and that he was finally safe from the beatings, Joey had been certain that the terrible feeling inside him was at last gone forever.

Yet it was strong tonight, stronger than it had ever been before.

He felt restless, like a caged animal, trapped within the confines of the house, trapped even within his own skin.

All he wanted was to disappear from the house, to disappear into the darkness outside, to roam in the night until he finally found release from the pain within his mind, and his spirit calmed once more.

But there was nothing to disappear *from*! This was his house, his room! He belonged here!

Except that on nights like tonight, when the feeling came over him, he knew he didn't belong anywhere.

Maybe it was because of those kids—the ones he'd seen in town today.

The ones who hated him.

Hated him even though he'd never done anything to them.

Or had he?

What about the times he couldn't remember?

But those times had been long ago, before he'd learned to conceal the strange nervousness that seemed to come out of nowhere, filling him with dark and violent feelings he didn't understand.

Tonight the feelings were back, setting his nerves on edge and making his skin itch so badly that no amount of scratching relieved it.

And the dark urges were already beginning to take form in his mind once more. The urges to strike out, to pass the pain his father had inflicted on him to someone else.

No!

He wouldn't give in to it! Not this time!

He slammed the window shut and forced himself to go back to the bed, stretching out on it, wrapping his arms around the pillow and burying his face in its softness.

Make it go away, he silently begged. Make it go away!

Storm, whimpering softly at his master's distress, jumped up onto the bed and stretched himself out next to Joey, licking gently at the boy's cheek.

But Joey, the dark urge within him increasing its grip on his soul, was completely unaware of the dog's gentle ministrations, for already he was preparing to slip out into the beckoning darkness of the night.

———

"I keep thinking maybe we should have just gone home," Tamara Reynolds said, snuggling closer to Glen Foster and stretching her feet out to toast her toes in the heat from the campfire. The darkness around her suddenly seemed threatening, and what had struck her as the gentle quiet of the forest the last time she and Glen had gone camping, now seemed more like an ominous silence. "I mean, after what those people said—"

"Come on," Glen interrupted, slipping his arm around her. "It was nothing. So a tent got torn up. They don't even know what did it, and no one was here when it happened. Besides, it was days ago, and nothing else has happened since, has it?"

"And there's hardly anyone here now, either," Tamara reminded him. "All the smart people went home."

"You mean all the chickens went back to their roosts," Glen replied. "As far as I'm concerned, this makes it even better. Just us, and one family on the other side of the campground." He flopped back, pulling Tamara with him, and stared up at the moon that was just visible through the treetops. "Now tell me anything's prettier than that."

Cuddling against him, Tamara told herself that he was right, that whatever had destroyed those people's tent was long gone. And besides, maybe the damage wasn't as bad as they'd heard. Stories always got exaggerated, didn't they? "It *is* nice." She sighed, some of the tension in her body starting to ease. As Glen rolled over to kiss her, she wrapped her arms around him, pressing herself even closer. "Tell you what," she whispered. "Why don't we go to bed early tonight?"

"What do you mean, early?" Glen teased, nibbling at her ear. "It's almost eleven."

"Then let's go to bed now," Tamara suggested, her fingers starting to work at the buttons of Glen's shirt.

"A good idea," Glen agreed. "Let's do it!"

Disentangling themselves from each other, they stood up, and Glen began banking the fire, covering the coals with ash so they'd still be alive in the morning. "Go ahead," he told Tamara. "I've gotta take a leak, then I'll be with you."

Tamara frowned uncertainly. "You're going to leave me here all by myself?"

"I'm going to leave you here for all of two minutes," he promised. "See that tree over there?"

Tamara nodded.

"Well, it looks like an outhouse to me, and that's as far as I'm going. Okay?"

"Okay. But I still think we should have just gone home."

Glen grinned wickedly in the flickering light of the dying flames. "Give me a couple of minutes, and I'll make you forget every fear you ever had."

As Tamara went into the tent, Glen moved to the far side of the campfire, stepped into the forest, and began relieving himself. But even as he emptied his bladder, he kept his eyes and ears open, for despite what he'd told Tamara, he, too, kept remembering what the family camping on the other side of the creek had told him. Yet all day, and through the evening, the most threatening thing that had come along was a family of raccoons that had crept out of the woods, circled carefully around them, and then tried to break into the ice chest. Glen had chased them off, moved the chest to the far side of the campfire, and put several heavy rocks on its lid. If a bear *did* come along, the rocks wouldn't stop it, but at least the chest was far from the tent.

Zipping up his fly, Glen paused to listen to the sounds of the forest once more.

He heard nothing except the squalling of a raccoon and the rustling of some small creature foraging in the brush by the stream. Satisfied, he returned to the tent, zipped the netting closed, and began stripping off his clothes in the darkness.

Naked, he slid into the double sleeping bag, feeling the soft warmth of Tamara's skin rubbing against his own. As his hand slid down her belly to the mound between her thighs, he pressed his mouth against hers, his tongue slipping easily between her teeth.

He groaned with pleasure as her fingers began to explore him, and held her closer, his excitement growing.

———————

Outside the tent, as Glen and Tamara wrapped themselves around each other, aware of nothing beyond the confines of the sleeping bag, the dark figure slipped out of the forest, moving close, waiting, listening.

The figure crept closer, twitching now with anticipation of what was to come.

It sniffed at the wind eagerly, nostrils flaring, gathering not only the acrid scent of the smoldering fire, but the scent of the enemy, as well.

The enemy that was hidden from its sight within the tent, but not hidden from its other senses.

The figure could hear them, as well as smell them, and now the mutterings and moans they made combined with the intoxicating odor to drive the shadowy being mad.

Crouching low to the ground, it tensed, every fiber of its being quivering with anticipation.

At last, giving in to the instinctive urges of its nature, it sprang.

The nylon above Glen Foster's head split with a quick ripping sound—no more than a tiny rent in the quiet of the night—and the brute was upon them, making no sound at all, slashing.

———————

By the time Glen realized what had happened, it was far too late.

Something had leaped on him, its weight pressing down hard,

and even as he started to struggle, the sleeping bag had been ripped apart and he felt claws digging at his flesh.

"Tammy!" he tried to call out, but before the word could even escape his lips, something sharp and vicious slashed at his throat and he felt a gush of hot liquid begin to flow across his chest. He gasped, trying to catch his breath, but only gagged on the blood that was choking him. Soundlessly, he thrashed against his attacker, but as more and more blood gushed from the torn artery in his neck, a terrible weakness overcame him, and he suddenly understood what was happening.

He was dying.

He tried to reach out, tried once more to push the attacker away, but it was too late.

His hands fell to his sides and he lay still.

By the time the attack was over, and the campsite deserted by the intruder, Glen Foster was already dead.

Tamara Reynolds, her skin torn by unseen teeth, her flesh cut deeply by invisible talons, lay moaning softly against pain so searing she could not move, could not even cry for help.

CHAPTER 10

*M*aryAnne was back in New Jersey, in her own house. Outside, she could hear sirens. At first she ignored them, going on with the endless task of packing up Alan's things. They seemed to be everywhere, his clothes heaped in suitcases that lay open and overflowed onto the bed, his books in cartons stacked against the wall. Other boxes held his back issues of *Architectural Digest*, still more his collection of old LPs. But the job seemed endless, and her closet still appeared to be filled with his things.

The sirens grew closer, and suddenly she knew what they meant.

They were coming here!

Coming for Audrey's body, which for some reason was lying in the far corner of the room.

How had it gotten there?

MaryAnne didn't know.

But as the sirens approached, panic seized her.

Her! They were coming for her!

They thought she'd killed Audrey!

But she hadn't! Surely she hadn't!

Suddenly the door flew open and she turned to see Joey, his hands covered with blood, an empty look in his eyes, a cold smile on his face.

He stepped toward her, his mouth opening, but no words coming out. His bloodied hands reached out to her, coming closer and closer as the din of the sirens grew louder in her ears.

She backed away from him, groping to steady herself against the wall, but instead of hard plaster, her hand brushed against something soft.

Soft, and cold.

Spinning away from Joey, she stared up into the dead eyes of Ted Wilkenson.

A scream rose in her throat, a scream cut short as she jerked awake, sitting straight up in her bed, her whole body trembling from the shock of what she'd just seen.

A dream, she told herself.

It was just a dream.

Except that she could still hear the sound of sirens.

Disoriented, she looked around her. Could she really still be at home in New Jersey? But she wasn't—she was in Idaho, on El Monte Ranch.

Shaking off the last vestiges of sleep, MaryAnne got out of bed and hurried to the window. Up on the hillside, a hundred feet above the valley floor, she could see a pale, silvery glow moving slowly through the forest, and every few seconds she could catch a glimpse of red and blue lights flickering among the trees.

"What is it, Mommy?" Logan's voice asked from the doorway. MaryAnne turned to see her son, rubbing his eyes, silhouetted against the lights in the hall.

"I don't know," MaryAnne replied.

"It's police cars," Alison said, joining her brother. "I saw them coming up the road, then turning off to go up that dirt road that leads to the campground."

The sirens died away, leaving an eerie silence. Up in the woods the glow of headlights had stopped moving. Turning from the window, MaryAnne pulled on her bathrobe and turned on the light on her night table, glancing at the clock. She frowned as she realized that it was one o'clock in the morning. What would have made the police go up to the campground at this hour?

"Let's go downstairs and make a cup of cocoa," she told the children, knowing they wouldn't go back to bed until they had an explanation for the disturbance in the night. "Go put on your bathrobes, and I'll get Joey, too. But you're going to be back in bed in half an hour. All right?"

As Alison and Logan, momentarily diverted from the police cars in the forest, ran back to their rooms, MaryAnne tapped at Joey's door. When there was no answer, she turned the knob, pushed the door open, and switched on the light, already certain that it was going to be a repeat of what had happened the night after his parents' funeral.

A knot of fear forming in her stomach as her mind instantly connected the police cars on the mountainside to Joey's absence, she hurried downstairs, quickly checking the rooms on the lower floor in the faint hope that Joey might be there.

He wasn't.

By the time she reached the kitchen, her children were already there, Alison getting mugs out of the cupboard above the counter, while Logan searched the pantry for cocoa mix. The smile on Alison's face faded as she saw her mother's expression of fear.

"Do you know where Joey is?" MaryAnne asked. "Did you hear him going outside?"

Puzzled, Alison shook her head. "Isn't he in his room?"

"He's not in the house at all," MaryAnne told her, her fear starting to rise into panic. What could have happened? Surely he wouldn't have gone up into the mountains in the middle of the night? And even if he had, how could the police cars be connected to him? How would anyone have even known he was there?

It couldn't have anything to do with Joey—it *couldn't*! But even as she tried to reassure herself, she remembered the dream from which she had just awakened, saw once again the blood dripping from Joey's outstretched hands, the cold emptiness in Joey's eyes. The same coldness she'd seen that morning—*No!* Whatever had happened on the mountainside had nothing to do with Joey! He had to be somewhere close by.

The stream! That's where he said he'd gone the other night.

Taking the Spotlighter off the charger mounted on the wall next to the back door, she snapped it on as she stepped out into the darkness. She swept the brilliant beam of light across the yard on the slight chance that Joey might be there, already on his way back to the house.

Her heart skipped as she saw a sudden flicker of movement in the beam, and she quickly brought it back, searching the darkness for whatever might have been there.

Two glowing eyes flashed green in the blackness, and Mary-Anne gasped, then relaxed as she recognized the creature that darted away into the night.

"What was it?" Logan demanded from behind her. "What did you see?"

"A baby raccoon," MaryAnne told him.

Logan crowded out the door. "Where is it? Can we catch it?"

"Not *now*, Logan!" MaryAnne snapped, her nerves fraying. "Go back into the house! I have to go look for Joey!"

"I want to come, too!" Logan demanded, excited at the prospect of an adventure into the darkness in the middle of the night.

"Logan, I'm not going to argue with you! Go back in the house, and stay there!"

Logan's eyes widened in shock at the harshness in his mother's voice, and he backed away.

"Please?" MaryAnne asked, her voice gentling as she saw the hurt in her son's eyes.

His feelings soothed, Logan turned and scurried back inside, slamming the door shut behind him.

MaryAnne started toward the front of the house, staying close to the wall as she hurried through the darkness. Reaching the corner, she swept the parking area with the light, then played it over the stand of trees that stood between the house and the stream.

"Joey?" she called out. "Joey, where are you?"

When there was no answer, she stepped away from the shelter of the house, crossing the yard, moving toward the woods. Then she stopped, hearing a sound from the barn.

A scraping, as if something inside were trying to get out.

Her blood ran cold and her hands began to tremble as she remembered the last time she had been out here in the dead of night and something had been in the barn.

Should she go back into the house and call for help?

Call whom?

The deputies must be up at the campground.

Bill Sikes?

She remembered his ominous words that morning, about the animals coming down out of the woods: *Somethin's out there, an' it's startin' to make me pretty nervous.*

Maybe she should get into the Rover and go up to his cabin. But she'd have to take Alison and Logan with her—she wasn't about to leave them alone in the house. "Joey," she called out again, her growing fear cracking her voice now. "Can you hear me?"

Again the scratching sound came from the barn, this time followed by what sounded like a growl.

MaryAnne turned, poised to take flight back to the house, but she didn't. Something was different tonight, she realized. But what?

Then she knew. The horses were quiet!

The last time, they had been whinnying nervously and stamping in their stalls.

Tonight there was only silence from the barn, a silence so complete it was as though no living creature breathed. As though . . .

Suddenly terrified, she ran, nearly stumbling, back to the kitchen, picked up the phone with one hand and opened the local phone book with the other, rifling the pages till she found the number. As the phone at the other end began to ring, she paced nervously. To her surprise, it was answered almost immediately, and she spoke in a rush of relief. "Oh, thank God you're there! It's MaryAnne Carpenter, Olivia, and I know it's late, but Joey's missing, and something's in the barn, and I'm frightened out of my wits, and I know I sound like the world's biggest—"

"I'll be right there," Olivia told her. "Stay in the house. Something's going on. I'll tell you about it when I get there."

Not more than five minutes later the glare of headlights swept through the yard as Olivia pulled up in her truck. When MaryAnne opened the door to let her in, the veterinarian was cradling a shotgun in her arms. "Let's take a look," Olivia said, starting toward the barn. Telling her children once more to stay in the house, MaryAnne fell in beside the other woman, her flashlight fixed on the barn door.

"You said something was going on," MaryAnne said. "Did you mean the police cars up in the forest?"

Olivia nodded. "Something attacked the campground again. I talked to the dispatcher, but she didn't know much. Just that some fellow came down a while ago, claiming someone was dead—maybe two people."

"My God," MaryAnne breathed. They were at the barn door now, and she hesitated, no longer certain she wanted to know what was inside. But Olivia, flipping the safety off the gun and pumping a shell into the chamber, nodded to her.

"Okay, I'm ready. Open the door."

Her heart pounding, MaryAnne lifted the latch on the heavy doors, and immediately heard a familiar whimpering sound from inside. "Oh, Lord," she groaned as she swung the door wide. "I feel like such an idiot! It's Storm!"

The big dog hurled himself out the door, rearing up to put his forepaws on MaryAnne's chest as he licked at her face. Olivia, removing the cartridge from the chamber and resetting the safety, lowered the gun to her side. "What are you doing out here, boy?" she asked. "Scaring us half to death like that! What's going on?"

As the dog shifted its affections to the veterinarian, MaryAnne stepped into the barn and flashed the light around. The three horses were lined up as usual, their heads hanging over their stall doors, blinking in the glare of the flashlight's beam. MaryAnne strode down the wide aisle in front of the stalls, found the light switch and turned on the big lamps suspended from the roof beams. As the darkness washed away, she snapped off the flashlight, then began searching the barn.

She found Joey, wrapped in a horse blanket in the empty stall at the far end of the aisle, sound asleep. Stepping into the stall, she stood still for a moment, gazing at him as he slept. What had brought him out here? And how long had he been here? She knelt down, gently touching his shoulder. He came awake instantly, rolling away from her, then sitting up, blinking in the light. Only when he recognized her did he relax, losing his startled, hunted expression. Then, as he realized where he was, a look of defensiveness—almost furtiveness—came into his eyes.

"Joey?" MaryAnne said, her voice gentle. "Joey, why are you sleeping out here? Why aren't you in bed?"

He frowned slightly, then his expression cleared. "It—It's just something I do sometimes," he stammered. "Sometimes I just can't sleep in the house. So I come out here, sometimes, and sleep with the horses." Then, more aggressively: "Mom and Dad never minded. They let me do it whenever I wanted."

"I see," MaryAnne said, though she didn't see at all. She wasn't quite sure she believed what the boy had just said. It didn't make sense that Audrey Wilkenson would let her son curl up in a horse stall. And yet, if Joey said his mother had let him do it, how could she argue with him? How could she ever know what Audrey had let Joey do, and what she hadn't? "Well, come on back to the house, all right?" she said. "Alison and Logan are up, and we're going to make cocoa. How does that sound?"

Leaving the blanket where it lay, Joey stood and brushed the loose straw off his disheveled clothes. The strange feeling—the frightening sensation of nervousness that had seized him earlier in the evening, finally driving him out of the house into the darkness of the night—was gone.

Something—something of which he was totally unaware—had released him from the torment of his own mind.

The *whup-whup-whup* of the helicopter blades drew closer. Rick Martin instinctively ducked as the downdraft of the great rotor struck him. A cloud of dust and pine needles swirled around him, and he shielded his eyes, peering up into the glare of the chopper's landing lights. From the belly of the machine, a rope was dangling; at its end hung the stretcher into which he and Tony Moleno would lift the torn body of Tamara Reynolds.

"You're fine!" he yelled into the radio, hoping the pilot could hear him above the din. "Hold position, and lower away!"

The stretcher began its slow descent, and Rick moved away for a moment to check on the young woman who still lay in the wreckage of the tent where they'd found her, unconscious. Her wounds were clumsily bound with bandages from the first-aid kit in his squad car, but fresh blood was already oozing through the white gauze. "How's she doing?" he asked Moleno, who was crouching beside her, his fingers pressed against her neck.

"Still got a pulse, but her breathing's getting worse."

"If she's still alive when we get her up there, she'll make it down to Boise," Rick replied, coming out of the tent. As the basket touched the ground a few yards away, the deputy glanced up at the man who had arrived in the village an hour ago to report the attack in the campground. Now he was standing at the edge of the campsite, a sheen of sweat glimmering on his skin in the firelight, despite the chill of the night. His arm was around his wife, who leaned into him heavily, seeming on the verge of collapse. Their children, a boy of about five and a girl a year younger, clung to their mother's legs. "Give us a hand!" Rick yelled. The man glanced at his wife as if he wasn't certain the words were actually being directed at him, but then realized there was no one else there. Leaving his wife to look after the children, he hurried over.

"Get the sling off the basket," Rick called to Tony Moleno, and while the assistant deputy ducked out of the tent, he told the young man—whose name had already escaped him—what they were going to do. "All three of us will lift her at the same time. I'll be at her head, and you take her feet. The idea's not to move her any more than we have to. Got it? Once she's on the stretcher, we'll take her out to the basket, strap her in, and she'll be on her way."

By the time he was finished, Tony Moleno was back, and the three of them carefully moved Tamara Reynolds—still unconscious—onto the stretcher, then carried her out of the wreckage of the tent. The basket sat on the ground, the line to the hovering aircraft hanging slack. The three men placed the stretcher in the basket, working against the blast of the chopper's downdraft. Rick Martin fastened the strap to hold the stretcher securely in place, then stepped back and waved the helicopter away. The line tightened, and the basket lifted off the ground, swinging as the helicopter moved slightly forward.

"Shit!" Tony yelled above the din of the engine as the basket moved toward a stand of tall lodgepole pines at the edge of the campsite. "What's he doing?"

The three men on the ground stared in horror as the basket

swung closer to the trees, but then the helicopter rose straight up, the basket soaring above the treetops as the winch hauled it in.

"Jesus," Tony said as the racket of the chopper's blades began to fade away. "Don't ever make me ride in one of those things, okay?"

Rick ignored his partner as he studied the man who had reported the attack on the campsite. "Is there anything else you want to tell me? Anything you've left out, Mister . . . ?"

"Jenson. Peter Jenson." He shook his head. "There isn't anything else to tell, really. We were sound asleep—the kids were in our tent, and Peg and I were outside. I was sound asleep, but Peg woke up. She thought she heard something, and woke me up. We listened, and didn't hear anything at first, but then just as I was going back to sleep, there was this sound. Not a scream or anything—more like a moan. Anyway, when I heard it again, I decided to go take a look. Peg went into the tent with the kids, and I took my flashlight and came over here." He glanced at the ruined tent, the carnage brilliantly lit by the halogen headlights of the two squad cars parked at the edge of the site. He flinched as he saw Glen Foster's torn body still lying where he'd found it, half covered by the remains of the ripped sleeping bag. "I didn't know what to do. I yelled at Peg to stay in the tent, then headed down to our car." He shook his head uncertainly. "Maybe that was kind of a dumb thing to do, huh? I mean, whatever did this is still out there somewhere. But what else could I do? The woman was still alive."

Rick Martin laid a reassuring hand on Jenson's shoulder. "Seems to me like whatever did this wouldn't have hung around here afterward. And the parking lot's only half a mile down the road."

Jenson's lips twisted wryly. "If you'd of asked me tonight, I'd have said it was more like ten miles."

"What about these two people?" Rick asked. "Did you know them?"

"I talked to them when they showed up, but that's all. Other than that, I've never seen them before." He glanced toward his wife, who had moved to the picnic table near the fire pit, her children still flanking her, her arms wrapped protectively around their shoulders. "Look," Jenson went on, "would it be possible for me to bring my car up here tonight? I'd like to pack us up and get out of here. No way the wife and kids are going to go back to sleep—not after what happened."

Rick nodded. "There'll be a whole crew coming up tomorrow. For tonight, I'm gonna have to leave the body where it is."

Jenson stared at him, a shiver running over him at the thought of the dead man being left in the tent until morning. As if he'd read Jenson's mind, Rick Martin's lips tightened into a grim line.

"Not much else I can do. No way the crime boys from Boise can get up here tonight, and I'm not gonna touch this site until they've gone over it with a fine-tooth comb. All I can do is post a guard for the rest of the night. If you want, I can give you a lift down to the parking lot. I'll just leave the gate open tonight with a police tape across it." He was silent for a moment, then spoke again. "I guess you know there's going to be a lot of people wanting to talk to you, the next couple of days." He kept his eyes on Peter Jenson, looking for any sign of discomfort his words might have caused the man. But Jenson only nodded.

"You've got my name and address." He took a deep breath, then let it out in a long sigh. "Hell of a way to end the summer, huh? We came up here for one last quiet weekend, and . . ." His voice trailed off, then he shook his head. "Why do you suppose it was this tent that got hit?" he asked. "Why wasn't it mine?"

It was the same question that had been running intermittently through Rick Martin's mind ever since Peter Jenson had first described the horror he'd discovered. But he had no answer, nor would there be any possibility of an answer until the crew from the crime lab had searched the site.

Had something attracted the attacker to this particular tent, this particular couple?

Or had it been a random attack, Rick wondered, as he'd assumed the earlier one against an empty site had been?

He didn't know, and deep down inside wondered if he ever would. But there was one thing he was sure of, with no doubt at all.

Coyote Creek Campground—the most beautiful in the area—would be closed.

Closed for the rest of the year, if not forever.

CHAPTER 11

The skies were leaden the next morning, and a steady drizzle had begun to fall, soaking the meadows and washing the trees free of the summer's dust. There was a new bite to the air, a dank cold that seemed to have plunged the Sugarloaf Valley into the coming fall virtually overnight.

"Why do we have to go to school today?" Logan complained in a last-ditch effort to put off his annual autumn agony for twenty-four more hours. "Nobody's going to be there! It's pouring outside, and I bet the creek's going to flood, and—"

"Everybody's going, and you're going, too," MaryAnne told him. "Now, do you want to go with Joey and Alison, or do you want me to drive you?"

Logan's eyes widened at the threat of going through the humiliation of having his mother take him school. Hurriedly, he shoved his arms into the sleeves of his worn jacket. "What if I freeze to death?" he asked, seeing no reason not to try a parting shot. "I should have gotten a new jacket yesterday. They had a really neat one! It's leather, and lined with fleece, and—"

"And you're not going to freeze to death," MaryAnne interrupted, cutting off Logan's monologue just as he was getting warmed up. "Now go, or you're going to miss the bus and have to walk all the way to town."

"I still bet nobody else is there," Logan muttered darkly, but he already knew that none of his arguments was going to work. He slouched to the back door, pulling the hood of his jacket over his head, then ran to catch up with Alison and Joey, who were already disappearing around the first curve in the driveway.

Fifty yards farther along, Joey veered off onto a path that led to the left.

"Where are you going?" Logan asked.

"It's a shortcut," Joey explained. "Come on."

Alison and Logan glanced at each other uneasily, the same thought in both their minds. Yesterday, when the sun had been shining brightly, it had been fun walking through the forest, hearing the pine needles crunch under their feet and playing along the banks of the stream.

This morning, though, in the drizzle of rain, with the overcast sky cutting off the light, the forest seemed to have closed in on itself; trees that only yesterday had offered shade from the brilliant sun had now taken on an oddly threatening aspect, as if something dangerous might be lurking just out of sight.

"M-Maybe we better stay on the road," Alison suggested. "I mean, what if we get lost?"

Joey's lips twisted scornfully. "We're not going to get lost. I always go this way." His grin broadened. "You're not chicken, are you?"

Logan's eyes narrowed at the slur on his sister's courage. He made up his mind. "I'm not," he declared, marching down the path that led into the woods. Under his feet the soggy pine needles squished damply, as large drops of rain splashed down onto the hood of his jacket from the dripping branches that spread over his head. "Come on, Alison," he pleaded. "It's neat."

But Alison still hesitated, wondering once more what the police cars had been doing up in the campground last night. Though neither her mother nor Olivia Sherbourne had told them anything, Alison had been almost certain the veterinarian had known something.

Something bad—or why wouldn't she have told them about it? To her, the woods now looked sinister, and she stood her ground. "I think we should stay on the driveway," she insisted. "It's going to be all muddy in there."

"Chicken, chicken!" Logan sang out. "Alison's a chicken!"

Her brother's teasing washed away the trepidation Alison was feeling. "All right, let's go," she challenged, striding off the driveway into the dripping forest.

The trees closed around them, the narrow path twisting and turning as they moved farther from the driveway, both Alison and Logan beginning to feel uneasy.

Strange sounds—sounds they hadn't heard before—came at them from every direction, and though Joey insisted it was nothing more than water dripping off the trees and squirrels rustling through the underbrush in their constant search for food, Alison startled when she heard the sharp snap of a twig.

"What was that?" she demanded.

"Wh-What?" Logan asked, though he'd heard the sound himself, and it had set his heart pounding.

"It wasn't anything," Joey replied. "Probably just a deer."

"What if it was a bear?" Logan piped. "What if it was a grizzly?"

"I'm telling you, it wasn't anything like that," Joey insisted. "Will you guys come on?"

They started walking again, but now Logan stayed close to his sister, slipping his hand into hers. The rain eased, but the trees kept up their constant dripping. Alison thought she could hear the sound of something moving through the forest a few yards to their left. She stopped again, her hand tightening on Logan's.

"What is it?" Logan asked, his voice dropping to a whisper.

"Shh!" Alison hissed, holding her finger to her lips. "Listen!"

Now Joey, too, had stopped, frowning as he strained his ears for the sound that had caught Alison's attention.

It came again.

A sharp snap, as if a twig had broken under a shoe. Then another snapping twig, followed by a rustling in the brush up ahead and to the left.

The three children stared at the spot where they'd heard the sound. An aspen shook, though there was no wind, its leaves shimmering as a mist of water fell from them. They froze.

Then they heard the voice: "You're going to die, Joey Wilkenson."

Her heart racing, Alison pulled Logan closer to her, slipping her arms around him protectively as he pressed himself against her. Joey, though, glanced around, then stooped to pick up a rotting stick from the forest floor.

"I'm coming for you, Joey," the voice whispered. "I'm going to get you. . . ."

There was another rustling movement in the brush. The aspen trembled again as something shook its trunk.

Bringing his right arm back so quickly Alison hardly saw what he was doing, Joey hurled the stick in the direction from which the threat had come. It whirled into the underbrush, then struck something with a soft thunk. A voice cried out. "Jeez! You could have hurt me!"

"Come out here, and I'll beat the shit out of you!" Joey challenged, his voice trembling with fury.

Now there was a loud rustling in the bushes, and a moment later two children, a boy and girl about the same age as Alison and Joey, pushed their way through the brush and appeared on the trail. Both of them had pale blue eyes and blond hair, and both were clad in blue jeans and denim shirts under their open slickers. Alison recognized them from the funeral the previous week, where neither of them had done more than nod to Joey. Nor had Joey been friendly to them. Now the boy was glaring angrily at Joey and rubbing his shoulder where the stick had struck him. "You're really nuts, Joey!"

Joey's jaw set, his eyes glittering furiously. "If I'd wanted to hurt you, I would have," he declared. "And I wasn't scared of you, either."

The girl's eyes rolled heavenward in scorn. "You almost threw one of your fits, creep." Turning away from Joey, she cocked her head to gaze quizzically at Alison. "You're Alison Carpenter," she said. "And he's your brother."

Alison, her heart still pounding with the terror she'd felt when she heard the voice whispering out of the forest, managed to nod her head.

"I'm Andrea Stiffle, and this is *my* brother, Mike. We're twins. We live up that way." She gestured toward the north, but Alison could see nothing beyond the thick stand of aspens that surrounded them. "There's trails all over the place," Andrea explained, flashing a smile at Alison. "This one starts at your driveway, but most of it's on our property. *You* can use it, though," she added, pointedly excluding Joey.

Alison remembered the group of kids who had blatantly snubbed Joey yesterday. Now, with Andrea and Michael Stiffle treating him with the same hostility, she wondered if she shouldn't just ignore both the girl and her brother. Before she could make up her mind, Logan piped up.

"How come you were trying to scare us?"

Andrea Stiffle's eyes mocked him. " 'Cause we figured after what happened last night, it would be easy. And it worked, didn't it?"

"After what happened last night?" Alison asked, remembering the guarded looks her mother and Olivia Sherbourne had exchanged while they were drinking cocoa the night before.

Andrea and Michael glanced at each other, then both of them started talking at once.

"Some guy got killed up at Coyote Creek—" Michael began.

"They had to fly the woman down to Boise," Andrea chimed in. Their voices tumbling over one another's, the two Stiffles repeated what they'd heard from their parents at breakfast that morning, while Logan Carpenter, his eyes wide as he pictured the dead man in the torn tent, pressed closer to his sister.

"But what was it?" Alison asked anxiously, the forest once more seeming to close in around her, and her curiosity overcoming her instant dislike of Andrea Stiffle. "What attacked them?"

Michael Stiffle shrugged. "No one knows. It might have been a bear." His voice dropped mysteriously and his eyes fixed on Logan. "Or it might have been something else."

"L-Like what?" Logan stammered, not sure he wanted to know, but unable to resist asking.

Michael Stiffle peered down at the little boy. "Maybe it was a Sasquatch," he whispered, raising his arms and drawing himself up so he loomed over Logan.

"What's a Sasquatch?" Logan quavered.

"No one's ever seen one up close," Andrea said, instantly picking up the story from her brother. "But they live up in the mountains, and they're seven feet tall."

Logan shuddered, his eyes darting to the thick underbrush as he imagined what might be lurking there. "That's not true," he said. Then, his voice small: "Is it?"

"It's just a story, Logan," Alison assured him, though the skin on the back of her own neck was starting to crawl as she, too, wondered what might be concealed in the tangle of vegetation that crowded the path on both sides.

"Maybe it is, and maybe it isn't," Michael teased. Then he called out to Joey, who had moved ahead, away from the little group. "Hey, Joey! Is that what got the people up at the campground? Was it a Sasquatch? Or was it you?"

Joey's face flushed scarlet, but he said nothing, only turned to shoot Michael Stiffle a dark glare. Michael snickered, and nudged his sister, who made a face at Joey's back.

Alison's mind whirled. What was Michael talking about? Was he kidding? He *had* to be! And yet there had been something in his voice that almost sounded as if he was serious. But what had Joey ever done to them? Before she could figure out how to ask Andrea Stiffle why she didn't like Joey, they came to the road. The school bus was pulling up to the stop fifty yards farther on, and Michael and Andrea broke into a run, each wanting to be the first to tell whoever might already be on the bus about the gory events at the campground the night before. Alison and Logan fell in beside Joey, but none of them said anything until they, too, got onto the bus, and were greeted by a burst of laughter from a cluster of kids at the back.

Kids who were listening intently as Michael and Andrea Stiffle whispered to them.

Every one of them, Alison noticed, was staring at Joey.

Feeling suddenly protective of the boy, though she'd known him barely a week, Alison slipped her hand into Joey's.

He made no move to pull away from her. The smile that came over his face, and the slight pressure of his own fingers on hers, made her heart beat faster. For the rest of the ride down the valley, they sat close together, their hands entwined, both of them pretending they didn't hear the whispers drifting from the back of the bus.

Maybe I should have stayed home, MaryAnne thought. She was sitting in the front seat of Olivia Sherbourne's pickup, her right hand clutching the armrest on the door to steady herself as the vehicle bounced up the rutted road to Coyote Creek Campground.

Maybe I should really go home—home to New Jersey. Just pack up the kids and get out of here as fast as I can. . . .

As Olivia maneuvered the truck up the track, MaryAnne's thoughts spun out of control.

A man had died horribly in the campground last night, and this morning the woman who had been with him was in intensive care in a hospital in Boise. And ever since Olivia had told her late last night what had transpired in the campground, Mary-Anne had been unable to reject the suspicion that kept crawling into her mind—the nagging idea that the campground attacks were somehow connected to the deaths of Audrey and Ted. Over and over, as she lay sleeplessly, tossing in bed, she'd told herself they weren't, that her friends' deaths had been nothing more than freak accidents, unfortunate, even bizarre events, linked to one another—for had Ted not been kicked by the horse, Audrey would never have been on the cliff that night—but not linked to this . . . this horror.

Yet the questions still gnawed. *Some*thing must have spooked Sheika, for in the week she'd been on the ranch, MaryAnne had gotten to know the gentle mare, and the horse had never so much as shied away from her, let alone shown any signs of aggression. Could whatever—*who*ever—attacked the campground last night have been in the barn as well?

How close had she come to being attacked herself the other night, when Joey was missing and something—something that had snarled and lunged at the door—had been lurking inside the barn?

She'd finally given up the quest for sleep as the gray dawn had begun to break. By the time she pushed herself downstairs to the big kitchen, the rain had started, only adding to her sense of gloom. Then, when the children had finally left for school and Bill Sikes had gone about his chores, the emptiness of the house began to set her nerves on edge, and she found herself prowling through the rooms, hearing sounds she couldn't identify, imagining some presence skulking through the house, stalking her.

The idea of going back to New Jersey—even to Alan—had begun to appeal to her.

When Olivia Sherbourne arrived, slamming the door of
truck and darting up the front steps with her head ducked l
against the rain, MaryAnne had felt a sense of relief far out o
proportion to the mere appearance of her neighbor. Opening the
front door, she'd made no attempt to cover her pleasure at seeing
Olivia, but the veterinarian had shaken her head at MaryAnne's
offer of coffee.

"I'm going up to the campground. I just thought I'd stop in
and see how you're doing." When MaryAnne registered surprise
that the veterinarian would be going up to the scene of the murder, Olivia quickly explained. "Rick asked me to meet him up
there and help look for tracks. Believe it or not, I'm a pretty
good tracker. Anyway, it struck me you might be feeling kind of
weird here with no one around except Bill Sikes." She glanced
toward the barn and the field, then turned back to MaryAnne.
"Sikes *is* still here, isn't he?"

MaryAnne nodded, remembering the few words the handyman had spoken that morning when he'd appeared briefly at the
kitchen door before setting about his chores. "Seems to me things
are goin' from bad to worse around here," he'd said. "You might
be wantin' to think about gettin' out."

Now, MaryAnne smiled thinly at Olivia. "Bill Sikes is here,
but I'm not sure for how long. He came in this morning suggesting that I might want to 'get out,' as he put it."

Olivia's brows had risen a notch. "And is that what you're
thinking?"

MaryAnne had sighed. "I wish I knew what I'm thinking."
Of one fact she was certain: this morning she didn't want to be
alone in the house. "Look, why don't I go with you, and then
maybe we can go into town for lunch. That is, if you have
time."

While Olivia paused, considering, MaryAnne had grabbed a
jacket from one of the hooks in the foyer, and started outside,
leaving the house before Olivia could protest and before she'd
really had a chance to think about what she was doing.

.ow, the truck hit a deep pothole, causing Olivia to curse ader her breath while MaryAnne braced herself against the dashboard. They had reached the campground. There seemed to be men everywhere. Olivia shook her head as she watched the activity around the ruined tent, from which Glen Foster's body was just being removed. "I sure hope they took a lot of pictures before they started tramping around. There can't be much left in that mud hole by way of tracks."

The two women got out of the truck. Though Olivia immediately strode toward the clump of men gathered around the body, MaryAnne hung back, knowing that if she let herself look at the wounds the man had suffered, the image would remain etched in her mind for years. Wishing she hadn't come at all, she went to the picnic table, brushed a layer of moisture off the bench, and sat down, stretching her hands toward the sputtering flames of the fire the guard had kept burning all night.

"I've never seen anything like that before," she heard someone say. "I've looked at a lot of bodies, but these wounds are new ones on me."

As MaryAnne turned away, trying not to hear the descriptions of Glen Foster's injuries, Olivia slipped into a space between Rick Martin and Whit Baker, who had been the county coroner for the last twenty years. "No tooth marks," she observed, gazing down on the pale form that now lay on a gurney next to the county ambulance. The corpse lay facedown, its back deeply lacerated by what looked like claw marks. The throat, too, had been laid open, but it was instantly clear to Olivia that if a knife had been used, it had not been sharp, for the tears in the skin were rough and irregular, the muscles beneath the skin mangled.

"That's what's bothering me," Whit Baker agreed, nodding a greeting to the veterinarian. "I've never seen an animal attack where there weren't any signs of bites." He glanced up questioningly. "That's what animals do, isn't it? When they attack, they use their teeth."

"As far as I've ever seen," Olivia replied. "Bears will use their claws as weapons, but once they've knocked down their prey, the first thing they do is go after it with their mouths. If they don't rip it apart, at least they drag it off somewhere." She bent closer, examining the lacerations that had ripped open Glen Foster's back from the shoulders all the way down to the waist. "You ever seen anything like this before, Rick?"

The deputy shook his head. "Sure looks like claws did it, but what kind? Spacing's not right for a bear, but what else does something like this?"

"Cougar?" Whit Baker suggested.

"That might be possible," Olivia Sherbourne said, her voice betraying her doubts. "It just doesn't look right, though. If it were a cougar, the lacerations would be deeper. And look at this," she went on, leaning forward to touch a discoloration on the right shoulder. "Doesn't this look like a bruise?"

"Looks like it would have been, if he'd lived long enough," Whit Baker agreed. "It almost looks like someone squeezed his shoulder. But those cuts sure don't look like any fingernail scratches I've ever seen."

"What about the tent?" Olivia asked.

"Come and take a look," Rick Martin suggested, nodding to the two medics as the coroner and the vet straightened up. "Any reason not to get the body down to the morgue?" As Whit Baker shook his head, the two aides slid the gurney into the ambulance. By the time the group had moved to the tent site, the vehicle was already turning around to start back down the road to the valley floor. With its departure, MaryAnne Carpenter finally trusted herself to join Olivia, Rick Martin, and the coroner.

"This is weird," she heard Rick say as she joined the group around the tent. "It's just like the tent that got torn up last week. It's as if someone ripped out the netting at the back window, then just tore the nylon open."

"So at least we know it was a man," Baker commented. "An

animal would just start tearing at it from anywhere. It wouldn't know to start at the window."

"Except that nylon's tough," Martin told him. "You don't just grab it and give it a rip. Even if you start by cutting through the seams around the netting, it's still too strong for me to rip. And look." He squatted down, pointing to the triple thickness of nylon that had been folded over and seamed to strengthen the hole that had formed the back window. "That's not cut," he said. "That's just torn apart. You got any idea what kind of strength it would take to do that?"

"More than any man I've ever met has." Whit Baker shook his head. "So where are we? Are we looking for a man or an animal? What about tracks? Anything?"

"I want Olivia to take a look around, but given the rain, and the pine needles, I'm not counting on any." He stood up, slapping the coroner on the back. "Thanks for coming up, Whit. I thought you'd better see the scene as well as the body, 'cause I have a feeling it's going to be up to you to figure this one out."

"Me and a good crime lab, from what I've seen so far," Baker replied darkly. "If you don't need me up here any longer, I'll be getting back to my office. You going to be interviewing the survivor any time soon?"

"This afternoon, if she's able to talk," Rick told him. "I'll let you know."

As a crew began packing up the ruins of the tent, the bloody remnants of the sleeping bag, and anything else that could possibly be construed as evidence, Olivia Sherbourne moved carefully around the perimeter of the campsite, searching for signs of tracks. But as Rick had suspected, the rain had obliterated anything she might have found. Then, when she was almost back to the point where she'd begun, directly behind the tent, she spotted something. Barely visible in a thicket of brush no more than ten feet away was what looked like the tail of a raccoon. "Rick?" she called. The deputy, with MaryAnne Carpenter trailing behind

him, came over to join her. "Did you see that?" she asked, pointing to the furry object protruding from the shrubbery. Martin
moved closer, finally reaching out to touch it with his foot. When
nothing happened, he squatted down, grasped it, and pulled it
free from the brush. When he stood up, the body of a dead raccoon was dangling from his right hand. Carrying it over to the
picnic table, he laid it down, and Olivia Sherbourne immediately
began examining it.

"No wounds," she said at last. "None at all. I'd guess it's been
dead maybe eight to twelve hours."

"What killed it?" Rick Martin asked.

"Its neck is broken," Olivia replied. "It's as if someone just
picked it up, grabbed its head, and give it a jerk. I think its spinal
cord is severed, which would have killed it instantly. But no
animal did this. Whatever killed this was definitely human. Animals just don't kill this way."

MaryAnne Carpenter, her eyes fixing on the dead raccoon,
suddenly saw a face flash in front of her eyes.

An indistinct face, surrounded by a wild mane of hair, flowing
down over the shoulders of a powerfully built man.

A man powerful enough to have snapped the raccoon's neck
with no more than a twist of his fingers.

"I saw someone," she heard herself saying.

Instantly, Rick Martin's and Olivia Sherbourne's attention was
fixed on her.

"You saw someone?" the deputy echoed. "What are you talking about?"

MaryAnne shook her head helplessly. "It doesn't make any
sense," she said. "I don't even know why I thought of it. But at
the funeral, I saw a man. He was standing way off to the side,
near the fence, almost hidden in the trees."

Martin's brow furrowed. "What made you think of him
now?"

"I'm not sure," MaryAnne replied. "It's just—he was so
strange-looking, and so strong, that when I looked at that poor

little raccoon, I thought of him. He was big, and looked terribly strong, and sort of—well, *wild* is the only word I can think of." She turned to Olivia. "Like one of those mountain men you were telling me about yesterday."

"A mountain man?" Rick Martin said doubtfully. "I know there used to be a lot of them living up here. Most of them were just harmless hermits, but I guess a few of them were pretty nuts. But I haven't even heard of any of them for years. Can you remember exactly what he looked like?"

MaryAnne did her best to describe the man she and Joey had seen at the funeral, but her glimpse of him had been so short, and he'd been so well hidden in the trees, that she could add little more than she'd already told him. "He was staring at Joey," she finished. "At least, Joey thought he was. Then he was gone, almost as if he'd never been there at all."

"Well, that puts a new twist on all this," Martin said. "Assuming, of course, that there's a connection between whoever you saw and what's been going on up here."

MaryAnne felt a chill of fear move through her body.

Someone living up here in the mountains. Someone who attacked like a wild animal.

Where—and when—would the next attack occur?

Maybe I should leave now, she thought, not for the first time that morning. Maybe I should just grab the kids—all three of them—and take them back to New Jersey.

To what? she suddenly found herself thinking. How many people got murdered in New Jersey every day of the week? Would she really feel any safer there than she did here?

By the time she and Olivia were back in the truck and headed toward town, her spirits felt as deeply shrouded in gloom as the mountaintops were in the cloud cover that had settled into the valley. The temperature had dropped sharply and the dank mist felt to MaryAnne even colder than the chill of fear that had seized her in the campground.

"We'll find out who did this," Olivia said as they approached the village a few minutes later. "Just don't make up your mind to leave too quickly, okay?"

MaryAnne forced a weak smile. "Was it that obvious?"

"It was pretty clear," Olivia replied. "But what's been happening around here lately isn't the way things usually are. Give Rick and Tony a few days, and don't forget that you'll have more people watching out for you around here than you ever will back home."

"I know," MaryAnne sighed. "I know you're right. But I have to tell you, this has shaken me up pretty badly. What if—well, what if the man who was watching Joey really did have something to do with this?"

"And what if last night was connected to Ted and Audrey?" Olivia asked, voicing the question MaryAnne had not yet brought herself to utter.

MaryAnne nodded.

"Believe me," Olivia went on, "it doesn't make any sense. What happened to Ted and Audrey were accidents. Horrible, yes, but still accidents."

"What if they weren't?" MaryAnne asked. "What if . . . what if someone killed them?"

To that question, Olivia Sherbourne had no answer.

———

Rick Martin stepped into the room where Tamara Reynolds lay on her back, her upper torso and head wrapped in bandages. A needle in her arm was attached to an IV bottle by a plastic tube, and another plastic tube extended from her nose, snaked across the bed and up the wall, where it was attached to an oxygen outlet.

"Miss Reynolds?" Rick asked softly. Though the duty nurse had told him the woman was awake, he found himself wondering if it could really be possible. "Can you hear me?"

The woman's lips barely moved, and her breathy voice was all but inaudible.

"I can hear. . . ."

"Can you tell me what happened?"

"Don't know . . . in the tent . . . someone . . ." She fell silent. Her chest heaved as she tried to catch her breath.

"Just take it easy," Rick said soothingly, pulling a chair close to the bed and laying a gentle hand on hers. "I'm with the sheriff's office in Sugarloaf, and we're trying to find out what happened. I'd like to ask you some questions, and I'll try to keep them simple. All you have to do is answer yes or no. And if you get tired, it's all right. Okay?"

"Yes," the woman breathed, the word drifting from her lips as a quiet sigh.

"Good. Now, were you able to see anything? Anything at all?"

"Yes."

"Was it an animal?"

"Don't . . . know . . ." The words came out with an effort, but before Rick could ask another question, Tamara Reynolds began speaking. "Big. Hairy. Touched hair."

"Hair on the head?" Rick asked.

"Don't know," Tamara Reynolds replied. "Couldn't see."

Rick Martin frowned. "Could it have been a bear?" he asked, knowing he was leading her, but seeing no other way to conduct the interview.

"Not a bear," Tamara moaned. "Not big enough."

"But you *did* see it?" he pressed, excited. "At least a glimpse?"

The young woman nodded, then groaned at the pain the motion had caused. Behind him, Rick heard the door open, then the nurse's voice: "Only another minute, please. She has to rest."

Very quickly, Rick Martin repeated the vague description of the man MaryAnne Carpenter had seen at the Wilkensons' funeral, but when he was finished, Tamara Reynolds only sighed helplessly. "Maybe," she whispered. "Maybe not. Too dark."

Martin's heart sank, for he knew that without a detailed description from Tamara Reynolds, neither he nor anyone else would have any idea of what it was they were looking for.

All he knew was that it was probably as large as a man, very strong, and very dangerous.

Mortally dangerous.

CHAPTER 12

*B*y the time the school bus dropped them off that afternoon, the rain had stopped and the clouds had lifted, revealing the dense stand of timber rising up the mountains' flanks. The tops of the mountains were still lost in heavy clouds, and as she gazed up at the leaden sky, Alison could almost imagine that the great cliffs rose on forever. As the bus turned around to start back down toward the village, and Andrea and Michael Stiffle disappeared up the driveway leading to their house without so much as a good-bye, Storm came bounding down the road, tail held high, to greet his master. Joey knelt down to hug the dog, then, as he stood up again, pointed to the road leading up to Coyote Creek Campground. "Want to go up and take a look?" he asked.

Alison shivered, but wasn't certain whether the chill had been caused by the damp breeze or by Joey's suggestion, which immediately reminded her of all the stories she'd heard at school that day.

Stories of bodies being found—ripped to pieces—arms and legs scattered all over the campground.

Rumors of a pack of wolves marauding down from the mountains.

Of a maddened grizzly, standing twelve feet tall when it reared up, its jaws dripping with human blood.

"Once they get the taste, they won't stop," one of her classmates had whispered excitedly at lunchtime. "They can't eat anything else, and just keep hunting for people!"

Ellen Brooks, her science teacher, had done her best to dispel the rumors that afternoon. Though she pointed out that one man had, indeed, been killed, a whole family had slept unmolested in another tent in the same campground. "There has never been a proven case of wolves attacking men," she had reminded them, "and while a grizzly certainly could have been responsible for what happened, there's no truth whatsoever to that story that they develop a taste for human blood. While you should certainly all be very careful, there isn't any reason for panic."

But the whisperings had continued between classes, embellished with ever bloodier detail, and by the time the day was over, the scene had become vivid in Alison's imagination—the mutilated body, the desecrated campsite, the huge, overpowering shape of the unknown creature, bear or Sasquatch, looming darkly in her mind's eye, claws outstretched, lying in wait.

Now, as Joey started up the road toward the campground, with Storm charging happily ahead, she hung back. "Why don't we go home?" she asked, hoping her own fears weren't showing in her voice.

Joey grinned at her knowingly. "Scared?" he asked.

"I just think we should go home, that's all," Alison insisted, but now her brother took up the same chant he'd used this morning.

"*Chick*en, *chick*en! Alison's a *chick*en!"

Alison stood her ground. "Mom said we should come right home after school!"

"She did not!" Logan crowed. "She didn't say anything like that at all. That's just what she said back in New Jersey! And I want to see the campground!" His fears at school all but forgotten in the thrill of actually seeing the spot where someone had gotten killed, he dashed after Joey. "Wait up, Joey! I'm coming, too!"

Alison hesitated, torn between wanting to stay on the road, where at least everything around her was familiar, and wanting to go along with her brother. In the end, as she, too, started up the road to the campground, she told herself that she was just looking out for Logan, making sure he didn't get lost.

The trail was steep and slick from the rain, and more than once Alison nearly lost her footing. Just as she was wondering how much farther they were going to have to climb, the campground opened out in front of them. As if obeying some unspoken command, all three of them came to an abrupt halt, their excitement at the prospect of seeing the murder site suddenly dampened now that they were actually there.

The silent campground spread out before them, its eerie emptiness oddly accentuated by the lonely appearance of the unused picnic tables scattered here and there among the trees. They glanced at each other uncertainly, none of them willing to be the first to voice what each of them had been counting on: that someone would be up here—one of the deputies, perhaps—guarding the scene of the murder.

But there was nothing.

Storm, his nose to the ground, was sniffing at the area where the tent had been, and finally the three children started toward him, Alison taking Logan's hand in her own.

"There isn't anything here," Joey said. They stood at the edge of the campsite, none of them wanting to venture any closer to the trampled area where only a few hours ago half a dozen people had searched for clues to the grisly murder and maiming. "I thought . . ." His voice trailed off as he realized he wasn't quite sure what he had thought, what he'd expected.

"I-I think we should go home," Alison said, her voice echoing oddly in her own ears in the empty campground. "I don't like it here." She stepped back and was about to turn around when Storm barked excitedly, a single, sharp outburst, then moved away, his nose still pressed to the ground.

"What's he doing?" Logan asked.

"He found something," Joey exclaimed. He was trembling with excitement. "He found a scent, and he's following it! Come on!"

"Joey, where are you going?" Alison cried out as Joey darted after the big dog, who was already moving into the forest, tracking the scent.

"I'm following him," Joey yelled back. "Come on!"

Logan watched Joey and the dog disappear into the woods, his eyes widening with fear as he gazed up at his sister. "What should we do?" he asked, the last of his bravado abandoning him.

Alison glanced around the campground nervously. "Let's just go home," she said, striving to sound less frightened than she was. "We'll just walk back down to the road, okay?"

Logan nodded mutely, and the two of them started back the way they had come, but all the excitement they had felt on the way up was gone now. All the way back down to the road that meandered up the valley's floor, it seemed they were being watched, that unseen eyes were following their every movement, that at any moment something might appear out of the woods in front of them, blocking their way.

Alison kept glancing behind them, watching and listening for signs of danger, plotting wildly what to do—turn and run back up to the campground? Or take off down the hill through the forest, toward the relative safety of the valley?

They were only a few yards from the road when they heard a rustling sound in the brush off to the left, then the sharp snap of a branch breaking.

"Run, Logan! Run!" Alison shouted. Tightening her grip on her brother's hand, she broke into a sprint, half supporting Logan, half dragging him, running madly, gasping for breath, until they burst out onto the paved road. Without slowing, neither of them willing to risk even a glance backward, they pounded up the drive, finally throwing open the back door, then slamming it shut behind them.

Hearing the commotion, MaryAnne appeared at the door to the dining room, her smile of welcome fading as she saw the frightened expressions on her children's faces. "Alison? Logan? What's wrong? What happened?" Then, as she saw no sign of Joey Wilkenson: "Joey!" she exclaimed. "Something's happened to Joey, hasn't it?"

"N-No," Alison stammered. "At least—I don't think—"

"He went off with Storm," Logan wailed. "He went off, and just left us up at the campground." He ran to his mother, throwing his arms around her. "We heard something, Mom. It was in the woods!"

As she wrapped her arms around her son, MaryAnne stared severely at Alison. "I think you'd better tell me exactly what happened," she said.

Haltingly, Alison explained where they had gone and what had happened at the campground. "We tried to stop him," she finished. "We told him not to go after Storm, but he wouldn't listen to us. He just went!"

MaryAnne said nothing for a long moment, remembering the nights Joey had taken off into the darkness, telling no one where he was going. "All right," she said, choosing her words carefully, as much to calm herself as her children. "Joey knows the ranch, and he's used to going off with Storm. And nothing happened to you two, so why should anything happen to him?" But even as she said the words, the knot of fear and anger in her stomach was already beginning to tighten. She would wait until six, but no later. If Joey wasn't back by then, she would call Rick Martin.

He sat on the single rough chair in his cabin, the wolf sprawled on the floor beside him. He'd awakened an hour ago, after having slept fitfully through the day, and gone out to the stream to bathe in the fresh running water. There wouldn't be too many days left during which he could enjoy the luxury of a bath—soon the temperature would begin to drop. Within a month the stream would begin to freeze over, but long before that the water would be far too cold for him to sink his body into it. Soon the long winter months would descend on him, with their short days and blinding whiteness and the icy chill that never left the cabin during the season he had come to dread. This winter would be his last winter here. Somehow, he knew that by spring he would be gone. But not now.

Not yet.

The wolf stirred on the floor, then sat up, her ears pricking, a low warning growl rising in her throat.

The man stiffened, his senses sharpening, alert for the noise that had disturbed the animal.

Then he heard it. Barely audible, it was the sound of small rocks being dislodged from their places as something moved up the rocky path toward the cabin.

The man sniffed at the air. There it was. The scent.

The scent that he knew well, for he often caught it on the breeze during the nights when he went down to the valley to prowl in the darkness around the great log cabin that nestled at the base of Sugarloaf Mountain.

Rising from the chair, he stepped to the door and gazed out into the clearing in which the cabin stood. Though he could see nothing, the scent was growing stronger, the telltale rattle of loose rocks steadily louder.

And beyond what he heard and smelled, a sense deep within him told him that the boy was near.

The boy who belonged to him.

Now the wolf, too, was on her feet, her sinewy body pressing close to the man's legs as she tensed, ready to leap at whatever intruder was approaching. The man's hand dropped to the wolf's head, silencing the menacing snarl before it could issue from her curled lips.

There was a flicker of movement at the far side of the clearing, and then the dog appeared, his nose barely above the ground as he sniffed along the trail. The wolf's snarl erupted, and the German shepherd stopped, one forepaw off the ground, his eyes fixing on the lean animal that crouched on the porch of the cabin.

Dog and wolf stared at each other, their eyes locked, their bodies trembling as they struggled for supremacy. But finally Storm dropped to the ground, whining.

The wolf, her snarl subsiding, trotted forward, stopped a few paces from the German shepherd and sniffed warily. Then, as she edged closer to him, a low growl rumbling in her throat, Storm rolled over, exposing his belly to the wolf. She sniffed at him, snarled once, then nipped at his flank. Instantly, Storm leaped up, whirled, but then dropped to the ground once more as a warning growl erupted from the wolf's throat. The wolf stood over him for a moment, confirming her status, then once more allowed him to get to his feet. Storm stood still, his body quivering as the wolf slowly circled him, her nose examining him, her teeth still bared as she maintained her aggressor's posture.

Suddenly distracted by a new sound, the wolf stiffened, and Storm seized the opportunity to dart away, disappearing back down the trail, only to return a moment later, this time followed by Joey Wilkenson.

As his dog had a few moments earlier, Joey froze when he stepped into the clearing, his eyes locking on those of the wolf, who was now crouched once more, her teeth bared, ready to strike.

But as Joey's eyes met hers and held them, the wolf slowly

began to relax, until at last she turned away, dropping her tail, and slunk back to her master.

Joey's gaze followed the wolf. It wasn't until she had pressed herself once again against the man's legs that Joey's eyes finally rose to take in the tall figure who stood just outside the cabin's door.

Their eyes met, their gazes held.

At Joey's feet, Storm barked nervously, pressing himself against Joey's legs, but Joey showed no signs of even noticing the big shepherd's fear. Then, as the man took one step forward, Storm broke from Joey, but instead of flying to attack the man, he turned and dashed from the clearing.

As before, Joey seemed not to notice his pet's terror. After a long moment, he started across the clearing toward the man and the wolf.

Pulled toward them as if by some unseen magnet.

Closer.

Closer.

Until Joey felt the large, cold hand on his cheek.

———

Five minutes to six. MaryAnne got up from the desk, where she'd been trying to concentrate on the packet of papers Charley Hawkins had given her when she'd stopped by his office after lunch that afternoon. So far, she hadn't absorbed a single word of the documents. Leaving the den after one last glance at the clock, she started toward the kitchen, pausing at the bottom of the stairs when she saw Alison coming down from her room, Logan following her.

"Hasn't he come home yet?" Alison asked.

"No, he hasn't," MaryAnne replied, keeping her voice as calm as possible. She went on into the kitchen and dropped into one of the chairs at the kitchen table, unwilling to pick up the phone until the last possible second had passed. As the clock began to strike a few minutes later, she stood up, but before she'd even taken a single step toward the phone on the counter, Logan cried out from his post by the kitchen door.

"There he is! Look! He's coming across the field!"

Relief flooding through her, MaryAnne hurried to the door as Logan dashed outside and across the yard, scrambled over the fence into the field and ran toward Joey. Storm, seeing Logan racing toward him, bounded ahead of Joey, leaping exuberantly atop Logan, bringing him down. Soon the dog and the little boy were rolling in the wet grass, Storm barking loudly as Logan tried to wrestle him to the ground. Joey, too, ran forward to join in the fray, but when he entered the house a few moments later, his happy grin faded at the look on MaryAnne's face.

"I think you'd better explain yourself, young man," she snapped, her relief at his reappearance giving way to anger at the worry he'd caused her. "Do you have any idea how frightened Alison and Logan were when you took off? And what were you doing up at the campground in the first place?"

The last of Joey's grin disappeared, and his eyes turned angry. "I wasn't doing anything wrong. We just went up there to look around, and then Storm took off. All I did was follow him!"

"Follow him!" MaryAnne shot back. "Do you know how long you've been gone? Two hours! Two hours, Joey!"

Joey's expression hardened. "So what?" he demanded. "It's not like I was lost or anything. And Mom always let—"

"I don't care what your mother let you do," MaryAnne cut in. "Don't you know what happened up at the campground last night? A man was killed, Joey! And whatever killed him is still out there somewhere!"

"But I'm okay," Joey protested. "Nothing happened! Besides, Storm wouldn't have let anything happen to me!"

"How can you know that?" MaryAnne shot back. "What if you'd run into a grizzly? You could have both been killed!"

"Well, we weren't!" Joey shouted. "Why don't you just leave

me alone? You're not my mother, and you can't tell me what to do!"

The angry words stung MaryAnne as painfully as if the boy had slapped her, and a furious reply rose to her lips before she checked herself, aware of Logan and Alison, their faces pale as they huddled together near the dining room door, more frightened by her outburst than by Joey's disappearance. With an effort she put her anger under control. "Joey, I'm sorry," she said. "But you have to understand how frightened I was. After what happened last night, for you to disappear like that was terrifying. Who knows what Storm might have been following? Can't you understand how worried I was?"

"There wasn't anything to worry about," Joey insisted. "Mom let me go anywhere I wanted, as long as Storm was with me!"

MaryAnne took a deep breath, then let it out as she struggled to control her emotions. "All right, let's assume she did, Joey," she began. "But she's not here anymore, and now I'm responsible for you. Whether you like it or not, I'm your guardian now, and I'm afraid you're going to have to do as I tell you. And I'm telling you—"

But Joey was no longer listening. "I don't need a guardian!" he shouted. "I don't need to be taken care of! Why don't you just go away?" Before MaryAnne could stop him, he was out the door again, Storm at his heels.

"Joey?" she called, hurrying to the door as he dashed back toward the field. "Joey, come back here—"

But the boy ignored her, vaulting over the rail fence that separated the field from the yard. He was halfway across the field as MaryAnne let the kitchen door swing closed.

Damn it, damn it, damn it! She'd handled it all wrong! Why had she thrown her authority in his face? He hardly knew her— had barely had time to get used to the fact that his parents were dead! What did she expect of him?

"Mom?" Alison said, her voice quivering. "What are you going to do?"

As MaryAnne hesitated, Alison and Logan exchanged a glance. "What if he doesn't come back?" Logan asked.

MaryAnne looked out toward the forest into which Joey had disappeared. "He will," she said. "When he calms down, he'll come home."

But even as she spoke the words, she wondered if she really believed them.

CHAPTER 13

"How long are we going to wait?" Alison asked. A fire was blazing on the hearth, but its dancing flames had done little to dispel the dark mood that had settled not only over Alison, but her mother and brother as well. Nor had the droning of the television distracted any of them from worrying about Joey. Periodically, as the evening wore on, one or the other of them found an excuse to leave the room, to tour through the downstairs rooms, peering out into the darkness, searching for any sign of either Joey or Storm. So far there had been nothing.

"We'll give him another few minutes." MaryAnne sighed, abandoning any pretense of watching the image on the television screen. As the clock began striking nine, she stood up. "Maybe I'd better check the barn again."

"Can I go with you?" Logan asked.

"You've already done that five times, Mom," Alison pointed out before MaryAnne could answer Logan's question.

"Then I'll do it one more time," MaryAnne replied. "And no, you can't go with me, Logan. I want you to stay in the house with Alison."

"But why?" Logan wailed. "I want to see the horses!"

"I'm not going to argue with you, Logan," MaryAnne told the little boy. And I'm not going to tell you why not, either, she thought as she went into the kitchen to put on one of Audrey's heavy jackets against the cold night air. She hadn't told either of the children of the terror she'd felt outside the barn the other night, and she had no intention of telling them now. Although every time she'd gone out to the barn tonight—each time hoping that this time she would find Joey and Storm curled up on the floor of one of the empty stalls—she'd found the horses calmly standing in their stalls, peering at her with placid eyes, apparently undisturbed by either her own presence, or the presence of anything else. Yet her fear had not diminished.

Taking her flashlight with her, MaryAnne stepped out the back door into the yard. She swept the field with her eyes, in the futile hope that she might see Joey Wilkenson coming out of the forest. In the dim light from the house, all she could see were a doe and two yearling fawns, grazing contentedly.

She paused outside the barn, listening. Hearing nothing, she pulled the door open far enough to slip inside, then snapped on the flashlight and shined it around the darkness. Sheika, her head hanging over her stall door as always, blinked in the brilliance of the glare, but didn't turn away. "Joey?" MaryAnne called out, more to break the silence of the barn than in any hope that the boy might reply. "Are you in here? Storm?"

The only answer she received was a soft nicker from Sheika, and she paused to scratch the horse's ears as she walked down the aisle, checking the empty stalls for any sign of Joey, but knowing even before she was through that he wasn't there. Re-latching the barn door, she hurried back to the house, stepping into the kitchen just as the phone began to ring.

She snatched up the receiver before it had a chance to shrill a second time, expecting to hear, if not Joey's voice, one of the neighbors', calling to tell her that he was there. "Hello?"

"That was quick," Alan said. "What were you doing, waiting for me to call?"

MaryAnne floundered at the unexpected sound of her husband's voice. "No—I—My God, Alan, it must be the middle of the night back there!"

"It's just a few minutes after eleven," Alan replied, a note of suspicion edging into his tone. "MaryAnne, is everything okay? You sound kind of—funny, I guess."

"No!" MaryAnne exclaimed, a little too loudly. "I mean, everything's fine! We're just finishing up the supper dishes, and—" Damn! Why had she said that? Why hadn't she told him the kids were at some friend's house? Now he'd insist on talking to them, and Logan, surely, would tell him the truth. "Actually, Joey got mad at me and took off a little while ago. I thought you might be him, calling for a ride home."

"A ride home from where?" Alan asked, his voice etched with sarcasm. "Your nearest neighbors are miles away, aren't they?"

"For heaven's sake, Alan, it's not that bad! We're not—" She cut off her own words. What was the use? If she tried to argue with him, they would instantly be in the middle of another pointless fight. "Look, I've got to go see if I can find Joey. Can I call you back—"

Alan's voice, dark with anger, interrupted her. "Don't bother," he said. "Just let me talk to the kids, or have you managed to convince them I'm the bad guy in this deal?"

If not you, then who? MaryAnne felt like snapping back, but held her temper in check. "I'm not sure this is the best time, Alan," she said out loud, but Alison was already at her elbow.

"Is that Dad? Let me talk to him!" She reached for the phone, and MaryAnne, after shooting her a look of warning, surrendered it. "Daddy? Are you coming to visit us?"

MaryAnne moved around to the other side of the counter, trying not to stare at her daughter, but not wanting to miss a word Alison said, either. As the girl talked to her father, though, she winked conspiratorially at her mother.

"What's the big deal, Daddy? Joey and Storm go out hiking every day . . . It's not like Canaan, Daddy. People aren't waiting to mug you on every corner, and we don't even have drive-by shootings! . . . He'll be *back* . . . Of course not! Why should we be scared? . . . Daddy . . . *Daddy!* . . ." Her eyes rolled up toward the ceiling. Then, as Alan apparently changed the subject, Alison grinned happily. "School's great! My classes are really small, and . . ." Her grin faded, and she took a deep breath. "Of course I miss you, Daddy, but I *like* it here! What's wrong with that?" She fell silent for a moment, then held the receiver out to Logan. "He wants to talk to you," she said, all the happiness in her voice when she'd first spoken to her father suddenly gone. As she surrendered the phone to her brother, she shrugged helplessly at her mother. "All he wants to know is when we're coming home, and he thinks we're living in the wilderness!" Then, as both she and her mother heard what Logan was saying to his father, she turned to glare at her brother.

"There was a *murder*, Dad!" the little boy said, his voice trembling with excitement. "Right up in the campground, practically next door to our house! It was a Sasquatch, and it ripped up a tent, and killed this guy, and everything! Everyone says—" Abruptly, he went silent, then looked up at his mother. "Daddy says he wants to talk to you. Right now!" he added, mimicking the tone his father had just used.

Her stomach already starting to ache with tension, MaryAnne reluctantly took the phone.

"Why didn't you tell me about the murder?" Alan demanded without preamble.

"It wasn't a murder," MaryAnne began.

"If someone's dead, what would *you* call it?" her husband shot back.

"Nobody's calling it anything yet!" she snapped. "And I didn't tell you about it because I knew exactly how ridiculously you'd react!"

"I don't call wanting you and the kids to come home 'ridiculous'! And I think I have a right to know what's going on with my family. I'm still your husband—"

"You lost your rights the night you walked out on us!" MaryAnne flared. Still trembling with anger, she dropped the receiver back on the hook, then turned to face the children, both of whom instantly looked away. "I'm sorry," she said, feeling depleted by the rage expended on her husband. "I wish you hadn't had to hear that, but—" She lapsed into silence.

"Is Daddy going to make us go back to New Jersey?" Logan asked uncertainly, looking much younger than his ten years.

"Daddy can't make us do anything," MaryAnne replied. "But he wants us to go back, yes. And maybe he's right. Maybe—"

"But I like it here," Logan protested. "It's lots better than dumb old New Jersey!"

A small smile played around MaryAnne's lips, and she reached out and pulled Logan close to her, but when she spoke, it was to Alison. "What about you?" she asked. "Do you think we should go home?"

Alison hesitated, but finally shook her head. "I think everything's a lot better here, too."

"What about last night?" MaryAnne asked. "Doesn't what happened up at the campground scare you?"

"I guess it scares me," Alison admitted softly. "But back home, I was scared every time I went to school. I mean, there were kids with guns there, Mom! It's not like that here. It's just not."

"Well, then, we're all agreed," MaryAnne said with a lot more confidence than she was feeling. "And it's time for both of you to be getting ready for bed."

"But Joey isn't home yet," Logan instantly objected.

"He *will* be," MaryAnne insisted. "Go up and get ready for bed, and when Joey comes back, you can both come down and say hello to him. All right?"

Sensing that their mother was in no mood to argue with them, Alison and Logan headed upstairs.

After taking a last look out into the night beyond the kitchen, MaryAnne picked up the phone and began calling the nearest neighbors, asking if any of them had seen her missing godchild.

———

The blackness of the overcast night closed down on El Monte Ranch. Ten o'clock. Joey finally stepped out of the shelter of the woods. For nearly four hours he'd been huddling in the refuge of the trees, watching as his godmother came outside over and over again, calling out to him, then going to the barn to search for him. Every time she'd appeared, Storm had risen to his feet, whining eagerly, ready to dash across the field to throw himself on her.

Joey himself had had to resist the same urge, holding fast to the dog's collar, keeping the big shepherd as firmly in control as he was keeping himself.

Why *should* he go back to the house?

All she'd do was yell at him again.

And he hadn't done anything wrong! All he and Storm had done was go for a hike, something they'd done thousands of times! And his mother had never gotten mad at him!

The thing was, he couldn't tell Aunt MaryAnne where he'd been, because he didn't really know. All he knew was that he'd started following Storm, and the dog had led him up the mountainside, higher than he'd ever gone by himself before. After a while he'd started getting that weird feeling again, as if all his nerves were exposed. But he'd kept going, kept following Storm, and by the time the feeling passed, he wasn't anywhere near where he'd started, and it had gotten a lot later than he'd thought it was.

How could he tell Aunt MaryAnne where he'd been when he didn't even know himself? Struggling against his own confusion, in the end he'd just gotten mad at all her questions and taken off.

At first he thought maybe he'd just stay outside all night long. He could sleep right here—he had his jacket on, and even if it wasn't very warm, he wasn't going to freeze to death. But as the hours crept by, and the temperature started to drop with the fading light, he'd changed his mind.

Maybe he'd just stay here until all the lights went out in the house and he was sure Aunt MaryAnne had gone to bed. Then he could sneak into the barn and go to sleep in one of the stalls, with the horses to keep him company. There were blankets in there, too, and the little bathroom off the tack room, where he could wash his face.

Now, though, as night pressed in around him, without even any moonlight to break the darkness, he started to shiver; the house, only a hundred yards away, looked warm and cozy with its lights glowing brightly. An hour ago he'd seen a wisp of smoke drifting up from the chimney as the fire in the den had been lit. As the cold of the night seeped through his jacket to chill his body, and loneliness wrapped his soul like a shroud, the last of Joey's anger faded away. Drawn by the warmth of the house, he started across the field, Storm racing ahead of him.

By the time he had climbed the fence between the field and the yard, the back door was open and his godmother was calling to him.

"Joey? Are you all right?"

He hesitated, but when he heard no anger in her voice, he dropped off the top rail of the fence and dashed across the yard, hurling himself into her arms.

"I'm sorry, Aunt MaryAnne," he apologized, struggling against the sobs that now threatened to overwhelm him.

"And I'm sorry, too," MaryAnne assured him. "But you're home, and you're safe, and it's not the end of the world. You and I are just going to have to learn how to talk to each other, okay?"

Nodding mutely as he tried to swallow the lump in his throat, Joey let MaryAnne lead him into the kitchen. "I didn't mean to get so mad," he confessed after he'd taken off his jacket. "I just—" But he was unable to explain his anger, any more than he could account for the time he'd lost in the mountains.

"We'll just forget about it, all right?" MaryAnne told him. "We'll call it a misunderstanding, and see if we can't do better from now on. Would you like me to fix you some supper?"

Joey shook his head. "I'm not hungry, I guess. I better go and get cleaned up." He looked down at his pants, smeared with mud from his long climb and the hours of sitting in the forest. "I guess I kind of messed up my clothes."

"I'll wash them in the morning," MaryAnne told him. "Just bring them down when you're done."

As Joey left the kitchen, MaryAnne called her closest neighbor once more, this time to report that Joey was back, that he was fine, and that she was sorry to have bothered her.

"Well, I'm glad he's back," Margaret Stiffle told her. "And I sure hope it doesn't mean he's starting to have trouble again. He sure put poor Audrey through enough, but we were all hoping it was over with."

MaryAnne's breath caught in her throat. "Trouble?" she asked. "What kind of trouble? What are you talking about?"

Margaret Stiffle said nothing for a moment. When she finally replied, it was guardedly. "Well, it's really none of my business, is it? And I'm sure I'm wrong. I'm sure Joey's just fine now, and I do thank you for calling." Before MaryAnne could say anything else, Margaret Stiffle had hung up.

Pensively, MaryAnne went back to the den, added another log

to the fire, and turned on the television. But Margaret Stiffle's words kept echoing in her mind. She turned the TV set off again, and went upstairs to Alison's room. Her daughter, clad in a bathrobe now, was lying on her bed, a book propped up in her lap. Closing the door, MaryAnne went over and sat on the edge of the bed. "Did you see Joey?" she asked.

Alison nodded. "He went in to take a shower."

"Did he say where he went?" MaryAnne asked. "I mean, tonight?"

Alison tipped the book over on her chest. "Didn't you ask him?"

"I guess I didn't want to run the risk of getting into another fight with him." She hesitated, then, studying her daughter's expression closely: "Alison, I just talked to Mrs. Stiffle, and she said something strange. About Joey." As Alison averted her face, MaryAnne frowned. "Do you know what she was talking about? Has someone else said something?"

Alison started to shake her head, but then changed her mind. "It's not like anyone really *said* anything," she began. "It's sort of—well, everyone acts like they don't like Joey." Haltingly, feeling like a tattletale, Alison told her mother what had happened on the shopping expedition and again today, on the way to school. "And this afternoon, Andrea and Michael Stiffle wouldn't even say good-bye to him. They all act real weird, like Joey did something to them, but nobody ever says what!"

For a long time that night, MaryAnne lay awake, thinking.

What could Mrs. Stiffle have meant?

What trouble was she talking about?

Somehow, MaryAnne knew, she was going to find out.

———

As midnight gave way to the small hours of the morning, the wind began to rise, howling down from the mountains to whistle through the trees, slamming against the house with a force that rattled the open windows of Joey's room. Waking, he sat up in bed, staring at the window, feeling the wind blowing on his face. He stayed still for a few moments, the pungent smells of the mountains filling his nostrils.

Though the night was still almost pitch-dark, the wind had torn at the clouds, and now and then a faint glow of moonlight glimmered outside. His nostrils flaring at the scent of a deer grazing in the field beyond the yard, Joey slid out of bed and padded silently to the door of his room. Storm, raising his head for a moment, watched as Joey slipped out into the hall, then dropped his muzzle back to his paws, his eyes closing once more.

Joey moved along the hall to the head of the stairs, then down to the first floor. Another scent caught his attention, and he followed it into the kitchen.

With no light to guide him except the dim glow of the waning moon shining through the scudding clouds, Joey went to the sink and knelt down by the door of the cupboard below it. As he opened the cabinet, the scent grew stronger. Joey reached into the wastebasket, his fingers closing on a piece of butcher's paper.

Clutching the paper in both his hands, he held it to his nose.

The tangy scent of fresh blood filled his nostrils now, and he felt saliva begin to run in his mouth.

His tongue flicked out, tasting the drying blood left on the paper, which only a few hours ago had wrapped the steaks his godmother had fixed for dinner that evening.

His tongue worked faster, licking the blood up, his mouth filling with pungent flavor.

Finally, when the paper was licked clean, he dropped it back into the wastebasket and moved to the refrigerator.

Opening it, he blinked in the glare of the refrigerator's light, but his eyes quickly adjusted to the brilliance, and he found what he was looking for.

On the lowest shelf were half a dozen more steaks, each of them wrapped in transparent plastic, stacked neatly on a large plate.

His stomach screaming with hunger now, he snatched up one of the steaks and began ripping the plastic away, the odor of raw meat nearly overwhelming him. He held the meat close to his mouth, then sank his teeth into it, tearing away a piece, swallowing it almost before he'd had a chance to chew it.

"Joey? What are you doing?"

The voice startled Joey. He spun around, the raw steak still clutched in one hand, the torn plastic in the other. Instinctively, he wiped the blood from his lips with one of his pajama sleeves. As the kitchen lights came on, he blinked, then recognized Logan standing just inside the kitchen door, staring curiously at him.

"You can't eat that!" Logan exclaimed. "It's not even cooked!"

"I'm not doing anything," Joey replied, thrusting his hands behind his back in a quick, guilty motion. "What are you doing down here, anyway? If Aunt MaryAnne catches you—"

But before he could complete the sentence, MaryAnne herself appeared behind Joey in the doorway. "Joey? Logan? Why aren't you two in bed?"

Logan's arm came up and he pointed accusingly at Joey. "He's got a steak, and he's eating it. It's not even cooked, Mom! He's eating it raw!"

Her eyes widening in shock, MaryAnne stared at Joey, until he finally pulled his hands from behind his back. "I-I wasn't eating it," he stammered. "I was hungry, and I found it in the refrigerator." He looked up despairingly at MaryAnne. "I thought—I was going to cook it, but—I'm not sure how."

The misery on the boy's face wrenched at MaryAnne, her annoyance that once again he'd gotten up in the middle of the night tempered by the knowledge that, having skipped dinner, he must be ravenously hungry. "Okay," she sighed. "Let me get Logan back in bed, then I'll fry it up for you. But then it's right back to bed for you, too, and no arguments. All right?"

Joey nodded silently, and MaryAnne spun Logan around, aimed him toward the stairs, then swatted him affectionately on the bottom. "Upstairs," she ordered. "Go on! Scoot!" Herding him ahead of her, she followed the little boy up the stairs.

The second she was gone, Joey's attention returned to the raw meat in his hand. Tearing at it with both his fingers and his teeth, he began cramming it into his mouth, swallowing all of it in less than a minute.

By the time MaryAnne had gotten Logan settled back in bed, Joey had thrown away the plastic the meat had been wrapped in, shoving it deep down to the bottom of the wastebasket.

He'd washed the blood from his hands and face and was wiping them dry as MaryAnne stepped into the kitchen. "I changed my mind," he said. "I just drank some milk."

MaryAnne frowned uncertainly. "You're sure that's all you want?"

Joey nodded, started toward the kitchen door, then impulsively hugged her. "I'm really sorry I messed up," he said. "I'll try not to do it again."

MaryAnne wrapped her arms around him, held him close for a moment, then released him. "Well, one of the things you can do is stay in bed all night for once." Tempering her words with a smile, she shooed him toward the stairs. "Now go on—scat! I'll shut off the light." Joey darted up the stairs, and MaryAnne reached for the light switch, then paused, her eyes on the refrigerator.

Feeling faintly silly, knowing the thought that had flicked through her mind was ridiculous, she nevertheless found herself crossing the kitchen and opening the refrigerator door.

She counted the steaks on the plate on the bottom shelf.

Earlier, there had been six.

She was certain of it.

Now, there were only five.

When she finally turned off the lights and started back up the stairs, her mind was spinning and her stomach felt nauseous.

She would get no more sleep tonight.

She was living with a boy she didn't know.

CHAPTER 14

"Going to be an early winter," Bill Sikes commented, glancing up at sky. It was much colder this morning, and though the rain clouds from the day before were gone, the first wisps of a new front were already visible. "See those?" he asked, pointing up to the streamers of white that were drifting out of the north. "Coming down from the Arctic. Be surprised if we don't get snow before the week's out."

"Snow?" MaryAnne asked. "But it's barely the beginning of September!"

The hired man shrugged. "Wouldn't be the first time it happened. Didn't hardly have any snow at all last winter." A cynical grin twisted his lips. "Damn near wrecked the ski season. Another winter like that one, and the developer fellas are gonna be real unhappy!"

"It doesn't sound like that bothers you even a little bit,"

MaryAnne observed. As a gust of wind blew down from the mountains, she turned up the collar of the heavy shearling jacket she'd found in the coat closet that morning. "Don't you think we'd better get the horses back in the barn?"

"They'll be spending enough time inside once the weather hits," Sikes replied, pivoting to watch the three horses he'd turned out of the barn two hours earlier. "It's good for them to be outside— it's where they belong. Not right, keeping them cooped up all the time. Ever wonder what they think about, just standin' in a stall all day?"

"I'm not sure they think at all," MaryAnne replied.

The weathered caretaker shook his head. "That's what lotsa people say, but don't you believe it. Just makes them feel better about how they treat the animals. They figure if the animals don't think, they don't suffer. But you just look at 'em!"

MaryAnne's gaze shifted to the field, where Sheika was cantering along the far fence, her head high, her tail streaming behind her. The other two horses—the dappled gelding that had been Audrey's, and the bay that was Joey's own—were standing together, head to tail, grazing contentedly. "Have you thought about what we were talking about the other day? Are you still thinking of leaving?"

"Well, now, I'll tell you," Sikes drawled, reaching down to pick up a piece of straw which he clamped between his teeth. "I *have* been thinkin', and it seems to me like it wouldn't be right for me to up and take off, if you're planning to stick with it." He glanced at her out of the corner of his eye. "That's what you're planning, isn't it?"

"I think so," MaryAnne replied. Then: "Bill, what can you tell me about Joey?"

The caretaker's eyes darkened slightly. "What about him?"

MaryAnne hesitated, choosing her words carefully. "Well, he doesn't seem to have many friends. I mean, the Stiffle twins live right down the road, and it seems like they'd all play together, doesn't it?"

"Joey's a loner," Sikes replied, his eyes still fixed on the horses in the field. "Nothin' wrong with that."

"But why?" MaryAnne pressed. "Did something happen between them? Alison says the other kids at school don't seem to like Joey."

Bill Sikes spit the remains of the straw he'd been chewing to the ground, and finally turned to face MaryAnne. "Far's I can see, there's two kinds of people in the world. The ones that get along with other people, and the ones that don't. Mostly, the ones that don't get along with people, get along with animals. Seems like Joey's one of the ones who gets along with animals. Nothin' wrong with *that*."

An hour later, as she headed down the road toward town, MaryAnne's thoughts circled over and around what Bill Sikes had told her. Could that really be all there was to Joey's lack of friendships with other children? Could it really be as simple as his preferring the company of animals? Certainly, that would explain his going out to sleep in the barn the night before last. And yet he seemed to get along just fine with Alison and Logan. By the time she pulled up to the building that housed all twelve grades of the Sugarloaf school district, MaryAnne was wondering if she really needed to talk to anyone at the school at all. When she'd called and made the appointment at eight o'clock this morning, it had seemed the logical thing to do, yet after her brief conversation with Bill Sikes, she was no longer sure. Sikes, after all, had known Joey practically all his life. Surely, if the boy had a problem, the caretaker would have known about it.

But would he have told her?

She slid the Range Rover into an empty slot in the parking lot and found her way to the principal's office, where Florence Wickman was waiting for her.

"I'm glad you called this morning." The principal was a heavyset woman with prematurely gray hair. She ushered MaryAnne into her office, closed the door, and indicated a worn leather chair in front of her desk. "As it happens, I was going to call you this afternoon."

MaryAnne lowered herself onto the chair, perching nervously on its edge. "You were going to call me?" she repeated. "Is there a problem with one of my children?"

Florence Wickman leaned back in her own chair. "Not at all. But I wondered how much you might know about Joey's . . ." She paused, as if looking for the right word, then sighed heavily. "Well, I suppose 'problems' is the best way to put it."

MaryAnne's heart sank. So there *was* more to it than Joey's simply being a loner. "I guess that's why I'm here. A couple of things have happened, and my daughter tells me that a lot of the children don't seem to like Joey. I guess I'm feeling as though I need some information."

Mrs. Wickman picked up a folder, opened it, and handed it to MaryAnne. "I think it's all in there. When Joey first came to kindergarten, he was the shyest little boy you ever saw. He hardly spoke to anyone—kept to himself. Nothing unusual about that— especially with only children. But as he started growing up, he didn't seem to become as well-socialized as the rest of the children. He never had a best friend, and never seemed interested in making one." She nodded toward the folder. "He also had a lot of trouble paying attention in classes," she went on. "Practically all his teachers have said he tends to daydream a lot. He often just sits staring out the window, as if he's seeing things nobody else sees." She paused, then spoke again. "And there were the fights."

"Fights?" MaryAnne echoed.

"Not terrible ones," the principal replied, her brows knitting into a thoughtful frown. "But strange ones. When he was in fifth—maybe sixth—grade, it seemed to be worst, and they never really started out as fights. It was almost as if it was no more than roughhousing that got out of hand. And the boys he fought with were always both older and bigger than Joey." She hesitated again, then seemed to make up her mind to go on. "I always wondered if perhaps it didn't have something to do with Ted."

"Ted?" MaryAnne asked, baffled now. "What on earth could it have to do with Ted?"

Mrs. Wickman spread her hands, a gesture meant to placate. "I'm not saying it did. But I always wondered if the fact that Joey invariably wound up fighting against bigger, older boys, wasn't some way of striking out at his father."

"I can't believe—"

"Again, Mrs. Carpenter, I'm not saying I understand it all. But if Ted was a strong disciplinarian, it would make sense, wouldn't it? If there was no way Joey felt he could win against his father, mightn't he try to win a fight with someone else—bigger and stronger than he—as a way of validating his own personality?"

MaryAnne's nerves began to tingle. Here it was again—the intimation that Ted and Joey had had frightening problems. "Are you saying that Ted was an abusive father?" she asked, struggling to keep her voice neutral.

"I'm not sure I'm saying anything at all," Florence Wickman quickly assured her. "I'm just searching for an explanation. At any rate," she went on, settling back in her chair once again, "it's all been much better, the last year or so. Joey was in counseling for awhile—"

"Counseling?" MaryAnne broke in. "Was it that bad?"

"I'm afraid it was, for a while. For a year or two, Audrey was quite worried about Joey. And although he's been much better lately, I can't help but think the loss of his parents might be a setback for him. It also occurred to me that you might not be aware of everything that's happened." She smiled. "You know what they say: 'forewarned is forearmed.' And it just seemed best that I have a talk with you."

"I see." MaryAnne let out the breath she'd been holding. "But you said things have been better?"

"Much," Florence Wickman told her. "I suspect that simply having two more children in the house will help him a great deal." She glanced up at the clock. "I hope all this hasn't upset you too much, but I did feel you ought to know about it. And if there's anything I can do to help . . ." She let the words hang in the air. MaryAnne rose to her feet.

"Thank you," she said automatically, still trying to sort out all the information the principal had given her.

As she stepped out of the office, the noon bell went off and the wide corridor began filling with children pouring out of the classrooms. Threading her way among them, MaryAnne didn't notice Joey standing at the end of the hall.

Standing silently, staring at her.

She'd been talking to Mrs. Wickman about him.

Spying on him . . .

———————

Rick Martin stared at the report from the lab in Boise in disgust. "What the hell is this?" he demanded rhetorically, but Tony Moleno, the only other person in the two-room office on the second floor of the firehouse, glanced up from the paperwork he was laboring over on the theft of a T-shirt from Francine Schildhauser's clothesline.

"A *pervert*!" Francine had insisted. "We have a pervert loose in town. The children won't be safe!" Seeing no point in arguing with her, Tony had dutifully taken notes, and was now stuck with the multitudinous forms the sheriff's department required.

"What's what?" he asked, glad for the diversion.

"This!" Martin spat, tossing the report to his partner. "Can you believe this?"

Moleno quickly scanned the document, an analysis of the minute quantities of matter that had been recovered from the tent and sleeping bags from Coyote Creek Campground and from the body of Glen Foster.

" 'Unidentified animal hair'?" Moleno read, his brows arching.

"What do they mean, 'unidentified'? Their whole fuckin' *job* is identifying stuff like that!"

"No shit," Rick Martin muttered, grabbing the receiver of the phone on his desk in his left hand as he jabbed angrily at the keypad with his right. "This is Rick Martin, up in Sugarloaf," he barked when a harried-sounding woman finally picked up his call on the tenth ring. "Let me talk to— Hold on a minute!" He reached for the report, snatched it out of Moleno's fingers, then spoke again, reading the name of the investigator from the bottom of the form. "Henry! Henry Henry!" He rolled his eyes at Moleno as he was put on hold. "Henry Henry? What the hell kind of name is that? Sounds like— Hello? Henry Henry? This is Rick Martin, up in Sugarloaf. I'm looking at your report on that stuff we sent you, and I'm not going to pretend I'm real happy with it. What the hell do you mean, 'unidentified animal hair'? What kind of crap is that, *Henry Henry*?"

In his office in Boise, Henry Henry took a deep breath, letting it out slowly. He'd been expecting this call ever since he'd given the report to his secretary an hour ago, ready to be faxed up to Sugarloaf. "You got all your steam blown off yet, or do you want to rant some more? It's your nickel, so either way is fine by me. Oh, and by the way," he added. "My name's Hank—my dad was a very sick man."

Rick Martin chuckled, his frustration at the report already dissipating. "Okay, *Hank*! Sorry I got cranky. But that still doesn't tell me what the hell's going on. What does 'unidentifiable animal hair' mean? In simple English, please."

"It means the hairs we recovered were animal—that's as opposed to nonanimal, I presume—and that we don't know what kind they are. Is that simple enough for you?"

"But you guys have samples from every kind of animal in Idaho down there, don't you?"

"And Oregon, Washington, Montana, British Columbia, and a lot of other places, too," Henry agreed. "But what you sent up doesn't match any of them. Closest thing is wolf, but it's not a match. Too thin, and too curly."

"All right, so where does that leave us?" Martin asked, already wondering what he was going to tell Milt Morgenstern when the editor and publisher of the local newspaper inevitably called him. " 'Unidentified animal' sounds awfully close to Sasquatch to me, and the last thing this place needs is for the tabloids to pick up something like that. You got any idea what it could do to our ski season?"

In the privacy of his office in Boise, Hank Henry shrugged. "But what if it *is* a Sasquatch you guys have got up there?" he asked with an air of exaggerated concern that slid across the line into parody. "Shouldn't the public be warned?"

"Come on, damn it," Martin replied. "You're going to have to do better than that, and you know it!"

"All right." Henry sighed. "You're right—it isn't good enough, and it's pissing me off as much as it is you. I've already sent the samples to the FBI lab. They've got the equipment to do a DNA analysis, and I put a rush on the job. With any luck, we should have an answer within twenty-four hours."

"What am I supposed to do in the meantime?" Martin demanded.

"Stonewall it," Henry suggested. "Tell 'em we're running behind and haven't gotten to it yet."

"This is a death we're talking about," Martin objected. "Not to mention the woman in the hospital down there! If I tell the newspaper guy up here that, he'll be on you so hard you'll feel like you got a yellow jacket in your jockstrap!"

"I'll try to bear up under the pressures of the fourth estate," Hank Henry observed dryly before he hung up.

Rick Martin got up from his desk, walked over to the window, and gazed down on the quiet street below.

Quiet for now, anyway.

But as soon as the first snow fell, the town would fill up, all the condominiums rented, the restaurants busy, the stores selling ski clothes as fast as they could ring them up. Though he had only a vague idea of how much of Sugarloaf's economy was currently based on winter sports, he knew there were a lot of people in town who wouldn't be able to survive a failed winter.

And every one of them would blame him for any rumors of an unidentifiable creature loose in the mountains.

For now, he decided, he'd do nothing at all about the strange report he'd gotten from Boise.

After all, there was no sense causing a panic, for surely there was nothing to panic about.

By tomorrow, he was certain—or the day after—they would know exactly what had killed Glen Foster. And only when he knew would he speak to Milt Morgenstern, or anybody else.

"Okay, you're doing fine," Olivia Sherbourne told MaryAnne. She glanced at her watch, then took the shotgun out of Mary-Anne's hands and began reloading the magazine. "I've got just about enough time for one more magazine, then I've got to go back to work."

"Why don't we quit now?" MaryAnne suggested. "I just stopped in to say hello—I wasn't really expecting a shooting lesson."

"No time like the present," Olivia replied. "Next time, you'll load the shells yourself. A gun you don't know how to load is a pretty useless weapon."

MaryAnne looked with distaste at the shotgun. Made entirely of metal, plastic, and hard rubber, it looked nothing like the ornately carved weapons she had occasionally glanced at in museums and sporting goods stores. This gun looked exactly like what it was—an instrument for cold-blooded killing.

"There's no point in even having a gun out here if it won't stop a grizzly," Olivia had told her when they'd brought the gun out to the pasture behind the large house that served the veterinarian as both home and office.

"But I'm not even sure I want a gun," MaryAnne protested.

"You've already got one," Olivia pointedly replied. "It's just like this one, and it's locked in the gun cabinet in your den. Audrey and I bought them at the same time, and you should know how to use it." Though she didn't mention the killing in the campground, both of them knew exactly what she was talking about.

"Why do I wish you'd been cleaning the oven when I arrived, instead of the gun?" MaryAnne groaned. "If you hadn't already had it out—"

"But I did have it out," Olivia cut in, "so let's just get to it, all right?"

She'd gone over the shotgun carefully, showing MaryAnne each of its parts and how it worked. "Never, ever, leave it loaded," she'd begun. "When you're done using it, empty the magazine, empty the chamber, and then fire it. Then try to load another cartridge into the chamber, and try to fire it again. Only when you can't make it fire—no matter what you do—do you put it away. Understand?"

MaryAnne had nodded, almost wishing she hadn't stopped in to say hello to Olivia at all, but at the same time knowing that her new friend was right—if she were going to live out here, she should know the basics of shooting. Reluctantly, she'd taken the gun, put it up to her shoulder, sighted along the barrel, and fired.

The kick of the gun had almost made her lose her balance.

"That's all right," Olivia had assured her as she steadied herself. "Just keep the stock hard against your shoulder. If you don't, it could break it when it kicks. The idea is to absorb the shock, not have it slam into you. Let's try it again."

And so, for almost half an hour, MaryAnne had practiced

shooting, and slowly the weapon had begun to feel less alien in her hands.

"With a laser sight, it's hard to miss," Olivia explained. "As soon as you squeeze the button, the laser comes on, and wherever you see the red dot is where the shot is going to hit."

Now Olivia handed her back the reloaded shotgun, and pointed to a bale of hay about fifty yards away. It was the farthest target she had set up. From this far, MaryAnne didn't think she had a chance of hitting it. "At night, you'll see the red dot even from this distance," Olivia told her. "What you'd do is aim the gun at the ground in front of you, and just walk the spot up to the target. During the day, it's actually trickier, harder to see the red dot. Take a shot."

MaryAnne shot the bolt, injecting a cartridge into the chamber, then lifted the weapon to her shoulder, her right forefinger curling around the trigger. Bracing the gun with her left hand, she pressed the button to light the laser.

No dot appeared on the target, so she concentrated, carefully lining the target up with the sights on the barrel. Finally she squeezed the trigger, pulling it with a slow, steady motion, preparing herself for the gun's kick.

As the shot exploded, the target suddenly appeared to have developed freckles.

"Bull's-eye," Olivia said. "Not bad. Not bad at all."

———

He had been asleep in his cabin when the first shot had roused him. Even before its roar had died away, he was fully awake and out of bed. He was half dressed when the second shot sounded, and by the time the third shot was fired, he was out of the cabin, moving quickly through the trees, following no path as he skirted the mountainside until he came to one of the massive outcroppings that commanded a view of the entire valley.

Crouching in a shadowed cleft, invisible from below, he gazed out over El Monte Ranch, his eyes searching out the source of the gunfire.

As MaryAnne Carpenter began firing the second magazine, the man's sharp eyes found the puff of smoke from the shotgun's muzzle, and he left his hiding place, ducking low to the ground as he raced along the mountain's flank, his bare feet silently carrying him closer to the veterinarian's property.

At last he came to a ridge directly above Olivia Sherbourne's pasture, where he crouched once more, still able to observe what was happening several hundred feet below him, invisible to the two women on the valley floor.

He cringed as yet another shot was fired, the blast of the shell resounding in his ears with a force that made him wince in physical pain. A moment later his flaring nostrils picked up the acrid scent of burnt gunpowder floating up from below. He saw MaryAnne pump yet another cartridge into the chamber, and he braced himself for the next shot.

Only when the echo of the last shell had died away and he saw the two women turn and head back toward the house, did the man leave the shelter of the ridge and start slowly back the way he came.

If she was learning how to use a gun, he would have to be more careful than he'd been before.

———

"You know what you need?" Olivia asked as they stepped through the back door into her large kitchen.

"I need a lot of things," MaryAnne replied wryly. "What's first on your list?"

"An evening out," Olivia replied. "An evening out of that house, an evening away from your kids, an evening spent entirely in the company of adults."

"And how do I arrange that?" MaryAnne asked. "Just call up some total stranger and ask him to invite me to a dinner party?"

"Not quite. All you do is come down here about six-thirty this evening. I'm having a few people in, and I think you should join us."

Though the idea instantly appealed to MaryAnne, she rejected it just as quickly. "What am I going to do with the kids?"

Now Olivia burst out laughing. "Come on, MaryAnne! Alison's old enough to be baby-sitting herself, and Joey's the same age she is. Let them sit Logan, and just tell Sikes to keep an eye on them. You're not going to be that far from home."

"You're on," MaryAnne quickly agreed. Except for the reception after the funeral, she'd barely spoken to anyone other than Olivia herself and Charley Hawkins. Olivia was right—it would do her good to get out of the house, even if it was only for a couple of hours. "What do you want me to bring?"

"Nothing," Olivia told her as they walked out to MaryAnne's car. "Just be here at six-thirty, and be ready to relax for a while. Deal?"

"Deal," MaryAnne replied.

As she climbed into the Range Rover and started up the road to El Monte, MaryAnne realized she was already looking forward to the evening. But as she emerged from the winding driveway into the open yard in front of the house, she suddenly had the uncanny feeling that she was being watched.

She glanced around. Bill Sikes must be somewhere close by. But there was no sign of him. Parking the Rover in front of the house, she got out, glanced around once more, then decided she was being silly. Why would anyone be watching her? Determinedly shaking off the feeling, she went into the house, unaware that from the shelter of one of the escarpments far up the mountainside, she was, indeed, being watched.

Watched by a man, and a wolf.

CHAPTER 15

*A*ll afternoon the sky had grown steadily darker, and when night finally fell over the ranch, it wrapped the house in a heavy blackness that set Alison's nerves on edge. Maybe she shouldn't have been so quick to insist her mother go to Dr. Sherbourne's for dinner, to assure her that she was old enough to take care of everything.

Her mother hadn't really wanted to leave them alone—Alison herself had insisted on it. But now that night had descended on them, she was beginning to regret it. She moved through the lower floor of the big house, turning on lights in every room, trying to drive the shadows away. Still, whenever she even glanced at one of the windows, she found herself shivering at the inky gloom that surrounded the house. She tried to shake off the feeling of apprehension that had come over her, tried to tell herself that she just wasn't used to having it so dark outside. Back in New Jersey, even on the darkest of nights, the streetlights still shined brightly and the neighbors' houses were always lit. Even late at night, after most of the neighborhood had gone to bed, there was a steady glow in the sky from Manhattan, only a few miles away, and every now and then a car would turn the corner a few yards away, the beams of its headlights sweeping the wall of the room she had shared with Logan.

There had been a steady background of noise, too. The familiar rumble of cars from the highway, the occasional drone of planes coming in to land at the airport. Here, silence had come along with the darkness, for the temperature had dropped quickly that afternoon, and not even the insects were buzzing tonight.

The only sound she'd heard was the howl of what she hoped was a coyote, but which Joey had insisted was a wolf.

"Really?" Logan had asked. The three of them had been in the kitchen, where Alison was adding extra cheese to the frozen pizza her mother had left for their dinner. "What's it doing?"

Joey's eyes had narrowed to slits and his voice took on a mysterious tone. "Hunting," he'd whispered in the silence that followed the wolf's haunting cry. "It's hungry, and it's looking for something to eat. And if it doesn't find anything, it'll come down here."

Logan had shivered with excitement, mixed with the thrill of fear. "It won't hurt the horses, will it?"

Joey's voice had dropped even further. "It won't even go after them," he said. "But if it's already tasted human blood, it might come after us!"

"Stop it!" Alison had cried. "You're scaring him!"

Joey, sitting at the table next to Logan, nudged the smaller boy. "Guess who's really scared?" he'd asked.

"Alison." Logan giggled. "Alison's scared of everything!"

"I am not," Alison shot back. But as the evening wore on, what had promised to be a great adventure when her mother told them she was leaving them alone in the house, was starting to turn into something else.

Twice already she'd had to resist the urge to call her mother at Olivia Sherbourne's and beg her to come home. All that stopped her was the certainty that if she did, she'd never hear the end of it from Logan. Besides, except for the blackness of the night, and the utter quiet outside, nothing had happened.

Nothing at all, except that as the minutes ticked by, she kept getting the feeling that something wasn't right.

She was becoming increasingly edgy. Something was outside, she thought, concealed in the night, watching the house.

Watching them.

Now she sat in the den with Logan, staring at the television screen, trying to concentrate on the movie her brother had found on one of the satellite channels, but every few minutes she kept glancing at the window, where, though the curtains were drawn, a small gap still allowed her to see a narrow strip of the blackness outside.

A gap that would let anyone—any*thing*—that might be out-side peer into the bright room.

At least once, she was certain, she'd seen a flash of movement just outside the window. It had only been visible from the corner of her eye, and when she'd turned to look straight at it, it was gone.

If it had been there at all.

There's nothing there, she told herself. Then why was she so nervous?

"Where's Joey?" she asked.

Logan, stretched out on the floor, his chin propped up on his hands as he stared at the television screen, spoke without looking at her. "I don't know."

Alison frowned. When he left the den a little while ago, she'd thought he was just going to the kitchen to get another piece of pizza.

But he hadn't come back.

She was about to get up to go look for him when her eye was

caught once more by what looked like a movement at the window, and suddenly she understood.

Joey was out there, trying to scare her!

Sitting still, giving no sign that she'd seen anything at all, she tried to figure out how to catch him at it. If she just got up and went to the window, he'd see her coming and disappear into the darkness. Then she had an idea. "I'm going to see if he went upstairs," she said. She stood and started toward the door, but at the last second she veered off, moving quickly toward the wall in which the curtained window was set. As quietly and as swiftly as she could, she went to the curtain and reached for the cord. With a quick jerk, she pulled the curtain open, fully expecting to see Joey standing there, grinning in at her.

But all she saw was the blackness of the night and her own reflection staring at her from the shiny glass.

"What are you doing?" Logan asked, finally turning away from the television to look at her.

Alison frowned uncertainly. "I-I thought I saw something."

"You're crazy." Logan groaned, rolling his eyes before going back to the movie once again.

Alison stared out into the blackness once more. *Had* she seen something at the window? Finally, she left the den, going through every room in search of Joey. But she already knew he'd gone outside.

The one thing her mother had made them promise not to do. "Remember, I want all of you *inside* the house, all evening. Agreed?" And all of them, including Joey, had agreed. What if he'd broken his promise? Should she call her mother down at Olivia Sherbourne's and tell on him? Or should she just go out herself, find him, and make him come back? But she knew she'd never work up the nerve to go out into the terrifying blackness beyond the house.

Coming to the top of the stairs, she saw light spilling from the crack under Joey's door. She paused uncertainly. Could he have left it on, just to fool her? Scowling, she went to the closed door and knocked. Storm whimpered eagerly in response, his claws scratching at the inside of the door. When there was no answer from Joey, though, she opened the door and peeked in. Storm reared up to lick her face, and Alison gave him a scratch before pushing him aside.

Then she saw Joey.

He was sitting on his bed, his back propped up against the headboard, his face pale, his eyes wide open. For a long time he stared at her and said nothing. At last he spoke, in a cold, flat voice. "I hate her," he said, his words falling from his lips like chips of ice. "She's spying on me, and I hate her."

Bill Sikes moved silently through the darkness outside the house, his senses sharpened, his well-toned muscles carrying him with a lightness and sure step that belied his years. He'd been outside for almost an hour now, just checking on things, like Mrs. Carpenter had asked him to. Not bothering the kids, not even going up to the back door to ask them if they were okay. Just checking around.

The horses were quiet in the barn, and though the night was cold and the light had faded faster than usual beneath the heavy cloud cover, the air was still, the valley peaceful.

He was less than a hundred feet from the barn when he heard one of the horses whinny loudly. The sound was followed by the sharp report of a hoof slamming against one of the wooden walls. Quickening his step, he hurried down to the barn. Inside the cavernous building, he turned on his flashlight.

All three of the horses were shuffling nervously in their stalls, and Bill Sikes spoke to them soothingly, talking steadily as he carefully searched the stable, the tack room and the storage areas, even mounting to the hayloft, where he found nothing but an owl, who hooted softly, then swept out into the night on silent wings.

When he'd finally gotten the horses calmed down, he headed back outside, making sure the barn door was securely latched behind him. He made a circuit of the house, moving silently, staying far enough away from the large log structure that he wouldn't be seen, but close enough that he could easily see in the windows.

All the lights had been turned on, but the rooms were empty, except for the den, where the little boy sprawled on the floor, watching television. Perfectly normal. Nothing wrong.

He'd started back toward his own cabin when it hit him. The certainty that lurking somewhere in the darkness, moving as silently as was he himself, there was another presence. He could feel it, as surely as he could feel the ground beneath his feet.

Feel it hunting him even as he now began hunting it.

He was near the back of the house, making his way slowly toward the stand of trees flanking the creek, when suddenly the quiet of the night was shattered.

A scream rang out, sharp and piercing.

As quickly as it began, it ended, cut off just as it reached its peak.

Bill Sikes froze. Waiting. Listening. But there was no other sound.

He started running toward the back door of the house.

———

Alison stood rooted at the door to Joey's room, waiting for him to speak again, but he said nothing. He lay perfectly still on the bed, staring at her, his face ashen. "W-Who?" Alison finally asked as the silence threatened to overwhelm her. The sound of her own voice breaking her paralysis, she took a step inside. "Who's spying on you, Joey?"

"Aunt MaryAnne," Joey replied after a long silence that made Alison wonder if he'd even heard her.

"Mom?" Alison asked, perplexed. "She wouldn't spy on you. She's not even here. She's—"

Joey spoke again, his voice harsh now. "She was at school today. She was talking to Mrs. Wickman. She was talking about me!"

Alison's first instinct was to back out of the room, go back downstairs, and call her mother. But what would she say? That Joey was acting weird? And what would happen if her mother came home and Joey was just as normal as he'd been a couple of hours ago, when her mother had left? But she had to do something! She stepped farther into the room and closed the door. "What do you mean, she was talking to Mrs. Wickman about you?"

"I saw her," Joey whispered, his eyes still fixed on Alison. But they were no longer the friendly eyes she'd grown used to. Now they had narrowed to slits, taking on a look that almost frightened her.

"S-Saw her when?" Alison stammered.

"Today. I saw her coming out of Mrs. Wickman's office, and I know why she was there."

His words made no sense to Alison. How could he have known why her mother might have been at the school? And if what he was saying were true, and he was as angry as he seemed, why hadn't he said anything earlier? After school, on the way home on the bus, he hadn't been any different from his usual self, and all afternoon he hadn't acted as if anything was wrong. "Joey, did something happen? How come you're mad all of a sudden?"

His hands clenched in his lap, his knuckles turning white. "Why shouldn't I be mad?" he demanded. "After what she did—"

"How do you know she did anything?" Alison broke in. "Maybe she wasn't talking to Mrs. Wickman about you at all. Maybe she wanted to talk to her about Logan, or me."

Joey glared at Alison, every nerve in his body shrieking with the horrible feeling that had come over him half an hour ago. At first he'd tried to ignore it, tried to concentrate on the movie they'd been watching, but it just kept getting worse.

He'd kept looking toward the window, feeling something outside, something that was calling to him. He wanted to go out there, out into the night, out where he'd be free of the confines of the house.

But he'd promised Aunt MaryAnne he'd stay inside, and he didn't want to break his promise. Finally he'd retreated up to his room and lain down on the bed, praying for the awful feeling to pass.

But the terrible feeling grew, a raw tingling that jangled his nerves and made him want to jump out of his skin. And then he'd begun having terrible thoughts.

Thoughts about his aunt. He'd known why she went to see Mrs. Wickman that day. She wanted to find out what was wrong with him. He'd been mad at her when he first saw her, but then he'd gotten over it, and by the time he came home, he'd almost forgotten about it. But ever since he'd come into his room, in the grip of the strange thing that happened to his nerves sometimes, his anger toward her had been building again. Now, as he stared at Alison, he felt a new fury boiling up inside him. A fury toward her. What was she doing here? Why didn't she just go away and leave him alone? "I wish you'd go away," he shouted. "I wish you'd all just go away! I hate all of you!"

Suddenly, he leaped off the bed, hurling himself toward Alison, his hands reaching out for her throat. Instinctively, Alison raised her arms against his attack, a scream rising in her.

A scream that was abruptly cut off as she lost her balance, stumbling backward into the wall. As she struggled to regain her footing, her knee came up, catching Joey's groin as he lurched toward her. Groaning and clutching at his crotch, Joey stumbled backward, and Alison seized the opportunity to dart out of the room, pulling the door closed behind her. She raced down the stairs, coming to the bottom just as there was a loud banging at the kitchen door. She stood still for a second, confused, then Logan came running in from the den.

"What happened?" the boy demanded. Seeing his sister crying, he looked past her up the stairs. "Where's Joey?" he asked. "Did you have a fight with him?"

Sobbing, her mind still reeling from Joey's attack, Alison staggered across the kitchen, forgetting her promise not to open the door for anybody, in her relief that someone—maybe even her mother—had arrived to help her. She jerked open the door, then gasped at the sight of a man in a worn jacket, his dark cap pulled down almost over his eyes, a shotgun clutched in his hands.

"It's okay," Bill Sikes told her, seeing the panic ignite in her eyes. "It's just me." Stepping into the kitchen, Sikes leaned his gun against the wall next to the door, taking in the sight of the sobbing girl, knowing instantly that it was her shrill scream he had heard less than a minute ago. Though she was obviously terrified, it didn't look as if she was hurt. "What is it, Alison?" he asked. "What's going on?"

Alison shook her head helplessly, struggling to speak through her sobs. Finally she managed to choke the words out. "J-Joey . . ." she gasped. "Upstairs . . . he—he was acting—I don't know—it's like he went crazy!"

"Call your mom," Bill Sikes told her. "Call her and tell her to come home. I'll go see what's goin' on with Joey." As Alison stumbled toward the phone, Sikes brushed past Logan and stamped up the stairs. He twisted the knob of Joey's door and pushed inside, having no idea what to expect.

What he found was an empty room.

Both Joey and Storm were gone. The bedroom window stood wide open.

Crossing the room in three quick strides, Sikes pulled his flashlight from the pocket of his jacket and switched it on. Casting the beam from side to side, he played it over the porch roof, just a couple of feet below the window, then searched the area around

the house. As he swept the light out into the field that lay between the house and the woods, he suddenly saw Joey, caught
in the beam like an insect on a pin. Running at full speed, Storm
gamboling ahead of him, Joey was already halfway across the
field, heading straight for the forest.

Cursing under his breath, Bill Sikes raced out of the room and
back down the stairs. He grabbed his shotgun from where he'd
left it by the kitchen door and started after the boy.

CHAPTER 16

*R*ick Martin was just about to let the dog out for the last time that night when the scanner in the kitchen came alive and he heard the dispatcher's voice from the sheriff's department in Challis, the county seat. "Unit 72–Sugarloaf, I have a report of a missing child at El Monte Ranch, end of Coyote Creek Road. Please investigate." Her voice changed, shifting out of its impersonally official mode. "Tony, what's going on up there? First a DOA and a critical injury, now this!"

His dog forgotten, Rick Martin hurried into the den of the little house on Pocatello Drive that he and Gillie had bought five years earlier, and switched on his radio. "Dispatch, this is Unit 71–Sugarloaf. I'll take the missing child myself. Seventy-two, are you copying?"

"I'm already on my way, Rick," Tony Moleno replied. "Any idea what's going on?"

"I know I don't like it," Martin told him, remembering the strange lab report indicating that some unknown creature was prowling in the mountains above the valley, but unwilling to talk about it over the airwaves. "I'm bringing my dog. Call Frank Peters and have him bring his hounds up, too. Do we know who's missing?"

"Joseph Wilkenson," the dispatcher replied. "Age thirteen, about five feet tall, brown hair—"

"I know what Joey looks like," Martin cut in. "We all do. I'll see you up there, Tony. Seventy-one–Sugarloaf, standing by."

Gillie followed him into the bedroom as he began changing back into his uniform, pulling on a pair of long johns before donning his pants and shirt. "I'm coming with you," she announced in a tone that said she would brook no opposition. Still, Rick felt constrained to try.

"What's the point? This could be a long night, and there's no point in your—"

"Sitting up, waiting to hear what's happening?" Gillie finished for him. "Thanks, but no thanks. At least if I'm up at El Monte, I'll know what's happening. Besides, I can give MaryAnne Carpenter a hand. If she's going to have a search party headquartered there, she's going to need all the help she can get." While Rick finished dressing, she went to the kitchen, found an empty shopping bag, and started filling it with provisions: the searchers would need sustenance. By the time Rick was ready to go, she already had her jacket on.

"King! Car!" Rick ordered, opening the back door. The big police dog that had been stretched out in front of the kitchen sink, warily watching the goings-on, pricked up his ears. His tail high, he bounded out the back door, then pranced impatiently until Rick let him into the backseat of the black-and-white Jeep. Not bothering with lights or siren, Rick sped away from the house, switching on the radio and picking up its microphone with one hand as he spun the car onto Main Street with the other.

"Will you slow down?" Gillie complained, though she knew it would do no good. "How can you help out with Joey if you wreck the car before we even get there?"

As they left town, and Main Street curved slightly to the right as it became Coyote Creek Road, Rick pulled into the left lane to pass a Nissan sedan. "Shit," he muttered as he recognized Milt Morgenstern's car. "Where's he think he's going?"

"Now, I wonder," Gillie mused with exaggerated sarcasm. "Let's see—he's the editor of the paper, and he's got a police scanner, and there was just a report that Joey Wilkenson is missing." She shook her head. "Nope, it's too deep for me—he's probably just out for a ride!"

Rick glanced at his wife sourly. "Smart-ass."

"Come on, hon. He's just doing his job, the same as you're doing yours."

"I guess," Rick sighed. "Just try to keep him away from me, okay? He's been on me all day about the lab report on Foster, and I've been dodging him."

Gillie's teasing smile vanished. "Why? Is there something in the report you don't want him to know about?"

Rick realized his mistake too late, but there was no way Gillie would let him off the hook now. As they approached the gate marking the entrance to El Monte Ranch, he quickly told her what the lab in Boise had come up with. "It's got to be some kind of snafu," he finished. "But unless Tamara Reynolds remembers something she hasn't told me about, and I know what really attacked Foster, I don't see any reason to let Milt Morgenstern cause a panic around here."

Gillie said nothing for a moment, then: "What if it's not a mistake, Rick? What if it's something—" She hesitated, then went on. "Well, what if it really is something no one's ever seen before?"

Rick pulled the squad car to a stop in front of the large log house at the end of the drive. He switched off the ignition and turned to face Gillie. "I don't believe in crap like Sasquatches or

Snowmen, and neither do you," he said. "So let's just leave that kind of garbage out of this, okay?"

"But—"

"Not a word!" Getting out of the car, he released King from the backseat, then strode up to the front porch and rapped sharply on the door.

Olivia Sherbourne opened it a few seconds later, standing aside to let the deputy and his wife in. "Everyone's in the kitchen."

MaryAnne Carpenter, her face pale, was sitting between her two children, an arm wrapped protectively around each of them. Across from her, taking notes, was Tony Moleno, and Charley Hawkins was leaning against the counter, listening intently. As Gillie tried to smile encouragingly at MaryAnne, Moleno filled Rick in on what had happened.

"Has anyone checked on Sikes's cabin?" Rick asked. "If he found Joey, and the boy was still acting strange, he might not have wanted to bring him back here."

"I checked," Olivia Sherbourne replied. "That's the first place I looked. No one's there, and if he came back now, he couldn't miss all the cars out in front—he'd be bound to come to the house."

Rick grunted his agreement, his one hope for a quick resolution of Joey's disappearance evaporating. When there was another loud knock at the front door, his expression hardened. "That'll be Milt Morgenstern," he warned. "Gillie and I passed him on the way up here. I'd appreciate it if all of you would say as little as possible right now. Just tell him the kids had a fight and Joey took off. I don't see any point in telling him Joey was acting strange." His eyes shifted to Alison, who sat huddled against her mother, her eyes still red from her tears, her complexion pale. "Think you can do that, Alison? I'm not asking you to lie—just don't tell him any more than you have to."

Alison hesitated, then made up her mind. "How about if I just go up to my room?" she asked. "Then I wouldn't have to talk to him at all."

"Perfect," Rick said. "How about you, Logan? I know how hard it is to keep a story as good as this one a secret, but it's important."

"I won't say anything," Logan promised. Then: "Can I go help look for Joey with you?"

Rick Martin made a show of considering the idea, then shook his head. "You could help me more by staying here and taking care of your mother. Could you do that for me?"

Though looking slightly crestfallen, Logan agreed, and by the time Olivia let Milt Morgenstern in, Alison had disappeared upstairs. The editor listened to the simple story Rick Martin had concocted, then zeroed in on Bill Sikes's absence. "You're sure he's out looking for Joey?"

"Both the kids saw him go," Rick Martin replied. "Isn't that right, Logan?"

Logan gazed steadily up at the newspaper editor. "He's the one who found out Joey wasn't in his room. He heard Joey and Alison yelling at each other, and came in to find out what they were fighting about. And when he went up to talk to Joey, Joey was gone."

Before Morgenstern could press the matter any further, Frank Peters arrived, his three bloodhounds barking from the back of his pickup truck. The question of exactly what had happened in the house was forgotten as Martin began organizing the search. With luck, they would find Joey and Bill Sikes together and on the way back to the ranch, but as they set out, Rick Martin had a clear feeling that tonight they were not going to have any luck.

He only prayed that they would find the boy and the caretaker still alive.

———

Bill Sikes moved steadily up the twisting trail, his breath only now becoming labored. He'd been away from the house for at

least half an hour—maybe more—and most of the tracking had
been uphill. Following Joey across the field had been easy: the
boy's footprints were clear in the soft ground, and even without
the tracks, the trampled grass where his feet had fallen made a
clear trail. But when he'd come to the woods, it had immediately
become more difficult. At the spot where Joey had disappeared
into the thick stand of lodgepole pines, there were no apparent
trails at all. Yet Sikes had had little trouble following the boy,
for Joey had still been running here, and every time his foot
struck the ground, it left a deep heel print and disturbed the
carpet of pine needles. Though his pace had slowed from what
it had been across the field, Sikes was still able to move rapidly.

The land was no longer level. A hundred yards into the stand
of trees, the floor of the valley had given way to the beginning
of the mountainside. Here, though, Joey had stumbled onto a
trail and begun following it. It was a hiking path—wide, and
clear of pine needles—and if it hadn't been for yesterday's rain,
Sikes surely would have lost the boy's trail completely. But the
rain had melted the hard-packed earth into sticky mud, and Joey
had run straight up the center of it, leaving deep footprints with
every step.

As he followed the trail up the mountain, Sikes broke into a
run: he was gaining on Joey; he had to be. But then the trail had
forked, and Joey had apparently taken the upper path, a much
steeper and narrower track.

Sikes's progress slowed significantly when portions of the trail
led over wide patches of bare granite, the only sign of Joey's
passage the clods of mud that dropped from his shoes.

For the last ten minutes Sikes had been moving on instinct
alone, for the terrain had changed once again. The path threaded
through a maze of immense boulders, some of them heaved up
when the mountains had been formed millennia ago, others
forced down from above by glaciation during the last ice age.
Here, the topsoil had long ago been ripped away, scoured out by

the advancing ice, the naked stone of the glacial moraine kept barren of any growth by the constant winds that swept down from the peaks above.

It was here that Bill Sikes finally paused, his heart pounding now, his breath coming in gasps after the long climb.

And yet he wasn't even to the timberline yet. Far beyond the great rampart that loomed above him, the thick forest of pines still climbed steadily upward.

Could Joey be up there somewhere, moving through the trees?

Sikes didn't know—couldn't know—for there was no longer any way of tracking the boy.

"Joey?" he called out, his voice sounding tiny in the vast reaches of the mountains. "Joey, where are you?"

He held his breath as he listened for even the faintest reply, but there was none, and finally he began breathing again, filling his lungs with the cold night air, taking one deep breath after another as his pulse began to slow and his panting eased.

Suddenly he stiffened.

Had he heard something? He froze, holding his breath once more, straining his ears.

Seconds crept by.

Long seconds of silence, unbroken by any noise except a sudden gust of wind blowing through the trees at the top of the great granite rampart.

And yet, despite the silence, Bill Sikes was suddenly sure he was no longer alone.

The same sensation that had come over him earlier, that had brought him to the perimeter of the house, was upon him once more, setting his nerves on edge, making the hairs on the back of his neck stand on end, setting his skin to tingling.

Something was out there in the darkness, not far away, watching him.

Joey?

But if it was Joey, why wouldn't the boy have answered his call?

Apprehension growing, unable to believe that Joey would have kept climbing through the massive boulders—difficult enough in the full light of day, and almost impossible at night without so much as a flashlight to guide him—Bill Sikes started back down the way he'd come.

Somewhere, before he'd reached this desolate area of upthrust rock, he must have lost the trail. Joey must have taken another direction, Sikes decided, must have found a path that he had failed to notice.

He worked his way back through the boulders, every one of his senses on the alert now, pausing every few steps to listen, expecting with each new turn in the narrow track to come face to face with—what?

A bear?

Not a bear. He would have heard the sound of a bear's claws scratching on the rocks as it moved, heard it snuffling and grunting, heard the rattle of small stones as it pawed them aside while it searched for tiny creatures that might be hiding beneath them.

He moved out of the moraine, back into the more open area of the forest, breathing easier here, where he wasn't trapped between massive boulders that would prevent him from fleeing an attack.

He continued downhill, keeping to the path, switching on the light every few seconds to examine the area next to the trail, searching for any signs that Joey had veered off, heading either up the mountainside or, more likely, back down toward the valley floor far below.

He was crouching, studying a disturbance in the soil a foot off the track, when he heard it.

Though it was barely audible, the snarl of an invisible creature nevertheless sent a jolt of fear down his spine. He froze, listening for it to be repeated, but the silence of the mountains closed around him once again. Even the wind of a few moments ago had died away, and now the quiet had taken on an eerie quality.

Sikes unslung the shotgun from his shoulder, flipped the safety off, and pumped a cartridge out of the magazine and into the firing chamber. He swept the area with the now-dimming beam of the flashlight, shutting it off when it revealed nothing. For a moment he was blind in the near pitch-blackness of the night, but then he realized that the cloud cover had thinned and there was a silvery glow of moonlight above. Certainly not enough for him to make out any details of the surrounding forest, but just enough that, by looking upward, he could see the break in the trees that marked the trail.

Now, though, as he moved through the darkness, he could hear something else moving, too.

Off to the right he could make out a faint rustling sound, a sound that stopped abruptly just a split second after he himself stopped moving. When he set out again, the same soft rustling drifted once more through the trees.

From the left, up the hill, he heard a soft sound, almost like a whistle.

A bird?

Perhaps a man . . .

Sikes froze, listening.

The rustling sound didn't stop this time, but grew nearer.

An animal, stalking him, moving closer and closer.

He switched on the flashlight, playing its weak beam through the tree trunks, finally holding it on a clump of brush ten yards away.

A clump of brush large enough, and thick enough, to conceal even the great bulk of a grizzly.

The rustling stopped as Sikes trained the light on the brush. He'd discovered his stalker.

Now the prey would become the hunter.

Silently dropping to his knees, he placed the flashlight on the ground, its beam, failing rapidly now, still focused on the mass of shrubbery. He raised the gun to his shoulder, gripped it firmly, and slowly pulled the trigger.

The attack came just as the gun fired.

As a roar of sound burst from the barrel and a load of heavy shot spewed from its muzzle, the gun flew out of Bill Sikes's hands as something pounced on him from behind, its weight flattening him to the ground, the shotgun pressed beneath his body.

An instinctive scream rose inside him, cut off before a sound escaped his lips, for before the air in his lungs could pass his vocal cords, his larynx was torn from his throat, and the huge artery carrying blood from his heart to his brain was ripped to shreds.

Bill Sikes died without uttering his final scream of terror.

———

The single report echoed back and forth across the valley. Frank Peters reached down and unsnapped the leashes that held his three bloodhounds in check. Giving them one last whiff of the shirt MaryAnne had brought from Joey's room, he spoke sharply to the trio of dogs. "Go get him! Go!" Baying with joy at being released from their constraints, the hounds raced ahead, quickly disappearing into the darkness. But as Peters, followed by Rick Martin, Tony Moleno, and Olivia Sherbourne—who had insisted on coming along despite Rick's strongest arguments—continued climbing up the trail through the pine forest, he knew there was no chance of losing the hounds. As long as they were on the scent, they would keep baying. In the event they lost it, the tone of their howling would instantly change as they began ranging around, searching for the lost scent, never giving up until he caught up with them and reattached their leads to drag them away. Even if their quarry went into a river, the hounds would keep on, splashing back and forth through the water, searching both banks, dashing up and down the river, constantly searching.

A few minutes later the baying did, indeed, change its tone, but not to the note of frustration that Frank Peters anticipated. Rather, it was the excited bark the dogs emitted when they'd succeeded in tracking down, and treeing, their prey. "Let's go," he said, heaving his heavy frame into a trot. "They've got something!"

It took them nearly ten minutes to catch up with the dogs. When they finally did, what they found was not what they were expecting. As Peters shined his flashlight on the object that had so completely distracted his dogs from their job, he stopped dead in his tracks, swearing softly. "Holy shit," he breathed. "Look at that."

Olivia Sherbourne, caught on the trail behind the three men, elbowed past them, terrified that she was about to see Joey Wilkenson's corpse spread out on the ground.

She stared instead at the body of Bill Sikes, his heavy jacket ripped from the collar downward, the flesh of his back shredded, his head twisted at an odd angle, connected to his body only by a few ligaments and some torn muscle. Though she knew he was dead, still she dropped to her knees, automatically feeling his wrist for a pulse.

"What the hell could have done that?" Frank Peters whispered, eyes fastened on the body in frozen fascination as his dogs, finally abandoning their examination of the corpse, gathered around his legs, whimpering eagerly.

Rick Martin and Tony Moleno, though, already knew the answer.

The marks on Bill Sikes's body were almost identical to the ones they'd seen on Glen Foster's corpse only a couple of nights ago.

Whatever was roaming the mountains above Sugarloaf had just struck again.

"Okay," Rick Martin sighed. "Here's what we're going to do. I don't want anything touched until the guys from Boise can get up here tomorrow. I don't want any footprints disturbed, I don't want Sikes's body moved—nothing. If there are any clues about what happened up here, I want them exactly in place tomorrow morning. Tony, how do you feel about staying up all night again?"

Moleno shrugged. "I survived the other night—guess I'll make it through tonight, too."

"Okay. Build a fire, and watch your ass." He shifted his attention to Frank Peters. "Any chance of getting your dogs back on the scent?"

Peters spread his hands helplessly. "I can try, but I don't know." For the next twenty minutes, he led the dogs around the perimeter of the area where Bill Sikes had been found, staying well away from the body itself, partly to keep the hounds from being distracted by the fresh blood, partly to avoid disturbing the killing ground.

But the hounds failed to pick up Joey Wilkenson's scent. It was as if he'd simply vanished into the blackness of the night.

CHAPTER 17

*T*he light of the rising sun crept down the rugged slopes of the mountains, diffused by the leaden sky so that the slow shift from the blackness of night to the gray of morning seemed to have no source at all. Slowly, out of the darkness emerged the ghostly forms of the great jutting cliffs and the towering trees that flowed down from the timberline to the valley below.

Joey Wilkenson, sleep finally beginning to release him from its tight embrace, snuggled deeper into the bed, fighting off the slow wakening of his mind and body. As the cold of the morning seeped into his body, he closed his fingers on the covers to draw them closer around him. But something was wrong—instead of the soft down of his familiar comforter, he felt something rough in his fingers. He came instantly awake; his eyes blinked open. He was lying on his side, and the first thing he saw was a window.

A window with no glass in its empty frame.

A window that shouldn't be there, for in his room at home, he could see no window when he was lying on his left side. His pulse quickened as he suddenly realized the bed in which he'd slept was not his own. Every muscle in his body ached, not just from the cold—which seemed to penetrate deeper within his very bones with each passing second, but from an unaccustomed stiffness, as well. Joey sat up, and the animal hide with which he had been covered fell away, leaving him shivering as the cold wind from the window struck his naked chest.

Where was he?

Why wasn't he at home?

He tried to remember what had happened last night. It began to come back to him in bits and pieces.

The feeling had come over him last night.

The terrible nervous feeling.

The urge to run out into the night.

The voice he'd heard calling out to him, whispering his name.

He'd tried to shut it out. But the harder he tried not to hear it, the more persistent the voice became.

He'd started wondering if this time he was actually going to go crazy, and that thought had scared him even more than the terrifying things happening to his mind and his body.

What if it never went away this time?

What if he had to spend the rest of his life feeling like this?

They'd lock him up. They'd put him in a hospital with all the crazy people, and never let him out again.

His emotions had fed on each other then, and he could feel himself sinking into a dark pit with a monster waiting for him at the bottom—a terrifying monster, which would suddenly attack him, coming out of nowhere, twisting its tentacles around him like a choking vine from which there would be no escape.

Finally the whole turmoil in his mind had congealed into rage, and he yelled at Aunt MaryAnne when she came looking for him.

No! He hadn't yelled at Aunt MaryAnne at all. It had been Alison who had come to his room, not Aunt MaryAnne!

His memory was getting fuzzy again, and he had to struggle to remember it all. Alison had come to his room. Why? And why had he been so mad at her?

He tried to remember what she'd said to him, but his mind failed him. But he did remember lying on the bed, staring at her, hating her. . . .

Hating *Alison*?

But that was crazy! He didn't hate Alison. He *liked* her. In fact, he liked her more than anyone he'd ever met. Yesterday morning, when she'd taken his hand, he felt wonderful, as if no matter what anyone said about him or how they treated him, it would be all right as long as Alison was next to him, holding his hand.

And then last night he'd said things to her—terrible things—things about her mother, and even about her. Snatches of it came back to him now.

. . . *wish you'd go away . . . wish you'd* all *go away . . . hate . . . all of you!*

He'd gotten off the bed, and he'd—

Oh, Jesus! He'd attacked Alison!

Except he hadn't! Not really! He wouldn't have!

But as he sat on the hard bed in the icy room, he knew that he had. He'd run at her, to put his hands around her neck and squeeze.

And keep squeezing.

But why? She hadn't done anything to him! She'd just been trying to talk to him, to find out what was wrong, to help him!

And he'd tried to kill her!

But she'd gotten away from him! He shoved her, and she fell against the wall, and—

All he remembered was a terrible searing pain, and then he'd been outside, running. Storm had been with him, and it had been very dark, and yet despite the blackness of the night, he'd been able to see.

See almost as clearly as if it was daytime.

Yet his memory after he'd left the house was nothing more than flickering images, images he could barely grasp before they flitted away again, skittering out of his reach before he could quite examine them.

Where was he? Wrapping the animal skin around himself, he went to the open door and peered out. He frowned. The clearing looked familiar, and when he finally went outside and turned to look at the crumbling cabin in which he'd passed the night, he had the certain feeling that he'd been here before.

When?

He went back into the cabin, his mind puzzling at the question, and suddenly he knew.

Day before yesterday.

Tuesday afternoon, when he had gone up to Coyote Creek Campground with Alison and Logan. Storm had smelled something, and gone off after it, and he followed. It hadn't seemed like they'd been gone very long, but when he got home it was a lot later than he thought it should have been.

Was this where he'd come? He gazed curiously around the cabin, stared at the single chair that stood next to a rough-surfaced table made of curling pine planks. There was an ancient cast-iron stove with a large kettle on it, a counter on which there were some badly chipped plates and mugs, and a few worn-looking clothes hanging from rusty nails hammered into the walls. So someone lived here, even if there wasn't any glass in the windows and the door barely shut. He looked at the windows once again, and discovered that there were shutters on the outside, shutters that could be pulled closed, and bolted. Once he'd secured them, he went to the stove, found the remnants of a barely smoldering fire, and added three pieces of wood to it from the box against the wall.

Under the counter, there was a lantern, an old kerosene one, but its wick was trimmed and its chimney clean. Yet if someone lived here, where was he?

And where was Storm?

He went to the door once more, whistled, and a moment later Storm appeared, slinking out of the underbrush, only to stop when he was still ten yards away from the cabin, dropping nervously to his haunches.

Joey frowned at the dog's behavior, then called out to him. "Come on, Storm! It's okay, boy!" The dog didn't move, but only whimpered anxiously. "Storm, come!" Joey commanded.

Still the dog didn't move from where he sat, but his body stiffened and he began quivering with nervousness. Scowling at the shepherd, Joey turned away, went back into the cabin, and set about searching for his clothes.

He finally found them, piled in the corner of the cabin's single room, and picked them up.

A strange, sharp odor filled his nose, and he carried the clothing to the bed, puzzled. Only when he shook them out did he understand.

Everywhere, dark stains covered his clothes.

Bloodstains.

Still wet, still sticky.

Where had they come from?

Had he done something? Something he couldn't even remember? He must have! If he hadn't, why were his clothes stained? Seizing them, he hurried to the stove where the wood he'd added had begun to sprout flames, and stuffed the clothing inside, slamming the door shut as soon as the bloodied material began to singe.

Terrified by the thoughts that now swirled through his mind, his eyes darted frantically around the cabin like those of a trapped animal. He had to get out! Get out now!

Shoving his bare feet into the pair of shoes that sat on the floor next to the bed, but with nothing to protect him from the cold of the morning except the animal skin beneath which he'd slept, he fled out the front door, Storm finally leaving his post to dash after him as he started down the trail. The horrible knowledge of what he must have done during the night building in his mind, yet having no clear memory at all of actually having done it, Joey charged down the mountainside, slipping and sliding on the stony trail, one hand holding the fur blanket around his naked shoulders as he used the other one to steady himself when he lost his footing. As he came into the forest and the path leveled out, he slowed. The cabin was now well out of sight. But what if someone found him up here? He left the trail, moving off into the shelter of the woods, then paralleled it, keeping his tread light.

He had gone perhaps a mile when he sensed something up ahead. He paused, listening, but heard nothing. Yet when he sniffed at the air, there was a trace of a scent.

A familiar scent.

Then he recognized it. The barely perceptible odor in the air was the same one he had whiffed back in the cabin, when he'd picked up his wadded clothes.

The scent of blood.

Now that same pungent sharpness was filling his nostrils again.

He began moving through the woods once more, careful to keep his tread absolutely silent. Storm, sensing his master's sudden fear, pressed close to him, his hackles rising.

Joey moved from tree to tree, the scent growing ever stronger. Finally, leaving the shelter of a large white-barked pine, he scuttled over to a clump of underbrush, dropped the animal skin that was his only protection from the chill air, and lay down on his belly to begin crawling forward through the shrubbery, toward the source of the coppery odor that lay just beyond. He worked his way through the tangle of vegetation, moving slowly, Storm at his side. At last he paused. Through a small gap in the leaves, he could make out the figure of a man seated on the ground, his back against a tree. A shotgun lay across his lap, and his head was tipped forward on his chest as he dozed. The head jerked as the man came suddenly awake, and Joey froze.

Had the man heard him?

But no—the man was simply struggling to stay awake, the way he himself sometimes did in the classroom, especially on the mornings after those nights when the nervousness had seized him and he'd been unable to sleep.

The man stood up, and now Joey recognized him.

Tony Moleno, his uniform rumpled from his night in the woods, his eyes puffy from lack of sleep. He stretched, then moved away from the tree, and as Joey's eyes followed the deputy's movements, he saw the source of the pungent odor that had caught his attention a few minutes before.

His eyes widened as he gazed at the body that still lay on the ground.

The body that Tony Moleno must have been guarding all night long, just as he had guarded the body of Glen Foster only two nights earlier.

Suddenly Joey was glad there had been nothing left to see when he and Alison and Logan had gone up to the campground the other day, for now, from his vantage point in the underbrush, he could stare right into Bill Sikes's face.

Stare at his dead eyes.

Stare at the gaping wound from which his blood must have poured.

Another image flickered in his head.

An image of the stains on his clothes came suddenly into his mind, as his eyes fastened on Sikes's face, and he imagined blood spewing from the great tear in his neck.

The two images fused in Joey's mind as his heart pounded heavily.

Could he have done this?

Was it possible?

Barely able to suppress the cry that rose in his throat, he began wriggling away, threading feet first back the way he'd come, until at last he was free from the underbrush. Shivering, his teeth chattering not only from the cold, but from the memory of what he'd seen—and the terror at what he might have done—he wrapped himself in the bearskin, clutching it tightly around his body.

A sob threatening to cut off his breathing completely, he stumbled on down the mountain, the trail now forgotten.

All he could think of—the single imperative that filled his soul and drove him onward—was his need to flee.

But even as he fled down the mountainside, he knew that no matter how far he ran, or where he finally went, the image of Bill Sikes's dead face—his vacant eyes staring straight at him, accusing him—would never leave him.

That image was burned in his mind forever, etched so deeply it would haunt him for the rest of his life. He would never be able to wipe it away.

Except, he realized, there *was* a way to erase that image from his consciousness, a way to escape not only from the vision of the dead man, but from the terror of the times when the nervousness came on him, making him want to flee.

There was a way, he realized, that he could escape it all.

Now he formed another image in his head.

An image of the cliff from which his mother had plunged less than two weeks ago.

But could he actually do it? Could he bring himself to stand at the top of the cliff, look down, and jump?

CHAPTER 18

"It's seven A.M., and this is Sugarloaf Sam, greeting the morning and lifting your spirits from now until ten! It's a cold morning in the Sugarloaf Valley, and promising to get colder before it gets warmer. Good news for the skiers, bad news for the farmers, but as Honest Abe Lincoln used to say, you can please some of the people some of the time, and some of the people all of the time, and none of the people some of the—all right, so that's not what he said, but you know what I mean! You *know* what I mean! And here we go with the first cut of the day!"

Sam Gilman hit the play button on the console in front of him, and the Montovani Strings began playing "Summertime," which struck Sam as absolutely appropriate for the unseasonably cold September morning. It was his station—all five watts of it—and if the audience didn't like it, that was their problem, not his. He swiveled around on the chair that took up nearly all the available floor space in the one-room studio, and began checking over the list of "guest hosts" his tiny radio station would be broadcasting that day. Arne Svenson was coming in for an hour starting at ten, to talk about getting cars ready for winter. Nearly everyone in town would be tuning in for that one. Though Arne had been running Sugarloaf's only gas station for nearly thirty years, his Swedish accent was still so thick as to make what he said nearly unintelligible, so he always brought his wife, Naomi, along to translate, and Naomi never failed to contradict everything Arne said. By the end of the hour they would appear to be on the verge of divorce, and then Arne would grab the mike. "Yust bring da damn car in!" he'd bellow. "I do it all for nuttin'!"

The rest of the day would be much the same, for Sam Gilman let pretty much anyone who had something he wanted to talk about come in and take over the mike for an hour or so. On days when no one wanted to talk, there were plenty of tapes for him to play. In a pinch, he had a few tapes that could run up to eight hours, and no one would ever be the wiser. But the kind of programming he loved best was the sort of unpredictability he got by inviting the townspeople to come in and unburden themselves. As long as what they had to say wasn't obscene or patently offensive to any particular minority (Sam's policy allowed for pretty much any kind of offensiveness to an *individual*), Sam liked people to speak their minds whether they agreed with him or not. Indeed, he had taken to running the disclaimer announcement stating that the opinions of the speaker did not necessarily reflect those of the station or its owner, even when he himself was on the air. When asked about that little ploy, he always replied that he often found himself in violent disagreement with his own thoughts, and was merely protecting himself from the possibility of "suing his own ass from here to Boise." Sam Gilman's methods of running his station hadn't made him much of a profit, but they certainly kept the town tuned in.

Thus, when Sam swung around on his chair and saw Milt Morgenstern, his eyes red, peering through the glass panel in the tiny studio's door, he immediately sensed that Milt had something he felt was too hot to hold for the next edition of the paper, which wouldn't come out until tomorrow. He waved the editor and publisher in, grinning mischievously. "You know, you and I could set up a media cartel around here, if we wanted to. Between us, we could have absolute mind control over this town. If we set our minds to it, we could probably elect a moose as mayor." Milt failed to respond to Sam's attempt at humor, and the broadcaster's grin faded. "Something going on, Milt?"

"We've got another killing," Milt told him. "And something's not looking right, and not smelling right."

The last traces of Sam Gilman's grin disappeared. "You mean it's the same as the one up at the campground?" he asked, slipping one of his tapes into the second player and pressing the start button just as the last chords of "Summertime" faded away.

"You got it," the editor replied. While the tape began to play, he told Sam what had happened the night before, from the moment he'd heard Rick Martin start organizing a search party until the deputy, together with Olivia Sherbourne, had returned to El Monte Ranch with the report of Bill Sikes's death. "The thing that really bothers me is that he didn't want me to go up there." Morgenstern's eyes hardened as they met Sam Gilman's. "I mean, he didn't want me at the ranch, he didn't want me to go along when they went out searching for Joey Wilkenson, and he sure didn't want me going up to take a look at the body."

Gilman's lips curved into a knowing smile. "Which I assume means that you went up there anyway."

"I couldn't," Morgenstern replied. "The son of a bitch wouldn't even tell me where it was."

"So what do you think's going on?" Sam asked, already sensing a major story brewing, one that could keep the phone lines ringing all day and get every radio in town tuned to his station as the news began to spread. "How come Martin's playing it so coy?"

"Have you seen the pictures of the man who was killed up there?" Morgenstern asked pointedly. When Gilman shook his head, the editor reached into the inside pocket of the heavily lined Gortex jacket he'd worn against the unseasonable cold and pulled out three photographs. "What do you think might have done that?" he asked as he handed them to Sam Gilman.

Gilman felt a touch of nausea as he studied the pictures, quickly returning them to Morgenstern. "I don't even want to think about it."

"Well, the lab in Boise doesn't know," Morgenstern replied. "I called them yesterday afternoon, and a guy named Hank Henry got real cute with me. So I called back, pretending to be—" He hesitated, catching himself just before blurting out the truth that he'd impersonated the county sheriff. "Let's just say I got some information." He paused, building the drama of the moment. "They don't know what killed him, Sam. They say it wasn't human, and it wasn't any kind of animal they can identify."

Sam Gilman felt a thrill of excitement. "You ready to go on the air with that?" he asked.

"Why do you think I'm here?" Morgenstern replied.

Squeezing an extra stool into the tiny studio, Sam Gilman handed Milt Morgenstern a set of headphones, checked the sound level on the microphone his guest would use, then cheerfully cut into the still-playing tape in the middle of Barbra Streisand's nasal wailing of "Memory."

"We seem to have a major problem here in Sugarloaf," he announced, carefully pitching his voice to its most sonorous level. "Milt Morgenstern just came in, and I'm going to let him tell you about it." He nodded to the editor, who leaned closer to the microphone.

"Bill Sikes, the caretaker of El Monte Ranch, and a man I always called a friend, was killed last night, apparently the latest victim of whatever it was that killed a camper in Coyote Creek Campground on Monday night."

"You say 'whatever it was,' Milt," Sam Gilman smoothly interrupted. "Does that mean there's some question about what might be up there?"

The editor's lips curved into a tight smile as he lit the fuse to his bombshell. "I'd say there definitely is, Sam," he replied. "All I can tell you is that we know it's not human, and it's not any kind of animal any of us have ever seen. In fact, from what I've been told by sources in Boise, it's not any kind of animal they can even identify. All they can say is what it's not. And it's not a bear, or a mountain lion, or anything else we normally think of as being in our mountains. But it's very large, and very strong, and very vicious."

To the satisfaction of both men, the term "Sasquatch" came up in the very first phone call. Within minutes all three lines coming into the studio had lit up. By saying as little as possible, and emphasizing Rick Martin's refusal to talk to Morgenstern, Sam Gilman and Milt Morgenstern quickly fanned the small spark of mystery supplied by the crime lab in Boise into a full-fledged panic.

———

MaryAnne Carpenter's bones were starting to ache from exhaustion. Nearly overcome by weariness, she nevertheless refused to surrender.

Not until Joey comes home, she whispered silently to herself as she began preparing yet another of the many pots of coffee she and Gillie Martin had brewed throughout the night.

It had become almost a mantra, which she endlessly repeated to herself as her eyes, puffy now from lack of sleep, began to sting, and her arms and legs began to feel oddly numb.

I won't go to bed—not until Joey comes home.

Sometime around three that morning, still in the throes of shock at the news of Bill Sikes's death, she'd made up her mind that tomorrow—perhaps even tonight, if the search party found Joey—she would pack up the children and drive to Boise to catch the first plane back to New Jersey. Better to go back—even back to Alan—than to try to cope with the horrors of what was happening here. Finally, as dawn broke in Idaho, knowing that Alan would be waking up anyway, she'd picked up the phone and called him.

She'd listened numbly when, instead of hearing Alan's voice, she'd heard a woman's voice. A wrong number, she thought; I must have misdialed. But something compelled her to ask for Alan. "He's asleep," she was told. Then: "Who is this?" She'd stared mutely at the phone for a moment, finally hanging up without saying anything more. So he'd moved someone in, and now she no longer had a home to go back to!

The hours had worn agonizingly on, with only occasional word from Rick Martin through the extra radio Gillie had brought in from the squad car. MaryAnne had felt fatigue bearing down on her like a physical weight, slowing her step, making it harder and harder to keep moving around the kitchen, fixing the sandwiches the searchers—seven of them now—used to fuel their stores of energy.

If they can do it, I can do it, she kept telling herself.

At six-thirty she'd gone upstairs to awaken the children. Alison was already up and dressed. "I didn't sleep very well," she admitted, and from the look of her daughter's reddened eyes, MaryAnne was fairly certain she hadn't slept at all.

Logan's first words when MaryAnne woke him up were to ask if Joey was back, and when MaryAnne shook her head, Logan had voiced the question that MaryAnne had refused to think about all night: "Is he dead?"

"No," MaryAnne had replied instantly, knowing even as she spoke the word that the wish was father to the thought. And yet she knew, deep down inside her, that somewhere up in the mountains, Joey *was* still alive.

But how had he managed to elude Frank Peters's hounds?

It was as if Joey had vanished from the mountainside, disappearing like a wraith into the night.

Now both the children were at the kitchen table, wolfing down the pancakes Gillie Martin had fixed for them, and MaryAnne was counting scoops of coffee into the basket at the top of the enormous restaurant-sized percolator she had found on the top shelf of the pantry behind the kitchen. She had just measured the last scoop when a flicker of movement far across the field caught her eye, and her pulse began to race.

Joey!

It had to be Joey!

She hurried to the back door, jerking it open, expecting to see the boy running across the field, only realizing as she stepped out into the yard that what she'd seen wasn't Joey at all.

It was Storm, standing at the edge of the forest. MaryAnne called out to him, but instead of breaking into a run toward her, the dog turned and disappeared back into the trees.

Joey! she thought. He had to be with Storm—he had to be! Surely the dog wouldn't leave his master in the middle of the wilderness. Wheeling around, she dashed back into the house. "How long before Rick gets back here?" she asked Gillie Martin.

"Maybe ten minutes," Gillie replied, staring in puzzlement at MaryAnne. "He said—"

"Let me have the radio," MaryAnne cut in. "Show me how to work it, and stay with the kids." She began to shove her arms into the sleeves of the jacket that had been hanging by the back door.

"Where are you going?" Gillie asked, alarmed.

"Storm is out there," MaryAnne told her. "He's in the woods on the other side of the field. Joey must be there, too! Don't you see? Storm wouldn't come back without him!"

Gillie Martin was about to argue with her, to urge her to wait until Rick got back, but even before she spoke, she realized that if she were in MaryAnne's place, she would do exactly what the other woman was doing. She picked up the small radio, handing it to MaryAnne. "All you have to do is press the button on the side and speak into the mike. It's already set on the same frequency as Rick's radio. But be careful what you say," she cautioned as MaryAnne started out the door. "Quite a few people in town have scanners, and every one of them will be listening in."

As MaryAnne started purposefully across the yard, Gillie closed the door and turned to Alison and Logan, who were still sitting at the table, worriedly watching through the window as their mother ran across the yard. "It's going to be all right," she assured them, sounding a lot more confident than she felt. Though she said nothing to the children, she was almost certain that if Storm led MaryAnne to anything at all, it would not be to Joey.

In all likelihood, the best MaryAnne could hope to find would be the boy's dead body.

————

MaryAnne climbed over the fence, terrified that by the time she got to the woods, Storm would be gone, vanishing into the trees long before she could catch up. Still, the thrill of at last being able to take an active part in the search for Joey caused a rush of adrenaline to surge through her blood, washing away the exhaustion and giving her a burst of energy that allowed her to break into a run. She was three-quarters of the way across the field when she spotted the shepherd again, barely visible in the trees, pacing nervously as he watched her. As soon as she caught up with him, he started off again, moving quickly up a trail that wound through the trees, but pausing every few seconds to look back at her as if making certain she was still following.

They came to a fork in the trail, and Storm bore to the right. As MaryAnne started after him, she realized where this trail led.

The great cliff from which Audrey Wilkenson had fallen to her death.

Could it be where Joey had gone?

Could he have spent the entire night up there, somehow needing to be close to his mother, and going to the last place she had been when she was still alive? MaryAnne's pulse quickened with the possibility that she might yet find him. She pushed herself harder, barely feeling the strain of the climb as the trail steepened.

Then, at last, she was at the top. As she stepped out onto the broad, flat area of bare rock between the edge of the forest and the vertical drop to the valley below, her heart began to race again.

He was sitting at the very edge of the cliff, his back toward her. It looked as if his knees were drawn up against his chest, and some kind of fur blanket was wrapped around him.

Storm, whimpering, had moved close to Joey, trying to lick at the boy's face, but Joey seemed oblivious to the dog's presence as he stared out at the valley that stretched away far below.

Something inside MaryAnne warned her not to call out to him, not to startle him in any way.

She started toward him, moving quietly, finally coming up beside him and dropping down to sit next to him. Still saying nothing, she slipped her arm around him and pulled him close. For a moment he seemed to resist, but then let himself go, his head dropping to her bosom.

"Are you all right?" MaryAnne asked, feeling no anger at all toward the lonely figure she had come upon less than a minute ago.

Joey hesitated, then shook his head. "No," he whispered, his voice barely audible. "I'm not all right at all, Aunt MaryAnne. I'm scared. I-I wanted to die."

A wave of pity for her tortured godson broke over MaryAnne, and she felt tears well in her eyes. She pulled him closer. "I'm very glad you didn't die," she told him. "We've all been very worried about you."

Joey said nothing for a long time. Then, in a tiny voice, sounding as if it were coming from a great distance away, he said, "I bet Alison wasn't worried. I bet she hates me."

"Nobody hates you," MaryAnne told him. "Nobody at all."

"But I tried to hurt her," Joey wailed. "Something awful happened to me, and I—" He fell silent for a moment, unable to finish. Then he spoke again: "Aunt MaryAnne, am I crazy? Is that what's wrong with me?" He began sobbing. "I didn't mean to hurt Alison," he wailed. "I really didn't! I just couldn't stop! A-And now Bill Sikes is dead, and—and—Aunt MaryAnne, what's going to happen to me?"

MaryAnne held Joey in her arms, gently stroking his head with the fingers of one hand. "It's going to be all right," she told him, as if crooning to a baby. "I'm here, and you're safe, and everything's going to be all right. You didn't hurt Alison at all, and whatever happened to Bill Sikes couldn't have been your fault."

"But—But I don't *remember*!" Joey sobbed. "I don't remember anything until I woke up, and I was all by myself, and . . ."

He went on, babbling almost incoherently, and though she tried to follow what he was saying, none of it made any sense to her. But slowly she realized that he hadn't been here all night, that he'd slept somewhere far up in the mountains, and that when he awoke, he'd been in a bed in a cabin, wrapped in the blanket that was now all he wore.

And when he'd come up here, just after dawn this morning, it had been his intention to kill himself.

"But you didn't do that," she told him as she finally helped him to his feet. "Instead, you waited for help to come. And that proves to me that you're not crazy."

Joey looked up at her, his wide brown eyes frightened. "Are you going to send me away?" he asked. "Am I going to have to go to a hospital?"

MaryAnne rested her hand reassuringly on his cheek, but couldn't bring herself to make any promises she might not be able to keep. "Let's not worry about that right now," she said. "Let's just get you back home, where you belong."

With Storm leading the way, they started back down the mountain, neither of them saying a word.

CHAPTER 19

*T*hey had set out an hour after MaryAnne had brought Joey down from the bluff, as soon as Joey got dressed and Rick Martin had heard his strange story of waking up in a cabin high in the mountains. Joey had led the way up the trails that Rick himself had followed through the long night. When they'd come to the place where Bill Sikes had been slain, Joey paused, staring at the spot where the corpse had lain, and where Tony Moleno—finally allowed to go home to bed—had stood guard when Joey passed just after dawn had begun to break. Bill Sikes's body was gone now, and the area, like the campsite at Coyote Creek a few days before, was being combed by the technicians from Boise, who this morning had redoubled their efforts, sealing everything they could find into plastic bags for analysis. Joey had said nothing as he gazed at the site, but finally turned away and started trudging again up the trail. Then, half an hour ago, he had veered off it and into the forest, sometimes following the narrow paths left by deer making their habitual rounds, more often than not winding his way through the trees.

Now they were high up, near the timberline, picking their way across the rubble of one of the glacial moraines. Rick shuddered as he tried to imagine anyone spending a winter up here, with the snow ten feet deep and the wind howling down from the mountains. He glanced at Joey, and the boy seemed to read the deputy's doubts.

"We're almost there," Joey said. "There's a trail up a little further." Fifty yards farther on, after they had slipped through a narrow gap between two immense boulders, the path developed, and a few moments later they emerged into a small clearing. At the far end, crouched against the rocky mountainside, was the cabin.

Its two empty windows seemed to stare balefully at them, and its open door formed a gaping mouth. But from the rusted metal chimney that rose from the shanty's patchy roof, a tiny wisp of smoke still drifted. The home of a mountain man, Rick Martin thought, though in the ten years he'd been in Sugarloaf, he'd never so much as set eyes on one. Until he'd talked to MaryAnne Carpenter yesterday, he'd heard only the vaguest of rumors that one of the strange hermits might still be living high above the valley. Yet here was exactly the kind of ruined cabin one of them would inhabit.

"See?" Joey said. "I told you it was here!"

Drawing his pistol from its holster, and telling Joey to stay where he was, Rick started toward the sagging door. "Hello?" he called out. "Anybody here?"

There was silence from the house, which, despite the telltale smoke from the chimney, exuded an aura of emptiness. At last Rick stepped up onto the porch and peered inside.

The inside of the cabin was as close to ruin as the outside, but it was obvious that despite the shack's condition, someone did, indeed, live here. "It's empty," Rick called to Joey. "I'm going to take a look."

Joey, still standing at the head of the trail, watched as the deputy disappeared into the shack, then he started across the clearing himself. If he showed Rick Martin where he'd slept, he'd have to believe him!

Abruptly he stopped, the hair on the nape of his neck standing on end as goose bumps crawled across his skin.

He was no longer alone.

He glanced around, certain he would see someone—or something—behind him.

There was nothing.

He stood perfectly still, listening for a sound that would betray the unseen presence, but the silence of the morning was broken only by the whispering of the wind in the trees.

He sniffed at the air, as an animal might search for a scent.

Nothing.

And yet he could sense the presence close by—so close he felt he could almost touch it.

Just as it, unseen though it was, seemed to be touching him.

He hesitated, then turned away from the cabin and darted back toward the trailhead, where he took refuge among the trees, screened from the cabin by the underbrush that thrived in the shelter of the tall pines.

The presence was stronger.

He moved quickly through the dense undergrowth, guided by nothing more than a whisper inside his own mind that seemed to tell him which way to go. He had gone no more than fifty yards when he saw the figure crouched among the trees ahead, watching him.

Joey stopped, staring at the man. He was clad in clothing so worn it was almost colorless. His hair was long, and his unshaven face was composed of rough-hewn features.

Joey recognized him instantly. It was the same man who

had been standing in the trees at his parents' funeral, watching him.

The man, he knew, who lived in the cabin.

Except for that one fleeting glimpse of him in the graveyard, Joey had no recollection of ever having seen the man before, his memory of two days ago wiped from his mind as completely as that of last night. Yet now, alone with him in the forest, a strange calmness came over him. Without thinking, he began to walk toward the man, stopping only when he was a few feet away from him.

The man held out his hand. "It's all right, Joey," he whispered, his voice as rough as his coarse features. "You know me, don't you?"

Joey hesitated, then slowly nodded, for inside him a conviction had already formed that he did, indeed, know this man, that somehow he was connected to him. He felt himself being drawn toward the rough countenance as though by some irresistible force.

"We're alike, Joey," the man whispered in his low voice. "You and me are just alike. We've got the same blood, boy." His dark eyes never left Joey's face. "That's right," he whispered once again. "We're not like the others, Joey. Not like anyone else. You understand me, Joey?"

Joey's brow knitted into a deep frown. The words had no meaning for him, but something in what the man had said struck a chord deep inside him, and unaware, he found himself nodding silently, his entire being focused on this stranger who seemed so familiar.

"You don't have to be afraid of me, Joey," the man whispered. "Come." As Joey drew closer, the man reached out to stroke the boy's cheek. The skin of his palm felt rough, but Joey made no move to pull away from the touch: his cheek, where the man's fingers grazed his skin, seemed electrified. Suddenly something inside Joey felt different from how he had ever felt in his life.

He no longer felt alone.

"Joey? Joey!"

Rick Martin's voice shattered the quiet of the moment, and Joey's eyes widened in alarm. The man's hand dropped away from Joey's cheek and his eyes narrowed. "Go back, Joey," he commanded, his voice dropping to a whisper. "It's not time yet. When it is, I'll come for you."

Laying his immense hands—his nails thick and long, curling like claws from the ends of his fingers—on Joey's shoulders, the man turned him around and nudged him, indicating that he was to go back the way he'd come.

Joey took a few tentative steps. When Rick Martin's call rang out again, he turned to glance back at the man whose first presence he had neither seen nor heard, but had nonetheless sensed.

The man was gone, and the spot where he had stood only a moment before was now empty.

There was no sign that he had ever been there at all. Joey's eyes raced over the whole area, searching for some proof that the encounter had been real, and not just another trick his mind was playing on him.

But there was nothing, and finally Joey turned away as he heard his name being called yet again. "I'm coming!" he shouted. Breaking into a run, he hurried back to the clearing.

"Where were you?" Rick Martin demanded. He had panicked at the realization that Joey was gone, and now his tone was gruff.

"I-I had to take a leak," Joey stammered. "I was right over there." He gestured vaguely in the direction of the forest.

"Well, don't do it again," Rick admonished him. "I promised your aunt I wouldn't let you out of my sight. I don't want you making a liar out of me, okay?"

Joey nodded, saying nothing of the man he had just seen in the forest, but listening carefully to every word Rick Martin spoke as the deputy laid plans to bring Frank Peters and his bloodhounds up to the cabin.

By nightfall, Martin was sure, the dogs would have tracked down the man who lived here.

———

"I'll be back to pick you up by three-thirty," MaryAnne told her children, pulling up in front of the school and leaning across Logan to open the far door of the Range Rover. "If I'm late, just wait for me. Don't take the bus. I don't want you walking anywhere by yourselves."

"Why do we have to go to school at all?" Logan began in a last ditch effort to be allowed to stay home that day. Before he could go on, Alison interrupted him.

"Will you stop being a baby, Logan? Mom's got enough to—"

His pleading abandoned, Logan wheeled around to glare at Alison. "I'm not a baby! I'm ten years old."

"Then stop acting like you're four," Alison broke in. She opened the back door and slid out. "Don't worry, Mom. I'll take care of him." She waved at her mother as the Range Rover pulled away from the curb, then turned to start up the wide walkway that led to the school's entrance. "Are you going to stand there all day?" she called back over her shoulder. Logan, after one last, longing look after the Rover, started up the walk.

"If you'd just kept your big mouth shut, I could've talked her into letting us stay home," he groused.

Alison ignored her brother, and Logan, finally bowing to the inevitable, followed her up the walk. But he hadn't gone more than a few steps before he heard a voice calling to him. "Hey, Logan! Did you see him?"

Logan turned. Michael Stiffle's lips were twisted into an unpleasant grin, and his eyes were fixed mockingly on him. "You didn't, did you?" Michael demanded.

"Who?" Logan countered.

"Bill Sikes!" someone yelled. A crowd quickly began to form around Logan and his sister. "Did you guys get to see the body when they brought it down?"

Logan hesitated. All he'd seen this morning were some men

coming out of the woods on the other side of the pasture. When they'd started toward the ambulance parked in the yard, his mother had made him stop watching. Now, though, he struggled to remember every detail of the glimpse he'd gotten of the large bundle the men had been carrying. Could it really have been Bill Sikes's body? A shiver ran through him as he decided that it couldn't have been anything else. "Sure, I saw it," he told them. "It took four men to carry it, and it was all wrapped up in plastic."

"But did you see the body?" someone else asked.

"We didn't see *any*thing!" Alison exclaimed before her brother could reply. Feeling slightly sick at her stomach, she took Logan's hand and started toward the door, hoping to get inside before anyone could ask anything else. But before they were even half-way up the steps, Mike Stiffle grabbed Logan's arm.

"Where's Joey?" he taunted. "Have they taken him away yet?"

Alison turned to glare at Michael, whose twin sister was right behind him, grinning knowingly at her. Sensing what was coming next, she pulled her brother away. "Come on, Logan," she said, dropping her voice so no one but her brother could hear her. "Let's go inside!" But even as she approached the doors, it began:

"I bet Joey did it!" Mike Stiffle sang out. "I bet he killed Bill Sikes!"

"Joey's crazy!" someone else called.

"Yeah! Everybody knows that!"

Alison wheeled around. "Stop it!" she shouted. "Just stop it! None of you know anything!"

"We know Joey!" Michael Stiffle yelled back. "We know—" His words died on his lips as the door opened and Florence Wickman stepped out onto the porch, Ellen Brooks beside her.

"That will be enough!" the principal declared in the forceful voice she'd developed years earlier to seize control of just such situations as this. "Nobody knows what happened to Bill Sikes, and there will be no more talk like that." Her eyes fixed on Michael Stiffle. "Do you understand me?"

The boy stared at his feet, nodding silently.

"Then I suggest you all get ready for classes," Mrs. Wickman told them. "And I don't want to hear any more talk about Joey Wilkenson! One more word out of any of you, and you can count on spending the next month doing laps after school! I mean it! One month, no excuses!"

As the principal's threat sank in, the murmuring among her students died away. Satisfied that the situation was under control, she turned and went back into the building. A few minutes later, though, when they were alone in Florence Wickman's office, Ellen Brooks spoke not only for herself, but for all the teachers she had talked to that morning.

"What are we going to do?" she asked. "The only thing the kids are talking about today is what happened last night, and I can't blame them. Did you hear Sam Gilman this morning?"

"He should be ashamed of himself," Florence Wickman snapped. "And Milt Morgenstern, too. It's as if they *want* to cause a panic!" She sighed, lowering herself into the chair behind her desk. "Still, I'm afraid Sam and Milt have a point. Until we know exactly what happened to Bill Sikes, the children should be scared. We should *all* be scared."

———

MaryAnne paced nervously in the kitchen as she waited for Joey and the deputy to return from the mountains. From the moment she'd let Joey go, she was certain she'd made a mistake. Yet what choice had she had? As soon as Rick had begun talking to Joey— just as he'd gotten dressed and settled down to try to eat something—she'd known where his questions were leading.

"Do you remember where the cabin is?" he'd asked. "Could you find it again?" Joey had hesitated, then nodded, and MaryAnne had listened in horror as the deputy suggested they go back up into the mountains immediately. Finally Rick had drawn her aside. "I've got two murders on my hands," he'd explained,

"and a woman in desperate shape in the hospital down in Boise. If there *is* somebody living up there, I want to talk to whoever it is right away. And if there isn't anyone there, or if there isn't a cabin at all . . ." He'd left the sentence dangling, but Mary-Anne had instantly caught his meaning.

"Then what?" she demanded, her voice cold. "Surely you can't be thinking that Joey had anything to do with the killings! My God, what are you saying? He's only a child."

"I'm not saying anything," Rick Martin had insisted. "But I have to follow up on this, and the only way I can do that is with Joey's help."

Still MaryAnne had hesitated, but in the end, when Joey himself had pleaded to be allowed to lead the deputy up to the cabin, she'd relented, albeit against her better judgment. "You have to let me go," Joey had protested. "If everyone thinks I'm lying, then everyone will think . . . they'll think . . ."

Though Joey had been unable to say the words, his meaning was clear, and after Rick Martin had promised not to let the boy out of his sight, she'd finally given in. "But you'll watch him every minute! Agreed?"

He'd agreed, and she believed him. But every minute since they'd left had been torture, especially the endless hour and a half that had elapsed since she'd dropped Alison and Logan at school. She went to the window one more time, glanced out, and felt a great wave of relief as she saw Joey coming across the field, Rick Martin beside him. Forcing herself not to run out to meet them, she waited by the door until they reached the house. When she looked anxiously at Rick, he was able to read her question as clearly as if she'd spoken it out loud.

"It's there," he said. "Right where he said it was, and exactly as he described it."

Some of the tension drained from MaryAnne's body. She slipped her arm protectively around Joey. "Was there anyone there?" she asked.

Martin shook his head. "Someone lives up there, though, but

don't ask me how." He described the cabin to MaryAnne. "It looked like he was there not too long before we arrived," he finished a couple of minutes later. "There was an empty coffee cup, still warm, and the fire had just been banked." He stretched, trying to ease the knots in his muscles, knowing he could push himself no further until he'd had at least an hour or two of sleep. "I'm calling Tony Moleno and sending him up with Frank Peters and the hounds. If the rain holds off, the dogs should be able to track the guy pretty easily."

MaryAnne started to say something, then changed her mind. "Joey? Why don't you go up to your room and change your clothes while I talk to Mr. Martin?"

Joey gazed up at her, his eyes filled with suspicion. She was going to talk about him—he was sure of it! "Why can't I stay?" he demanded.

Reading the fear in his voice, MaryAnne smiled at him. "Because I want you to put on clean clothes," she told him. "We're going to go see your doctor and try to find out what's happening to you."

Joey's eyes widened. Was she going to make him go to a hospital? Was she going to send him away after all, even though she'd promised not to? "But you said—" he began, but Mary-Anne gently put her finger over his lips, silencing him.

"It's going to be all right, Joey. We're just going to go see your doctor, and maybe he can help you remember what happened last night. I promise you I'll be right there with you, and we'll come home afterward." As Joey still hesitated, she spoke again, her eyes fixing on his. "I promised to take care of you, Joey. I promised your parents when you were born, and I promised you this morning. I won't break that promise, Joey, I swear I won't."

Joey gazed up at her, seeing nothing in her face to make him think she might not be telling him the truth. But what if she wasn't? What if she sent him away to a hospital somewhere? Then, even as the question formed in his mind, he knew the answer.

I'll run away. If they send me to a hospital, I'll run away, and go up in the mountains and find the man. I'll find him, and he'll take care of me.

Satisfied with the answer that had come to him, he left the kitchen and started up the stairs to his room. When he was gone, MaryAnne turned back to Rick Martin.

"There's something I don't understand," she said. "If you think whoever lives in that cabin might have killed Bill Sikes, then why didn't he hurt Joey last night?"

It was exactly the question Rick Martin had been puzzling over for the last half hour as they had climbed back down the mountain.

It was a question for which he still had no answer.

———

Joey opened the door of his room and whistled at his dog, who was stretched out on the bed, his head resting on his forepaws. But instead of bounding off the bed to trot over and greet his master, Storm only whined softly, then slithered to the floor and disappeared under the bed. Frowning, Joey dropped down to his hands and knees, peering into the chasm between the box springs and the floor.

Storm snarled and retreated a few more inches.

Suddenly Joey understood.

The scent of the mountain man was on him.

"It's okay, Storm," he whispered. "You don't need to be afraid of him. He wouldn't hurt me. He loves me, boy. He loves me."

Once again he reached out to the dog, but the shepherd's frightened whimper did not subside.

As the scent of the man who had laid his hand on Joey's face filled Storm's nostrils, his whole body began to tremble, and he shrank even farther away from the boy who had been his master his entire life.

A boy who, right now, he instinctively feared.

CHAPTER 20

"Well, now, that wasn't so bad, was it, Joey?" Clark Corcoran asked, standing up and coming around to perch on the corner of his desk. Built like a quarterback, Corcoran's youthful look belied his forty-four years, and his easy manner had always made him popular with kids.

But Joey shifted nervously in his chair, and the worry in his eyes was apparent as he gazed up at the doctor. "You mean we're done?" he asked.

Corcoran nodded. "All done," he replied, instilling a heartiness in his voice that he knew wasn't justified by the results of his examination of Joey. Still, he had reached some conclusions about the boy during the last hour, encouraging Joey to keep talking while he checked him over physically, knowing that with someone of Joey's age, he would gain a lot more information from an informal talk than he ever would if they'd merely sat face-to-face across his desk.

Physically, the boy was in good condition. Though he wasn't large for his age—his height was actually a bit below average—his muscular development was far beyond his years, and already hair was beginning to sprout on his well-developed chest. His pulse and blood pressure were perfect, and the only abnormality about the boy was his temperature, which measured a full degree above normal. Corcoran wondered about that, and checked for any other symptoms of illness, but found none. Finally he'd taken Joey's temperature once again, getting the same reading and noting it on the chart as an anomaly to be checked again the next time he saw Joey.

Though he hadn't yet discovered the exact reason for Joey's memory lapses, he suspected he knew the answer, and it was simple enough—the loss of his parents had been a tremendous trauma to the thirteen-year-old, and there were bound to be times when the boy's grief would simply overwhelm him, leaving his mind with no options except to close down. In Joey's case, Clark Corcoran was almost certain he was right, for no matter from which direction the doctor approached the boy's reaction to the loss of his parents, Joey consistently replied that he was all right, that he was adjusting to his new life, and that he liked his aunt MaryAnne. He'd even admitted to developing a crush on Alison Carpenter.

All of which, when Corcoran put it together, told him that Joey was repressing his grief; refusing to face the reality of what had happened to him, and dealing with his loss by simply pretending that nothing of terrible importance had happened.

None of which could possibly be true.

He suspected that during those times of which Joey had no memory, the boy had simply hidden himself away, unwilling to expose his pain to anyone, even himself. Corcoran was equally certain he knew the source of Joey's unwillingness to share his pain.

"All I need is a few minutes with your aunt to fill her in on how healthy you are, then you're off. But I'll want to see you again next week."

Joey's eyes clouded with suspicion. "I thought you said I was okay."

"You seem to be," Corcoran assured him. "The only thing wrong with you physically is a slight temperature, which I assume will be gone by tomorrow. But we still have to find out what you were up to when you took off last night, don't we?"

Joey was quiet for a moment, taking on the wary look of a cornered animal. "L-Lots of people can't remember things," he finally ventured. "What's the big deal?"

"Who said it was a big deal?" Corcoran countered. If he lent too much importance to the memory loss, Joey would retreat even further within himself. "But aren't you even curious? I know I am!"

An image of Bill Sikes's corpse flashed into Joey's mind. What if he *did* remember what he'd done last night, and it turned out that he'd— *No!* He shut the thought out of his mind before he even completed it. "I-I guess I am," he finally said.

"Then next week we'll work some more on figuring it out, okay?" Corcoran opened the door to the inner office and walked Joey down to the waiting room where MaryAnne Carpenter was nervously flipping through the pages of a magazine. "Would you come into my office for a couple of minutes, Mrs. Carpenter?" Corcoran asked.

As Joey settled onto the sofa she vacated, MaryAnne followed the doctor back to his office, seating herself on the very edge of the chair in front of his desk. Corcoran dropped into his chair and picked up Joey's chart, handing it to her so she could read for herself the notations he'd made. "Except for a minor temperature," he remarked as MaryAnne began scanning the record, "Joey's in good shape physically. Very good shape, in fact." For the next several minutes he spoke without a break, explaining his theory about Joey's memory lapses.

"I wish I thought it was that simple," MaryAnne said pensively when he was finished. She still remembered the day she had arrived in Sugarloaf, and Joey, bursting into tears, had thrown himself into her arms. "The boy you're describing sounds a lot more—well, *stoic* is the word, I guess. And Joey isn't stoic. If anything, he's volatile. His moods seem to change so quickly, I sometimes wonder if I know him at all."

"Joey's always been like that," Corcoran agreed. "And I'm not sure there's a conflict. Even when he was very small, there were times when he seemed to retreat completely within himself, and other times when he could be an absolute demon." He paused, and when he went on, his voice had taken on a guarded quality. "How well did you know Ted?"

Ted, MaryAnne echoed silently. *With everyone I talk to, it always comes back to Ted.* "I'm beginning to wonder if I knew him at all," she finally replied. "And I suppose I didn't. I mean, I've known him almost since Audrey married him, but I certainly never spent much time with him."

"He was a complicated man." Corcoran leaned back in his chair. "I liked him—I want you to understand that. But he could be very strict with Joey sometimes, and at other times he'd let him get away with murder. I always got the impression that Joey never quite knew where he stood with his father. What seemed to please Ted one day might not the next, so Joey was always kept off balance. And the last couple of years, Ted seemed to be getting harder on the boy."

MaryAnne's expression tightened. "Are you saying he'd gotten abusive toward Joey?" she asked, finally deciding the time had come to press the issue everyone else—from Charley Hawkins to Rick Martin, and even Olivia Sherbourne—had dodged away from.

For a long moment Clark Corcoran was silent, then he heaved a long sigh. MaryAnne could not help but notice that when he spoke, he avoided meeting her gaze. "The thing is, not many people around here were ever willing to stand up to Ted. Even me, I'm afraid." He reached out and picked up a pencil, which he nervously twirled between his fingers as he talked. "You know that Ted was very wealthy, and a couple of years ago he established a fund to build a clinic out here. We should be ready to start construction next spring."

He fell silent, but MaryAnne, already certain she knew what was coming next, refused to let him avoid his own guilt. "Go on," she said.

Corcoran slumped lower in his chair. "Well, I'm afraid that while I did my best to help Joey, I wasn't very willing to confront Ted. I'm not proud of it, but there it is. So whatever Joey's problems may be, I'm afraid I have to share in the responsibility, too. But try not to worry too much—I've gotten Joey this far. I'll get him through this, too."

"How?" MaryAnne asked, a surge of anger coursing through her. "How do you propose to help Joey, when you knew what was going on and did nothing to stop it? Dear God, Dr. Corcoran! How could you do it? Did everyone in town know Ted was abusing Joey? And didn't anyone do anything about it?"

"I'm not sure anyone actually *knew*—" Corcoran began, but MaryAnne didn't let him finish.

"Don't split hairs, Dr. Corcoran," she cut in. "You just told me you suspected Ted was abusing Joey. Which means that you should not only have made notations in Joey's records, but you should have reported what you suspected to the police!" She began flipping through the records in Joey's folder, scanning them for anything that would reflect what the doctor had just told her.

There was nothing.

Nothing at all!

Finally she came to the back of the folder where a copy of Joey's birth certificate, Xeroxed on both sides, appeared as the first document of his medical records. She stared at it for a long moment, started to flip back through the records, then went back to the birth certificate.

Something was wrong.

She studied the document for another moment, then looked up at Clark Corcoran. "Audrey told me Joey was born prematurely," she said. The doctor appeared totally baffled by the sudden shift in her thoughts. "Did you handle Audrey's pregnancy?"

Corcoran shook his head. "I wasn't here then. And Joey was born in San Francisco, wasn't he?"

MaryAnne nodded, studying the birth certificate once more. "Audrey told me she felt lucky to be there when Joey arrived almost two months early."

"I'd have to agree with her," Corcoran replied. "If he'd been born that early out here, he'd have been lucky to survive."

"But it says here he weighed eight pounds nine ounces when he was born," MaryAnne said. "That's awfully heavy for a seven-month preemie, isn't it?"

Corcoran frowned and reached for the record, which Mary-Anne passed across the desk. Now he studied the birth certificate, along with the records of Joey's first few days of life. There was no evidence of his having been in an incubator, no mention of an abnormal birth or any neonatal problem at all. "Are you sure Audrey said he was premature?"

"Absolutely," MaryAnne replied, her heart beginning to beat faster as she calculated when Audrey must have gotten pregnant if Joey had been a full-term child. "It certainly explains why Ted would have been so hard on Joey," she finally said, her voice trembling slightly.

"I don't understand—" Corcoran began, but MaryAnne didn't let him finish.

"If Joey was full-term, then Ted couldn't possibly have been his father. Ted and Audrey only knew each other for a month before they got married, and Joey was born seven months after the wedding. Which means that if Ted was the father, Joey would have to have been no more than a month premature, and Audrey told me it was two months."

Corcoran studied the records from the hospital in San Francisco once more, then shook his head. "Unless someone faked these records, she wasn't telling you the truth," he finally said. "It looks like he was full-term. In fact, if anything, his size at birth would indicate the possibility of an extra week or two. But not premature. And Audrey certainly never mentioned anything about his being a preemie to me."

MaryAnne shook her head. "She probably didn't tell anyone except me and a few friends back East. But if Ted wasn't his father, who—" She went silent as she remembered the man who had been all but hidden in the trees at Ted's and Audrey's funeral.

The man whom both Rick Martin and Olivia Sherbourne had said must be a mountain man, living by himself up in the mountains.

The man who had been watching Joey at the funeral.

The man whose cabin Joey had awakened in only this morning?

Was it possible?

But it was insane!

Surely, whoever Joey's father had been, he couldn't have been living up in the mountains above Sugarloaf! Audrey would never have fallen in love with one of those men!

Unless he hadn't been a mountain man when Audrey had met him.

Suddenly, one of Olivia Sherbourne's fleeting remarks rose out of her memory: . . . *when Audrey married him a month after she met him, I had plenty to say! Told her she was just on the rebound, that she hardly knew Ted . . .*

On the rebound.

Now MaryAnne remembered it, too. There *had* been someone, but it hadn't lasted long. Just a few weeks. And then Audrey had never mentioned him again.

But Ted must have known the truth. MaryAnne could imagine how the knowledge would have eaten at him all these years, until he'd finally turned against the boy he knew wasn't his son.

Suddenly everything made sense—and nothing made sense at

all. A headache hammered behind her eyes. If the man she'd seen at the funeral was the same man who was living up in the cabin . . .

Could he be Joey's father?

Could Joey know Ted wasn't his father: could he have felt that Ted hated him for it?

The questions spun through her mind, building upon themselves until finally she could stand it no longer. "Dr. Corcoran," she said carefully, her voice quavering, "if Joey's real father were . . . to show up . . . would there be any way to prove it? Through blood tests, or something?"

Clark Corcoran shook his head. "Not through simple blood tests. All we can do is eliminate certain groups of people from paternity through impossible blood-type matches. The only way we could actively prove paternity would be through a DNA analysis. And that's expensive."

MaryAnne's features set in determination. "I want you to take a sample of Joey's blood and get a lab working on the analysis. I have a feeling we're going to need it."

A few minutes later, as Corcoran took the sample from a vein in Joey's right arm, he made no mention of its true purpose, explaining only that MaryAnne was concerned about the slight temperature and they were going to run some tests. The sample, in a vial, was marked for shipment to a lab in Boise.

As MaryAnne drove Joey back up to the ranch, she wondered if she should ask him any more questions about his relationship with Ted Wilkenson. In the end, though, she decided to wait, at least until she found out whether the man who was living in the cabin had been found.

Found, and identified.

———

The man paused to listen.

The dogs were still far away, but they were getting closer.

He'd been stupid—right from the start. He should have stayed near the cabin, listened to what the deputy had said. Instead, intent only on staying well out of sight, he had slipped away into the forest, climbing up the cliffs to crouch on a ledge, the wolf growling softly beside him, until he had seen the man and the boy—*his* boy—working their way back down to the valley. Only then had he returned to the cabin, certain that he would find it in ruins, possibly even burned to the ground.

It had been untouched. After he'd built up the fire, knowing there was no longer any point in concealing his presence by burning the stove only at night, he'd eaten his fill of boiled potatoes from the store in the cave behind the shack, and fried rabbit from last night's kill, for now, during the hours of daylight, the hunger for raw flesh was not upon him.

When at last he'd stretched out on the bed, he had intended to have no more than a few minutes rest while he decided what to do.

The cabin must be abandoned—he knew that. Surely the deputy would be back, bringing more men with him.

And dogs.

The same dogs that had been out last night—tracking Joey— losing his scent only when they came to the spot where he had found the boy wandering in the woods, his eyes glazed over as he moved through the trees, following . . .

Following what?

A voice inside himself, that only he could hear?

An instinct deep within him, imprinted so strongly that he had no choice but to obey when the urge came upon him?

The madness had been in Joey since the day he was born. Even when he'd been nothing but a toddler, lurching around the yard of the house the Wilkensons had built in the valley, the man had seen the yearning in the boy as he'd watched from the ledges above.

He'd seen Joey start toward the shelter of the woods, his eyes fixed on the trees and the shadows they cast, his soul already seeking the solace that only the wilderness could provide.

The man had known what the boy was feeling, even known the cycles of his madness.

How many times had he gone down to the valley when the hunger and the thirst came upon him—in the years when the urges were still weak enough for him to control—and felt Joey's own needs, seen him at the window of his room, staring longingly out into the night, even felt the mind of the child reaching out to his own?

Two minds, with a single instinct.

Were there more of them? How many might there be?

How many like him, prowling in the darkness, fighting the hunger, resisting the thirst, only, finally, to lose the struggle against their very nature?

People were dying now.

Was it only happening here? Or were there others like him, living in other cabins on other mountains?

In other places—in cities, where they would hide during the day in cheap apartments, creeping out only at night, foraging for food in the Dumpsters as he himself foraged in the campsites, struggling against the demons inside them?

Struggle as he had struggled.

As Joey Wilkenson had just begun to struggle.

Now the cabin had been found. He had to abandon it and find a place to hide.

To hide, before they came to kill him.

For that was what they were going to do. Surely, anyone who looked upon him would know him for what he was.

Know him, and hate him.

As they would come to hate Joey, too.

With Joey, though, it was barely beginning, the change within. No one else would see it yet; to the others, the people unafflicted with the sickness, Joey would still seem normal.

No, they wouldn't see it until it was far too late, until Joey himself would finally be unable to resist the urges within him.

He'd closed his eyes for a moment, trying only to blot out the vision of Joey turning into the monster he himself had become, but his body, exhausted from the night before, had betrayed him. He had fallen asleep, awakening only when the wolf issued a warning growl.

It had been too late to do anything but flee, and he had been running ever since, the wolf at his side.

Now he was tired—exhaustion weakening his muscles, seeping into his bones. Soon, he would have to stand and fight.

Fight, or die.

He glanced around, his sharp eyes scanning the landscape, searching for a place of sanctuary. Then, high up, he saw it.

Above the timberline, where the granite surface of the mountains was fully exposed to the wind, he saw a cleft.

A narrow cleft, which would give him protection on three sides.

Give him protection, but trap him, too.

He stared at it for a moment, making up his mind, then began climbing, the wolf scrambling ahead of him, as if it knew where he was going.

Below him the baying of the hounds grew louder.

———————

"Unleash one of them," Tony Moleno said as an icy rain began to fall from the leaden sky above.

Frank Peters stared at the deputy. "You nuts? How long do you think we can keep up with him? He'll be gone before—"

"We're close enough," Moleno interrupted. "I can almost feel him. He's somewhere nearby. And if we don't find him within the next fifteen minutes or so, we're not going to. This rain'll wash away the scent faster than a jackrabbit can go down a hole."

"Maybe we better call Rick," Peters suggested, still unwilling to release his dogs to whatever quarry might be hiding on the mountainside.

Tony Moleno scanned the landscape that towered above them. They were just above the timberline; from here to the summit there was nothing but naked rock.

Broken rock, shattered by a millennium of rain seeping into the cracks of the mountains, then freezing and expanding through the long winters, slowly working their way deeper, until at last huge chunks of the mountain broke free, tumbling downward, clearing great swaths of timber as they fell, the masses of rock disintegrating into rubble studded with enormous boulders, piled at the bases of sheer cliffs.

Everywhere, there were clefts in the rock. In any one of them the man for whom they searched could be hiding.

A dog, though, could find him within minutes, and from where they stood, they would be able to watch until the last few seconds of the hunt.

"Let Rick sleep," Tony replied, making his decision. "He's not here, and we are." Reaching down, he unsnapped the leash from the collar of one of Frank Peters's hounds. The dog leapt forward, his eager baying rising to echo from the cliffs as he followed the scent of the creature he was tracking.

The hound moved quickly, for the scent was strong and unlike anything it had smelled before. There were no false trails, no similar odors mixed in with the pungent aroma it had picked up from the bed in the cabin.

His head low, he bounded up the mountainside, a flash of brown and white against the gray of the rocks, disappearing for a few seconds as he scuttled around the huge boulders, only to reappear as he scrambled up the rubble that would soon be covered by yet another layer of snow and ice.

The man braced himself.

One of the dogs was close now, very close.

The men had unleashed it, which was good.

It meant he'd have time before they got here, for while the dog would leap and scramble along the shortest route once it caught his scent, the men with the other dog would have to pick their way slowly, searching for the path that had led him up here, struggling to find each foothold.

The rain was coming down harder now, but it was too late for it to do him any good, for the wind was gusting down the mountainside as well, sweeping down on him, chilling his skin and stiffening his fingers.

And picking up his scent, to carry it to the dog below.

The tenor of the baying changed suddenly, and he knew that the time had come. The hound had his scent now, and would charge up the hillside, no longer confined to the trail he himself had left.

But he was ready—as ready as he would ever be.

As the wolf snarled a low warning, the man dropped his hand to her head, quieting her.

Suddenly the dog was there, silhouetted in the opening of the cleft.

It stopped dead in its tracks, silent for a moment, as if surprised to have come upon its prey so quickly. Then it let out a howl of victory as it leaped toward him, its jaws wide, saliva dripping from its tongue. From its throat, yet another round of baying rose, its signal that its prey was cornered and under attack.

But the baying was cut short, its echoing note of victory changing in an instant into something else.

The valley was filled with a wailing scream of agony as the wolf leaped forward, catching the bloodhound in the air, her jaws closing on the dog's throat, her fangs sinking deep into the dog's flesh.

CHAPTER 21

"What the hell happened up there?" Frank Peters asked as the last terrified yelp of his best hound died away.

Tony Moleno's eyes narrowed. "I'd say whatever's cornered up there just killed the dog. Come on." Turning away from Peters, he started up the steep slope, picking his way carefully in the loose rubble that was scattered at the base of the cliff, wondering how long he could fight off the exhaustion his three scant hours of sleep had failed to put at bay.

The wind, which had been growing steadily out of the north during their long climb up the face of the mountain, was howling across the peaks now. As the temperature dropped, the icy rain that had begun falling a few minutes before quickly turned to sleet.

Frank Peters stared at the deputy. "Are you nuts? If we don't get down from here right now, we're going to get stuck! Look at that!" He pointed up into the sky where roiling black clouds were already beginning to darken the day, though the afternoon had barely begun.

"We've got time!" Moleno insisted. "We've got a chance to get this guy right now, and if we blow it, he'll be gone! We'll never find him again!"

"Son of a bitch will freeze to death if we just leave him where he is," Peters countered, but when Tony Moleno ignored him and started working his way up the slope, Peters followed, clutching at the lead of his remaining dog.

Reaching the boulders piled at the base of the cliff, Tony Moleno waited for Frank Peters to catch up. "How the hell did he get up there?" Peters complained, turning his back to the driving wind and wiping the sleet from his face with the sleeve of his parka. He reached into his pocket, pulled out a pair of heavy gloves, and shoved his hands into them.

"Looks like he must have gone up over there." Moleno pointed to a place twenty yards to the right, where a jagged gash in the granite bluff seemed to lead the way to a wide ledge above. Somewhere on that ledge, the cleft that concealed the mountain man lay. He began working his way around the boulders, envying the dog who only a few moments ago had dashed into gaps far too small for Moleno himself to wedge through. He moved slowly now, for below him the ground had sheared away into a steep slope that ended at the lip of one of the stone ramparts that reared above the treetops like the lookout tower of some great castle.

The rock glistened. Already the sleet was forming a thin layer of ice that would be even slicker than the mossy rocks lining the bottom of Coyote Creek. A slip here would lead to far worse than the sprained ankle Tony had suffered the previous spring on his first fishing expedition of the year.

Steeling himself, he edged around one of the boulders, feeling for secure fingerholds before groping with his toes for the narrow ledges that would bear his weight. After what seemed an eternity, but was no more than a minute, he ducked into the relative shelter of the great gash in the face of the cliff, and waited for Frank Peters to catch up.

For Peters, the going was even rougher, for he realized too late his mistake in pulling on the thick gloves. He edged around the boulders slowly, warring against the temptation to look down the steep slope that yawned below him, knowing that if he so much as glanced at what lay below, a wave of dizziness could destroy his already precarious sense of balance. Suddenly he felt a tug at the hound's leash. He dropped it instantly as the dog, far more sure of its footing than Frank himself, leapt from one boulder to another, then scrambled the last few feet, its claws finding a purchase on the bare rock where Frank could see no crevices at all.

Turning his back to the steep grade, he pressed close to the boulder, knowing he should take the thick gloves off before proceeding to scuttle crabwise around the great rock, but his fear of heights began to close in on him. Still, with the gloves hindering his fingers, he'd never be able to find a purchase on the increasingly slippery rock. Finally he released the grip his right hand held on one of the boulder's protrusions and began pulling the glove off with his teeth, finger by finger. As soon as his hand was free of the constricting object, he spat it out, then went to work on the other.

"Okay," he yelled to Tony Moleno, whom he could no longer even see. "I'm coming!"

He stretched his right hand out as far as it would extend, feeling the stone cold against his fingers. At last he found a tiny crevice, slid his fingers in, and curled them tight. His right foot was next. He moved it slowly, probing for a purchase, found one, tested it, then began easing his weight from his left foot to his right.

He had just released the grip of his left hand when he felt something give beneath his right foot, and suddenly he lurched, his fingers slipping out of the crevice.

Instinctively, he dropped into a crouching position and rolled over onto his back, bending his knees to try to use the soles of his shoes as brakes, but the rubble beneath him began to move. All at once he was sliding toward the precipice forty feet below. "Tony!" His shout for help dissipated instantly into the wind. He rolled over again, scrabbling against the broken rock, searching in vain for something—anything—to hang on to.

From above, Tony Moleno watched in hopeless horror as Frank Peters slid downward. The whole hillside seemed to be moving now, and Peters almost seemed to be trying to swim upstream against a river of pebbles.

"Tony! Do something!"

But it was far too late. Even if Moleno had brought a rope with him, he wouldn't have had time to throw it to his friend. Unable to tear his eyes away, he watched as Frank rolled over one last time, tried to stand, finally managed to lurch to his feet, only to plunge over the edge of the cliff. His scream of terror as he fell rose above the wind for a moment. Then it, like Frank Peters himself, was gone.

Tony Moleno took a deep breath. Still staring at the spot at which Peters had disappeared over the abyss, he took his radio from its holster and flipped it on. Shouting to make himself heard over the steadily growing wind, he reported to the dispatcher in Challis what had just happened, and described the cliff upon which he stood.

"I'm not sure I can get back down," he finished. "So I'm going on up." At last he turned away and started grimly up the rock face at whose base he now stood. Above him the second hound was baying excitedly. Tony redoubled his efforts, scrambling up the slippery rock, finally coming to the ledge that formed a narrow shelf running for a hundred yards along the sheer face of the slope. At a sudden change in the tone of the hound's baying, he dashed forward, his gun drawn, but he was still ten yards away when the dog darted into a cleft in the rocks and a moment later uttered the same brief howl of pain that Moleno had heard only minutes before.

Moleno slowed his pace, moving carefully, until he was only a yard from the deep cut that sank into the cliff. Squatting down, he picked up a rock, then threw it into the opening, listening carefully for a reaction from the man he knew was hidden inside.

There was nothing.

At last Moleno edged closer, unconsciously held his breath, then sprang out to the center of the cleft, his gun braced in both hands, his finger ready to squeeze the trigger the moment he found a target.

Immediately, he saw something coming at him. Even before his eyes had truly focused on the object, he fired.

The wolf howled with pain as the lead slug ripped into her flank. Whimpering, the animal backed away.

Stunned by the unexpected attack of the wolf, Tony lost his concentration for a fraction of a second, but that fraction was still too long.

The mountain man dropped out of the narrow crevice he'd wedged himself into, sprang from the rock his legs had been braced against, and fell on Tony Moleno, the clawlike fingernails of his left hand sinking into the deputy's eyes as his heavily muscled right forearm slid around Moleno's neck. With a quick jerk, he snapped Moleno's neck, then picked up the twitching body and pitched it off the ledge. It glanced off the steep slope, flipped over in midair, then fell once more, skidding down the incline toward the edge of the rampart.

As he shot off the precipice, Tony Moleno's arms and legs spread wide, giving his final fall to the rocks below the appearance of a dive.

A dive gone horribly wrong; a dive made in the silence of death.

———

"Rick? Rick, wake up!"

Gillie Martin jostled her husband's shoulder, then shook him harder. He moaned, rolled over, then came slowly awake, blinking at his wife. "What the hell are you doing?" he groaned, still feeling the exhaustion of having been up all night, and certain that he'd only sprawled out on the bed a minute or two ago. "I barely got to sleep—"

"You've been out cold for three hours, and I'd have let you sleep, but we've got a problem," Gillie said, the tone of her voice bringing him instantly wide-awake. "I was listening to the scanner, and I heard Tony Moleno calling down to the dispatcher in Challis." She hesitated, then went on, knowing there was no way to break the news gently. "Frank Peters is dead, Rick. He lost his footing on the mountain, and Tony couldn't get to him."

Gillie's words cleared the last of the fog from Rick's mind. "Oh, Christ! Where's Tony? Is he okay?"

"That's the rest of the problem," Gillie replied, her voice grim. "He thinks he's got whoever lives in that cabin you found this morning trapped, and he's going after him."

"What?" Rick said, sitting up and swinging his legs off the bed. "By himself? That's nuts!"

"He said he didn't think he could get back down. There's a storm coming in—"

But Rick wasn't listening anymore. He'd snatched up the telephone, punching in the numbers for the dispatcher's office. "Debbie? Rick Martin. Let me hear the recording of Tony's last call."

"I told him to come back down, Rick, but—"

"Just play it, Debbie," Rick cut in. He listened intently to Tony's voice, barely audible over the storm and the static, as he'd reported to the dispatcher. At least, Rick thought, Tony had remembered to tell Debbie where he was. Though it might not mean much to the dispatcher at the other end of the county, Rick knew exactly the area Tony had described.

"I'm going up there," he told Gillie, reaching for the jacket of his uniform. "I can get pretty close by going through Coyote Creek Campground and up the firebreak."

"Are you insane?" Gillie demanded. "Rick, look outside! It's freezing cold, and raining, and the radio says it's going to start snowing in Stanley within the hour. Which means it will start snowing here, too, and it already is up in the mountains."

"Then I'd better get going," Rick said, brushing her words aside. He pulled on thick wool socks and a pair of boots in place of his usual shoes. "What time is it?"

"A little after one-thirty. You've only had a few hours of sleep—"

"I'm fine," Rick cut in. "A hell of a lot finer than Frank Peters, and I'm damned if I'll let Tony try to get off that mountain by himself." He headed out into the garage, found a three-hundred-foot length of nylon rope, some pitons, and a grappling hook. Gillie followed him out to the car, still protesting as he tossed the mountaineering equipment into the backseat. "Don't worry," he told her. "I'll be all right."

Twenty minutes later he passed through the deserted campground in which Glen Foster had died and started up the steep firebreak, shifting the Jeep into four-wheel drive and throwing the lever into the low range. The engine raced and the transmission whined, but the vehicle started up the rutted dirt track, rocks flying from under the tires, the car itself slipping and sliding over the rain-slicked mud.

After a mile he turned off onto an old logging road, now almost overgrown with brush, and dropped the transmission into the lowest gear, working the engine hard as he pushed his way through. When the road finally became impassable, blocked by a fallen tree, he pulled a plastic slicker on over his parka and scrambled out into the storm.

From what Tony had said, he was no more than a half mile from the spot where Frank Peters had fallen.

Shoving the pitons in the pockets of his raincoat, he slung the rope over his arm and picked up the grappling hook, then clambered over the fallen tree and began threading his way through the forest of seedling pines that had all but obliterated the unused road.

It was another quarter of an hour before he came to the base of the cliff from which Frank Peters had fallen. Ten minutes after that, he found Frank's body.

Only a few yards from Frank Peters, he found Tony Moleno.

His partner was sprawled on his back, his head twisted grotesquely against his left shoulder.

As he stared at Tony's face, the eyes no more than two bloody holes in his skull, nausea rose in Rick Martin's stomach. He bent over as a great retching seized him.

As he threw up on the ground at the base of the cliff, then waited, still doubled over, for the nausea to pass, the mountain man slipped through the forest a thousand yards away.

Descending from his sanctuary on the sheer face of Sugarloaf Mountain, he was once more moving through the wilderness, the force of the storm only spurring him on as the feral instincts within him, fueled by the attack on Tony Moleno into a ferocious blood lust, surged to the surface.

MaryAnne Carpenter gazed around the storage attic under the house's steeply sloped roof, searching for one more box—a trunk—anything she might not yet have looked through in her hunt for some reference to the man Audrey Wilkenson had been dating before she met Ted. But there was nothing. Every box and suitcase in the attic had already been opened, but there was no trace of what she was looking for.

Except a picture.

A single picture in the photo album downstairs, showing Audrey with a group of people MaryAnne hadn't recognized.

The snapshot was blurry, but Audrey had been standing next to a tall, broad-shouldered man with heavy features, whose arm was draped over her shoulders in a way that could have meant they were no more than casual friends, or could have signaled something else entirely.

So she had kept searching, hunting for a diary or a hidden packet of photographs Audrey might not have wanted Ted to see—anything that might have given her a clue to the identity of Joey's real father. But there was nothing. Brushing her sleeve across her eyes in a futile effort to free herself of the dust that had been swirling around her for the last three hours, she finally abandoned the attic and went back down to the desk in the den. Knowing another search of its drawers would prove futile, she picked up the phone and dialed Olivia Sherbourne's number one more time, once again getting only the veterinarian's answering machine. "Call me as soon as you get this message," she said, essentially repeating the same message she'd left twice already. "Olivia, I have a weird idea about who the man up in the mountains might be, but I can't remember his name! If the man is who I think he is, he might have thought he had a reason to kill Ted, and maybe even Audrey, too! I know it sounds nuts, and I hope it is, but please call me as soon as you can!"

Hanging up the phone, she glanced at her watch. It was almost three, time for her to go pick up the kids at school. And she'd take Joey with her, since she'd already made up her mind not to leave him alone until she knew exactly who the man was the police were hunting for.

"Joey!" she called up the stairs. "It's time to go get Logan and Alison!"

When she heard nothing but silence from the second floor, a terrible feeling of foreboding came over her. She rushed up the stairs, not even pausing to knock at his door before pushing it open.

The room was empty!

Instantly, her eyes went to the window. Closed. She felt a strange sense of relief that at least if he'd gone out, he hadn't slipped away through the window, dropping down off the roof of the porch.

But where was he?

She strode across to the window and looked out, only then realizing that it had begun to rain. It was coming down hard, and it looked as if there were snowflakes mixed in with the large drops.

Snow? But it was only the beginning of September. Then she remembered Bill Sikes's words, uttered only a couple of days before. *Going to be an early winter . . . be surprised if we don't get snow before the week's out.*

The rain was streaking against the glass, and heavy clouds had dimmed the daylight so that it almost looked like evening. As she raised the window to gain a clearer view of the yard and pasture, a gust of icy wind blasted in at her, and she quickly slammed the window shut again, then hurried downstairs. She was rushing through the kitchen on her way to the back door when she stopped abruptly. A note was propped against the salt shaker on the table. Frowning, she picked it up.

"I'm out in the barn," she read in neatly blocked letters. "The horses need to be fed and the stalls have to be mucked out and I didn't want to bother you." It was signed "Joey," and at the bottom he'd scribbled a P.S.: "Don't worry—I'm okay!"

The fear that had gripped her when she'd realized Joey wasn't in the house released its hold, and she dropped into one of the kitchen chairs, a brittle laugh rising in her throat as she realized how close to panic she'd been. As her nerves calmed, she went to the closet behind the stairs and pulled the heavy shearling jacket off its hook. Buttoning it all the way up, she fished a knitted cap off the shelf above the coats, donning the cap and turning up her collar as she went back through the kitchen. The back door threatened to blow out of her control as she opened it, but she managed to pull it closed, and started across the yard to the barn, leaning into the wind and holding up her arm against the rain. The barn door was propped open. She pulled it shut as she went through, the wind slamming it behind her.

"Joey?" she called into the gloom. "Where are you?"

All she heard was the soft nickering of one of the horses, and she hurried across to the light switch, blinking in the glare as the bright floodlights washed the darkness away. "Joey? Are you in here?"

Two of the horses were in their stalls, their heads hanging over the closed half doors, but the third stall—Sheika's—was empty. Her pulse quickening, MaryAnne moved closer to the empty stall, peering inside.

Though the horse was gone, her feeding trough was full, and the floor of her stall was covered with fresh straw. But surely Joey wouldn't have gone out riding in weather like this!

She moved to the tack room, scanning the equipment. All the saddles were in place.

Her concern deepening, she left the tack room and started back toward the barn door. When she was still ten feet away, she saw it begin to move, opening a crack, then slamming shut again as the wind caught it. Outside, she could barely hear Joey's voice, shouting above the storm.

"Back up, Sheika! Come on! Back up! Thata girl. Good girl!"

The barn door opened again, but once more slammed shut, and MaryAnne ran forward. "Get her back!" she called, putting her weight against the big door and pushing it against the force of the wind. "I'll push the door open!"

"Okay!" Joey called back.

She shoved again, bracing herself this time, and finally got the door open. As it swung wide, Joey, mounted bareback on the big mare, rode through the opening. Both the boy and the horse were soaking wet, but Joey was grinning broadly. "You should have seen Sheika!" he said. "She loved it!"

MaryAnne stared at the dripping boy. "Loved what? What were you doing? Where were you?"

"I took her out for a ride," Joey said. "It was great—I've never ridden her bareback before."

"In the rain?" MaryAnne asked. "Joey, it's pouring out there!"

"It wasn't when we started. It was just sort of drizzling. But you should have seen her! When it really started pouring, and the wind started coming down from the mountains, she really took off. You should have seen us coming across the field just now! Her tail was up, and she was really prancing!" He patted the big horse on the neck, then lithely swung his leg over her neck and slid to the floor, already leading her toward the cross ties. "You liked that, didn't you?" he asked as the horse nuzzled his neck. "Didn't you like that?"

The horse whinnied, tossing her head and almost pulling the lead from Joey's hand.

"Well, come into the house," MaryAnne told him. "You have to get dried off and put on clean clothes, and then we have to go down to school to pick up Alison and Logan."

"I can't," Joey replied, settling Sheika into the wash stall and snapping the leads to her bridle. "I've got to get her wiped down and blanketed, or she'll catch cold."

"And what about you?" MaryAnne replied. "Dr. Corcoran said you were already running a fever—"

"I'm fine," Joey broke in. "As soon as I get Sheika back in her stall, I'll go in and get changed."

MaryAnne started to protest, then decided she had neither the time nor the inclination to argue with the boy. Besides, she wouldn't be gone more than half an hour, and by now the police had probably either caught the mountain man or chased him out of the area. "Okay," she sighed, "but promise me you'll stay in the house and not go anywhere."

Joey hesitated, his eyes clouding for a split second, but then he nodded. "I promise," he agreed. Then, his grin flashing once again: "But you better hurry. It's really starting to snow out there. Hey! Maybe we'll get snowed in! Maybe there won't be any school tomorrow! Wouldn't that be neat?"

MaryAnne smiled ruefully; she would be hearing exactly the same chorus from Logan the minute she picked him up. At least Joey's just like all the rest of the kids where snow is concerned, she thought as she climbed into the Range Rover and turned on the ignition, the more the better, and if school closes, it's just a lucky break!

Putting the car in gear, she turned it around and started down the drive.

Joey, watching her go, felt the grin he'd been struggling to maintain begin to slip away.

Deep inside him, he was once again feeling the first stirrings of the same nervousness that had come over him the night before and driven him out into the darkness.

Only a moment ago, when he'd been out on Sheika, racing across the field in the freezing rain, he'd felt wonderful, an exuberance building in him that had made him whoop with pure joy. The moment he'd come into the barn, though, the joy had drained out of him, and the first feelings of being trapped had begun to form in the pit of his gut.

Now, as he began rubbing down the big mare, he could feel his nerves taking on that familiar edge, feel the howling elements outside beckoning to him, the wilds of the mountains summoning him.

He tried to ignore the feeling, tried to pretend it wasn't happening, but as he continued working on the horse, the urge inside him grew stronger.

Sheika, sensing something different about the boy, began to grow nervous, pawing at the floor, and jerking her head against the restraining lines that held her in the cross ties.

CHAPTER 22

*T*he rain had turned completely to snow by the time MaryAnne got to the school, and as Logan and Alison dashed down the steps and raced across the lawn, she gazed worriedly up at the gray sky. She had never experienced the kind of storm that sometimes came raging down from the Arctic at this time of the year, and the blackness of the clouds made her shiver even in the warmth of the Range Rover. She pulled the shearling coat tighter around her neck.

"Isn't this neat?" Logan asked, scrambling into the front seat and slamming the door behind him. "I bet they don't even have school tomorrow! I bet we get snowed in!"

MaryAnne smiled at her son. "I wouldn't start getting my hopes up. It's barely the middle of September, and I suspect this is going to blow over. By tomorrow it'll probably all be melted."

"It will not!" Logan argued. "Mike Stiffle says it'll be eight feet deep and we won't even be able to get out of our house! He says—"

"It sounds like what he says might be just a little exaggerated," MaryAnne cut in, pulling away from the curb and turning up the windshield wipers to clear away the thickening snow.

"Michael and Andrea Stiffle are jerks," Alison announced from the backseat, causing her mother to glance at her in the mirror.

"Oh? And what brought that on?"

Alison slouched moodily in her seat. "I just don't like them, that's all."

"They were talking about Joey," Logan offered, his voice taking on an angry edge. "They said—" But before he could finish his sentence, he noticed that Joey wasn't in the car. "Where is he?" he asked, his anger at the Stiffle twins giving way to concern about the boy he already thought of as his big brother. "The doctor didn't make him go to the hospital, did he?" Though he wasn't exactly sure what kind of hospital Joey might have been taken to, he still remembered how frightened Joey had been this morning that he might have to go to one.

"He's fine," MaryAnne assured him. "He's at home taking care of Sheika."

Mollified, Logan's ten-year-old mind immediately shifted gears again. "I wish *I* could have stayed home and taken care of the horses today."

"Oh, really?" MaryAnne drawled. "Well, let's see—all you would have to do was muck out the stalls, then get some hay out of the loft, then feed all three of them. Then after that, you could have started grooming them, and there's a lot of things to do in the tack room. The saddles need to be polished, and—"

"He didn't have to do all that," Logan interrupted her, finally figuring out that his leg was being pulled.

"What did the doctor say?" Alison asked from the backseat. "Is something really wrong with Joey?"

MaryAnne hesitated, wondering just how much she should tell Alison and Logan about what Dr. Corcoran had said this morning. They were on the edge of town now, and as they headed up the valley she could see that the snow was sticking to the pavement ahead. It seemed to be coming down harder every minute. Her fingers tensing on the wheel, she finally spoke. "He's having some trouble adjusting to his parents' dying. The doctor doesn't think it's anything terribly serious, but Joey's bound to have some times when he feels very angry about what happened."

"Well, why shouldn't he be?" Alison asked, the fear of Joey she'd felt the previous night giving way to a wave of sympathy. "It's not fair—both of his parents are dead, and now all the kids are starting to talk like it's his fault! Mom, it's really awful! The way some of them are talking, you'd think Joey was some kind of monster or something!"

MaryAnne felt a sharp pang of guilt as she realized that only this morning she herself had asked Clark Corcoran a question that certainly could have been interpreted in exactly the same way. And she clearly remembered the moment of panic she'd experienced less than an hour before, when she'd come down from the attic to find that Joey was not in the house. If she herself was starting to wonder if Joey's problems went much deeper than the grief he was feeling, what must everyone else be—

She felt the car lose its traction as she started into a corner, and she automatically stepped on the brake, then remembered that was the worst thing she could do, and just as quickly released the pressure on the brake and steered into the skid. An eternal second later the tires caught again. As she slowed down to a crawl, she expelled a sigh of relief.

"Watch out, Mom," Logan complained. "You almost went off the road. Dad always says women can't drive in snow!"

"Your dad's not here to do the driving, is he?" MaryAnne snapped with more annoyance than Logan's comment had deserved. "I'm sorry," she said. "But I didn't go off the road, did I?"

As Logan lapsed into sulky silence, MaryAnne focused her concentration on driving. A few minutes later they pulled into the yard in front of the house, which was already covered with an inch of snow. She steered the Rover around to a spot near the back door, and all three of them piled into the kitchen. Outside, the snow was falling harder. The wind coming down from the mountains was churning it across the field and low drifts were already forming against the storage sheds beyond the barn. "It makes me cold just to look at it," MaryAnne said. "Alison, why don't you build us a fire in the living room, and I'll make some hot cocoa. Call Joey down from his room, will you, Logan?"

She was just starting to heat milk for the cocoa when Logan came back. "He's not up there," her son reported. "He's not here at all."

Struggling to conceal her sudden panic from Logan, Mary-Anne quickly pulled the shearling coat back on, added the knitted cap, then wound a scarf around her neck and lower face. Finally she opened the back door and ran out to the barn, opening the door just far enough to slip inside. Sheika was back in her stall, but there was no sign of Joey.

"Joey?" she called out, her fear rising. He couldn't have taken off—he just couldn't have! He'd promised to stay in the house! "Joey!"

She heard a movement from the loft, and peered vainly upward into the darkness above. "Joey? Are you up there?"

"I'm coming down," she heard him call, and instantly her panic began to subside. But when he scrambled down the ladder a moment later and turned to face her, she gasped.

Joey's face—and the front of his clothes—were covered with snow.

"Joey?" MaryAnne breathed. "What on earth—"

The boy moved toward her, his step slow, almost uncertain. "I was watching the snow," he said, so quietly that MaryAnne could barely hear him. "I opened the door up there. You can see all the way up into the mountains." He frowned, as if puzzled about something. Then, sounding worried: "I was just standing there, Aunt MaryAnne. I wasn't doing anything." His voice changed again, and MaryAnne thought he seemed frightened. "I really wasn't doing anything wrong!"

He's afraid, MaryAnne thought. He's afraid of me! She went to him, slipping her arms around him. "Of course you weren't! But look at you—you're all covered with snow. You must be freezing!" She could feel him shiver as she hugged him close. "Let's get you inside. We're going to build a fire and have hot chocolate, and you can take a nice long hot bath. How does that sound?"

Silently, not trusting himself even to speak as the terrible sense of panic began to close in on him once more, Joey nodded and let MaryAnne lead him back to the house. As they stepped out of the barn, though, and MaryAnne pulled the shearling tight around her throat, Joey felt himself begin to relax again.

And he wasn't cold, he realized. Despite the driving snow and subfreezing temperature, he wasn't cold at all.

Joey stared at the steaming bathtub. He had stripped naked in what had felt to him like the stifling heat of his bedroom, and now as he gazed at the tub full of hot water, he felt no desire to lower his body into it. He was already sweating in the tiny room, and even as he prepared to step into the tub, he felt a strange heat deep in his bones.

A heat that had nothing to do with the warmth of the room, for even when he'd sat in the open door of the hayloft, facing directly into the wind as it blew down the valley, driving the snow before it, he hadn't noticed the cold against his skin.

All he'd felt were the calming effects of the wind and snow, driving out the terrifying nervousness that had been building inside him. With the wind whipping his hair and the snowflakes biting at his face, the hollow, empty feeling in his belly and the strange urge to escape—not just from the house, or the ranch, but even from himself—that almost indescribable feeling of wanting to crawl out of his own skin had instantly eased. It had seemed to him as if the elements outside were calling to him, the forest beckoning, the mountains whispering in his ears.

He remembered it all, every detail of it etched into his mind. It had been almost like living in a dream, and he'd imagined he could hear sounds that he knew were impossible. The wind in the trees certainly would have blotted out what had sounded to him like a deer pushing through the heavy underbrush down by the creek, and he knew that he couldn't possibly be hearing a rat skittering across the floor of the barn twelve feet beneath him.

Yet it had seemed that he could, and when he'd seen the Rover come into the yard, he hadn't been surprised, for he'd even heard the sound of its quiet engine mixed into the whistling of the wind.

He'd even imagined that he could see each individual snow-flake, picking one out as it rode on the wind, following it as it twisted among the others, only losing it when it finally fell to the ground to disappear into the white blanket that was building in the yard.

Even his nose had detected scents he'd never noticed before, faint aromas of the creatures of the forest—no more than wisps carried to him on the wind, but each of them distinct, each of them exciting something deep inside him.

Even when he had finally responded to MaryAnne's call, re-luctantly pulling himself away from the euphoria of the elements outside, he had had no sense at all of the chill in the barn. Now, as he sat in the tub, the heat of the water against his skin com-bined with the peculiar warmth that radiated from somewhere deep inside him to make him feel almost faint.

Sweat was pouring from his forehead, and his mouth kept fill-ing with saliva.

Leaning forward to turn on the cold water tap, he cupped his hands under the icy stream spewing out of the faucet, poured the water over his head, then picked up the bar of soap and began washing his hair.

As he worked the lather into his scalp, he realized that something about his hair seemed different. He could feel a slight roughness he'd never noticed before. Puzzled, he slid down, holding his breath as he dipped his head beneath the surface, running his fingers through his hair to wash the soap away. Only when his lungs began to hurt did he sit back up, his breath exploding as he released the tension in his diaphragm. He picked up the soap again, this time rubbing it on his arms and chest. The strange, tingling sensation worsened. Without warning, a wave of claustrophobia broke over him.

The tub seemed suddenly tiny, and the walls of the bathroom felt like they were closing in on him. He stood up, shaking his body violently, water spraying around the room. The stifling heat choking him, he raised the window over the tub and breathed deeply of the cold air that poured in from outside. Feeling better, he stepped out of the tub, took a towel from the rack on the wall and began drying himself off. Catching a glimpse of his foggy image in the mirror over the sink, he reached over and wiped the steam from the glass.

He stared at the image in the mirror.

It was no longer the image he'd seen this morning.

His eyes seemed to have narrowed slightly.

The down on his cheeks seemed to have darkened, so he almost appeared to have the shadow of a beard.

He ran his fingers through his damp and matted hair, and once more felt the strange roughness on his scalp. Leaning forward, he examined his scalp more closely.

Tiny hairs were coming out of his skin, no more then specks, almost invisible to the naked eye.

Yet they were there.

He swallowed, staring at the image in the mirror.

What was happening to him?

Panic welled up in him. Suddenly, despite the open window, the bathroom, the house—everything was closing in on him once again.

Rick Martin dropped to the ground, sheltering himself in the meager protection of a fallen tree. The snow was deepening rapidly, and drifts were starting to build as the wind churned down the slope, picking up the icy crystals almost as soon as they touched the ground, tossing them back into the air to mix with the thick, fluffy flakes that seemed to drop out of an invisible sky. He should have been back in the Jeep half an hour ago, but he'd taken a wrong turn somewhere, and now he knew he was lost. The quickly building blizzard had cut visibility down to only a few yards.

Should he keep looking for the Jeep?

If he did, and couldn't find it, he could end up lost in the forest, with no protection against the storm. If that happened, he knew what the end of the day would bring.

He could wander in circles for hours, telling himself that he was getting closer and closer to the safety of the Jeep, but never finding it.

Eventually the cold would begin to affect him. Sooner or later—possibly not until dark—he would sit down to rest. And with his energy drained, fighting panic as well as exhaustion and hunger, he would feel the urge to sleep.

Not for long—only for a few minutes.

A few minutes that would turn into eternity.

Abandoning thoughts of searching for the Jeep, he considered that he could move upward, hoping to find a cave—or at least a deep enough cleft in the rocks in which to hole up until the blizzard passed. If he was protected from the wind, and blocked himself inside with a wall of snow, he would have a fighting chance of surviving through the night. Then, in the morning, with the storm over, he would recognize where he was, and either go back to the Jeep or simply make his way down the mountainside into the valley.

His other option was to try to walk out now.

He rehearsed it in his mind, trying to picture the route he might have taken since he'd left the bodies at the base of the rampart. How far had he come? Half a mile? Two miles? No matter which direction he looked, everything looked the same now.

A blanket of white, snow swirling among the trees, the wind wailing forlornly through their tops.

Nothing looked familiar, and he knew it wouldn't, not as long as the storm lasted. Snow changed everything.

The contours of the mountains.

The look of the forest.

He could no longer even trust the footing beneath him. As the snow deepened, it covered rocks and filled crevices, turning the whole mountainside into a mine field through which he would have to thread his way carefully, testing every step before risking transferring his weight to his lead foot.

Better to go back up and try to find shelter.

He stood up, shaking the heavy snow from his boots, and started off, his head low, working his way back up the hill. He moved steadily. The slope was relatively gentle here, and the underbrush not so thick that he couldn't make his way through it with reasonable ease.

He sensed the base of the cliff before he came to it, for as he worked his way into its lee, the wind began to ease and he was able to stand straight up without having snow driven instantly into his eyes and nostrils.

He paused for a moment, stretching the muscles in his back, then moved on. Finally, out of the snow, a black wall of stone slowly emerged, and he felt a surge of hope that renewed his energy, letting him push forward until he was close enough to actually rest his weight against the vertical surface. The snow was already more than a foot deep at the base of the cliff, and falling steadily, drifting down gently here where the wind could not seize it. Though he could still hear the howling gale, its roar was muffled by the snow; it seemed to be coming from a great distance, and he could almost forget how it had felt only a few minutes before, when it had driven the snow at him with the force of a thousand needles, stinging his face whenever he'd lifted his head to try to get his bearings.

But where was he?

He tried to visualize a cliff such as this, but his heart sank as he realized that Sugarloaf Mountain—indeed, every mountain in the range—was studded with sheer rock faces exactly like this one.

He could be anywhere.

He started moving along the cliff, carefully working his way over the rubble that had sheered off its face. Somewhere there was bound to be a cleft, a deep overhang, something that would offer him shelter. At last he found one—nothing more than a shallow gash in the rock, but offering him some protection if the wind shifted.

He knelt down and began building a rough wall out of snow, then groped for fallen branches, shaking the snow loose from them and piling them in the gap between the face of the cliff and the wall he had built. If he could find enough dry wood and get it lit with the stock of matches he always carried in a waterproof container in his pocket, he had a better than even chance of surviving the blizzard.

He'd begun ranging farther and farther from his rudimentary shelter, when the toe of his right boot touched something.

Something that gave slightly.

He knelt down and brushed away the snow that covered the object.

And looked into Tony Moleno's savaged eyes.

He swore softly. For all his efforts, he had only circled around, coming back to the spot from which he'd set out—how long ago?

An hour?

Two hours?

A wasted eternity.

Then, as suddenly as the hopelessness had washed over him, it receded, for he realized that at least he knew where he was.

Pulling the radio from the holster on his belt, he switched it on, and a moment later began talking to the dispatcher in Challis. Gillie would be listening in on the scanner at home.

"It looks like I'm going to be spending the night on the mountain," he said, forcing his voice to reflect more confidence than he felt. "The snow's really coming down, but I've found a spot to hole up, and I'm going to be building a fire. Give Gillie a call in case she's not listening, and tell her I'm all right, but I don't want to try to climb back down in the middle of a blizzard. And Gillie," he added, "in case you're listening, don't worry about me, and don't try to do anything stupid. Just put your feet up and relax, and I'll see you sometime in the morning." He hesitated, but knew there was no way he was going to reveal the long circle he'd made. "I doubt I'll be able to get the Jeep out in the morning, but it should be great weather for snowmobiling, so if someone wants to bring a sled up, they can find me at the base of Castle Cliff."

There was a second of silence before the dispatcher's voice came back, sounding puzzled. "That's where you found Moleno and Peters, isn't it?"

"That's right." Rick Martin sighed, realizing he'd let his secret out. "But I'm telling you right now that anyone who tries to rag on me about getting lost is going to get a fat lip for their trouble. Talk to you in the morning."

If I'm still alive in the morning, he thought as he clicked the radio off.

Right now, he figured he had about a fifty-fifty chance. If the blizzard got worse, he knew those chances would go down.

Way down.

CHAPTER 23

*M*aryAnne threw another log on the fire. As the pile of burning wood shifted, the flames leapt up, already licking at the fresh fuel, and MaryAnne held out her hands to absorb the warmth. "Now this isn't so bad, is it?" she asked. Outside, the snow was falling so heavily that it seemed to form a white shroud around the house, and even as she spoke, MaryAnne wondered if her words had been intended to reassure Alison and Logan, or herself.

"It's cool," Logan replied. "It never snowed like this at home! I bet we get snowed in for a week. Wouldn't that be neat?"

Not if I don't have enough food in the house, MaryAnne thought silently. And what if the electricity goes off? What if the pipes freeze? What if something happens and we can't get out?

They were questions that had never even occurred to her in New Jersey, where even in the worst of storms, the streets were always cleared within a few hours, and there was a store only a block away. Power outages rarely lasted more than an hour or two, and if the pipes froze, all she'd had to do was call a plumber. But out here . . .

Would they even plow the road as far up as the gate to the ranch? They must—it was a county road, and surely she couldn't be expected to do it herself. But what about the driveway? Who would clear it?

She thought of the tractor stored in one of the sheds out behind the barn. Was it really only yesterday that Olivia Sherbourne had promised to teach her how to drive it? They'd talked about doing it next week, but now MaryAnne wished they'd done it right away. Still, if push came to shove, she supposed she could get it started and figure out how to operate it at least well enough to clear the snow off the driveway.

But it won't come to that, she told herself. This will only last an hour or two, and then it will be over. Telling herself the nervousness she was feeling was caused more by her fears of who the man in the mountains might be than by the storm, she struggled to calm down.

Don't panic over what's probably a very stupid idea, she told herself. But a second later her ruminations were interrupted by Storm, who trotted into the den, whimpering softly as he pawed at MaryAnne's leg, then trotted back out again. He uttered a sharp bark, and the fears MaryAnne had only a moment ago put firmly aside came flooding back.

Was something outside the house? Was that what Storm was barking about? She started to get up to go after the big dog, but Logan had already slid off the couch. "I'll take him out!" her son said as he dashed after the shepherd.

"No!" MaryAnne cried, her fears suddenly rising. "Logan—"

She got to the kitchen just as the little boy was pulling on his jacket. Her hand closed on his arm as he reached for the door-knob. Storm, crouched by the door, was whimpering and scratching at the painted wood. "Logan, you're not going out-side! It's freezing out there, and you'll catch pneumonia!"

"I will not!" Logan objected. He pulled the door open just far enough for Storm to slither through, but then his mother pushed it closed again. "Aw, Mom, I never get to have any fun at all!" Logan wailed. Just then the telephone began to ring. MaryAnne glared at her son.

"Open that door, and you'll spend the rest of the afternoon in your room. Is that clear?" Logan's eyes narrowed angrily, but he made no move to go outside, instead moving over to the win-dow where he could watch the dog, who was now standing in the yard a few yards from the house, his head up, one paw lifted as he sniffed at the wind. A moment later he broke into a loud baying, and raced off around the back corner of the house, dis-appearing from view.

"Hello . . ." MaryAnne said distractedly, picking up the phone even while keeping a watchful eye on Logan.

"MaryAnne?" Olivia Sherbourne asked anxiously. "What's go-ing on up there? You sounded terrified when you left those mes-sages."

"Olivia!" MaryAnne cried. "Thank God! Tell me—what do you know about—" She hesitated, seeing Logan watching her, listening to every word she said, then sent him back to the den. Only when he was gone did she explain her strange idea to Olivia. "Olivia, Joey wasn't premature at all. So Ted can't be his father!"

There was a silence at the other end of the line, and for a moment MaryAnne wondered if the connection had broken. Then Olivia spoke, her voice hollow. "His name was Slater," she said quietly. "Shane Slater. But that's not the name we knew him by."

MaryAnne's blood ran cold. "Olivia, what are you saying?"

Another silence, then: "He was a strange man, MaryAnne. He showed up in Sun Valley in the spring that year. He told everyone his name was Randy Durrell. Everybody liked him, and Audrey was crazy about him. I mean, really crazy about him. And then he disappeared one day."

"Just disappeared?" MaryAnne asked.

"We found out why the next day," Olivia went on. "Two FBI agents showed up, looking for someone named Shane Slater. They had pictures, and there weren't any mistakes. It was the same guy Audrey had been seeing."

"Dear God," MaryAnne whispered. "What had he done?"

"I don't know," Olivia replied. "They never told us. They just told us he should be considered very dangerous, so I've always assumed he must have killed someone."

There was a long silence, which MaryAnne finally broke. "They never caught him, did they?" she asked.

"If they did, we never heard about it," Olivia told her. "But it was nearly fourteen years ago, MaryAnne. It couldn't be the same man! It—"

"Why not?" MaryAnne broke in. "What if he just disappeared up into the mountains and has been living in them ever since? What if he knew Audrey was pregnant? What if he knows Joey's his son?"

"MaryAnne, calm down," Olivia interrupted as MaryAnne's voice began to take on an hysterical edge. "It's all just speculation. You don't know—"

"I know Ted wasn't Joey's father, and I know he abused him!" MaryAnne shot back. "I know everyone around here looked the other way, and I even know why! Ted was rich! So rich no one would blow the whistle on him. But what if Joey's real father was up in the mountains, and he knew what Ted was doing? What would he do, Olivia? What would *you* do?"

MaryAnne's outburst was met with a long silence, but when she finally spoke, Olivia Sherbourne's tone was quietly somber. "I would have killed Ted, I suppose. And I might even have killed Audrey for letting Ted abuse my son."

"Which is exactly what I'm thinking," MaryAnne said, her voice trembling.

Almost feeling MaryAnne's fear coming over the wire, Olivia spoke once more. "MaryAnne, until we know exactly what's going on up in the mountains, I think you'd better pack up the kids and bring them down here. It's starting to look like this is turning into a real blizzard, and I don't like the idea of you getting stuck up there. Even if you're completely wrong—which I have to say I think you are—you're going to be terrified if you get snowed in."

MaryAnne gazed out into the darkening yard. If anything, the snow was coming down faster than ever. Already, she could see it drifting deeply against the side of the barn. "I wonder if I can even make it," she said. "It looks like it must be a foot deep already."

"If you leave now, you shouldn't have any trouble," Olivia assured her. "That Range Rover is built for weather like this. I've got plenty of room, and—"

"Mom!" Alison yelled from the den. "The roof's leaking!"

"Oh, God," MaryAnne groaned. "Olivia, let me call you back in a couple of minutes. Alison says the roof's leaking!"

Olivia groaned. "Want me to come up and give you a hand?"

"I'll call you back," MaryAnne repeated, then dropped the phone back on the hook and followed her daughter to the den. By the time she got there, both children were staring up at the ceiling, where a damp stain was spreading across the cedar planks and water was starting to drip down to the floor.

"Get a pan to catch the drip, Alison," MaryAnne told her daughter. "I'll go see if I can find out where it's coming from." Trying to picture which room was above the den, MaryAnne ran up the stairs, then instantly knew.

The children's bathroom!

Though its door was closed, she could see a dark water stain spreading across the carpet. She dashed down the hall, calling out her godson's name. "Joey? Joey!"

There was no answer. She knocked loudly on the door. "Joey? What's going on in there!" She tried to turn the doorknob, found it was locked, and banged on the door once again.

"Joey! Answer me!"

She could hear water running now, the sound of a steady stream pouring into the bathtub, which obviously had begun overflowing.

Why didn't Joey answer her?

Suddenly she had a vision of him, lying in the bathtub, his head under the water, his skin the horrible gray of death.

Could he have slipped? Lost his footing, his head banging against the hard edge of the porcelain tub as he fell?

But he would have yelled, wouldn't he? Surely they would have heard him, even with the storm raging outside!

Then she saw another vision of him, this time as she'd found him early this morning, wrapped in the bearskin, huddled on the edge of the cliff from which Audrey had fallen.

His arms wrapped around his legs, staring mournfully over the abyss almost as if he wished—

Oh, God! No!

"Alison!" she screamed. "Logan! Come and help me!"

She tried to twist the knob again, willing it to turn in her hand, but it held fast. As she heard her children pounding up the stairs in response to her cry, she slammed her weight against the door. The wood of the frame creaked, but held.

"Mom? What's wrong?" Alison asked as she raced down the hall.

"The door's locked," MaryAnne cried, her voice rising toward hysteria. "Joey's locked himself inside, and the tub's running, and he won't answer me, and—"

"I'll get the axe!" Logan yelled. He raced down the stairs, coming back a moment later with the small hatchet that stood on the hearth, ready to be used for splitting extra kindling. Her fear for Joey far outweighing her reluctance to ruin the door, MaryAnne snatched the tool out of Logan's hands and swung it at the door. The blade sunk deep into one of the panels, sticking tight, but MaryAnne twisted it free, then lashed out again. On the third blow the panel finally split, then shattered. MaryAnne reached through the smashed plank, fumbled for a moment, then found the inside knob, giving it a quick twist. The lock clicked and the door swung open, releasing a blast of icy air into the hall.

With Alison and Logan pushing in behind her, MaryAnne stared at the overflowing tub.

Joey wasn't in it. He wasn't in it!

Relief energizing her, she bent down and spun the water valves, cutting off the flow into the tub, then reached down into the cold water and pulled the plug out of the drain.

Cold water?

Why would he have—

The thought unfinished, she looked up at the open window, shivering as more wind-driven snow blew in. "His room, Alison," she commanded. "See if he's there! Now!"

As Alison turned to dash down the hall to Joey's room, MaryAnne leaned forward over the tub, struggling to pull the window closed, but her awkward position made it impossible, and the window held fast. Then Alison was back.

"He's not there, Mom! His clothes are all piled up on the floor, but he's gone."

MaryAnne felt a wave of panic rising in her once again, and as she glanced frantically around the little room, her eyes fell on Joey's bathrobe, still hanging on a hook on the back of the bathroom door.

No!

It was impossible! He couldn't have climbed out of the window stark naked, with a blizzard howling outside! Was he crazy? As the water continued to swirl down the drain, she leaned toward the window once again, though even as she tried to peer out into the blinding snowstorm, she knew it was useless. If he'd been gone long enough for the bathtub to overflow, then wherever he was, he wouldn't be close enough to the house for her still to see him.

Racing down the stairs, MaryAnne ran to the front door, pulled it open and stepped out onto the porch.

"Joey!" she called, straining her voice to make herself heard over the howling wind. "Joey, where are you? Come back!" She was about to leave the porch, instinctively wanting to go out into the storm to find Joey, when she heard Alison shouting at her from the hall.

"Mom! What are you doing?"

Distraught, MaryAnne turned to stare at her daughter. Though she was only a few yards from the porch, she could barely see Alison. "Mom, come back!" Alison wailed. "You'll get lost out there! You'll freeze to death!"

MaryAnne hesitated, torn between her need to go after Joey and her certainty that Alison was right. Only a few more yards and the house would disappear into the snow, and she could wander around for hours, never finding it again.

A feeling of hopelessness washed over her. Choking back a sob of despair, she lurched back to the porch.

"What's wrong with Joey, Mom?" Alison asked as MaryAnne came back into the house, closing the door behind her. When she spoke again, her voice trembled with fear. "Are the kids at school right? Is he crazy?"

MaryAnne leaned against the door, trying to gather her wits, to think what to do next. The police—she had to call the police.

Ignoring Alison's question, she ran to the den and picked up the phone, stabbing the three emergency digits into the keypad.

It wasn't until she'd finished dialing that she realized that no sound at all was coming out of the telephone's receiver.

Now Joey was gone, and the phone was dead.

———

The man moved through the blizzard with the instincts of an animal, so familiar with the woods, so used to moving in darkness, that even the storm barely hindered his progress. He'd left the injured wolf in the protection of the cleft, certain that even if he didn't return for her, she would survive. Her wound was clean, and within a day she would be back on her feet, limping badly, but still able to feed herself. Satisfied that she was safe, he moved steadily downward, angling across the flank of the mountain to Coyote Creek. It had been even easier after he'd come to the stream. All he had to do was follow its course, a route he'd taken often in his years of patrolling the territory he'd subconsciously staked out as his own.

The route he'd been on the night the camper had died, when the irresistible urge to attack had come upon him under the moon. He'd tried to resist it, tried to pull away from the campground, but instead he'd lurked in the shadows, staying as far as he could from the light of the campfire, watching the two people as they cuddled by their fire.

Cuddled and snuggled together in a way that was only a dim memory for the man, and a memory that he had long known was never to be relived. IIe was alone, and would be alone the rest of his life.

Alone.

Alone, with nothing but a wolf for company.

How had the animal known him? How had she recognized him so many years ago, when he himself had not yet understood what was happening to him?

Was the smell already on him?

Had the smell of the wild—the feral odor of the beast that was even then growing inside him—already begun seeping through the pores of his skin?

Was that how she had known she had nothing to fear from him?

She'd crouched beside him that night in the campground, silently watching with him, silently sharing his struggle as he tried to pull himself away into the woods, to leave the man and woman alone in one another's company.

He'd failed, for the urge to hunt had been strong within him.

So strong as to be irresistible.

And at last, giving in to the urge, he'd struck.

The tent had torn apart like tissue paper in his hands, and the man himself . . .

He shut the thought out, wishing he could blot what he'd done from his memory, but knowing he couldn't.

It would haunt him, torture him, until finally he died.

Not long.

But not yet.

Not until he'd talked to Joey one more time.

He passed swiftly through the campground and moved on down the stream until it spilled out of the mountains into the valley floor, its water slowing as it drifted gently along its winding course.

It was beautiful in the gray light of the afternoon, a silver cut through the mounding snow driven by the wind, every branch of the trees along its banks laden with sparkling crystals.

No tracks showed in the freshly fallen snow, for even the forest animals had hidden themselves away from the force of the storm. When it passed on, and the air was still again, they would creep out of their holes, scampering across the fluffy white surface, leaving deep tracks, trails so clear that any predator could stalk them easily.

He turned away from the stream at last, slipping though the trees toward the house. Only forty yards away, it was totally masked by the swirling snow.

He was still twenty yards from the building when he heard the cry from the house.

"Joey! Joey, where are you? Come back!"

He broke into a trot, moving toward the sound, and finally the outline of the house took shape, lights glowing in the windows, the front door open.

He paused, still concealed by blowing flakes, unwilling to move close enough to risk being seen.

He watched as MaryAnne Carpenter lurched back to the shelter of the house, helpless against the force of the storm. As the front door closed, he understood what had happened.

Somewhere in the gloom of the afternoon, Joey was searching for him.

The man crouched low, his senses alert, his body tense as he searched for some hint of where the boy might be. At last he began moving again, circling the house slowly, staying just far enough away to conceal himself from anyone who might be watching from within. Finally he came around to the yard between the house and the field, and the barn loomed ahead of him.

The barn, with one door ajar, held open by the drifting snow.

Knowing now where Joey was, the man silently loped across the yard with animal grace and slipped through the space provided by the open door.

His eyes adjusted instantly to the dim light. In their stalls, the three horses backed away from the half doors that separated them from the wide aisle down the center of the barn, instinctively wanting to distance themselves from the being that had just invaded their domain. As Buck and Fritz whinnied nervously, Sheika reared up, snorting, her forehooves striking out at the danger she sensed.

The man ignored the horses as his nose picked up a scent drifting down from the hayloft.

Joey.

He moved forward silently, mounted the ladder, and a moment later was in the loft. Crouched by the doors at the end of the loft, Joey was nestled deep in the hay, his knees pulled up to his chest, his arms wrapped around his legs. As the man approached, the boy looked up, his head cocked, his eyes frightened.

The man dropped down next to him, reaching out with his gnarled hand, touching Joey's cheek, just as he had this morning when Joey had come to him in the woods near the cabin.

"Don't be frightened, Joey," he said, his voice low. "I won't hurt you. I'll never hurt you."

Joey looked up at the man, his eyes wide as he stared into the distorted face. Joey's whole body was trembling, though he was neither frightened of the man who crouched in front of him nor shivering from the cold in the barn. The trembling was caused by something else—his fear of the feelings inside himself, feelings boiled into turbulence by the presence of this man. "Wh-What's wrong with me?" he asked. "Why am I like this?"

The man said nothing, fighting his urge to end Joey's misery right now.

But he couldn't do it, even if he was certain it would be for the best.

"It's my fault," the man finally whispered, the words choking in his throat. "All my fault, Joey. But I didn't know—I swear to you I didn't know."

"Know what?" Joey asked. What was he talking about?

"I tried to tell them," the man said. "I came down to talk to them, so they could help you. It should have been safe that day, Joey. The moon wasn't up, and I was feeling good. Really good. But when I came into the barn, the horse shied—"

Suddenly Joey understood. "My dad," he whispered. "You killed my dad!" He started to stand up, but the man's strong fingers closed on the boy's naked shoulder, holding him down.

"I wanted to talk to him, Joey—I wanted to tell him what was going to happen to you. I wanted him to stop hurting you, to stop the things he was doing to you." His voice trembled, then broke. "I thought if he knew, maybe he could have helped you."

"He hated me," Joey whispered. "He always hated me." His breath caught in his throat, and then, for the first time, he uttered the words he had been unable to speak to anyone else. "I was *glad* when he died!"

The man held onto Joey, forcing the boy to look directly into his eyes. "I killed that man in the campground, Joey. And I killed Bill Sikes. That's why I'm here. I have to tell you what's going to happen to you, Joey. It's starting. It's starting already. You can feel it, can't you, Joey? The emptiness in your gut, and the tingling on your skin? Can't you feel it, Joey? Aren't you feeling it right now?"

Joey's eyes widened with wonder as he heard this strange man reciting all the things that happened to him. Almost involuntarily he nodded his head.

"It will get worse, Joey," the man whispered. His voice was barely audible, but it carried an intensity that burned each of his words into Joey's mind. "Soon you'll be like me. You'll have to hide in the woods, Joey. If anyone sees you, they'll want to kill you. It'll only get worse as you get older. You'll hunt, Joey. But you won't hunt for animals. You'll hunt for people."

"N-No—" Joey stammered, but the man kept talking, whispering Joey's future relentlessly into his ear.

"You'll start hating them, Joey. All of them. You'll creep through the night, peering into their houses, watching them. And then you'll start killing them." Joey gasped, but the man went on, murmuring more to himself than to the terrified boy. "You won't want to. You'll try not to, but you won't be able to stop yourself. It's in your blood, Joey, just like it's in mine. You'll start changing soon. Your fingernails will turn into claws, and hair will grow all over your body. You'll look like me, Joey. Me! Look!" Releasing Joey, he stood and ripped off his shirt, dropping it on the floor of the hayloft.

Joey stared in awe at the man's powerful torso, his muscles rippling under the curling hair that all but covered his skin. "Touch it," the man whispered. "Not human, Joey—something else—something terrible, Joey."

Almost as if he was hypnotized by the words, Joey reached out, his fingers brushing against the thick mat of hair that covered the man's skin.

Fur.

It almost felt like fur! If he closed his eyes, he could imagine he was stroking Storm, the hair was so thick and soft.

"It's going to happen to you," he heard the man say, and then he remembered the strange hairs that were growing on his head, the dark shadow the down on his face had formed.

"Why?" he moaned, the word cracking as a sob closed his throat.

The man's arms went around the boy, and he held Joey close. "Because I'm your father, Joey," he whispered. "My name is Shane Slater, and I'm your father."

———————

His mind churned, and he could feel insanity rising inside him. It would be so easy to end it for Joey right now, so easy to close his fingers around Joey's throat. A squeeze—a quick jerk, crushing the bones of the boy's neck—and it would be over.

So easy . . .

He felt his fingers tightening, felt Joey stiffen as the pressure grew.

All he had to do was move his hands, slide them up to Joey's neck.

In a split second it would be over.

"*Nooo!*" The word rose out of Shane Slater's throat in an anguished howl. He hurled Joey aside, staggered to the hayloft door and threw it open.

A second later he was gone, disappearing into the storm so quickly that it was as if he had never been there at all.

Yet his words still hung in the air, etched in Joey's memory, echoing in his mind.

. . . your father, Joey. My name is Shane Slater, and I'm your father. . . .

In the depths of his soul, Joey knew it was true.

CHAPTER 24

Logan gazed up at his mother, his face pale, his eyes wide with fear. "What are we going to do, Mom?"

MaryAnne stood trembling by the desk in the den, the dead telephone still in her hand, a tide of hysteria rising once more, threatening to overcome her. She felt herself losing control, felt a scream of frustration and fear building in her throat. She couldn't deal with it—couldn't stand any more of it! Where could Joey have gone? Why would he have climbed out the window, naked, and run away into the storm? If he was out there, how long could he even survive?

The questions twisted like serpents in her mind, her confusion growing every second. All she could think of was that she had an overwhelming urge to give in to her tears, to collapse onto the sofa, to close it all out of her mind.

Her eyes began to sting with the threatened tears, but she knew she had to put the hysteria aside, had to keep going, had to at least appear to be in charge of the situation, if not for the sake of her own sanity, then for Alison and Logan. They were watching her expectantly, Logan with the trust of his ten years, but Alison clearly seeing the panic inside her. She took a deep breath and finally put the phone back on the hook, resting her hand on it for a second, certain that it would tremble the moment she removed it from the instrument that should have brought her help, but instead had betrayed her.

She cast about for something to say—something to do—that would at least occupy their minds, distract them from the fact that Joey was no longer in the house. Then she heard a splash as a drop of water fell from the ceiling into the pan Alison had placed on the floor.

"The bathroom," she breathed, her mind numbly grasping at something—anything!—with which to deal until she could once again begin thinking clearly. "Get some rags from the pantry, Logan." Her legs almost refusing to obey her commands, she left the den and crossed the living room into the foyer. The stairs stretched ahead of her, and for a moment she wondered if she could even climb them. Then she heard Alison's voice behind her, trying to offer her comfort.

"It's not your fault, Mom! And we'll find him! I know we will!"

Nodding, but unable to speak, MaryAnne mounted the stairs.

As his mother and sister started up to the second floor, Logan went through the dining room into the kitchen, and was just starting toward the pantry when he thought he heard something at the door.

A scratching sound!

Storm! Or maybe even Joey!

Without even pausing to call his mother, he darted across to the back door and pulled it open, certain that the dog—or Joey— would slip inside.

Nothing.

Frowning, Logan peered out into the blizzard. For a moment he saw only the swirling snow, but then he caught a glimpse of something else—something barely visible—moving in the storm.

"Joey?" he breathed, but even as the word left his lips, the phantom disappeared into the storm.

But he'd *seen* it!

He *knew* he had!

It was right outside! Without thinking, he stepped out onto the small back porch, cupping his hands around his mouth. "Joey!" he yelled. "Hey, Joey! Is that you?"

His words were drowned by the wind, and he hesitated, wondering whether to go a little farther—just a yard or two—and call again, or whether he should go back into the house. But then the wind made the decision for him, lashing at him, driving snow into his eyes, blinding him for a second. He turned around, about to stumble back into the kitchen, when suddenly the wind shifted, creating a brief vacuum within the house and the back door slammed shut in Logan's face.

He reached for the knob, trying to twist it.

Locked!

Why hadn't he checked it before he'd come out?

"Mom!" he yelled, pounding on the door. "Mom, I'm locked out! Let me in!"

Once again his words disappeared into the wind as quickly as he uttered them, and Logan felt a stirring of panic as he realized that the bathroom was on the other side of the house. They'd never hear him yelling unless they came downstairs.

The window! Maybe he should break the window in the back door.

But his mom would kill him! He could almost hear her: "For heaven's sake, Logan, don't you ever think before you do something?"

He could go around the house, staying real close to it so he wouldn't get lost in the storm, and try all the windows on the way. And if he hadn't found one that was unlocked before he got to the other side, then he could yell right up at the bathroom. They'd have to hear him then! They'd have to!

He shivered in the cold, the wind cutting right through the sweater he'd put on earlier, when he'd still been hoping he might get to go out and play in the snow. Now, though, he wished that at least he'd put on his jacket before he came out on the porch. But who thought the dumb old door was going to blow shut!

Hunching his shoulders against the blowing snow, he left the back porch and started toward the front of the house, testing each window as he came to it.

All of them were locked.

He was just coming to the front of the house when once more he saw a movement out of the corner of his eye. He turned toward it, straining to get a better look, but this time it didn't disappear back into the swirling white blanket.

Instead, he saw the massive shape come toward him, emerging out of the snow like some horrible demon from a nightmare. As Logan stared up into the coarse, heavily bearded face of the mountain man—his mane of black hair matted with snow and blowing wildly in the wind—the little boy's voice died in his throat and he turned to run. The house forgotten, the danger of the blizzard driven from his mind by the twisted features of the terrifying vision that had appeared out of the storm, Logan raced away, slogging through the drifting snow, lurching farther out into the yard, until even if he'd turned around, he would no longer have been able to see the house which was only ten yards away.

When he tripped, sprawling facedown in the snow, he felt the hands on his body.

Strong hands, with nails so long and sharp he could feel them even through his sweater.

Now he found his voice, uttering a scream of terror, but it was too late.

He felt himself being lifted up, held immobile in the man's arms.

"*Nooo!*" he screamed once again. "Let go of me! Help me! Mom! Mom!"

"Shh, shh," Shane Slater said, struggling to hold onto the squirming boy. "Have to get you—"

But before he could say anything else, there was a sudden howl of canine fury and a blur of motion as Storm hurtled out of the blizzard, charging toward Shane Slater, his teeth bared, his eyes glinting as they fixed on the hated man whose scent alone had always terrified him.

Now, though, the dog saw no more than the threat to the little boy, and his instincts to guard the child overcame his fear of the man. His eyes glowing, he launched himself into the air, leaping toward the throat of the man whose arms were wrapped around Logan Carpenter.

Shane Slater, momentarily stunned by the dog's sudden attack, reacted instinctively, raising his arms to protect his throat from the animal's dripping fangs.

Raised his arms, in which he still held Logan Carpenter.

Too late, he tried to turn away, tried to protect the boy as well as himself from the German shepherd's jaws.

Storm twisted his body in midair as his intended victim tried to duck away, his great jaws snapping closed as they came in contact with human flesh.

Logan Carpenter's flesh.

The dog's teeth sank into Logan's neck, piercing the jugular. Shane Slater instantly dropped down to lay the boy on the ground, and seized the dog, grasping its muzzle with one hand and its neck with the other. With a quick twist he broke the dog's grip on Logan. Storm uttered a high-pitched yelp of agony as his mandible shattered under the uncanny strength of Slater's hand.

Leaving the dog lying where it fell, twitching in pain in the snow, Slater picked up Logan, holding him close to his massive chest, bending over him to protect him from the icy wind.

Blood was gushing from the wound in Logan's neck, pouring into Shane Slater's thick beard, matting the curly hair that covered his body.

"No," Slater whispered, his voice barely audible even to himself, and taking on a strange singsong tone. "Don't die . . . Please don't die . . . Have to stop it . . . can't stop it . . . didn't want to . . . never wanted to . . . no more . . . please, no more . . . let it stop . . ."

He began rocking, crouching low, his body curling protectively around the dying child, his murmuring voice fading away into a low sob.

At last, when the blood stopped flowing from Logan's neck and the boy's body lay limp and lifeless in his arms, Shane Slater laid him gently in the soft snow, then straightened up.

He knew what would happen when they found the boy. They would blame him, for they would never understand that he had been trying to protect the child, trying to save him from freezing to death.

He staggered away into the snow, his lips moving, though no sound was any longer emerging from his throat, for his mind was beginning to fail, fragmenting into tiny pieces.

Once more he began circling the house, peering in through the windows, seeing the fire dancing on the hearth, the comfortable furniture, the brightly lit kitchen, filled with the kinds of food he hadn't tasted for nearly fourteen years.

Almost fourteen years since he had been in a house like this, fourteen years since he had seen the men who had come to town looking for him, and had chosen to disappear into the mountains rather than let them take him away and lock him up again.

Tonight, one more time before he died, he would go into the warmth of a house.

A real house.

This house.

CHAPTER 25

O livia Sherbourne paced nervously in the small living room of her house down the valley from El Monte Ranch, moving to the window every few seconds to gaze out at the raging blizzard.

Was it wishful thinking, or was the wind starting to slack off a bit?

Probably my imagination, she decided. The snow was drifting in distinct patterns, for the wind was coming out of the north, sweeping down the slope across the valley from Olivia's house, so that, though the front of her house was already banked with drifts that came nearly up to the windowsill, the small fenced pasture that extended from the back of her house out to the narrow band of aspens and cottonwoods that edged Coyote Creek as it wandered along the border of her property was still relatively clear. She tried to visualize the road, running almost straight up the valley floor. Most of it would still be passable;

though drifts would be building on the south side, the north lane should be open.

Twice she'd picked up the telephone to call MaryAnne Carpenter back, but both times it had been busy.

Now, though, when she tried a third time, her phone was dead, and she realized what must have happened.

MaryAnne's phone hadn't been busy at all—it had just gone out before her own.

But if her phone was out of order, why hadn't MaryAnne simply put the kids in the car and come down? As she glanced out the window once more, Olivia thought she knew the answer. Surely MaryAnne would stay in the house rather than risk getting stuck in the car with the three children with her.

Especially if she thought Shane Slater might be somewhere in the vicinity, possibly looking for Joey.

Was it really possible? The idea seemed so farfetched.

And yet, as she remembered back fourteen years—was it really that long ago?—Olivia began to wonder.

She'd never warmed to Slater, even by his alias, "Randy Durrell." Even when she'd first met him, she hadn't been able to put the name together with the person. "Randy" had always seemed like a warm, boyish sort of name to her, but Randy Durrell hadn't fit her image at all. From the very beginning she'd seen something in his eyes—a strange hard glitter—that made her wonder if he was quite sane.

He'd been big, and quiet, but not the kind of quiet that instilled a sense of calm and comfort. Rather, it had been a tension within him, as if a spring somewhere inside was being wound tighter and tighter, and every day he was getting closer to flying apart.

But Audrey had been wild for him, and when she found out that he was being hunted by the FBI, she'd simply closed down.

Had she known even then that she was pregnant?

More important, had Shane Slater known?

Even if he hadn't known Audrey was carrying his son, he might still have been the kind of man who'd enjoy disappearing into the mountains, depending only on himself while he thumbed his nose at the men who were trying to find him.

He would have seen it as a challenge.

And a further challenge, Olivia now realized, would have been to stay in the area and watch Audrey.

Watch her, and become obsessed with her?

Perhaps even to try to come back to her once the hunt for him had died down?

If he had, then MaryAnne's theory wasn't so farfetched after all, and as that realization came into Olivia's mind, her concern for MaryAnne and the children grew into genuine fear.

Even if they stayed safely locked in the house tonight, the problem would come in the morning. Assuming the blizzard had spent itself by dawn, Olivia knew that the town plow would be up as far as her house by eight or eight-thirty, but El Monte Ranch would undoubtedly be ignored completely. Ted and Audrey had usually taken responsibility for the last mile or so of the road themselves, attaching a snowplow to the tractor and pushing their way out in half an hour.

MaryAnne didn't even know how to operate the tractor yet, let alone hook up the snowplow. Which meant they'd have to try to hike out.

Better, Olivia thought, if she just took her truck up there right now and led them down herself. Her five-year-old pickup had made it though a lot worse snow than this.

She brought her heaviest coat down from the closet upstairs— a bulky wool one, lined with down, which she usually didn't need much before December—pulled her gloves on, then wrapped a muffler around her neck and head. Parked behind the house, sheltered from the worst of the storm, the pickup was covered with only a couple of inches of snow, but beneath the snow Olivia found a layer of ice. Starting the truck, she held her foot on the gas to speed the warming of the engine, then turned on the powerful defroster. A blast of cold air, quickly heating up as the engine began to warm, blew against the cold glass. As she waited for the ice on the windshield to melt, Olivia turned on the cellular phone and called the Sugarloaf deputy's office. When no one answered, she punched in Rick Martin's home phone number.

Gillie answered on the first ring, which told Olivia as much as did Gillie's frightened voice.

"It's Olivia Sherbourne, Gillie. What's wrong?"

"Oh, God, Olivia—it's awful. Frank Peters is dead, and so is Tony Moleno, and—" Her voice cracked as a sob choked her throat.

"Where's Rick?" she asked.

"He's up in the mountains," Gillie told her. "He went up to help Tony, but by the time he got there—" Another sob cut off her words. Several seconds went by before she managed to regain her self-control. "Something terrible is up there, Olivia! I tried to call you a few minutes ago, but all the phones are out! I tried to call everyone in the valley to tell them to come into town. It's not safe up there, Olivia. If—"

"Gillie, listen!" Olivia cut in. "MaryAnne Carpenter and I think we know who it might be. If we're right, his name is Shane Slater, and he's probably been up there for years. The FBI was looking for him in Sun Valley fourteen years ago."

"What?" Gillie demanded. "Olivia, what are you talking about? Fourteen *years* ago!"

"Look, just let the sheriff know, okay? The name is Shane Slater," she repeated. "We're probably wrong, but if we're right, at least the sheriff will know who he's looking for. And I'm heading up to El Monte right now. I'll stop at the Stiffles' on my way and warn them to leave."

"Are you sure you can make it?" Gillie asked. "If you get stuck—"

"I won't get stuck," Olivia replied. "And even if I do, I'll be all right. I've got the phone, and I'll let you know what I'm doing." The cellular signal began to break up, and all Olivia could hear was static crackling in her ear. "I'll call you back, Gillie!" she shouted into the microphone that was tucked away in the headliner above the rearview mirror. She switched on the windshield wipers, watching as the thin sheet of softened ice was broken up and cleared by the first oscillation of the twin wipers. She was about to put the truck in gear when Gillie's words suddenly came back to her.

Something terrible is up there. As the words echoed in her mind, so also did the memory of Shane Slater's strange, veiled eyes.

Shutting off the engine, she took the keys out of the ignition and fitted one of them into the lock on the glove compartment. The door dropped open and she reached inside and pulled out a box of shotgun cartridges, then used another key to unlock the gun rack that spanned the space behind the truck's wide seat. Taking her shotgun out of the rack, she carefully loaded the magazine, checked the safety, then put the gun back in the rack.

She stopped herself just in time as her fingers reflexively moved to relock the gun rack. If she needed the gun tonight, she suspected she might not have time to mess around with a key.

Restarting the truck, she put it in low gear, made a wide U-turn, and started down the driveway to the road. As soon as she left the shelter of the house, the snow deepened, and for a moment she wondered if she ought to stop and put on chains.

No time for that.

She switched the truck into four-wheel drive. It surged ahead, breaking through the drift in the driveway. When she came out onto the road, it was just as she had expected. Though the southbound lane was lost under a bank of snow that had built to almost three feet in some areas, the lane she was using was almost clear.

Though she increased her speed slightly, Olivia kept the truck in low gear, for even with the four-wheel drive she could feel the tires struggling to hold their traction on the snowy roadway, and every blast of the arctic wind made the truck swerve. The run up to El Monte Ranch, which normally took no more than a few minutes, was going to take a lot longer this afternoon.

———————

"Logan? Where are those rags?" MaryAnne stood impatiently at the top of the stairs, calling down to her son. It had been more than ten minutes since she and Alison had come upstairs, and the towels in the bathroom were already sopping wet, while water still puddled the floor, and the carpet in the hall had squished under her feet as she'd gone to the head of the stairs.

The diversion of dealing with the flood in the bathroom had given her enough time to compose her nerves. She had already decided that she had no choice but to go out into the blizzard to look for Joey. If he hadn't gotten lost in the storm, the only place he could be was the barn, where she'd found him twice before. She knew which direction the barn was, and it wasn't more than thirty yards from the house. Certainly she could make it that far without getting lost, couldn't she?

"Logan, do you hear me?" she called out, her annoyance at her son's lollygagging growing by the second. When there was no answer from the floor below, she took a deep breath, resisting the urge to give in to her temper, and hurried down the stairs. She moved quickly through the dining room and was halfway across to the pantry door when she stopped short, staring at the floor just inside the door.

A small pile of snow was rapidly melting into a puddle.

The panic she'd only a few minutes ago succeeded in conquering flooded back into her now, and she dashed to the door, jerking it open. "Logan!" she cried. "Logan, come back here! This instant!"

As the wind struck her, she stepped back into the house, slamming the door behind her, then heard Alison pounding down the stairs. "Bring my coat, Alison!" she shouted. "Hurry!" A few seconds later Alison dashed into the kitchen, the heavy shearling clutched in her arms. "Logan's gone!" MaryAnne told her, grabbing the coat and shoving her arms into its sleeves. "How could he have done something so stupid?" Without waiting for a reply from Alison, MaryAnne jerked the door open once more and stumbled outside.

In the kitchen, Alison ran to the open door, calling after her mother.

"Mom, don't! Don't leave me alone!"

But it was too late. MaryAnne was already disappearing into the swirling snow, but she turned around for a moment, calling out to her daughter. "Stay inside, Alison! Don't leave the house!"

The words were almost lost in the wind, but Alison heard them. A moment later, as her mother finally disappeared into the white miasma, she helplessly retreated into the kitchen, closing the door behind her.

Suddenly the house, which had seemed so warm and cozy only a little while ago, now seemed very large.

Very large, and very empty.

———

MaryAnne stumbled through the snow, almost blinded by the wind-driven powder, uncertain of where she was going. "Logan!" she called out. "Honey, where are you? If you can hear me, just yell! I'll find you, Logan."

She paused for a second, but heard nothing. She looked around, realizing she could no longer see either the house or the barn.

Where was she?

Desperately, she tried to remember which direction she'd gone when she left the back porch.

She'd started toward the barn, but when Alison had called out to her, she'd turned around.

Stupid!

But the action was instinctive, just as the overriding imperative to come out into the blizzard and find her son had been.

Too late, she realized that she'd brought nothing with her. Not a flashlight, certainly not the shotgun from the rack in the den.

Suddenly an image formed in her mind. An image of a large ball of nylon string, sitting in the bottom drawer of Audrey's desk. All she'd have had to do was tie the end of it to the doorknob!

She shoved the thought aside, unwilling to waste time condemning herself for her own stupidity. If she didn't find Logan soon—

Which way?

Which way was the house?

The barn?

Which way should she go?

Tentacles of panic closed around her. She felt her lungs constrict as if metal bands were being tightened on her chest. She took a step, then changed her mind, and started off in another direction. A few steps later, suddenly certain she was going in the wrong direction, she stopped again, hesitated, then veered off toward the left. This time the terrible fear that she was only moving farther from the house stopped her after only three steps.

Think! she commanded herself.

The wind!

From which direction had it been coming?

She stood still, concentrating hard, then remembered the kitchen door and the wind pushing at it every time she'd tried to shut it.

The north!

It was coming down the mountainside from the north, and sweeping across the pasture.

If she walked into the wind, sooner or later she would come to the fence around the pasture, and then she could move along the fence to the barn. Hope surged in her heart, for as well as shelter, she might find Joey and Logan there, too!

Her panic receding slightly, she turned slowly, until at last the wind was blowing directly in her face. Leaning into it, shielding her eyes with the sleeve of her jacket, she started moving slowly forward, the stinging crystals lashing at her cheeks, her eyes starting to water from the cold.

After five steps she felt her left foot strike against something.

Something that gave as her shoe struck it.

Dropping to her knees, she brushed the snow away from the object that lay in the yard, and stifled a scream as her fingers touched Storm's fur.

Her mind raced as she dug the snow away from the dog's lifeless body. Was that what had brought Logan outside? Had the dog come scratching at the back door, only to run away when Logan opened it?

She brushed the last of the snow away, and found herself staring at the dog's broken jaw, twisted away from his muzzle, hanging open, his pink tongue dangling over his teeth.

Not pink—

Red!

MaryAnne saw the stains in the snow around the dog's head, and a wave of nausea hit her. What could have happened out here? Storm must have attacked something.

Something that had fought back, and killed him.

Had Logan heard Storm barking, or even heard only his last howl before whatever attacked him finished the kill?

"Logan?" she called out once more. "Oh, my God! Logan!"

Whatever had killed Storm must still be out here. The dog's body was still warm, the blood in his mouth still fresh—he couldn't have been dead more than a few minutes!

Her eyes streaming now, partly from the blizzard, partly from the terror she felt at the thought of what must be out here— possibly only a few yards away, possibly already catching her scent and beginning to stalk her—MaryAnne started to stagger away, still intent on reaching the fence and then the comparative safety of the barn.

But once more she stopped, for this time, through the tears in her eyes, she saw the object that was blocking her path before she tripped over it.

Once more a scream rose in her throat, but this time she made no effort at all to mute it.

As she dropped back to the ground to gather the lifeless body of her son into her arms, another scream emerged from her throat, a high, keening wail of despair as Logan's head flopped backward, exposing the terrible wound in his neck.

Clutching the body of her son in her arms, MaryAnne began to sob, the pain in her soul threatening to destroy her sanity as she rocked back and forth, cradling Logan as she had when he was only a tiny baby.

The blizzard howled around her, engulfing her in its white shroud, but MaryAnne was no longer aware of anything except the terrible agony of holding her dead son in her arms.

An agony, she felt with searing certainty, from which she would never recover.

———

Olivia Sherbourne was easing around the bend in the road, slowing almost to a stop as she prepared to turn into the Stiffles' narrow driveway, when she saw their car—a small Subaru station wagon—making its way toward the road. Pulling over as far as she could, she waited until Mark Stiffle had swung around in front of her, then rolled the window down just far enough to be able to talk with him.

"We're heading into town," Mark called, raising his voice to a shout to make himself heard above the wind.

"I was coming up to check on you!" Olivia called back. "Can you make it in that?"

Mark nodded. "I've got chains on all four wheels!"

"Okay! I'm going up to El Monte to get MaryAnne and the kids. We'll hole up at my house if we can't make it all the way into town!"

Mark glanced uncertainly into the rearview mirror of his car, past the twins, who were giggling excitedly at the prospect of spending the night with friends in town, to the trackless snow-covered road leading up toward El Monte Ranch. "You sure you can make it?" he called.

Olivia nodded. "I'll be fine. But MaryAnne's scared stiff, and her phone's out." Her eyes narrowed. "Did you hear about Frank Peters and Tony Moleno?"

Now Margaret Stiffle leaned forward to peer past her husband. Olivia glanced at the kids in the backseat of the little station wagon, and when she spoke again, her voice dropped slightly. "Gillie says they're dead. And Rick's trapped up in the mountains."

"Jesus!" Mark Stiffle exclaimed. "What the hell's going on around here?"

"I bet it's Joey," Michael Stiffle said from the backseat. "I bet he's finally gone totally nutso!"

Margaret Stiffle glared at her son, but Olivia chose to ignore the boy's accusation. "I don't think any of us is going to find out until this blizzard's over. Just be careful—if the car breaks down, stay with it! Okay?"

"Don't worry about us," Margaret told her. "Just take care of yourself!"

Olivia nodded, rolled up the window, and waved to the twins in the backseat as Mark slowly pulled the car away, following the tracks Olivia herself had cut in the snow on the way up. Putting the truck back in gear, Olivia continued up the road, but the farther she went, the deeper the snow got.

She shifted the truck down into its lowest gear, and the engine surged as the vehicle began creeping forward once again. She was still a quarter of a mile from the entrance to the ranch, steering more by the feel of the road under the tires than by any ability to see the pavement in front of her, when suddenly she felt the right front tire leave the pavement.

Instantly, she moved her foot from the accelerator to the brake, stepping hard on the pedal before her winter driving instincts kicked in.

As the brakes locked the wheels, they lost their traction on the ice that had formed beneath the snow. Moving as if in slow motion, the truck slewed around, drifting into a four-wheel skid that took it completely off the road.

Olivia's hands tightened on the wheel as the truck tipped steeply to the right, both wheels on that side now leaving the road and sliding into the deep ditch that paralleled the road.

The truck jerked to a stop, throwing Olivia against the steering wheel. For a moment she did nothing at all, silently cursing herself for being stupid enough to apply the brakes in snow like this.

Finally deciding there was no point in wasting any more energy kicking herself, she put the transmission in reverse and tried to back the vehicle up, turning the wheel to the left so that the front end would swing around and force the right rear tire up the steep incline.

A moment later three of the truck's four wheels were in the ditch, and Olivia furiously slammed her fist on the dash.

Getting out of the truck, she went around the front to see how badly she was stuck, and knew instantly that there was no hope of getting the pickup back on the road without the help of a tow truck. Sighing with disgust, she climbed back in the cab and picked up the cellular phone.

No bars were showing on the screen, and the two words "No Service" seemed to taunt her as she stared at them. What good was the damned thing if it didn't work when she needed it?

She sat for a couple of minutes, wondering if she should stay in the truck or walk on up to the ranch.

All her common sense told her to stay where she was, to run the engine only often enough to keep the cab warm, and to make sure the snow didn't pile up under the exhaust pipe to the point where it blocked it. The last thing she needed was for the snowplow to find her dead in the truck sometime tomorrow.

Except she was only a quarter of a mile from the gate to El Monte, and she'd walked up the driveway literally thousands of times over the years. All she had to do was stay on the pavement until she reached the gate. From there it would be easy. The driveway was cut through the forest; there was no possibility of getting lost.

Except that a tiny voice in the back of her mind warned her that this was exactly how hundreds of people had lost their lives in storms like this one. People had even been known to freeze to death halfway between their houses and barns.

But she was convinced that the wind was finally beginning to slacken, and even if it didn't, this wasn't the great plains, where there were hundreds of miles without even a tree to use as a reference point. This was Idaho, and the forest was everywhere. All she had to do was stay out of it, and she knew damned well she could walk from here up to the ranch blindfolded, if she had to.

Making up her mind, she took a flashlight out of the glove compartment and her shotgun from the rack behind the seat. Leaving the keys in the truck's ignition, she pulled on her fur-lined gloves, wrapped her muffler around her head and neck, and got out.

She started up the road, feeling each step with her foot, kicking the snow aside to make certain she was still on the pavement.

When she turned around, the blizzard had closed in on her, and even the truck, which couldn't have been more than fifty feet away, had disappeared into the blinding snow.

Olivia Sherbourne felt completely alone.

CHAPTER 26

*T*he freezing wind, driving the snow before it, finally began to penetrate the thick shearling coat that was MaryAnne Carpenter's only protection from the blizzard. As the cold crept through her flesh into her very bones, her mind at last began to emerge from the shell into which it had retreated. She stared down into Logan's face and had the odd sensation that she was looking into the face of a stranger.

This was not her son—it *couldn't* be her son! This was someone else, some stranger who only looked like Logan. Logan was still alive—he *had* to be still alive. And she would find him.

She would carry this child—this stranger she refused to recognize as her own flesh, her own blood—into the barn, and then she would go on looking for Logan.

She staggered to her feet, stumbling as she struggled to clutch the body in her arms closer to her chest, and something deep inside her reminded her to walk into the wind. A few moments later she came to the fence and paused, leaning against it for a moment as a great sob racked her body. She shuddered, her knees weakening, and for a second thought she might collapse under the load she was bearing.

And why not?

Why not give in to the impulse to simply lie down in the snow—which suddenly seemed to her as soft and inviting as a warm blanket—and go to sleep? Not for long—just for a little while, just for a few moments, to give herself time—

Time for what?

Time to die!

The words galvanized her, and she knew with perfect certainty that they were true.

If she lay down, even for a moment, she would die.

And Alison would be alone, alone in the house, alone with whoever was out here, hidden somewhere in the blizzard.

But who was it? Who was out here, concealed in the blinding whiteness, striking out with the viciousness that had killed her son?

A stranger named Shane Slater? A man whose name she'd never even known until a few minutes ago?

She must be wrong! She must have simply grasped at a straw, invented a story to fit what was happening but mask the truth of it.

Joey!

Could it possibly be that her own godchild had done this?

She tried to imagine it, but her mind refused to entertain the thought.

And yet . . .

Joey had been out the night the man in the campground had died.

He had been out the night Bill Sikes had died, too!

And he'd had reason to hate his father.

Memories—cruel memories—flickered in her mind, quick visions of Joey glaring at her furiously, his temper suddenly flaring, a frightening darkness coming into his eyes.

No! She wouldn't believe it—it couldn't be possible! He was only a little boy! Yet even as she tried to reject the thought, it lingered in her mind, refusing to be dismissed.

But it *had* to be someone else! The man in the cabin—even if her theory about Shane Slater was completely wrong, there was still someone up in the mountains, someone Frank Peters and Tony Moleno had been tracking all day!

But what if there was no man? What if there was no one at all?

She'd heard nothing from the deputy, nothing from anybody!

What if Joey had found the cabin years ago, and only led Rick Martin up to it to protect himself?

Was he capable of such a thing?

She didn't know. She didn't know what he was capable of, or even what he might be thinking. She didn't know him at all!

But if it was Joey, who would he strike out at next?

Alison?

Herself?

He could be anywhere—stalking her, circling around her even as she stood by the fence, pressing herself against it as if it alone could somehow protect her. Steeling herself, she willed the rising panic away, then felt a surge of strength course through her body. No more!

Whether it was Joey or something else who was out here, she wouldn't let herself fall victim to it. She would survive.

She and Alison both would survive!

She moved quickly now, her step more sure, following the fence to the barn. Then she was there, holding Logan's body tightly as she fumbled with the door latch with fingers already gone numb from the cold.

Inside, she thought. Have to get him inside. Can't leave him out here, can't leave him to be buried in the snow! The latch finally opened, and she pulled hard on the door, forcing it open against the mounding snow just wide enough to wriggle through.

Her eyes darted around the gloomy interior of the barn, and she heard one of the horses nicker softly. Carrying Logan's body with her, she hurried past the stalls the horses occupied and opened the latch of the fourth one. It was here that only a few nights ago she had found Joey sleeping on a bed of straw. Now she gently laid Logan's body on the floor, kneeling beside him, her hand resting on his cold cheek, her eyes fixing on his face. But for the terrible wound in his throat, she could almost imagine that he might be only asleep, might awaken at any moment.

Suddenly the horses began moving restlessly, and then Buck, in the next stall, whinnied loudly. A second later MaryAnne heard a sound behind her. Whirling, she saw the wrought-iron latch of the door that led from the stall directly into the pasture move, and realized what had spooked the horses.

Someone was outside, trying to get in!

Joey!

It had to be Joey!

No! The horses had never been afraid of Joey!

As whatever was outside gave vent to a terrifying howl, MaryAnne's heart began to race. Panic once more welled up inside her, and this time she was powerless to put it down, powerless to regain control of herself. She fled from the stall, her feet pounding on the wooden floor of the barn as she raced toward the door. Shoving it open against the wind that had blown it closed, she dashed outside, oblivious now to the wind and the snow, her only goal to reach the safety of the house.

———

The unearthly howl rose over the wail of the wind in the trees, then died away, choked into silence by the driving snow. Olivia Sherbourne stopped in her tracks, a violent shudder passing through her, her skin crawling as the cry faded into the blizzard.

Not human, but unlike any animal she had ever heard, either.

Even the mountain lions that could still occasionally be heard, their terrifying yowls echoing across the valley, had lacked the strange note of anguish that Olivia had heard in that one brief cry.

Anguish, and rage.

It was as if whatever being had emitted the sound were so filled with inexpressible emotions that it had finally been reduced to a single, unintelligible howl of fear, confusion, and anger.

Suddenly Olivia knew where she had heard that sound before.

It had been years ago, long before she'd moved west. She had taken an apartment near a mental hospital, attracted by the cheap rent. It had not taken her long to discover why the rent was so low, for no more than a week after she'd moved in, she'd begun hearing the screams from the institution next door. Looking out her window, she'd seen a heavily screened porch, high up on the fourth floor. Although it was the middle of winter, and the temperature was nearly zero, there had been a woman on that porch.

Her hair unkempt, wearing only an overcoat over her nightgown, the woman stood at the heavy metal screening like an animal in a cage, her fingers clenched around the cold metal, her lips stretched into a painful grimace as her anguished cry welled up from her lungs, exploding from her mouth with the same mixture of terror and fear that Olivia had just heard floating on the winds in Sugarloaf Valley.

Inhuman, and yet uttered by what was—or once had been—a human being.

Gillie Martin's frightened words of warning echoed once more in her mind: *Something terrible is up there.*

Something that had killed at least four people.

And something that was no longer up in the mountains, no longer hiding itself in the wilderness, but had come down into the valley.

Olivia glanced around. Though she could feel the wind finally beginning to slacken, the snow was still falling heavily, and the powder scoured up from the valley floor mixed with the new flakes dropping out of the sky to reduce her visibility to only a few yards. As the whiteout closed around her, she felt a stab of fear.

What if the tortured being that had uttered that chilling cry had already caught her scent, was already moving closer to her, searching her out?

She cast her fear firmly aside. Whatever was out there could be no more aware of her than she had been of it only a few seconds ago.

Indeed, as the soul-numbing howl echoed once more in her mind, she wondered if whatever had uttered it could be aware of anything beyond the confines of its own mind, or whether it was, as it sounded, trapped in some inescapable hell from which it could never again emerge.

A gust of wind lashed out at her, and Olivia set out once more, finally coming to the stone columns that marked the entrance to El Monte Ranch. But as she crossed the cattle guard, coming into the narrow lane that was the ranch's driveway, which wound through tall trees whose trunks were surrounded by heavy underbrush, her fear came back, for whatever being had given voice to the unearthly cry of a few minutes ago could now be only a few feet away from her.

Which meant that she would have no more than a second or two to prepare herself for any attack it might launch.

Unslinging her shotgun from her shoulder, she clicked the safety off and pumped a cartridge into the chamber.

Holding the gun in both hands, she continued her slow progress up the driveway, slogging through the blizzard, the forest seeming to close in on her.

She had taken no more than three steps when she heard something moving in the woods, somewhere off to her left. Swinging around, she raised the shotgun, but nothing appeared in the sights.

Nothing except a thick curtain of white, swirling in front of her eyes, almost blinding her as she strained to see what might have made the sound.

When she heard it again, closer now, but still could see nothing, she turned and fled, plunging into the woods, her resolve not to leave the driveway evaporating in the face of the unseen creature.

By the time the deer that had been disturbed by her passage jumped out onto the driveway, then bounded toward the road in a series of graceful arching leaps through the snow, Olivia had disappeared into the storm, already lost.

MaryAnne burst through the back door, slamming it behind her, her numb fingers fumbling with the lock. Her whole body shaking, she turned around and slid the chain into place, then peered out into the blinding whiteness outside.

Was there a movement out there?

Had something moved, just barely within the range of her vision, then disappeared back into the snowfall even before she could quite see it?

"What is it, Mom?" Alison asked, her voice quavering. "Where's Logan? What was that sound?"

MaryAnne felt tears flood her eyes as Alison spoke her brother's name, but she refused to give in to them, refused right now to try to explain to Alison that her brother was dead.

"I don't know," she said, bracing herself against the back door for a moment while she marshaled her courage. "There's something out there, Alison. I thought I saw it just now." Suddenly she remembered the blood on her clothes, the stains that Alison would see as soon as she turned around. "It killed Storm, Alison. He's out in the yard. I—" Her voice cracked, and finally she turned around. Alison gazed at her for a moment, and Mary-Anne realized that despite her words, despite her determination not to tell her daughter what had happened to Logan, the tragedy was clear on her face.

Alison's eyes glistened with tears and she shook her head as if to shut out the truth she could see written on her mother's features. MaryAnne went to her daughter, put her arms around her and held her close. "Don't say it," she whispered. "Not now. If you say it, I won't be able to stand it. There's nothing we can do for him, darling. Nothing at all."

"Oh, Mommy," Alison moaned, a terrible constriction forming in her throat. "What's happening? What are we going to do?"

"I don't know," MaryAnne replied.

Suddenly she sensed another flicker of motion out of the corner of her eye. When she turned to look, she caught a glimpse of something at the window over the sink.

A face—

But not a face—not a face such as she had ever seen before.

It was gone almost before it registered on her mind, but even as she stared at the now empty window, a vision of a pair of eyes lingered in her memory.

Narrow, feral eyes, glittering outside, reflecting the light from the kitchen.

Eyes that had fixed on her, bored into her, filling her with terror.

"Help me," she said, her voice taking on a hard edge of urgency as she pushed Alison away from her. "Don't ask any questions—just do as I say!"

She began jerking the chairs away from the heavy oak kitchen table, then shoved the table itself toward the door. "Help me!" she cried again, and her voice, cutting through the fear and grief that had paralyzed Alison, brought the girl back to life. She moved next to her mother, and together they pushed the table up against the door.

"What is it, Mom?" Alison pleaded. "What's out there?"

"I don't know," MaryAnne replied, her voice shaking. "I saw— there was something looking in the window, Alison. I barely saw it, but—" She shuddered, once again remembering those terrible slits of eyes staring in at her. "Oh, God! It won't hold!" Her mind raced, trying to think of something—anything—that might prevent whatever was outside from getting into the house. But there were too many windows, too many doors.

The gun!

"Come on!" she yelled. Turning, she bolted out of the kitchen, raced through the dining room and the living room, into the den. She fumbled with the door to the gun cabinet, then remembered it was locked!

The key!

Where was the key?

Rushing to the desk, she jerked open the center drawer with enough force to pull it all the way out. Instantly, its contents cascaded to the floor. A collection of pens, pencils, paper clips, and all the other detritus that had collected in the drawer spread around her feet. She fell to her knees, scrabbling through the mess with trembling fingers, finally finding what she was looking for.

"Open it!" she yelled to Alison, throwing her daughter the keys as she started jerking the other drawers open, searching for the box of shells she'd put away after Olivia had given her the shooting lesson.

She found the box and opened it, her eyes widening as she saw there were only two left. Clutching them and throwing the empty box aside, she ran to Alison, jerking the gun out of the rack as soon as Alison opened the door.

"What's going to happen, Mom?" Alison asked as MaryAnne fumbled with the gun, Olivia's instructions on how to load it suddenly gone from her mind.

"It's all right," MaryAnne told her, her trembling voice belying her words. "We're going to be okay!" A moment later her mind cleared, and her fingers found the release that opened the magazine. She slid the two shells inside, closed the magazine, then pumped a shell into the firing chamber.

"Put some more wood on the fire, Alison," she said, though she knew the chattering of her teeth and her shivering body came more from fear than cold.

Alison started toward the fireplace, then froze, the color draining from her face as she stared at the window.

MaryAnne's gaze followed her daughter's, and she gasped.

Peering in through the window were those same eyes she'd seen only a few moments ago in the kitchen. Now, though, the rest of the face was visible as well.

The heavy features, the eyes sunken deeply and glittering almost as if electricity was surging from within them.

The tangle of matted hair, caked now with snow.

The man was bare-chested, and MaryAnne could see the corded muscles of his arms, his powerful shoulders.

Suddenly she knew.

It wasn't Storm who had killed Logan at all.

It was the evil creature that stood outside the window, impervious to the storm, glaring in at her with eyes filled with an insane fury that chilled her soul.

She raised the gun, pressing the stock firmly against her shoulder, then squeezed the forefinger of her right hand on the button that would turn on the laser sight.

An instant before the red light flashed on, its brilliant beam slashing through the storm outside, the face disappeared from the window.

"Who is it?" Alison wailed, backing up to cower against the wall opposite the window. "What does he want?"

MaryAnne said nothing, holding the gun steady, the barrel pointing toward the window, but when the face did not reappear, she finally lowered it. "I don't know," she whispered. "I don't know."

Wearily, she went to the fireplace, pulled a log from the wood box and threw it onto the pile of glowing coals.

The flames leaped upward, curling around the fresh log, which began to crackle as its sap ignited.

Then, a second later, there was a pounding on the front door. Alison's eyes widened, and she came over to stand by her mother, pressing close to her.

The pounding at the door was repeated, followed by a long silence. MaryAnne felt her pulse racing and imagined she could hear the thudding of her heart. She was about to take a step toward the door to the living room, when there was a crash, followed by the tinkling of glass.

"He broke in!" Alison screamed. "He's inside the house!"

"Don't move," MaryAnne told her. "Just don't move at all." Once again she raised the gun, training it on the doorway to the living room, her finger already pressing the button on the laser sight.

A brilliant red dot appeared on the far wall of the living room, its edge crystal clear, despite the light in the room.

She heard a scuffling sound, then a grunt.

A shadow appeared on the living room floor. MaryAnne's eyes fixed on it, watching it change shape as the man who cast it moved slowly toward the door to the den.

As her eyes caught a movement just beyond the door, she jerked the gun to the right, instinctively squeezing the trigger.

The gun roared, and a hole appeared in the wall that separated the den from the living room, instantly followed by a howl of pain. A split second later the man appeared in the doorway.

His chest was covered with blood and his left hand clutched the wound in his side where the buckshot had penetrated the wall and slashed through his skin to lodge in the muscles of his belly. He started toward them, staggering into the room, his right hand reaching out toward them, its clawlike nails slashing at the air.

Despite the panic rising in her, MaryAnne pumped the second cartridge into the chamber, raised the gun, and once more pressed her finger on the laser switch. The red light flashed on, centered on the man's stomach.

Holding her breath, she once more squeezed the trigger.

Again the roar of the gun filled the room, and MaryAnne felt the impact of its kick wrench her shoulder, but she held her balance.

His eyes opened wide as the buckshot, unhindered by the wall of the den, tore into his stomach, knocking him backward. Blood began spewing from the wound, but he seemed unaware of it. He leaned against the door frame, his eyes flicking around the room as if he were searching for something, and then he began to sink down to the floor.

His legs gave way, and suddenly he dropped, rolling over on his back.

His right hand, which only a second ago had been reaching out toward MaryAnne, now went to the wound in his belly, moving spasmodically, as if he were trying to pack his ruined intestines back inside his shredded skin.

Then, his eyes closing, his whole great frame shuddered and he lay still.

MaryAnne and Alison Carpenter stared in shock at the body, still oozing blood, that now blocked the door to the living room. Neither of them moved, neither of them even breathed.

Time seemed to stand still.

Outside, the howling wind of the blizzard, finally spent, died away.

Silence—a terrible silence—filled the house.

CHAPTER 27

"Wh-Who is he?" Alison stammered, her voice barely audible. Her whole body trembled as she stared at the man lying on the floor, blocking the door to the living room.

MaryAnne opened her mouth, but no sound came from her throat at all.

Her knees felt weak and her heart was still pounding, but slowly she managed to get her breathing back to normal.

She had done it.

She had actually killed a man.

A twinge of nausea wrenched her gut, but she put it down, refusing to give in to it.

He's not a man, she told herself.

Even if he has a name, and it's Shane Slater, he's still not a man, but a monster.

A monster covered with her son's blood.

This was what had killed her son. This—this *creature* whose corpse was sprawled on the floor had killed her little boy.

She understood it all now.

It was this man whom Logan must have seen.

How long had he been out there, creeping around the house under the cover of the blizzard?

Was this the first time he'd come?

But she knew better than that.

It was this—thing that had terrified the horses in the barn and set Bill Sikes to prowling in the dark, searching for the source of their fear.

She shuddered now as she thought of how often he must have been out in the yard, concealed in the darkness of the night, peering in through the windows, watching them.

Spying on them.

Had they ever been safe from those eyes as they sat in the den or the kitchen?

And what had he been looking for?

But she knew why he was there, for as she gazed at him now, she was absolutely certain who he was.

The man whose picture she'd found in Audrey's photo album only that morning.

And now that she could see him in the flesh, even through the distortions of both his life and his death, she recognized the resemblance to Joey Wilkenson.

The same strong brow line, the same firm jaw.

The ears set close to the head, though Shane Slater's were large—unnaturally large.

She knew why he'd come. He was watching Joey.

Watching his son.

But what had he wanted tonight?

Had he come to kill them and take Joey away with him? Or had it been something else, something she could never even guess at? She took a step toward him and stared once more into his twisted face, his open eyes seeming to be fixed on her as if he were still alive.

Insane!

He looked insane, and she knew he had to be to have stayed up in the mountains year after year, keeping himself alive while he watched his child grow up as the son of another man.

At last she found her voice. "He's the man from the cabin," she replied to Alison's question, her voice sounding preternaturally loud in the hollow silence that had fallen over the house now that the wind had died away. Should she tell Alison he was also Joey's father?

No.

At least not now.

"They must have chased him down," she said, not answering Alison's question. With an effort, MaryAnne forced herself to relax her grip on the shotgun, her clenched fingers sore from the force she had been exerting on the hard rubber of its stock. "We have to get him out of here."

Alison's eyes widened with fear and she said nothing, her mouth going dry as she thought of actually touching the horrible bleeding thing on the floor.

MaryAnne leaned the shotgun against the stone chimney and took a tentative step toward Shane Slater's hulking form, then stopped.

What if he wasn't dead?

Her eyes darted around the room, searching for some weapon other than the empty shotgun, and finally fell on the fireplace poker, a heavy black wrought-iron rod whose end bent at a right angle, the tip of which had been forged into a sharp point. Her hand trembling, she reached out and took it from the hook below the heavy mantelpiece. "Help me, Alison," she whispered as she started once more toward Slater's prostrate form, her feet heavy, her legs threatening to give way beneath her. "For God's sake—I can't do this by myself!"

"Mommy, I—"

"Help me!" MaryAnne said again, her voice rising now, taking on a sharp edge that finally penetrated the fog that had gathered around Alison's mind.

Slowly, forcing herself to take each halting step, Alison moved away from the fireplace and started toward her mother. "Wh-What are we going to do with him?" she breathed.

"We'll take him outside," MaryAnne replied. "We're snowed in, Alison. We can't get out of here until someone comes for us, and we can't stay in here with"—she hesitated, searching for the right word, but nothing came—"with *that*! You have to help me get him out of here!"

Alison nodded wordlessly, edging toward her mother, staying as far away as she could from the bloody stain that was still spreading across the floor. "H-How?" she asked. "How are we going to move him?"

"We'll have to drag him," MaryAnne replied. "If we each take an arm—" A shudder passed through her at the mere thought of actually touching the bloody corpse. But what choice did she have? If she left him there, even covered him up, she would never make it through the long night ahead. When they finally found her, she would be cowering on the floor, gibbering nonsense, her mind no longer functioning at all. Even now, she could feel the edges of her sanity beginning to fray, feel a terrible urge spreading through her to give in to the impulse to scream for help.

Scream, even though no one would hear her.

They were alone—completely alone—and outside the snow was still falling, piling higher with every minute that passed.

How long would it be before help could get to them, before they could get away from this terrible place forever?

She didn't know.

All she knew was that unless she got the body of the man who had killed her son out of the house, she would go mad.

"Now!" she told Alison, her voice cracking. "Let's do it, and get it over with!"

She bent down and took one of Shane Slater's wrists. Alison, still not certain she could actually bring herself to touch the ruin of what had once been a man, forced herself to reach tentatively toward the other.

Alison's fingers were still a few inches from Shane Slater's arm when suddenly he raised his hand, his clawlike fingernails closing around her wrist.

Alison screamed as MaryAnne realized her worst fear had just come true—Slater wasn't dead at all. His eyes were wide open now, and as his fingers clamped down, his nails digging into the flesh of Alison's arm, his head turned and his mouth began to work.

Dropping his arm, MaryAnne rose up, fury rising in her as she glared down into the dying face of the man she thought she had already killed. Alison, immobilized, was staring down into Shane Slater's face, too. His lips worked spasmodically as he struggled to speak. MaryAnne's grip tightened on the poker. She raised it high above her head, its sharp point aimed directly at Shane Slater's forehead.

As the poker began its deadly arc, Shane Slater's words finally formed on his lips.

"*I'm . . . sorry . . .*" he whispered. "*Tried to . . . save . . . him . . .*"

They were the last words he spoke, for even as he uttered them, MaryAnne brought the poker down with all the force she could muster, plunging the point through his forehead, tearing his brain to shreds.

As his hand fell away from Alison's wrist, the girl looked up at her mother, her face ashen. "Did you hear him?" she asked, her voice trembling. "Did you hear what he said?"

MaryAnne dropped the poker to the floor, saying nothing, but when Alison repeated the dead man's final words, she shook her head.

"He couldn't have said that," she breathed. "He killed Logan, Alison. He killed him! Now let's get him out of here!" Certain he was dead this time, MaryAnne bent down and grasped both of Shane Slater's arms, then dragged him through the living room and dining room.

It wasn't until Alison heard her mother in the kitchen, pulling the table away from the back door, that she finally found the strength to go and help her. But even as the two of them dragged the body outside and across the yard to leave it out of sight behind the barn, Alison kept hearing the man's last words over and over again.

He must have killed Logan! *He must have!*

But Joey was somewhere outside, too!

Now Shane Slater's words were replaced with the ones she'd heard in school that morning.

I bet Joey did it, she heard Andrea Stiffle saying. *He's crazy, and I bet he did it!*

What if Andrea was right? What if Joey, not this man, had killed her brother?

A shudder of pure terror went through her, and she knew that the day was not yet done.

———

Joey Wilkenson came slowly out of the dark reverie into which he'd fallen after the man from the cabin had leaped from the loft into the yard below, disappearing instantly into the howling blizzard. The sound of shotgun blasts echoed in his ears, but as his mind came slowly into focus, he wasn't sure whether they had been real or whether he had only imagined them.

Finally, for the first time, the biting cold of the afternoon began to penetrate his body, and he shivered, then burrowed into the comparative warmth of the thick layer of hay on the loft's floor.

Burrowed like an animal seeking shelter from the elements.

A moment later, though, he heard a faint scream, and then the wind began to die away, and some voice deep inside him whispered to him that something had happened.

Something terrible.

He crept forward once more, but stayed away from the open door to the loft, his instincts telling him to keep himself concealed. Still almost buried in the hay, he pressed his eye to a knothole in one of the barn's heavy planks.

For a moment he saw nothing, but then, as the windblown snow began to settle back to earth, the outline of the house began to take form. As he watched, the back door opened and a figure emerged.

Then there were two figures.

Two figures, backing out of the kitchen, dragging something after them.

A body!

The body of the man who had been in the loft with him, who had spoken to him, who had touched him.

Who had claimed to be his father.

Could it possibly be true?

Joey didn't know, but as he watched MaryAnne and Alison drag the corpse out into the snowy yard, each of them clinging to one of its arms, he felt a dark rage rising inside him.

They had killed him, shot him as if he'd been no more than an animal in the woods!

As MaryAnne and Alison moved around the corner of the barn, disappearing from his line of vision, Joey slithered free from the hay and moved toward the ladder. A moment later he was back downstairs, slipping silently into the tack room.

There were clothes there—clothes his mother had deemed no longer good enough for school, and had relegated to the barn for him to wear as he went about his chores until either he outgrew them or they wore out. Rummaging in a trunk, he found a pair of torn jeans, a stained flannel shirt, and a thick sweater, frayed around the cuffs.

He pulled them on, then shoved his feet into a pair of shoes that were already half a size too small.

Dressed, he left the tack room and moved silently toward the back of the barn, where a small door led to the outside. He paused inside the door, listening, but heard no sound. Finally he opened the door a crack and peered out into the pale light of the afternoon.

The body of the mountain man lay in the snow, next to the shed where the tractor was stored.

MaryAnne and Alison had disappeared. Joey could see the tracks they'd left in the snow as they started back to the house.

In the silence of the now gently falling snow, Joey left the shelter of the barn and walked slowly to where Shane Slater lay, then dropped to his knees to look into the mountain man's face.

His father.

He tried to deny it, tried to tell himself it couldn't possibly be true.

Yet deep inside, he knew it *was* true, had known it even as the man had spoken the words.

Shane Slater.

The name was burned into Joey's memory, though he'd only heard it once.

How long had he been up in the mountains?

Had his father been there all his life, watching him?

He had.

Joey knew it, felt it in that hidden place deep inside him where all his most secret feelings had always lain concealed.

Now he knew why he'd never been afraid of the forest, never been afraid to wander alone up into the mountains.

His father—his real father—had been there, too, though Joey had never consciously known it.

Now, too, he knew why he'd never made friends, never fit in with the rest of the kids in Sugarloaf.

He was different!

Something inside him was different from everyone else.

That was why he'd spent so much of his time alone, or with the animals on the ranch.

It wasn't just the way his dad had treated him. It was something inside himself; only the animals had never turned away from him, never acted like there was something wrong with him, never shut him out the way the kids at school had.

And always, for as long as he could remember, the mountains had beckoned to him, calling out to something in his soul, whispering to him that they were the place where he truly belonged.

Now he understood why.

The mountains were where his father was; his real father, who had been there all along, watching over him. As he knelt in the snow, Joey began to remember all the times when he'd stood at the window of his room, feeling the strange, unseen presence reaching out to him, trying to resist the urge to go out into the night.

Now he knew that this man had been there, outside the house, hidden in the dark, so close by that Joey had felt his presence.

He'd been there all along, watching over him, and in the end, when his mother's husband had begun beating him, his father had protected him.

Loved him.

Even now Joey could feel the mountain man's touch on his cheek, feel the love that had warmed him as the man crouched beside him.

The man who had been his father, and whom he'd betrayed.

For today Joey had showed Rick Martin where his father lived, led him up the mountainside, so they could begin tracking him down.

But his father had forgiven him.

Even after they'd hunted him all day, driven him down from the safety of the mountains, he'd forgiven him.

His father knew he was going to die—had told Joey he was going to die that very day.

But still his father had forgiven him.

Forgiven him, and loved him.

Reaching out to caress Shane Slater's cheek as earlier Slater had caressed his own, Joey Wilkenson opened his mouth, and out of his throat rose an unearthly howl of anguish.

Anguish, and rage.

At long last, Joey had truly become his father's son.

———————

Olivia Sherbourne heard the howl rise out of the silence of the falling snow, heard it echo across the valley, no longer muffled by the wind that had driven the blizzard, then suddenly die away.

The same howl she'd heard before, the same inhuman venting of twisted emotions, the same painful wail that had made her blood run cold only a few minutes earlier.

Could it really have been only a few minutes? It felt like hours—endless hours—that she'd spent stumbling through the snow, desperately searching for some recognizable landmark.

Now, though, as the windblown snow that had all but blinded her began to settle, something familiar at last emerged from the whiteout.

Twenty yards away stood one of the white-barked pines—the strange trees that bore no resemblance at all to the tall lodgepoles that blanketed the flanks of the mountains. Its twisting branches spread from a gnarled trunk, and its oddly leaflike clumps of needles had trapped great masses of snow, so that it looked as if it were covered with great puffs of cotton.

She recognized the tree—she had seen it every time she came up to the ranch, its unique form always catching her eye as she emerged from the narrow driveway into the large clearing that was dominated by the house.

But this afternoon she was approaching it from a different direction. Suddenly she understood what had happened. She had moved north through the woods, instead of west, so instead of paralleling the driveway as it wound up the valley, she had been moving across the valley floor. Still, though she couldn't quite see them yet, she knew the sheds and barn were just beyond the tree.

As was whatever creature had uttered the howl of rage whose echoes still lingered in the valley. Removing her shotgun from her shoulder, Olivia checked the chamber to be certain a cartridge was ready, then started toward the ranch's outbuildings. A surge of new energy ran through her as she realized she was no longer lost, was no longer at risk of dying in the snowstorm. Her shotgun held at the ready, she pushed her way through the snowdrifts, moving as quickly as she could.

———

Kneeling by his father's corpse, Joey Wilkenson's ears picked up the faint sound of snow crunching under walking feet. His body tensed and he unconsciously sniffed at the air, trying to catch the scent of whatever might be approaching.

A low growl rumbled in his throat, and then he scuttled away, disappearing around the corner of the shed, crouching in the shelter of the little building, all his senses alert as he watched and waited.

———

The tractor shed was visible now, and Olivia redoubled her efforts, her goal finally clearly in sight, for beyond the shed was the barn, and beyond that she could at last make out part of the house itself. Only a few more yards.

She stopped dead in her tracks, her eyes widening as she saw the pair of feet that stuck out from the corner of the tractor shed.

A pair of feet—bare, their soles thick with calluses, the toes twisted and bent, ending in curving nails that looked almost like claws. Her pulse quickening, Olivia changed course, veering toward the pair of feet, and a moment later found herself staring down at a corpse.

A corpse that was lying in the snow, the great gaping wound in its belly still oozing blood.

Two eyes stared up at her, gazing sightlessly from their sunken sockets.

In the man's forehead was a deep wound, as if someone had driven a spike into his skull, then torn it loose again.

Olivia gazed at the man's face, fear building inside her as the twisted features began to look faintly familiar.

But surely she had never seen this man before—if she had, she would never have forgotten him, for the face had a feral look to it, a strange mixture of something partly human, partly animal.

Suddenly, a menacing snarl penetrated Olivia's thoughts. She froze, every muscle in her body tensing, then swung around, raising the shotgun to her shoulder, her left hand gripping its stock, her right forefinger curling around the trigger.

A second later Joey Wilkenson sprang at her from the opposite end of the tractor shed, his body smashing into her back with enough force to knock her to the ground.

The shotgun went off, and Olivia felt her right arm rip free from its socket as the weapon kicked back into her shoulder. She screamed at the searing pain that shot out from the dislocated joint, then tried to roll over, tried to free herself from the weight of the creature that had attacked her.

But even as she tried to move, she felt an arm snake around her neck, felt the pressure of it cutting off her breath.

She had to move. Had to do something—anything!—to free herself from her attacker.

She struggled, her good arm flailing in the snow, a keening cry of pain and terror rising from her throat, but it was too late, for the pain from her right shoulder was already draining her energy, and her right arm was worse than useless in her attempts to defend herself.

As Joey Wilkenson's teeth sank into the back of her neck, Olivia Sherbourne was all but unaware of the new pain that assaulted her body, for her mind had already begun its inevitable withdrawal into the soft, painless darkness of unconsciousness.

When his grisly work was finally done, and he felt Olivia's body lying still beneath him, Joey stood up.

Fresh blood glistened on his sweater, and he wiped more of it from his face with his sleeve.

His breath was coming in panting gasps, but as he stared down at the corpse of the woman he had known all his life, the woman he had just killed, a surge of heat poured through him.

He felt strong and powerful, energized by the kill. His nostrils flared as he sucked in the intoxicating aroma of fresh blood, and he finally understood who and what he was.

Turning away from Olivia Sherbourne's corpse, he made his way through the drifting snow to the fence that separated the yard from the field and the forest beyond.

Vaulting the fence in a single graceful motion, he loped toward the forest, his swift stride carrying him easily across the pasture, which the wind had swept nearly clean of snow. Only when he was at the edge of the forest did he stop to look back.

Through the falling snow, the house was just visible, and he gazed at it for a moment, then turned away.

It was no longer his home, would never be his home again.

From now on, his home would be the mountains, where he would live as his father had lived, hiding during the day, concealing himself from the enemies who lived in the valley below, coming out only at night.

Coming out to hunt in the darkness.

CHAPTER 28

MaryAnne came awake slowly, her eyes blinking in the bright sunlight that flooded through the large east windows of the living room. For a long moment she resisted awakening at all, for as consciousness returned, so also did the paralyzing fear that had all but immobilized her through the long evening and night that had preceded this oddly sunny morning.

It shouldn't have been sunny this morning—given what had come before, there should have been rain falling from the sky. Drizzling rain, dropping from leaden clouds, tapping a mournful dirge on the house's roof.

For a long time MaryAnne didn't move at all, even closed her eyes against the sunlight, as if by that simple act she could shut out the reality of yesterday, pretend to herself for a few more minutes that none of it had really happened at all, that it was simply a nightmare lingering in her mind as she slowly awakened, and any second she would realize the truth—that Logan was asleep in his room upstairs, and Joey was back in his, as well.

Perhaps Bill Sikes might even now be coming down from his cabin, tramping through the glistening snow to begin his chores.

And Olivia—perhaps she would call Olivia, ask her to come up for coffee, and tell her about the terrible dream she'd had last night.

The dream in which she'd come back to the house with Alison, huddled with her daughter in the kitchen, her mind spinning as she tried to decide what to do.

Then she'd heard a howl rising from somewhere beyond the barn, and her blood had run cold as the unbidden thought that Shane Slater—whom she'd shot, then killed with the fireplace poker—had somehow come back to life. She had clung to Alison, cradling her adolescent daughter protectively, almost as if she were still a baby, and stared out the window into the snowstorm, terror building in her as she waited for Slater to appear, his belly torn and bleeding, his chest smeared with Logan's blood, and an oozing hole in his forehead.

Dead, but not dead, and coming inexorably back toward the house.

Toward her. Toward Alison.

And she'd known that the next time he appeared, she would be able to defend neither her daughter nor herself, for her courage was spent, and her body, as well as her mind, were exhausted.

But he hadn't come.

Instead, a terrible silence had followed the bestial howl of rage, a silence that seemed to go on forever, and then there had been a shot.

A single blast of a shotgun, its roar echoing off the cliffs high above the mountain, followed only a moment later by a scream of pain and terror.

A woman's scream.

Olivia Sherbourne's scream.

From the moment she heard it, MaryAnne knew who had uttered it, knew too that even as the scream's echoes faded away, Olivia had died. Her arms tightened around Alison, whose face was buried against her bosom, but she had said nothing as she continued to stare out the window, waiting silently for whatever might come next.

Then she had seen Joey.

He appeared from somewhere beyond the barn, running across the field with the grace of a young animal, and even before he stopped at the edge of the woods and turned to face the house, she understood that it was he who had just killed Olivia.

When he paused in his flight and turned to gaze at the house for a moment, the brilliant red stains on the white sweater he was wearing only confirmed the bitter truth that had formed in her mind. She watched him silently as he gazed at the house, then finally turned away and disappeared into the forest.

MaryAnne had lost track of time after that. She had no idea how long she sat in the kitchen, gently rocking Alison, waiting not only for her daughter's terror to pass, but for her own fear to release her from its paralytic grip as well.

At some point they'd moved into the living room, nailed a blanket over the smashed window through which the intruder had entered the house, even spread more blankets on the floor to cover the already darkening stains of drying blood.

She'd built a fire on the immense stone hearth in the living room, and the two of them sat silently on the sofa, MaryAnne sitting up, Alison curled on her side, her head on her mother's lap, neither of them saying anything.

Both of them staring into the flickering flames.

Each of them dealing with what had happened in her own way.

MaryAnne wasn't sure when they finally fell asleep, couldn't have said whether night had yet fallen when their exhausted minds and bodies gave themselves up to unconsciousness.

Now, though, as she opened her eyes, at last giving up the wish to retreat back into the warm oblivion of sleep, she knew that it had not been a terrible nightmare at all—it had all happened.

She stirred, her stiff muscles protesting, then eased herself from beneath the weight of Alison's head, gently slipping a pillow beneath her daughter's cheek and spreading an afghan over her curled body. A few coals still glowed in the fireplace, and after she checked the telephone—still dead—MaryAnne added three logs to the guttering fire, then used a worn leather bellows to breathe life back into the flames. As the fire flickered up, twisting between the logs, she went to the window and peered out into the brilliance of the morning.

Snow must have been falling all night, for now a blanket nearly two feet deep covered the yard, the roofs of the barn and outbuildings, even the top rail of the pasture fence. A single line of deer tracks broke the glistening surface of sparkling crystals, and the branches of the trees bordering the stream were sagging under heavy loads, for their leaves, barely starting to change color, had caught far more of the glittering flakes than the naked branches alone could have supported.

Overnight, the valley had been transformed from early fall into deep winter. MaryAnne shivered as she gazed out on the monochromatic fantasy. But the chill, she instantly realized, stemmed more from her certain knowledge of the nightmare the snow now covered than from the cold beyond the window.

"Mommy?" Alison said, her voice sounding sleepy. MaryAnne turned to face her daughter, who this morning looked much younger than her thirteen years. "It all really happened, didn't it?" Alison breathed, her eyes fearful, her face pale.

MaryAnne could only nod, unable to summon any words at all.

"What are we going to do?" Alison went on. "Are we going to go home? Are we going to go back to Daddy?"

Mommy . . . Daddy . . .

Only yesterday morning Alison had still been calling her

"Mom," and it had been years since she'd referred to her father as anything but "Dad." Now, after the terrible trauma of the previous day, she had reverted to the terms of her babyhood. Her heart going out to the girl who was now all she had left, MaryAnne went back to the sofa, sat down, and put her arms around Alison once more. "I don't know what we're going to do, darling," she said quietly. "All I know is that right now there isn't anything we can do at all. We're snowed in, and the telephone isn't working yet. We have to wait for someone to come and help us."

"What if no one comes?" Alison asked.

"They will," MaryAnne promised her daughter. "As soon as they can, someone will come to help us." She started toward the kitchen, knowing that she had to do something—anything— before the horror of last night closed in on her all over again.

But as she started fixing a pot of coffee, she glanced out the window, out across the field to the spot where Joey had disappeared into the woods.

A thought came into her mind.

What if Joey comes back?

What if no one comes to help us, and Joey comes back?

———

High up in the mountains, Rick Martin stirred, then came slowly awake. Every bone in his body ached with cold, but he had survived the night. The small fire he had built had long ago died away, and he shoved his hand in his pocket, feeling for the hard plastic case that contained his meager supply of matches. He finally found it, pulled it out, then realized his fingers were too numb even to unscrew the cap of the small gray cylinder. He began massaging the fingers of his right hand, then unzipped his jacket and slipped his hands inside, burying them in the warmth of his armpits. While the feeling slowly began to seep back into his fingers, and the agonizing itch of frostbite settled in as well,

he glanced around for something to add to the black coals that
were all that was left of last night's fire. A moment later he began
with pain-curled fingers to break up one of the branches he'd
used as a makeshift bed, piling the pieces carefully to allow as
much air as possible to circulate through the damp pine needles.
When he was at last satisfied, he struck the first match and held
it in the center of the small pile. The flame burnt brightly. Some
of the needles sputtered, started to catch, then died away as the
match burnt down to a smoking stub.

He was down to the next to the last match when the fire finally
caught. He cupped his hands around the tiny flame, blowing
gently on it as it spread through the needles. Only when it was
burning strongly did he risk adding more fuel, but the fire held,
and it wasn't long before he felt the heat begin to seep through
his clothing.

He broke up the rest of the branches that had both cushioned
him from the hard ground and helped insulate him from the
snow that had fallen through the night, adding it all to the fire,
building it up until finally the heat grew intense enough that he
had to stand up and back away from it a pace or two. Finally
he turned away from it altogether and began kicking down the
snow barrier he'd built to protect himself from yesterday's gale
winds. The barrier was far thicker than he'd built it: snow had
drifted as long as the wind had blown. Its base was now almost
four feet thick, and it rose nearly as far above the ground. But
the snow was soft, and within a few seconds he had leveled the
wall, freeing himself from the tiny cavern in which he'd weathered the storm. He gazed out over the valley, covered now in a
thick layer of white, only the sheer granite outcroppings still free
of snow. Far below him, barely visible in the distance, was the
village, looking for all the world like a tiny hamlet caught in a
crystal paperweight, its roofs forever buried in white, candles
eternally glowing in tiny painted windows.

He pulled his radio from its holster and flipped it on. This morning, with the blizzard no longer turning the signal into hissing static, he could hear the dispatcher down in Challis as clearly as if they were talking on the telephone.

"Gillie's been on the phone all night long. If I don't patch you through, I think she'll drive up and kill me, even if she has to plow the road herself. Jeez, Rick, do you believe this?"

"It's almost three feet deep up where I am," Rick told her. "How soon can you get a helicopter to lift me out?"

"I'll start working on it right away," the dispatcher promised. "And we have a possible ID on the man you're after. Someone named Shane Slater, who's been a fugitive for almost fifteen years." Before Rick could reply, Gillie's voice came through the radio, her relief apparent.

"Rick? My God, are you really all right?"

"As all right as I can expect, considering I didn't get any dinner, I missed a football game, and I might just be getting too old to sleep on nothing but a pile of branches. But I'm alive, so I guess I can't complain. How'd you make out?"

"I'm fine," Gillie replied, "except I haven't had any sleep at all. But I'm worried about Olivia, and MaryAnne Carpenter. Both their phones are out, and the only thing I've been able to find out is that the Stiffles saw Olivia on their way down to town yesterday afternoon. She said she was going to get MaryAnne and the kids and take them back to her place."

"Then that's where they probably are," Rick told her. "Olivia knows what she's doing."

Gillie hesitated, wondering if she should even tell Rick the other detail that was worrying her. Before she could make up her mind, he hit on it himself. "Have you looked out the back window? We can see her chimney from there."

"I already did," Gillie replied. "There's no smoke, and you know Olivia—she won't heat any other way, if she can help it. If she were there, she'd have kept a fire burning all night."

Once again Rick scanned the valley, then saw what looked like a wisp of smoke drifting up from the area where the Wilkenson house stood. "I think they must all have holed up at El Monte," he said into the radio. Then the dispatcher's voice cut in.

"Rick, it doesn't look like we can get a chopper up to you for a couple of hours. We've got people stranded all over the place, and most of them need medical help. Can you just sit tight for a while?"

"I can do a hell of a lot better than that," Rick replied, his voice grim. "If I could get myself in here in the middle of a blizzard, I can damned well get myself out again now that it's over."

"Rick, you stay right where you are!" Gillie interrupted, her voice rising. "You're lucky to be alive, and you know it! Just stay where you are until someone can come and pick you up."

Rick shook his head, despite the fact no one was there to see him. "No way! I'll be a hell of a lot better off hiking out than dangling from a rope underneath one of those whirlybirds. They'd probably drag me through the trees and wind up killing me themselves. Talk to you later."

Snapping off the radio before Gillie could argue with him, he kicked snow onto the already dying fire, then set out. He pushed his way through the drifts until he came to the edge of the forest, where the going got much easier, since most of the snow had been caught by the dense canopy of branches overhead. Here, for the most part, the ground was still nearly bare, and he started back the way he'd come, threading his way through the underbrush until at last he came back to the spot where he'd left the Jeep.

He circled the snow-covered vehicle, assessing the situation, and finally decided he had a better than even chance of driving himself out the way he'd come in, if he could just get the car turned around. He brushed the tailgate free of snow, then lifted it up. Inside, half buried under the collection of odds and ends that always seemed to gather there, he found the set of chains that he always left there, even when he cleaned the Jeep out, and a shovel he carried for situations such as this one. The hard part, he decided, was going to be digging away enough snow to get the chains onto all four wheels. Once he had them in place, the rest should be easy.

An hour later, after more cursing than he'd done in the past twelve months combined, and with the skin missing from at least half of his knuckles, the chains were secured. After digging as much snow as he could away from the area around the car, he got in and tried the engine.

It ground for a few seconds, coughed, then caught, and he babied it along, giving it small spurts of gas to digest as it slowly warmed up, its uneven chugs slowly settling into a steady purr. He turned the heater on full blast, then held his hands in front of the dash vents until he felt them begin to thaw out once again. Finally he checked the transfer box, then put the transmission in reverse. The Jeep began to move, and he heard the crackling of snapping twigs as the rear end left the road and plunged into the dense underbrush. When the car would go no farther, he shifted into forward, spun the wheel around, then nosed into the brush on the other side of the narrow track.

After three back and forths, the Jeep was finally turned around, and Rick shifted it once more into its lowest forward gear. As the engine labored, the vehicle began pushing its way through the snow.

Thirty minutes later he was back in the campground, and twenty minutes after that he finally gave up, for the road had left the protection of the forest, and the snow blowing across the valley the day before had drifted nearly six feet deep. Turning the car around once more, Rick went back up the road until he judged he was as close as he could get to the ranch house. Switching off the engine, he abandoned the car once more, but knew it didn't matter. He was back in totally familiar territory, and only a quarter of a mile from El Monte. He switched the radio on, reported his position, and asked the dispatcher to call Gillie for him. "I'd talk to her myself, but I doubt she's speaking to me right now. Talk to you when I know what the situation is up here."

He made his way down the gentle incline toward Coyote Creek, moving quickly through the forest, finding a place to cross the stream only a hundred yards out of his way, then emerged from the forest and gazed at the house some forty yards away.

The Range Rover, covered in snow, was still parked in the yard, and a grayish plume of smoke rose from the chimney.

Only when his eyes fell on the blanket hanging inside the smashed window did Rick realize that, though the house seemed peaceful now, something had gone very wrong.

Wading through the snow, he finally made it to the front porch and banged loudly on the door.

Hearing nothing but silence, he pounded again, and was about to leave the porch to go around to the kitchen door on the side when he heard MaryAnne Carpenter's voice, its trembling clearly audible, despite the muffling of the heavy wooden door. "Wh-Who is it?"

"It's Rick Martin, Mrs. Carpenter!" the deputy called. "Are you all right?"

The door opened the slightest crack, and MaryAnne peered suspiciously out at him for a second, then pulled the door wide as she recognized him. As the door swung open, Rick could see by her ashen complexion and the look of pure terror in her eyes that something had, indeed, gone very wrong.

"They're dead," MaryAnne said, her voice numb, tears beginning to run down her pale face as she realized that, at last, it was safe to give in to the shock. "They're all dead. Logan— Olivia—Slater—all dead. All dead . . ."

Rick stepped into the house, guiding MaryAnne gently back to the kitchen, his radio in his hand once again.

"I'm at El Monte," he said. "And we're going to need help. A lot of help. Get a plow up here, now! We may have three people dead!" As they came into the kitchen, he saw Alison, her face as pale as her mother's, sitting at the table, an untouched glass of orange juice in front of her. He glanced around once more, then turned to MaryAnne. "Where's Joey?" he asked.

MaryAnne's eyes fixed on Rick's face for a moment, then drifted toward the window, and the soaring mountain peaks that loomed high above the narrow valley. "Gone," she whispered. "That man—his name was Shane Slater, and he was Joey's father. And now Joey's gone." Her voice turned hollow as her eyes fixed on the towering peaks. "Like his father," she murmured. "He's gone up into the mountains, just like his father did."

———

Joey's eyes snapped open, his senses instantly alert. He was in the cabin—his father's cabin—and once more he'd slept in his father's bed, curled beneath a mound of animal skins.

He was no longer alone.

He could sense a presence somewhere close to the cabin, though he could neither hear any sound nor see anything moving through the empty windows or open door.

Yet he was certain that something was there. He crept out from under the heavy furs, still dressed in the clothes he'd found in the tack room yesterday afternoon. His bare feet made no sound as he moved to the door. Finally, he stepped out on the porch.

The snow was deep, and even the tracks he'd made as he climbed up to the cabin had long since disappeared. The air was still, and the morning was silent, all sound muffled by the layer of snow that had fallen during the night. And yet Joey could still sense that invisible presence lurking somewhere nearby.

He whistled, a single soft, low note. A moment later he heard a faint sound, a barely audible whimpering, and then there was a movement in the brush at the edge of the clearing.

As he watched, the wolf emerged from the dense bushes, her head low, her tail curled between her legs, the mangled carcass of a rabbit dangling from her jaws. She gazed steadily at Joey, her eyes glittering in the sunlight. After a few seconds Joey dropped to a crouch, holding his hand out toward her. "Come on, girl," he said. "It's okay—come on."

The wolf hesitated for a moment but then moved forward, limping on three legs, her right hindpaw held off the ground. When she was still six feet from Joey, she stopped short, whimpering again, then dropped down into the snow, stretching herself out, except for the right hindleg, which stayed curled against her chest.

"What's wrong?" Joey asked, leaning toward the wolf. "Did they hurt you? It's okay, though. You're safe now, and I'll take care of you." Talking steadily, keeping his voice low, he moved closer, finally dropping down into a crouch again when he was next to the animal. He held out his hand, letting her sniff at his fingers, then reached out to stroke her head. She trembled under his touch, but made no move to shy away, then Joey stroked her sinewy body. When the wolf made no move either to snap at him or to run away, Joey spoke to her once more, eventually standing up again and starting toward the cabin. As he urged her along, the animal struggled back to her feet and limped after him, dropping to the floor as soon as she was inside the cabin.

As she rolled over onto her left side, Joey saw the mat of bloody hair around the wound Tony Moleno's bullet had torn in her flank.

He went to the stove and added some wood to the fire he'd banked the night before, then took a battered pan outside and filled it with snow. As the snow melted in the pan on the stove, he talked steadily to the wolf, sitting next to her, stroking her fur gently. When the water was finally warm enough, he found a rag and began cleaning the wound.

The wolf, trembling under his touch, seemed to understand that he was helping her, and made no move to pull away, uttered no snarls of warning.

At last the wound was clean, and Joey discovered that the bullet had gone completely through her leg, leaving a wound on each side. He found more rags, and tore them into thin strips, then began binding up the wound. When he was finished, the wolf sat up, favoring her right side, and licked his hand.

"Good girl," he said. Realizing he was hungry, Joey glanced around the cabin, looking for something to eat. Then remembered the rabbit the wolf had been carrying when she'd crept out of the brush a few minutes ago. Leaving the cabin, he went outside and, at the far side of the clearing, perched on the carcass of the rabbit, saw a hawk pecking out the little creature's eyes. Joey ran toward it, shouting and waving his arms, and the bird screamed with sudden fury, its wings flapping in a gesture of defiance. As Joey came closer, though, it launched itself into the air, its talons still clutching the body of the rabbit. Only when Joey was a few feet away did the hawk, its instinct for self-preservation overcoming its desire to guard its prey, finally drop the rabbit and soar into the sky, out of the boy's reach. Snatching the rabbit up out of the snow, Joey trotted back to the cabin.

He found a knife and began clumsily skinning the rabbit, finally abandoning the knife altogether and using his fingers to strip the skin away from the meat below. Twisting one of the legs to snap the joint, he tore the tendons loose from the bone, then began ripping at the raw meat with his teeth. Only when his own appetite was sated did he throw the remains of the little creature to the wolf, who instantly snatched it up, swallowing the rabbit's guts in great gulps without bothering to chew.

While the wolf finished eating, Joey took the bloody skin outside to bury it in the snow, and for the first time became aware of an ominous sound echoing off the rocky cliffs above. Dropping the rabbit's hide, he scanned the valley below.

A moment later he found the source of the sound.

A helicopter was moving up the valley. As Joey watched, it hovered in place for a moment, then began dropping down.

Down into the field at El Monte Ranch.

Joey's mind began to race. They would start looking for him soon, and he already knew where they would look first.

Here, in the cabin to which he had led Rick Martin yesterday.

His eyes went to the chimney, and he saw the plume of smoke rising from it.

Smoke that would be clearly visible from the valley, since there was no wind to disperse it.

He darted back into the cabin, already searching for things he could take with him, things he might be able to use while he hunted for a place to live.

He found a knife, some rope, and a trap.

But there were other things, things he could use but knew he couldn't carry with him.

He would have to come back!

Come back some other time, at night, when no one would be watching.

But for now, he had to get away.

Filling his pockets with whatever came to hand, he wrapped himself in one of the bearskins piled on the bed, then whistled softly to the wolf.

A moment later Joey was gone, the wolf hobbling after him as the boy began climbing higher up into the mountains, following his instincts.

Higher up, where the landscape was rougher, and where whatever wind might come up as the sun rose higher would wipe away the tracks he left in the snow.

Higher up, where there were caverns in the rocks, caverns in which he could hide while he learned how to live as his father had lived.

Like his father before him, Joey would disappear into the mountains, leaving no trace behind him.

CHAPTER 29

*L*ate that afternoon, in his office in Boise, Hank Henry gazed disbelievingly at the coroner's report that had just arrived on his desk. As he stared at the fax, his mind rejected the words the doctor up in Challis had written.

The cause of death of Shane Slater, who had been positively identified through a fingerprint check within an hour of the body's arrival in the Custer County morgue, had been simple and straightforward: a twelve-gauge shotgun wound had lacerated his abdomen, wounding his kidney, liver, stomach, and intestines. Even without the puncture wound in the center of his forehead, which had killed him instantly, he would have died within a matter of minutes, perhaps even seconds. By the time Mary-Anne Carpenter had swung the poker—which, along with the shotgun, had been delivered to the sheriff's office at the same time the body had been flown up to the coroner—Slater had already been dying. Indeed, the wounds he'd suffered from the two shotgun shells should have made his grasping of Alison Carpenter's arm—his last act before he'd died—impossible.

And yet there was a great deal about Shane Slater that seemed to be impossible.

The description of the body alone made no sense.

The coroner had made many notes, and as Hank Henry studied them, disbelief grew in his mind.

Fingernails like claws, twice as thick as those of a normal human being, but much narrower.

Canine teeth that were developed far beyond those in a normal human mouth, much longer than the teeth that flanked them, and ending in sharp points.

Points ideally suited to tearing meat.

Slater's jaw, too, was different, the chin protruding forward, the normal pattern of the dental arch distorted into an oddly wedge-shaped form.

And there were anomalies about Slater's eyes and ears, neither of which conformed to the human norms.

The contents of his stomach showed that his diet had consisted, at least in part, of raw meat.

The fat content of his body was exceedingly low, and his muscles were in a far better state of development than seemed warranted for a man of his age, though that, at least, Hank Henry could dismiss. The man had been living alone in the mountains for years—his muscles damned well *should* have been well-developed.

What confounded him were the samples of hair and blood that had been flown down to Boise along with the preliminary report of the autopsy.

Hair samples that the coroner up in Challis had described as "body hair inconsistent with available human samples," and blood that he had described as "unresponsive to testing by local lab."

It had taken Henry no time at all to find a match for the hair sample. He had simply sent it downstairs to his own lab, where it had instantly been matched to one of the samples scraped from the fingernails of Tamara Reynolds.

At least he now had proof of who had killed Glen Foster, and he suspected that when the evidence gathered from the site of Bill Sikes's death was analyzed, that link would be established as well.

But what the hell did it mean? "Body hair inconsistent with available human samples"? Blood that was "unresponsive to testing by local lab"? As far as he could tell, the coroner's report was nothing more than a coy bureaucratic method of saying they didn't think Slater had been human at all, but weren't about to commit their thoughts to paper, where they might be held responsible for them.

Not that he could blame them—after all, he had bucked the hair samples his own lab had been unable to identify up to the feds within minutes of reading the report. And he could still hear the scorn in Rick Martin's voice when the deputy in Sugarloaf had called him to discuss his own report. What must he be saying about the coroner's report?

Sighing, he turned to his computer and typed in the information that would bring up Shane Slater's criminal record, then waited as the program went to work, culling through the combined records from several data banks in various parts of the country. A few seconds later the report came up, and Hank Henry began reading it.

Nothing major—the man was arrested nearly twenty years ago on charges that had been nearly a decade old even then. He'd been involved in various antiwar movements during the early days of Vietnam, and finally a warrant had been issued after he'd taken part in the blowing up of a Selective Service office. No one had been injured, but the office had been destroyed. Standard campus radical stuff that had gotten out of hand. Slater had disappeared, but after living underground for a few years, he'd finally turned himself in, apparently tired of being a fugitive.

Sentenced to fifteen years, he'd been a model prisoner, but then something strange had happened.

According to the record on Hank Henry's computer screen, he killed two nurses during an escape from a prison hospital, and had been a fugitive ever since.

Henry frowned, then picked up the telephone and called the federal prison where Slater had been held until his escape fourteen years earlier. After being transferred three times, he finally found himself talking to the warden.

Hank Henry identified himself, then announced the reason for his call. "I've got a body up here that I've identified as being a former prisoner of yours. His name's Slater. Shane Slater."

The warden was silent for a moment. When he finally replied, his voice was guarded. "I'm not sure the name rings a bell. We've had a lot of people over the years—"

"How many that were model prisoners, until they went into the hospital, killed two nurses, and escaped?" Henry interrupted.

"You've been doing your homework," the warden commented.

"My question is this: Why was Slater in the hospital? What was wrong with him?"

The warden's tone hardened. "I'm afraid I can't tell you that. All the public information on Slater is in the report I assume you're looking at right now. Everything else is classified."

Hank Henry's mind instantly translated the warden's words: the government was up to something, and they didn't want anyone to know what.

His translation was confirmed a moment later when the computer screen suddenly went blank. When he tried to recall the record he'd been looking at only seconds earlier, a single line came up on the screen:

All Data Banks searched—no records found.

Shane Slater had just disappeared from the files of the United States government.

———

What's going to happen to the horses?

The thought came into MaryAnne Carpenter's mind out of nowhere. She and Alison were ready to leave the house, the few meager belongings they'd brought with them barely two weeks ago already packed into their suitcases.

It was the middle of the afternoon, and all day long the house had been filled with people, some of whom she knew, most of whom she didn't. Charley Hawkins had pulled up shortly after the snowplow had opened the road, following on the heels of the hearse and ambulance that arrived to take away the bodies of Logan and Olivia Sherbourne. Shane Slater's corpse had been removed in the helicopter, flown immediately to Challis for the autopsy. Men had appeared out of nowhere, swarming over the house and yard, photographing everything, taking samples of blood from the floor of the den and living room, even packing away the broken fragments of the smashed window through which Slater had entered the house.

Even Storm's carcass had been dug out of the snow and packed into a plastic bag.

MaryAnne had watched none of it, unable to bring herself even to go out to the barn when they'd moved Logan out of the stall where she'd left him in order to put him into the hearse.

"I can't do it," she'd told Margaret Stiffle, who had arrived a few minutes after Charley Hawkins. "I know how it must look, but I just can't do it!"

"It doesn't look like anything at all," Margaret had insisted. "If it were me, I wouldn't be able to go out there, either. After what you've been through, I'm just amazed you can function at all!"

But she wasn't functioning. All she was doing was hanging on, going through the motions of dealing with whatever came to hand, certain that if she stopped moving and let herself think, her mind would finally shatter.

At ten that morning, the phone had finally come back on, and she could no longer postpone the inevitable.

She'd called Alan, and done her best to explain what had happened.

"He's dead," she'd whispered. "Logan's dead!"

There was a short silence at the other end of the line, and then Alan's voice had come through, any grief he might be feeling concealed by fury. "How the hell could you have let that happen?" he demanded. "I'm coming out there on the first flight and taking my daughter home!"

Stunned, MaryAnne wasn't certain for a moment that she'd heard him correctly, but then she realized that his reaction was exactly what she should have expected:

Whatever was wrong—whatever had happened—it had to be her fault. The last of the feelings she still had for him dissolved away.

"Never mind," she sighed, her mind clearing for the first time that day. "We won't be here, Alan. Alison and I are going away." Unwilling to listen to him further, knowing that he would only hurl accusations at her, MaryAnne quietly hung up the phone.

She'd started packing then, not really certain where she was going yet, but knowing that she'd told Alan the truth. By this evening she and Alison would be gone from the ranch, and after the funeral for Logan, they would be gone from Sugarloaf as well.

Gone forever.

She trudged upstairs, pulled her suitcases out of the closet, and begun folding her clothes, finishing the job in far less time than she would have imagined possible. Yet she'd brought so little with her, why had she expected that the simple act of repacking a suitcase would take more than a few minutes?

She'd gone to Logan's room next, intent on packing his things, too, but hadn't even been able to bring herself to open his door, let alone look at his clothes.

"I'll arrange to have his things sent to you," Charley Hawkins had told her, finding her standing outside the door to her son's room, her whole body trembling.

MaryAnne had nodded, but said nothing as she struggled with her emotions. It wasn't until she was back downstairs, trying to eat a bowl of the soup Margaret Stiffle had made, that she finally told the lawyer not to send Logan's things. "I won't even be able to open the box," she said. "And there must be someone here who can use them. Just—" Her voice faltered again, but Charley nodded.

"Don't worry about a thing. I'll take care of it." He'd hesitated, then spoken again. "I've already gotten you and Alison a suite at the lodge. I told them I didn't know how long you'd want it, but you can stay as long as you need to."

She'd looked up at him blankly. "I can't stay in Sugarloaf," she said. "I just can't."

The lawyer smiled understandingly. "Of course not. But I assume you'll want to be at Olivia's funeral. I thought we'd have a service for Bill Sikes at the same time."

"And Logan," MaryAnne heard herself saying. "I'd like Logan's funeral to be part of it, too." Though she had no idea why she'd spoken the words, she knew even as she uttered them that it was the right thing to do. Though he'd barely arrived here, Logan had already fallen in love with the ranch, and she realized that although most of his life had been spent in Canaan, New Jersey, this was where he belonged.

Now, finally, she was ready to leave. The suitcases were in the back of the Range Rover, and she and Alison stood on the porch.

She turned back to Charley Hawkins and Margaret Stiffle, who had accompanied her out of the house. "We're going to have to arrange for someone to look after the horses," she told Hawkins. "Is there someone you can think of who could come up and feed them and muck out the stalls? Maybe someone who could be a caretaker—"

"Michael can do it," Margaret Stiffle told her. "We're just down the road, and he loves horses."

"Do you think he would?" MaryAnne asked anxiously. "After what happened . . ." Her voice trailed off, and she felt a shudder pass over her.

"He'll be fine," Margaret assured her.

"Of course I'll pay him," MaryAnne began, but Margaret held up her hand in a gesture of protest.

"You'll do no such thing! Just let him ride them, and he'd pay you for the privilege! My goodness, what are neighbors for if they can't lend a hand?"

Still MaryAnne hesitated, something in the back of her mind telling her to refuse Margaret's offer, to insist on having Charley Hawkins find someone to move into Bill Sikes's cabin, or even the main house. And yet who would want to live here, after the carnage this house had witnessed? "All right," she sighed at last, following the path of least resistance. "Tell him he can ride them whenever he wants, and to call Mr. Hawkins if he needs anything. And I'm sure it won't be for long, anyway." She glanced at the house, which only a couple of weeks ago had appeared so warm and welcoming. Now, it had taken on a foreboding look. "I think we'll probably be selling the ranch as soon as we can, won't we, Charley?"

"I think we'll talk about it later on," the lawyer said. This was not the time to remind MaryAnne that for the moment, at least, nothing at all could be done, for the ranch was not hers to sell.

It was in trust for Joey, and unless either Joey or his body was found, nothing could be disposed of at all for the next seven years.

Seven years, after which Joey Wilkenson could be declared legally dead.

"We can sort it all out after things have settled down a bit," he went on. "You're sure you don't want me to drive you into town?"

MaryAnne shook her head. "I can do it. And I think Alison and I need to be alone for a while."

She got into the Range Rover, and Alison climbed into the passenger seat next to her. The car was already warmed up, and she put it in gear, turning it around to start down the narrow driveway, certain that she would never return again.

As they left the house forever, neither she nor Alison even glanced back at it, wanting only to forget the terrible things that had happened there.

———

Rick Martin stared out at the sling dangling from the winch fastened to the outside of the helicopter. Did they really expect him to climb out of the cabin, fasten himself into that sling, and be lowered to the ground fifty feet below? They must be nuts! He glanced over at the pilot, who was grinning wickedly, then heard his voice coming through the headset clamped over his ears. "It looks a hell of a lot worse than it is! Try it—you'll like it!"

"Did you ever try it?" Rick yelled into the microphone suspended in front of his mouth.

"Hell, no!" the pilot cracked. "I'm scared shitless of heights!"

Glaring darkly at the pilot, Rick unfastened his seat belt, took off the headset, and pulled on a thick knitted cap, then finally slid the door open. Instantly, a gale of freezing wind, driven by the rotor above him, slashed through the cabin. All his instincts told him to slam the door shut again and have the pilot take him back down to the valley, where at least they could set the chopper down on solid ground. But if they did that, it would only mean that he and the two men in the back of the helicopter would have to set out on foot, and after the snowfall of the night before, the trek up the mountainside to Shane Slater's cabin would take most of the day, assuming they could make it at all. Resigning himself to the inevitable, he took a deep breath, then reached out and grabbed the sling, pulling it in next to the seat and carefully transferring himself into it, securing the harness. He let himself swing outward, and the pilot began lowering him to the ground. A few seconds later, as his legs sank into the soft snow and his feet touched solid ground, he realized that the pilot had been right—the anticipation of the drop had been a lot worse than the reality. Releasing himself from the sling, he gave the pilot a thumbs-up, then waded through the snow toward the cabin, twenty yards away.

By the time the two deputies from Challis joined him, he had already begun his search of the cabin. Joey Wilkenson had been here. He had left tracks through the snow when he'd abandoned it.

They had been clearly visible from the air. The pilot followed them as far as he could, until they'd neared the crest of the mountains and begun to feel the effects of the wind that was blowing in from the west. As the chopper began to bounce around in the wind, the tracks in the snow had also begun to peter out.

"Snow's blowing down there," the pilot had called over the headset. "No point in trying to follow those tracks any farther, and if we go any higher, I'm not going to guarantee we'll get back down again!" A moment later they swung around, returning to hover in the air above the structure in which Rick Martin now stood.

Once again he marveled that anyone could have survived a winter in the shack, yet it was obvious that Shane Slater had. Though the fire had all but burned out, the stove was still warm, and a few embers still glowed inside, embers that Rick fanned back to life, adding wood until the fire blazed up once again. Not that it would do much good, even if he closed the shutters and door, which he wasn't about to do, given that they were his only source of light.

"Jesus Christ," Tom Singlefeather breathed as he stepped through the door. "This looks like something the feds would give us for the reservation! Why the hell would anyone live up here?"

"That's exactly what we're going to find out," Martin told him. He glanced around the cabin. He'd searched it only twenty-four hours ago, but this time he was determined to find something—anything—that he might have missed before. "If we have to, we'll tear this place apart. There's got to be something here that will tell us what the feds won't!"

He pulled the suitcase he'd found yesterday out from under the wooden bed, opened it, and began going through the contents one more time. "Damn it," he muttered as he realized there was nothing there he hadn't seen the day before, "there's got to be something—"

"What about this?" Tom Singlefeather asked. He was kneeling on the floor, prying up a loose floorboard.

A floorboard Rick Martin had missed completely yesterday. The board came up, and Singlefeather reached down into the hole it had exposed and felt around the space beneath the house. A moment later he pulled out a brown metal box, its paint peeling and the underlying steel rusting. It looked like a small filing box, and there was a wire handle on top, by which it could be carried. The clasp on the front was locked, but Martin pried it open easily with a bent knife that Singlefeather found on the counter that had served as Slater's kitchen.

Inside, Rick found a small book, its leather cover worn, its pages beginning to mold from the years in the box beneath the house. The book, he realized as he carefully opened the crumbling cover, was Shane Slater's diary.

He needed only to scan the first page before he knew that he'd found what he was looking for, for the first words told it all:

I've made a deal. There's a new medical program being tested in the hospital, and they're looking for volunteers. It has to be dangerous, because they're promising early release to any of us they can sucker in, and they're making us suckers sign the kind of waivers they only use if they figure we might sue them. But what the hell—at best I find out what the government is up to, and at the worst, I die. So no big deal. Anyway, I'm going to write it all down, just in case.

Rick Martin carefully turned to the last page of the book. Shane Slater's handwriting had changed. No longer the easily legible script of the first entry, it was now a barely readable scrawl:

I keep changing, keep getting worse. It's not just my body that's changing now, it's my mind, too. I'm ready to die— I want to die, some days—but I can't. Not yet. I have to warn Joey, have to tell him what's going to happen to him. I have to tell him I'm sorry. Why did they do this to me? Why would they do it to anybody? And why did I let myself fall in love with Audrey? But it's too late—I can't change any of it, and I know I won't be able to kill Joey, even though I know I should. I think I could kill anyone now, except him. I can't stop myself anymore. I'm no longer a human being. When the night comes, and the instincts take over, I have to hunt. Hunt like a wolf. Kill my prey like a wolf. I suppose I'll die like a wolf, too. Some day, someone will hunt me down, and then it will finally be over. Over for me, anyway. But what about Joey? What will happen to my son?

At the very bottom of the metal box, there was one more envelope, containing a copy of the release Shane Slater had signed more than fifteen years earlier when he'd agreed to take part in the experiment in the prison hospital.

It had authorized the injection into his system of a serum containing the DNA of "a nonhuman species," DNA that would hopefully merge with his own, strengthening his resistance to certain kinds of disease.

But it also might possibly—and the release italicized the word *possibly*—permanently alter the structure of his own genes.

The "nonhuman species" specified for Shane Slater was *canis lupus*.

The timber wolf.

CHAPTER 30

*C*lark Corcoran gazed at the documents on his desk, barely able to believe what he was seeing. Yet there was no question of the validity of the test results performed on tissue taken from various parts of Shane Slater's body. Two labs had run the tests, not only on samples of Slater's blood, but of his sperm, as well.

Corcoran had run his own tests, too, over the last two days, tests it had never occurred to him to perform in all the years that Joey Wilkenson had been in his care. With every test result he'd studied, the evidence became clearer. No matter how his mind might resist the facts, the facts simply could not be denied. He sighed and leaned back in his chair, scanning the faces of the three people gathered around his desk, then taking off his glasses to polish them, knowing that the gesture was merely a way of giving himself a few extra moments to organize his thoughts.

MaryAnne Carpenter was sitting between Charley Hawkins and Rick Martin, her face pale, her fingers twisting at a handkerchief that had already been crumpled in her hand when she'd come in with Hawkins ten minutes ago.

Hawkins himself, his face drawn, was doing his best to maintain a certain judicial impassivity, but Corcoran wondered exactly what thoughts must be going through the attorney's mind this morning. It was obvious that Hawkins hadn't slept much the night before. Not, he suspected, that anyone in Sugarloaf had slept well last night. This morning it was apparent that all day yesterday, and through the night, rumors had been flying.

The Sugarloaf werewolf.

Corcoran had first heard the term when he'd switched on the radio this morning and listened to Sam Gilman talking about the events at El Monte Ranch. Though the disk jockey's facts were sketchy at best, it had been no trick at all for "Sugarloaf Sam"— an appellation that had always vaguely annoyed Clark Corcoran—to inflate the story into a tale of proportions large enough to make everyone in town feel he had been lucky to survive at all. To hear Gilman tell it, Shane Slater had been prowling the village every night for years, searching out victims to satisfy his "blood lust." The fact that until a week ago there had apparently been no victims at all seemed to have occurred to nobody. Finally Corcoran, fed up, had called in himself, suggesting that Gilman switch his nickname to the "Sugarloaf Ghoul." Gilman, uninterested in talking to anyone who wouldn't feed the flames of his rumor-mongering, had promptly cut Corcoran off, and the doctor had retaliated by shutting off his radio—a pyrrhic victory at best, since whether he listened to them or not, the rumors were going to go on. And once the reports on his own desk were made public, which he knew they would be, it was only going to get worse.

A lot worse.

Rick Martin, his eyes rimmed with red from lack of sleep, finally stirred in his chair. "Well?" he asked. "What's the verdict?"

Corcoran cleared his throat, then leaned forward, choosing his words carefully. "I'm not sure what to say," he began, though he knew all too well that there was no way of avoiding the truth. "I wish I could tell you differently, but there's no question that MaryAnne was right. Shane Slater was Joey Wilkenson's biological father."

MaryAnne nodded grimly. "I got the impression from Olivia that Audrey felt really stupid about the whole thing. Apparently she had no idea about 'Randy Durrell' at all. She didn't even know his real name, but she was crazy about him, according to Olivia."

"Except it turns out Slater was the one who was crazy," Rick Martin said. No one in the room even chuckled.

"I suppose that's why she fell in love with Ted so fast," MaryAnne went on. "She was on the rebound, and at least she knew exactly who Ted was. I thought she'd made a mistake, a terrible mistake, but—"

"She did," Clark Corcoran interjected. "She'd already gotten pregnant by Shane Slater."

MaryAnne's gaze slowly lifted from the faded photograph of Audrey and the man who had called himself Randy Durrell. "But you said Joey is all right," she whispered. "You said—"

"I was wrong," Corcoran told her, his eyes dropping to the open file on his desk. "From what I've seen, there is no possible way Joey can be all right. When they experimented on Shane Slater, they actually succeeded in altering his genetic structure. His genes aren't those of a normal human being, MaryAnne. A great deal of them are, but there are differences, too. There are strings in his DNA that simply don't match anything human at all." He flipped to another page of the file, then another. "The same DNA is in his sperm. The reports are all here, and they don't leave any room for doubt. Almost certainly, he passed some of his—" Corcoran hesitated, searching for the right word, unwilling to use the one that came instantly to mind.

A man of his education simply didn't use the word *werewolf*.

"He would have passed some of his *mutations* on to Joey," he finished.

MaryAnne's lips tightened, but she said nothing.

"Which ones?" Charley Hawkins asked. "Are you saying we have to consider him to be as dangerous as Shane Slater was?"

"For Christ's sake, Charley, we already know he killed Olivia Sherbourne!" Rick Martin shouted.

"But Clark said—" the lawyer began, his voice taking on an edge of desperation.

"I know what I'm going to do," Rick stated, standing up. His eyes went to the window, narrowing as he saw the thick layer of snow that was not yet showing any signs of melting. "As soon as this thaws out, I'm putting together a team. We're going to search those mountains until we find him, and when we do—" He cut his own words short just in time, knowing that if he'd uttered them, they not only would have sounded like a line from a grade-B movie, but they would have incriminated him as well.

Officers of the law, he knew, simply did not set out to gun down a thirteen-year-old boy on sight.

But that was exactly what he intended to do.

And it might happen a lot sooner than anyone thought, if the hunch that had been growing in him all morning long was right.

As the meeting in Corcoran's office broke up, Rick Martin got into his Jeep and headed up to El Monte Ranch.

Joey would come back there, he was almost certain of it.

He might be Shane Slater's son, but he wasn't like his father yet.

He didn't know how to live in the woods, didn't know how to take care of himself in the wilderness.

So he'd come back to the ranch.

He'd come back, if for no other reason than hunger.

By now, he must be very hungry, indeed.

———

Michael Stiffle gazed at the deep snow burying the trail that be-gan at the edge of his family's pasture and wound through the woods to come out at the driveway of El Monte Ranch.

He'd been using the path all his life and knew every one of its turns so well that even on the night when he and Andrea had gone out to scare Joey Wilkenson, he'd never felt even slightly lost.

It wasn't the snow that kept him from using the trail today. In fact, all morning long he'd been thinking about how much fun it would be to get out his snowmobile and race through the woods, then streak across the big pasture at El Monte, mak-ing figure eights in the fresh white blanket that would still be almost unmarred even by grazing deer. But every time he thought about it, he also remembered what had happened up at the ranch two nights ago, and remembered, too, the shadowy figure he and Andrea had seen up at the ranch the night before that.

Had it been Shane Slater?

Michael shivered with excitement every time he thought about it. He could hardly wait until school started again to tell every-one what he'd seen.

And he had been the only one to see the werewolf, despite what Andrea might say. He could remember it perfectly, and she'd stayed close to the house, too scared even to go out and throw some rocks at Joey's window! She might have seen some-thing—maybe a shadow, or something like that—but only he had seen the monster that killed Logan—and maybe even Dr. Sherbourne, too—with his own eyes!

Of course, he'd heard that it was Joey that killed Dr. Sher-bourne, but he didn't believe that. Joey was nuts, but he just wasn't strong enough to kill someone with his bare hands. So the fact that Shane Slater was dead should have made the trail through the woods less scary.

Yet when he was finally ready to go up to El Monte Ranch and feed the horses—and check out for himself the place behind the barn where they'd found Shane Slater and Dr. Sherbourne— he felt no temptation at all to take the trail, with or without his snowmobile. In fact, he wasn't supposed to be going at all, since his folks had made him promise to wait until they got back from town, when his father would drive him up there and wait while he did his job.

Wait, just like he was still some ten-year-old kid who couldn't take care of himself.

And his father, he knew, wouldn't let him go anywhere near where they'd found the bodies. But his folks wouldn't be back from town for at least an hour, and he had plenty of time to get up there, take a good look, feed the horses, and get back.

He set out walking, moving quickly down his driveway to the main road, then turning right to head up toward El Monte. The road was plowed, and there had been enough traffic going back and forth that the pavement was clear. In less than ten minutes he had come to the driveway.

It wasn't until Michael was halfway up the drive, and the forest had begun to creep in on him from both sides, that he began to feel nervous. The thick snow covering the trees and ground seemed to cast an unnatural silence over the forest, and suddenly he felt as if he was being watched. The hairs on the back of his neck stood up, and he felt gooseflesh forming even under the heavy sweater and jacket he was wearing. Glancing around, half expecting to spot Andrea hiding behind a tree ready to jump out at him, he scanned the woods on both sides, but saw nothing. Finally, when he was certain there was no one there to see him lose his nerve, he broke into a trot, and ran the rest of the way up to the ranch, not stopping until he burst out of the mouth of the driveway into the yard.

He stopped to catch his breath, then gazed around. Over by the shed behind the barn he could see the bright yellow strips of plastic that marked the area where they'd found the two bodies. Michael immediately headed over to take a look, feeling vaguely disappointed when he found that there was nothing much to see. The snow around the shed was trampled down, and he wasn't even sure where the bodies had been lying, except that some of the snow was stained with what he figured must be blood. He shivered as he stared at the reddish stains, but finally turned away and started toward the barn.

But as he approached the enormous, looming structure, he began to wonder if maybe, after all, he should have waited for his parents to come back from town. Though the sun was shining brightly, and the sky was clear overhead, the barn seemed somehow forbidding.

Then he remembered.

It was inside the barn that they had found Logan Carpenter's body, his throat torn open, blood soaking his clothes.

His heart pounding, Michael slowly moved around the barn until he came to the two huge doors.

Maybe he shouldn't go in at all. Maybe he should just go home and come back later with his father.

Chicken! he told himself. *You're just being a chicken! There's nothing in there except some horses, and maybe a few rats!*

Putting down the fear that was threatening to make him turn and flee, Michael resolutely lifted the latch and pulled the barn door open.

As the hinges creaked, the horses inside began to snort and paw restlessly at the floors of their stalls. "It's okay," Michael called loudly, more to steady his own nerves than anything else. "It's only me. I'm going to feed you!" But he made no move to go into the barn yet. He stood at the door, poised now to take off if he heard anything from inside that didn't sound quite right.

But except for the horses, he heard nothing, and finally he slipped into the barn, leaving the door standing open.

Ten minutes.

Just ten minutes and he would be done and he could go back home. Then, at school tomorrow, he could tell everyone what he'd done and what he'd seen.

And he'd tell them he hadn't been scared at all.

———

Joey moved silently through the woods, slipping from tree to tree, darting across the open places only when he was certain there were no human eyes to see him. He'd been circling slowly around the ranch for more than an hour, starting at the head of the trail that opened into the pasture directly across from the kitchen door. Even when he'd descended the trail, he'd been careful to avoid the small clearing adjoining the pasture itself, staying a few yards into the shelter of the forest, crouching low in the snow as he watched the house, unaware of the cold wetness seeping through his clothes. Finally he'd changed his position, moving to the west, finding a vantage point from which he could survey the back of the house as well as the side facing west. When he'd still seen no signs that anyone was there, he'd moved on, working his way through the forest, keeping himself concealed, patiently examining the house from every angle, satisfying himself that it was, indeed, deserted.

Now he retraced his steps until he was once more at the back of the house, screened by the large log building itself from the mouth of the driveway and the barn. He crouched at the base of a low white-barked pine, nearly invisible in the shelter of its twisting branches.

He sniffed at the air, searching for any trace of a scent that would betray the presence of someone hiding inside the house, listened for any sound that might be made by someone waiting within.

Nothing.

His muscles tensed, and at last he made his move, darting from the shelter of the tree to sprint across the snow-covered yard, ducking into the sanctuary of the house itself. Pausing for only a moment, he slipped around to the west side and scuttled to the broken window through which his father had entered the house two days ago.

Two days.

And more than a full day since he'd left the cabin, climbing high into the mountains until at last he'd found a cave that had offered him shelter. He'd crouched inside it, watching unseen as the helicopter had flown above, searching for him, then nestled down into the bearskin he'd brought with him from the cabin, sleeping fitfully through the night.

But this morning he had woken up hungry, his stomach growling, a cold knot of pain lying sullenly in his belly. He'd eaten some snow, but while his thirst had been satisfied, his hunger had not, and as the morning wore on, he thought more and more about the food in the house.

More food than anyone needed.

And surely no one would be there.

Not after what had happened.

Leaving the still crippled wolf in the cave, he'd started down the mountain, his hunger growing with every step, but never driving him past the limits of caution.

Now, though, he was there, and, as he'd thought, the house was deserted!

Except that someone had nailed a sheet of plywood over the broken window. He reached up, working his fingers under the edge of the plywood, and tugged at it. It held fast for a moment, but then he felt one of the nails give way, and a second later the gap was wide enough for him to slip the fingers of both hands into it. He pulled again, and the corner came loose, then all four of the nails along the bottom of the plywood sheet gave way and he was able to pull the wood far enough from the window frame to slither over the sill and drop to the floor inside.

Once again, like a wary animal, he crouched where he was, listening.

The house was silent.

He rose to his feet and moved quickly into the kitchen, pulling open the refrigerator door.

On the bottom shelf, still on the plate where MaryAnne had left them, were the five steaks, wrapped in plastic. Ripping the plastic off one of them, Joey began tearing the raw meat into small chunks, shoving them into his mouth, swallowing them almost without chewing them.

The knot of pain in his stomach eased, then disappeared entirely as he finished the first steak and started on a second.

His hunger sated, he turned away from the refrigerator, leaving it open, and moved into the dining room, then to the bottom of the stairs. He started slowly upward, his nose filling with familiar odors, scents that stirred emotions within him.

He came to the door of his own room but passed it by, moving on to another door.

The door stood ajar.

Inside the room, the odor of its occupant was still strong, and he breathed deeply of it, an odd warmth spreading through him as he inhaled the scent.

Alison.

Alison, who had always been kind to him, even after he'd attacked her.

He went to the closet door and pulled it open.

The closet was empty—all her clothes were gone. His eyes darted around the room, finally coming to rest on a scarf that hung over the footboard of the bed.

The scarf that he'd chosen for her himself.

He snatched it up, holding it to his nose, breathing in the smell that clung to it. Finally he wrapped the plaid cashmere around his neck, comforted by the scent of the girl who had been the one friend he'd ever had.

A minute later he was back downstairs, throwing as much food as he could into a large plastic bag. When he'd filled the bag, he slipped out through the back door, and was about to head back toward the creek and the safety of the mountains when he saw the barn door standing partway open.

He hesitated, almost turned away again, then sniffed at the air.

A breeze was wafting up from the direction of the barn, and Joey could smell the scent of the horses, their familiar odor triggering memories of days that now seemed a lifetime ago, when he'd spent endless hours with them, feeding them and grooming them, training them and riding them.

Days that were gone forever.

He breathed deeply of the comforting smell, wanting to capture it in his memory, but then his muscles tensed. There was another odor coming from the barn as well.

An odor he'd never truly been aware of before, but which now filled him with sudden rage.

Michael Stiffle.

Michael Stiffle was in the barn, and his scent, unfamiliar as it was, still triggered memories in Joey.

Memories of Michael taunting him, telling him he was crazy, whispering about him when he didn't think he was listening.

More memories welled up out of his subconscious, and suddenly Michael Stiffle seemed to personify every slight and insult he'd suffered at the hands of his classmates for as long as he could remember. His fury building, Joey dropped the bag of food to the ground and started toward the open barn door.

———

Michael Stiffle was pouring feed into the trough in Sheika's stall when the big mare snorted, tossed her head, and began backing away from the door, her hooves drumming on the wooden floor, her eyes wide.

"What is it?" Michael asked, looking up from the trough to gaze quizzically at the horse. Only a moment ago the mare had been nuzzling at his neck, trying to nose him aside in her efforts to get to the fresh food in her trough. Now, though, the horse looked terrified, and when Michael reached up to pat her neck, she shied away with a loud whinny. She backed farther, her rump finally coming to a stop as it hit the stall's far corner. She started, then reared up, her forehooves striking out, forcing Michael to duck out of the way.

"Jesus Christ!" the boy burst out, scrambling toward the stall door. "What the hell's wrong with you?" Keeping his eyes on the still-rearing horse, Michael groped behind him for the latch to the stall door, finally found it and twisted it. As the door swung open, he slipped out into the wide aisle that ran in front of the stall and slammed the lower half of the door shut, even though Sheika—still in the far corner of her stall—made no move to try to bolt.

Now Michael realized that it wasn't only Sheika who had spooked, for Buck and Fritz were also pawing nervously, and suddenly Fritz reared up, his hooves striking out to crash against the planks that walled his stall. A moment later Buck followed suit, and then Sheika, too, joined in the melee. "What the hell's going on?" Michael asked out loud.

Then he knew, for suddenly he had the same feeling of being watched that he'd felt in the woods a few minutes before.

Except this time it was stronger.

Much stronger.

His whole body broke out in goose bumps, and a terrible chill seized him as he felt the presence in the barn.

A presence that wasn't human, but wasn't an animal, either.

Then he heard a sound—a single step—but instead of making him jump, the sound paralyzed him.

His eyes darted quickly around, searching for something he could use as a weapon.

A pitchfork.

It was only two steps away, just across the aisle.

Gathering what little courage he could muster, Michael Stiffle forced himself to overcome the paralytic fear that had seized him, then leaped across the aisle and grabbed the pitchfork.

Just as his hands closed on the fork, he heard another sound, much closer this time, directly behind him. Whirling around, the needle-sharp tines of the fork pointing straight out, Michael Stiffle found himself gazing at Joey Wilkenson.

Joey was staring back at him through narrowed eyes that glittered with menace, and an image suddenly came into Michael Stiffle's mind.

An image of a wolf.

For a moment that seemed to go on forever, neither boy said a word.

It was finally Michael Stiffle who broke the silence: "Wh-What do you want?" he asked, his voice quavering.

Joey glared at the boy who had taunted him all his life. "I'm crazy," he whispered. "It's finally true, Michael. All the things you ever said about me are finally true."

"L-Leave me alone," Michael stammered. "I never hurt you. I never did anything to you!"

"Yes you did," Joey replied. "And it wasn't just you, Michael. It was your sister, too. And all your friends." Joey's eyes locked on to the other boy's, and Michael felt himself powerless to turn away. "Do you know what's going to happen to you, Michael?" Joey finally asked.

As he felt his knees begin to give way beneath him, Michael tried to speak, but found that his voice had failed him. Mutely, he stared at Joey.

"I'm going to kill you, Michael," Joey whispered. "Some night, when you think you're safe in your room, I'm going to come and kill you."

Michael Stiffle stared at Joey, the other boy's words echoing in his mind.

I'm going to come and kill you, Michael. I'm going to come and kill you.

"N-Nooo," Michael wailed, finding his voice at last. He rushed at Joey, the tines of the pitchfork pointed directly at Joey's chest, but at the last second Joey stepped aside, his own hands closing on the fork's handle as it lunged past him.

A fraction of an instant later, Joey had jerked the fork from Mike Stiffle's hands, and as the other boy realized what had happened, he turned to flee.

He was almost to the tack room when Joey hurled the fork with a force that drove the tines deep into the wood of the door through which Michael had been trying to flee.

Michael's head was pinned to the door, two tines of the wide fork straddling his neck.

A third tine, though, had pierced Michael Stiffle's neck, missing his spinal cord by a fraction of an inch but puncturing his carotid artery.

A scream burst from Michael's throat, but it almost instantly died away to a bubbling moan as his throat filled with blood that poured out of his mouth and nose.

As he died, the last words he heard were Joey Wilkenson's: "It's only the beginning, Michael. This is only the beginning."

Then, as Michael Stiffle died, dark laughter welled up from the depths of Joey Wilkenson's soul, and he walked out of the barn, back into the bright sunlight outside. As his ears detected the sound of a car coming up the road toward the driveway, he loped to the house, picked up the bag of food that would get him through the next several days, and started across the pasture toward the shelter of the woods.

Rick Martin arrived less than a minute later. As he pulled into the yard in front of the house, he saw Joey across the field, only a few yards from the forest. His heart racing, he slammed the car to a halt. "Joey!" he yelled as he scrambled out of the front seat and jerked his gun from its holster. *"Joey Wilkenson!"*

Joey stopped short and turned as Rick took aim.

Too quickly, Martin pulled the trigger, and the shot went wild.

By the time he was ready to fire again, Joey was gone.

His laughter still echoing among the rocky ramparts above, Joey Wilkenson disappeared back into the mountains.

EPILOGUE

*A*nother hour, MaryAnne thought. Another hour, and we can leave this place forever.

The funeral was over, and she had gotten through it, though she wasn't quite certain how. Now that she was back in Charley Hawkins's Cadillac, though, with Alison beside her, she could finally allow herself to think about it.

There had been something surreal about the caskets that had been buried in the cemetery that morning. All through the memorial service and the interment that had finally come to an end a few minutes ago, she had the feeling that she was about to wake up, about to rouse herself from this terrible nightmare to find herself back home in Canaan.

Yet it had all happened, and the memories would remain etched in her subconscious for years to come.

Last night, and the night before, she had awakened from the

real nightmare, when she had once more been trapped in the blizzard, carrying Logan's body through the driving snow.

Except in the dream, Logan hadn't been dead.

He had been alive, blood pouring from the terrible wound in his throat, and he'd kept begging her to help him, not to let him die.

Holding him in her arms, she'd kept moving through the blizzard, but no matter which direction she went, it was always the same.

Snow. Endless snow, driving into her face whatever direction she turned, and Logan endlessly dying in her arms.

Both nights she awoke screaming, and both nights Alison had finally crept into bed with her, holding her while she shook with the terrible memory of the dream.

Now, she was sitting in the backseat of Charley Hawkins's car, and Alison was beside her, her daughter's fingers intertwined in her own. In a few minutes they would be at the lodge, where the funeral reception was being held. After that, it would finally be over. She and Alison could leave Sugarloaf.

Would they ever be back? Would they ever be able to bring themselves to come back here, even to visit the grave of her son, Alison's brother?

Right now she didn't think so, and yet already she knew that sooner or later the numbness would wear off, and even the memories of what had happened here would begin to fade, losing their sharp edge.

But where would they go?

They hadn't decided yet, though MaryAnne already knew that Alison was no more willing than she to go back to Canaan, and try to pick up the threads of their existence. The memories of Logan would be too strong, for everything either of them saw, everything they touched, would remind them of the little boy and renew the pain of their loss.

"But what about your father?" MaryAnne had asked when they discussed it last night. "Don't you want to see him?"

"He's not even coming for Logan's funeral, is he?" Alison had asked bitterly.

"He can't afford it," MaryAnne reminded her, but Alison was unmoved.

"He could have gotten the money if he'd really wanted to." She'd smiled, but there was no joy in the expression. "I guess I'm finally figuring out why you don't want him back."

They'd left it at that last night, both of them knowing they didn't want to go back to Canaan, but neither knowing where she did want to go.

Now, in the car, Alison asked, "Mom? Where will we go?"

It was as if the girl had read her mind. Coming out of her reverie, MaryAnne turned to look at her daughter, who had stood beside her throughout the long service, their hands grasped in mutual support. Suddenly Alison seemed older. Her eyes had changed, had lost their childish innocence, had darkened with a new maturity. It's not just her brother she's lost, MaryAnne thought. It's her childhood, too.

"I haven't even thought about it," MaryAnne said.

"Well, I have," Alison told her. "You remember how Logan always wanted to go to California? How he was always talking about going to Disneyland, and learning to surf, and all that stuff?"

MaryAnne felt her heart breaking a little more as she thought of all the things Logan had been looking forward to and now would never experience. Not trusting her voice, she could only nod mutely.

"Let's do it for him, Mom," Alison said. "Let's go out to California, and do all the things Logan wanted to do."

The car came to a halt, but MaryAnne made no move to get out. She sat quietly, thinking about what Alison had just said.

Could they do it?

Could they set out alone, just the two of them, and build a whole new life for themselves?

Charley Hawkins spoke from the front seat: "You can leave

right now, MaryAnne. You don't even have to think about it. All you have to do is pack your bags and put them in the Range Rover, and you can take off."

MaryAnne suddenly felt disoriented. "But I can't. I—I have to think about it—I can't just *do* something like that."

"Of course you can," Charley said, his eyes meeting hers in the rearview mirror. "It's exactly what Ted and Audrey did. They met each other, and they knew they were right for each other, and that was that. And neither one of them ever regretted a minute of it, despite how it ended. Even if they'd known what was going to happen, they'd have done it anyway."

"You're right," MaryAnne said. "You're both right. Let's do it."

The weight of her grief lifting slightly, she got out of the car. Ten minutes later she and Alison had finished packing. Putting their luggage into the Range Rover, they climbed into the front seat. "Are you sure you don't want to say good-bye to anyone?" she asked Alison.

Alison shook her head. "I said good-bye to Logan at the cemetery. I think we should just go."

MaryAnne put the car in gear and drove away. As they left the town of Sugarloaf forever, neither of them looked back.

If they had, they might have seen Joey Wilkenson, watching from the mountainside until the car finally disappeared.

Only when it was gone did he at last start back up into the safety of the high country, the wolf, whom he had named Lobo, limping at his side.

"Don't worry," he said softly, dropping one hand to the wolf's head while the fingers of the other stroked Alison's scarf, which was still around his neck. "We'll find her again. Wherever they go, somehow we'll find her."

ABOUT THE AUTHOR

JOHN SAUL's first novel, *Suffer the Children*, published in 1977, was an immediate million-copy bestseller. He has since written such *New York Times* bestsellers as *The God Project*, *Nathaniel*, *Brainchild*, *Hellfire*, *The Unwanted*, *The Unloved*, *Creature*, *Sleepwalk*, *Second Child*, and *Darkness*, each a riveting tale of supernatural, technological, or psychological terror. His sixteenth novel was *Shadows*. John Saul lives in Seattle, Washington, where he is at work on his next novel.

Readers of John Saul now can join the John Saul Fan Club by writing to the address below. Members receive an autographed photo of John, newsletters and advance information about forthcoming publications. Please send your name and address to:

The John Saul Fan Club
P. O. Box 17035
Seattle, Washington 98107